Adam Runaway

Adam Runaway

PETER PRINCE

BLOOMSBURY

To the memory of my friend Peter Conboy,
this story about a promising young man
is dedicated

First published in 2005
This paperback edition published 2006

Copyright © 2005 by Peter Prince

The moral right of the author has been asserted

Bloomsbury Publishing Plc, 36 Soho Square, London W1D 3QY

A CIP catalogue record for this book
is available from the British Library

ISBN 0 7475 7941 5
9780747579410

10 9 8 7 6 5 4 3 2 1

All papers used by Bloomsbury Publishing are natural,
recyclable products made from wood grown in well-managed
forests. The manufacturing processes conform to the
environmental regulations of the country of origin.

Typeset by Hewer Text UK Ltd, Edinburgh
Printed by Clays Ltd, St Ives Plc

www.adamrunaway.com

To the traveller who was fortunate enough to first approach it by water, the city that existed three decades and a half before the famous devouring earthquake of 1755 appeared like a lofty amphitheatre. Palaces, convents, houses, churches, rising tier upon tier from the edge of the Tagus river, and all of them seeming large and cleanly built, many in white marble. From this favoured point of view, there was nothing mean, dirty or criminal in sight.

The city began then on the western side at the Alcântara gate, near which was a harbour for the King's ships, and a small fort; the eastern end terminated at the market for slaves. A person walking at three miles in an hour could have gone from the west gate to the slave bagnio in an hour and twenty-seven minutes. Halfway along, his route would have passed through the great square before the royal palace, where the city's principal merchants and financiers met to do business, where the customs house was, and where great spectacles were held: bullfights and bull-runnings, army exercises, the erection of triumphal arches.

A quarter of a mile behind this was another extensive piazza. This was the square of the people, where the hospital was, and a multitude of small shops and outdoor markets, and where the most obstinate heretics were burned alive in front of the Palace of the Inquisition. Or – if they were less hardened, and the servants of the Holy Office inclined to be merciful – strangled before they were burned.

The climate is agreeable, tempered by sea breezes; the view from the battlements of the castle of St George sublime; on summer evenings the scent of lemons and oranges wafts in from the numerous groves beyond the city, and fills its narrow streets and broad avenues alike with a cool sweetness.

'Quem nunca viu Lisboa, nunca viu uma coisa boa,' the natives used to say.

'He who never saw Lisbon, never saw a fine thing.'

From *A Visit to Portugal in the Time of King João V*, by a Pennsylvania Merchant (Philadelphia, 1771)

BOOK ONE

Gomes

G omes woke at exactly ten minutes before dawn, just as he always did. His first action, also his daily habit, was to drive from his bed the girl who had shared it with him in the night. There was always a girl – without her presence, whoever she might be, Gomes found it difficult to sleep. Last night he had used the new one, Doroteia, a skinny wench who thought she was aged thirteen or fourteen, she wasn't sure, who had arrived in the city from the Trás-os-Montes a couple of weeks ago. Gomes – whose duties as head clerk in the firm of Hanaway's also encompassed the supervision of the household – preferred to hire new serving-girls from that or another part of the kingdom distant from Lisbon. This pretty much removed from the realm of possibility the danger that he would be visited by irate masculine relatives, demanding satisfaction or reparation for the loss of their daughter's or sister's innocence.

Last night's wench had pleased him very much. There was a quality of outraged modesty about her, and an unavailing resistance to him, that had excited his ardour and caused him to perform prodigiously upon her body. Bartolomeu Gomes had an iron rule that none of the serving-girls was allowed to stay with the household for more than two or three months. He was too aware of the danger that sloth and slovenliness, both at her housework or in bed, could easily infect a little *puta* who felt herself too secure in either part of her employment. So after two or three months she was invariably shown the door and left to shift for herself thereafter. The same thing ought to happen with this Doroteia. But lying in bed, waiting for dawn to finally break, Gomes thought seriously that he might allow this wench to stay well beyond the usual time. Even as long as four, five, even six

3

months. So much had she pleased him in the night, as she had wept for him to desist, not to do that, oh please, senhor, don't do *that* . . .

The one flaw in his arrangements was that his master, old Felix Hanaway, was starting to show signs of curiosity lately at the steady stream of young provincial girls that passed through his house. Last time Gomes had reported with regret that the latest was failing in her duties and would have to be replaced, the old *bugre* had said, 'My goodness, we have no luck at all with our servants, do we?'

Gomes, after experiencing a moment of unease, had pointed out that indeed their other servants – Inês who supervised in the kitchen, Sebastiana the housekeeper, Álvaro who used to drive Old Felix's coach-and-four in more prosperous days when the household had boasted such a luxury – had all proved most satisfactory for several years.

'It's just these girls, Sir,' Gomes explained. 'They come off their father's little farms where they've been worked like mules all their lives, and they get to Lisbon and think they will take it easy from then on. At our expense,' he complained righteously.

'Well, that will never do,' Old Felix had nodded. 'Carry on as you see fit then, Bartolomeu. D'you think you can find a replacement soon? Mrs Hanaway will be staying here a couple of nights next week and I should like to see that we have a full complement of staff by then.'

'I'll do my best, Sir,' Gomes promised.

As he had told the old fool, it was only the serving-girls that always had to be replaced. Gomes had no intentions of dismissing any of the upper servants. Each in his or her way was of use to him. Inês, a fine, big woman of thirty, knew it as part of her duties to come to his bed when they were between serving-girls, or whenever he had a taste for riper flesh and more experienced love-craft than the average girl in her teens could offer. Sebastiana, though too old and fat herself to excite any man's appetite, had excellent connections among the stews and brothels of the Remolares district next to the water, and was the conduit by which these country girls were diverted from beginning a whore's life – for a couple of months at least – and sent to the Hanaway house to become servants.

As for Álvaro: by rights, having lost his occupation as coach-driver when the coach had to be sold, he should have been dismissed and the few trivial tasks that remained to him turned over to a boy who would do them for a fraction of what he earned. But he had come to an agreement with Gomes whereby, in return for being allowed to stay on in Old Felix's employ and household, and to spend his days in near complete idleness at the tavern next door, he turned over a quarter of his wages to the head clerk.

Gomes turned on his side as the first rays of light came in through the window that he always left unshuttered. He wanted to see dear São Bartolomeu – his own, his name saint – first thing, and give him thanks for his easy life, and for the new girl, and everything else. But this morning the saint, in the shape of the woodcut in its golden frame that he had purchased for half a *moeda* off a stall under the arches of the Rossio, regarded him not. Only the back of the frame – which, too late, Gomes had discovered to be made of tin, lightly covered with gold paint – was on view from its perch on top of the chest-of-drawers.

For a moment, he panicked, thinking that somehow the *beato Bartolomeu* had become angry with him, and had in the night turned himself around so that he would no longer have to look at Gomes. Perhaps he had witnessed once too often his child's favourite way with the serving-girls, his preference, as it were, for the less travelled path. Gomes wanted to assure the *beato Bartolomeu* it was only with the bitches that he diverted himself in this way. He was not a damn *maricão*, a queer, a dirty *sodomita* – even though it was a man, the Captain Merriweather, who had introduced him to the practice years ago, forcing his long English cock nightly into Gomes' youthful hindquarters.

Well, in time he had paid the Captain in full for that service. What he had done to him certainly ought to have been enough to have convinced the saint that he was serious in his hatred for the foul congress of men with men. But perhaps it hadn't been sufficient punishment after all – as Gomes had begun to fear? Really he was growing frantic. He was on his knees. He even thought of promising the blessed one that he would take no more serving-girls to his bed, or at least if he did he wouldn't use them in the way the saint obviously disapproved of. Fortunately the words did not pass his lips, for Gomes knew that it was a habit he'd have had much more difficulty giving up than, say, the drinking of wine, or the smoking of *charutos*, and abandoning it would have placed a great strain on his affection for São Bartolomeu. He was saved from this rash step by a sudden memory – which must have been temporarily expunged by the pleasures of the night – that it wasn't the saint who had turned his countenance away from Gomes, but Gomes who, as a punishment, had turned the saint around himself, so that he would no longer have the luxury of gazing upon a pleasant room, decent furniture, and a window that looked out on to a tree-shaded courtyard, but was forced every hour of the day to stare at a blank wall.

Gomes got to his feet. He felt such relief at remembering this, and gratitude too that he had not pledged himself to give up a practice he loved, that he was almost moved to relent towards the *beato Bartolomeu*, and turn him to face the room again. But then the memory of why he had punished him in the first place returned and hardened his heart. The saint had a long way to go before he earned his remission, for the offence he had committed – the bringing of the young Englishman, another fucking snooping Hanaway, into Gomes' life – was very serious.

Today was Wednesday, the day appointed by Felix Hanaway for the young man to appear at the house, and be permitted to see his uncle. Gomes still had no idea what the result of that interview would be. It was true that Felix still bore a great deal of ill will towards his late brother and because of him towards all his family. And why should he not? Gomes thought piously, for had not the older brother through his folly and misrepresentation made substantial inroads into the younger brother's fortune too? Gomes felt personally involved in this disaster. For Felix's being so much less wealthy today than he was eighteen months ago meant there was that much less available for Gomes to steal.

Knowing Old Felix's current aversion to the London-based Hanaways and all their members, living or dead, Gomes confidently expected him to show anger when, last Saturday, he had brought his master the news that a runner waited below with a message from his nephew, this Adam Hanaway, who had apparently fetched up in Lisbon after all. One might have hoped that, since previous letters to Felix from the same source had been ignored, the little *filho da puta* would have got the idea that he would not be welcome here.

Old Felix had certainly frowned and blown out his cheeks, and had shaken his head.

'Shall I tell the man to go away, Sir?'

And for just a moment Gomes was certain that this was what he would hear, and so he would go back down, and dismiss the runner with the words 'No message', and the whole threat would be blown away in a moment.

But Felix said, 'No, I can't do that to Adam,' and Gomes' heart sank.

His master had turned and strode across to his own room. He was in there for forty minutes by the office clock. At one point, curious as to what he could be doing, Gomes had walked past the open door and looked in. Old Felix had the office Day Book open on his desk and was studying it with furious concentration. It didn't bother Gomes much. He had learned his craft from good masters and the first rule of business – the thieving business – was that there were always two sets of books. Old Felix could study the Day Book before him as long as he liked. Reality was in the other book, and that was the one Gomes always kept to himself.

At last the old man had quitted his office and had said to Gomes – not exactly the words the clerk had absolutely dreaded to hear, not an order to write out an immediate invitation for the nephew to appear in this house – that he should send instructions for the boy to attend him in a few days' time. In other words young Hanaway still had his chance to worm his way into his uncle's favour – that is, if he was feeble enough not to resent this discourteous, almost contemptuous treatment.

'Try and make the invitation as kind as may be,' Felix asked him. 'As far as the circumstances permit.'

'I'll do what I can, Sir.'

And Gomes went into his own office and wrote out the message, made it as cool and unwelcoming as it could be, short of outright rejection, and took it downstairs to the runner who was growing pretty restless and clearly expected he should be compensated for his time of waiting. Gomes advised him to seek any such favour from the fellow who had sent him hither, and dismissed him from the premises. And between that hour and this morning, Gomes had not been able to do much to affect the situation one way or another. He had done what he could in bringing to Old Felix's attention certain hitherto unnoticed costs and losses in the accounts, which could be directly traced to the disastrous influence of his chief's late brother, father to this unwanted new arrival. Gomes had sat up till late at night inventing these transactions and working them into the office Day Book and Ledger. But, when he showed them to his employer the next day, the old *bugre* had hardly glanced at them. It had been a waste of time and skill.

Other than that there was only one more thing that Gomes could come up with. But it was a serious step and he had to think hard and long before doing it. In the end he could see no alternative. The *beato Bartolomeu* had never hesitated to do Gomes wrong if he was displeased with him. Now the shoe was on the other foot, it would be weak of him not to show the same stern countenance to the saint. Having come to the right decision, the job was done in a moment. Which was why São Bartolomeu was now staring at the wall, in which posture he was able to contemplate his cruelty towards his beloved child, without any distractions at all.

Adam

1

At the end of the infamous bubble year of 1720 my father Matthew Hanaway, for many years a leading merchant in the City of London, had the misfortune to break to the tune of ninety-two thousand pounds. Within a few months the condition of his family was changed utterly. I, his only son, was removed from my studies at Oxford University; my mother and two sisters were found dubious shelter in a cottage in the woods near the village of Bromley in Kent where Mother had grown up; and Father himself was dead as a result of what I shall maintain until my own dying day was an accident that befell him while he was cleaning his guns.

Upon me alone now rested any hope that the family would ever again rise in the world. Whatever ambitions for a polite or distinguished career I (and my parents) had once entertained for me all had to be set aside now, of course. Money was what was needed, and soon at that, and it seemed the only hope of getting it was for me to follow in Father's footsteps into trade. It was resolved after several anxious conferences between my mother and myself – assisted at all times by Mr Solomon Marks, who had formerly been my father's trusted head clerk – that it were best my entrance on to the scene of commercial life should not be in London where the collapse of the firm of Hanaway's was too fresh in men's minds. I had an uncle, my father's younger brother, who was established in business in Lisbon, and it was decided at last that my career should begin in that city. Several letters were sent to Uncle Felix warning him of my early arrival.

Within the month I had followed the letters. My Uncle Felix

welcomed me to the Portuguese capital, without much enthusiasm, it seemed to me, and rather grudgingly too accepted me into his firm in the informal position of apprentice clerk. This half-hearted attitude pained, but did not really surprise me. My father in the latter part of what can only be described as his stock-buying frenzy was not only purchasing as much of the South Sea and other companies' subscriptions as he could lay his hands on, but was recommending them to all his friends and colleagues and relatives. I knew Uncle Felix had taken some of this paper – so soon to be nearly worthless – perhaps a great deal of it, and had also lost greatly therefore when the bubble broke. It was not quite fair for him to blame me for this disaster, who had no hand in creating it, but yet as I say I understood.

Thereafter six days of my week were consecrated to hard work in the great customs house of Lisbon, the Alfândega. The seventh day was spent by me mostly in exhausted sleep in a room on the fourth floor of a house in the Rua do Parreiral, which was in that part of town which is called the Baixa. I shared this room with a Portuguese fellow called Bento, who was employed as a general labourer in this and several other tenement buildings in the street, and who I rarely saw. I remember this time, in fact, as one of almost unremitting toil. Apart from my principal and official duties, which comprised the keeping of a true written record at all times of our firm's goods – their numbers, quality, provenance, destination, etcetera – as they arrived first at the wharves, then in the customs house, I often found myself being told off by Senhor Gomes (my uncle's head clerk, a Portuguese, who generally supervised me) to lower myself to the condition of a mere labouring man, working alongside the casual hands who were hired by the day every morning outside the Alfândega's front gates. Many of these fellows were freed negroes from Portugal's colony in Angola, dubbed 'snowballs' by their white fellow-workers. I worked beside these black fellows too, my coat off my back, sometimes without my shirt, the sweat pouring off me in the summer heat, heaving great bales of cloth or rolls of tobacco or whatever it was from the shelves to the floor, where they could be assessed by the customs officers, then from the floor to the storage areas that my uncle rented in various nearby warehouses.

I am not complaining now, nor did I then – or not very much – at this hard life I was living. Always before me was the spectacle of my poor reduced family at home and how I must raise them back up to a decent mode of living by my own exertions here in Lisbon. This was my holy grail, and I thought I would endure far greater tests of my resolve and strength than what I did in order to lay my hands upon it.

In this time of constant labour, I can recall very few particular incidents that separate themselves out from the surrounding darkness. Such as there were seem in my memory like mountain peaks rising above a dark and endless plain. I do certainly re-member the first true encounter I had with Allen Hutchinson, for that was a surprising and, for me, an uncharacteristic moment. I had learned from my new landlord almost as soon as I had arrived in his house that an apartment on the second floor of the building was occupied by an elderly fellow-countryman of mine, a Mr Hutchinson, who lived there with his daughter. I had passed an old gentleman on the stairs a few times who I thought might very well be the man my landlord had spoken of. We had exchanged polite nods, and I might have stopped to speak with him except I was always rushing to be at the Alfândega or else dragging myself upstairs to my bed, too tired even to be civil.

But about a month into my stay, one Saturday evening, I was out in the Rua do Parreiral in search of food at one of the cheap *tabernas* or the food carts that lined this street. I could hardly though concentrate on what I was doing for I was so conscious of having just made a fool of myself. My Uncle Felix, possibly feeling that his distant attitude towards me was not really worthy of the natural obligations of family, had been kind enough to ask me to drop in at his town house at dinnertime to meet a few people he would like me to be known by. I accepted the invitation very gladly. I had grown increasingly hurt by Felix's behaviour. He had not yet, for instance, asked me out to his country house, his *quinta* as they called it here, where his wife, my Aunt Sarah, and their two daughters dwelled.

He made it clear that they would not be at the house in town that night, but still I felt that his invitation was a promising first step in reuniting at last the family that had been fractured by my father's distracted folly. It further increased my sense that our relationship was turning a corner into something more suited to our old affection for each other in that my uncle allowed me to leave the Alfândega early on Saturday in order, as he said, that I should 'make myself look respectable' for the evening ahead. I wanted to do much more than that. For the first time in Lisbon I took out of my trunk the handsome suit of clothes I had brought with me. Legally, all these, as items of certain value, should have been a sacrifice to my father's creditors, along with almost everything else we possessed. But my mother had insisted that I must still be able to make an appearance of some distinction if I was to give a decent first impression of myself to the world. That it was absolutely necessary I should give. Mr Marks had taken care of all, letting me store what I had saved at the back of the draper's shop he had recently opened in the Royal Exchange at Cornhill, until the day of my departure. Now all that precious hoard, like myself, was removed to a foreign shore, and beyond the range of avaricious duns.

Silently thanking my mother's forethought, I surveyed myself in the cracked mirror that stood near to the bed. I knew I had grown thinner and gawkier in the last few months, but still I thought the clothes sat on me very well. The coat was of burgundy cut-velvet, full-mounted and trimmed with silver lace. I was wearing it somewhat unbuttoned to present a pretty good view of the waist-coat of grey silk, trimmed with broad-figured gold lace, that I wore under it. Below that, my breeches were of black velvet, my stockings of white silk, ending at a pair of russet pumps of the finest calf, with silver buckles and, according to the latest mode, squared-off at the toes. Under my waistcoat I wore a ruffled shirt, and around my neck a plain white silk cravat, one of whose ends, again according to the 'military' fashion of the day, was threaded through the top buttonhole of my coat. The whole ensemble was topped off by a full periwig, the product of a certain Monsieur Baye: 'late of Paris, where he was apprenticed to the celebrated M.

Duvallier, currently of Oxford, where he is Perruquier to the *Bon Ton* and to the University'.

Finally I hung at my waist my sword, and silver knot and scabbard, a gift from my father on my twenty-first birthday, a scant nine months ago when he'd believed he was worth at least half a million pounds. I had hired a chaise tonight so that I might be set down outside my uncle's house without my person, or more importantly my clothes, having once come into contact with the amazingly glutinous filth of this city's streets. I intended my appearance to be as fine as I could manage it, for my own sake and more important to the credit of my uncle before his friends.

In fact, as I say, I made a complete ass of myself. The half-dozen middle-aged gentlemen – Felix's colleagues and co-projectors, representatives of that great and powerful assemblage of Lisbon merchants, known collectively as the English Factory – who were assembled in his drawing room that afternoon were all clad in the most sober of hues. In fact, invariably, in black or brown. The wigs they wore were of the most restrained and sober design, there were no military affectations in their plain white neck cloths, gold or silver trim was conspicuous by its absence upon their coats, above all there were certainly no other swords than mine on view. In the midst of these formidable cits I stood out in fact like a vain peacock in a flock of industrious sparrows and starlings. I could see that my uncle was mortified. I had let him down in front of his friends. I dangled miserably trying to make conversation with them and then, when my uncle had left the room for the moment, I fled from it and from the house too. I did not know how I was going to face him ever again.

In this mood, still in my gaudy finery, I turned off the Rua do Parreiral into an alley where I knew there was a pretty good stall where I could buy a bit of fish on a slice of bread for only a couple of *reis*. My mortification was turning into anger. I was terribly angry – at my uncle for not giving me fair warning of how I should dress for his dinner, at the other guests for not disguising in the least their amazement and scorn for how I appeared, most of all at myself for blundering into this social quagmire. Oh, I was angry. Which must be the reason why when I came upon the bullies in the alley who were pushing and jostling and striking at an elderly man who was trapped in their midst I did not, as prudence would have suggested, turn around and walk away from the scene. Instead I was now actually congratulating myself that I had thought to wear a sword tonight, and my right hand was gripping its handle.

It was between five and six o'clock, still light enough in the city's squares but turning to gloom in all the little alleys and passages like this one. I estimated there were three of these bravos setting upon the single man, possibly four. I didn't care. Let there be five of the rogues, or six or seven. I drew my sword. The victim was down on the ground now and his assailants were taking turns to kick at him. I rushed down the alley towards them. The bullies looked up to see me come. I must have made a sight in the gloom. Two of them fled immediately, the other turned to me as if he would make a stand. He pulled free the dagger he wore at his waist. I levelled my sword. Perfect balance 'twixt arm and blade (my old fencing master would have been proud). And slipped it past the fellow's slashing knife.

I was not sure where the point had landed. It might have gone through the sleeve into the upper arm, or even punctured the breast. Wherever it went, the bully immediately set up a loud shrieking, and dropped to his knees. I pulled back my sword arm as if preparing to deliver another thrust. The other louts, who had only retired a few yards into the alley, came rushing back. I prepared to deal with them too. But they made gestures of surrender, and then seized their friend under the arms and dragged him, still squalling, from the scene. I stood over the fallen man, in the correct *en garde* position, glaring after them until they were entirely gone.

Then I kneeled beside the victim. He was stirring feebly, groaning. In the dim light I saw there was blood on his face. I dragged the cravat from my neck and tried to staunch the flow. Close up, I saw that the man was even older than I had first thought. Perhaps seventy or seventy-five. His wig had fallen off in the struggle, and his own hair was white and sparse, the pink scalp showing through.

And then I realised that I knew him. It was the old fellow who lived in my building. The words he was murmuring through his broken lips were English. I must say that it was most gratifying to me to know that the man I had rescued not only might be my compatriot, but also was definitely my neighbour, the very gentleman who I had nodded to once or twice upon the stairs of our mutual home.

I persuaded the poor old fellow to come with me to a *taberna* near by where he could take a glass and recover from his ordeal. He had already declined my suggestion of a doctor: 'Nonsense. Just a scratch. I shall be right as rain in a moment.' But I could see that, when I had got him upright again, he was quite unsteady on his legs, and he confessed to me that he would be glad to sit for a while, before he had to tackle the stairs up to his apartment.

We went in at the nearest *taberna* to the scene of the assault, though my companion declined to give it his approval and told me that if he had his strength he could show me a far better establishment than this. I had no doubt he could, once I had looked around me. It was a filthy, dark little room, occupied by a handful of ruffians, most of whom were sprawled out in their seats, apparently dead drunk. The service was by another ruffian, who lacked grace, politeness and also his left arm. When he came to our table he looked down suspiciously at my companion and grunted out a few surly words. At the time my knowledge of Portuguese was as close to zero as made no difference and I had to rely on my new friend for a translation.

'He says he wants to see some money before he brings us anything to drink,' explained the old man, wincing a little at the effort of speaking.

Indignantly I pulled out a handful of change – actually, my entire fortune until I received another instalment of my meagre salary on Tuesday next – and the rascal grunted again and shuffled off to fetch us wine. When it arrived, and I sipped at it, I found it as vile as was everything else in this reeking hovel.

My elderly companion however was sipping at his glass with every appearance of satisfaction. I was very glad to see this. I really had feared his brutal attackers would have done much more damage than it seemed they had. I told him that I was happy to see him so soon recovered, and added – which was the truth –

that I was the more pleased I had been able to assist him in that I guessed, like me, he had the good fortune to be an Englishman.

'Assist me?' said the old man, quite as if he was surprised at what I had said. 'How do you mean, Sir?'

'Why, I . . .' I was quite nonplussed. 'Well,' I started again uncertainly, 'there you were on the ground and – well, those fellows were kicking you –'

'And how did you know, Sir, that I had not in fact adopted this posture deliberately, and was only biding my time before springing to my feet and laying about those slubberdegullions right and left who, surprised as they must have been by my sudden resurgence, would have certainly taken to their heels, and I would have been left with the honour of having dealt with that whole scurvy pack by myself, alone?'

The old man stopped, quite out of breath after this speech. While he was recovering, I took the opportunity to study him more closely than I had before. He was dressed in a rather remarkable costume. Indeed I think in most English houses it was what would have been relegated to the playroom long ago for the children to dress up in. Everything about it was flowing and ambiguous and peculiar. There was a vast deal of ruffled dirty-white linen at the neck and at the huge sleeves of his coat, and bunches of ribbons, equally grubby, stuck on all over as ornament. The whole assemblage was topped off with a towering periwig, the hair of which was jet-black in colour, with two points in front and – except where it had been torn off in lumps, during some misadventure presumably – descending below the shoulders in a lank mass of fulsome curls. Surely, I thought, nothing like this has been seen in London since the happy day in the previous century when the second King James was chased from the throne. It was also presently displaying a couple of other unusual features in the shape of two long streaks of slime among the curls and bald patches from where the piece had become detached from its owner and had rolled in the dirt of the alley during the late altercation.

Which the old man appeared now to be pretending had not happened. Or not in the way that, in spite of the gloom, I had clearly seen it had.

'I am sure,' I said slowly, 'that you could, and would have done just what you say, Sir. Except that – as far as I could see – you were not in possession of the means of "laying about" anyone. No sword, for instance. Or club. Not that I could see, at any rate.'

The old man looked for a moment as if he would keep up his posture of injured dignity, but then, rather suddenly, he sighed, and his shoulders came down.

'You are right, Sir. Forgive me – foolish pride. I didn't have a single damned thing to defend myself with against those bung-nappers. It is my daughter's fault. She will not allow me to go abroad armed. She says it only incites others to pick quarrels with me.' Now he put his hand out to me, and I seized it gladly. 'Allen Hutchinson,' he said. 'The first name is spelled with two Ls, and an E in place of the second A. And you, Sir, are –?'

'Adam Hanaway.'

'We live in the same building, do we not, Mr Hanaway? I think I have seen you on the stairs. You too are a tenant of Onofre Montesinhos?'

'You have and I am, Sir.'

'Your servant, Sir. It makes me doubly gratified to be rescued by a neighbour.' And he took my hand and shook it warmly, quite as if he had not done the same thing only a minute before.

This was the high point in Mr Hutchinson's recuperation for this night. The excess of confidence and energy brought on, I suppose, by his great relief at having escaped from the bullies, ebbed away pretty soon. He asked me in a while if I would mind helping him back to the house on the Rua do Parreiral. I did what he asked very gladly, and then assisted him up to the second floor where he lived. I asked him if he would like me to come in and explain matters to his daughter, who I understood lived in the same apartment. He said it would not be necessary, and I had the impression that he hoped to conceal his recent beating from his fond offspring. I did not really see how he was going to be able to do this. At the scene of the assault I had done what I could with my neck cloth to stop the bleeding, but the marks of conflict were still pretty clear on his face. As well as the graze on his temple, there was an ugly bruise forming at one side of his mouth.

Just before we parted, Mr Hutchinson asked if I would let him take me to dine at a nearby tavern. He wanted to do this, he said, to show his gratitude and also to reassure me that our neighbourhood boasted some establishments that were above the level of the squalid hole we had drunk in tonight. I said I would be very glad to accept his invitation. Mr Hutchinson found a bit of paper in his pocket and the stump of a pencil and, in the light of the tallow candle that was sputtering on the landing wall, he wrote out an address. We arranged to meet there the following day, Sunday, planning to sit down to our meal at the peculiarly late hour of four o'clock, as was the fashion here.

2

The next morning I rose at dawn. I had slept poorly. The wretched lumpy state of my bed had contributed to this, even more so the fetid heat of the town, so unnatural for May, which had lain on me like a bear's breath all night. But the real culprit lay beyond my windows. On three separate occasions I had been woken out of a shallow sleep by what sounded like fighting in the street below. The second time of waking, my consciousness had barely raised itself above a doze, and so I could not be sure afterwards whether, as I had imagined at the time, I had really heard a clash of swords from down there.

I thought it more likely it was the product of some nightmare connected with the wild events of the evening before. The memory of them had kept me an hour and more from settling down for the night. The risks I had run charging into that gang of bullies . . . that fellow with the dagger . . . oh, it was not to be thought of. Yet I could not help thinking, though it set up a trembling in all my limbs and made me thrash about miserably under the single sheet that was covering me.

The truth was that my behaviour had been greatly out of character. Mine was a curious disposition then: although I was not disinclined to seek confrontations with others, it was too much my habit to abandon them very precipitously. And even in my own heart, I was not sure that in thus rousing up trouble and then taking pains to avoid its most serious consequences I hadn't often strayed across the boundaries of prudence into something that appeared very like plain cowardice. Except that it seemed to me the true coward would not have risked inviting trouble in the first place, so that there would have been nothing to back away from.

Indeed, my conduct in these matters was often a puzzle to me. Sometimes I placed its origins in unhappy childhood memories of my Grandfather Jack. When he died at last I had been happy for it, though I knew it was wicked of me. In the days surrounding the funeral, my father would walk around the house – the old house in the City, where Grandfather Jack had lived with us for the last six years of his life – shaking his head and intoning in sad and reverential accents, 'What a character!' and then again, 'What a character!' With that opinion at least, I could agree. No question Jack had been a character, an old bully of a character who, when he found that his son's only son was of a somewhat apprehensive and timid disposition, made it his business to work on that flaw until it was on the way to becoming an unbridgeable gulf, directing against me a whole battery of surreptitious pokes, pushes, threats, teazing and general malevolence.

Whether or not it was fair to blame my failings on one nasty old man, I am not sure. At any rate, it was undeniable that I had not always shown proper spirit in the numerous schoolyard- and street-fights of childhood. Not invariably, but often enough so that it was remarked upon by the other boys, and I had got a certain unflattering reputation by it in my neighbourhood. It made me glad when the rising state of my father's fortune meant that the family moved out to our new estate in Surrey, and I could leave my old critics behind. But the propensity to – well – *caution* had not left me. At Oxford, a couple of times, I had ducked the final stage in confrontations with other undergraduates that perhaps, if I'd had a greater respect for myself, I would have faced up to. I had once been struck on the mouth by Sir Giles Barry of my College, a hulking red-haired youth, heir to a great estate in the north. In no time Barry had apologised for his insult, and had gone on, quite unconcerned, to ask to borrow ten guineas off me as the price of an Irish wolfhound he particularly wished to buy.

There was perhaps no occasion for pressing the matter further. In some ways I had provoked the argument in the first place. And after the unfortunate incident, I had got my apology, and Giles and I were friends again – but I could not help knowing that the general opinion was that I should have resented the blow much more than I had. Indeed, I was informed by obliging friends that I had been given a nickname after the incident that was sometimes muttered behind my back: 'Adam Runaway'.

(Oh, need I mention? I lent the sum that Giles had asked for, and never pressed him when, as I'd expected, he failed to pay me back.)

Adam Runaway. When I was fifteen my father had insisted that I learn the art of sword-play and I had dutifully obeyed him in this, as in everything else. For the next eighteen months, in the school holidays, I had gone twice a week to Mr Jonathan Cryer's celebrated establishment in Fenchurch Street. In the course of this attendance I discovered myself quite an adept at the short sword. But I was never self-deceived so much as to think that what I could do with blunted foils against patient, methodical Cryer, or my inexpert and complaisant fellow-pupils, could translate to the hurly-burly and the gore of an actual encounter. It simply, I felt, wasn't in me.

And yet here, yesterday, I had done exactly what I had always feared. Launched myself, sword in hand, at an enraged opponent – and for once had actually carried through the assault rather than, as might have been expected, excusing myself from danger at the last moment. What had I been thinking of? Thank God I had done no more, as far as I knew, than scratch the fellow with the point of my hanger. Perhaps I hadn't done even that, just torn his sleeve a little bit.

With the morning, a careful glance out of my window discovered no evidence of serious disturbances from the night before. No bodies in the street – I smiled at the unlikely notion. In fact it was entirely empty, except for two or three starved-looking dogs who were rooting around in the nearest dung-pile. And if there had been any fresh bloodstains upon those cobbles below then they would long since have disappeared under the latest cascades of offal and waste from the windows of the various buildings around that I had listened to while I still lay abed.

Feeling very relieved at the innocuousness of the view from my window, I turned back into the room and began to consider how I would dress for the dinner that Mr Hutchinson had promised me. I didn't want to make any more foolish mistakes in this area; yesterday's at my uncle's had been quite enough for me.

The tavern my neighbour had selected for our feast was located a few winding alleys and one broad street away from my own lodgings. It proved a quite handsome edifice, built in the old Moorish style with a flat roof and whitened façade. When I looked inside the door, I found a long, low, clean-looking room with a handful of diners of the better sort seated at the tables. There was a mouthwatering aroma of roasting meat in the air. Smoked hams hung from the rafters and the walls were lined with bottles in straw. Two neat serving wenches brought food to the tables from a door that must have led to the kitchen. A dignified negro man in a buff-coloured livery also attended the clientele in the capacity of drawer. The whole impression was one of distinguished ease and comfort. It was exactly the establishment that I would have chosen myself for a special dinner. I congratulated myself for having taken the precaution to practically starve myself today in preparation for the feast.

A small, withered woman in a green mantua, hooped to reveal white petticoats – who I took to be the lady of the house – approached me then and, after I had asked for Mr Hutchinson, indicated politely that I should follow her through the parlour. She led me through a doorway in the rear of the room, and I found myself outside again, in a delightful little walled garden, abounding with flowers. There were a couple of tables out here too. Only one of them was occupied. Not by Mr Hutchinson though, but by a lady: a handsome woman of mature years, who wore her own lustrous black hair under a very tall variety of headdress, which I think was called a 'commode'. (It was not, I believe, still in fashion at home, but I had seen its like on the heads of several Portuguese women during my rambles in the town.) I was about to turn to my guide and say – how? In what language? – that there had been a mistake, when the lady before me looked up, discovered to me a very fine pair of eyes, and then spoke herself.

'*Muito obrigada, Dona Ana,*' she murmured to the lady of the house, who nodded and turned away from us. The woman at the table started to rise.

'Madam, please,' I said, rather shocked to see a lady rising in her place to me, and then, supposing she would have no idea what I had said, begged her with a gesture to sit down again.

'Won't you join me, Mr Hanaway?' she said when she had settled herself.

I was so startled to hear her, though whether most because she spoke in English or because she knew my name I am not certain. In any case her words had the effect of making me grope for the other chair at her table and sit myself upon it. I'm afraid I was gaping at her as I did so in a prodigiously inelegant fashion.

'I am right to address you so?' the lady said. 'You are the Senhor Adam Hanaway?'

I closed my mouth, and nodded. I was still staring at her. If my reaction sounds a little excessive, I would point to the fact that I was in a foreign city, where I knew no one except my Uncle Felix and the handful of people I came across daily in the Alfândega. I had not spoken to another soul in an impromptu fashion, as it were, for a long time.

'I am Dona Maria Beatriz Fonseca.'

This information advanced my understanding of what we were doing in each other's company not at all. She studied my evident incomprehension and nodded. 'I changed my surname in the English fashion to that of my husband when I married, for I was fond of Ruffino Fonseca. I was very sorry when he died.'

She paused here as if to take a breath. Her English was faultless, I noticed, with only the least trace of an accent. Yet there appeared to be a minute gap between each word she spoke as if, for just a fraction of a second, she needed to think what she was about to say before bringing it forth.

'But if I was following the Portuguese way I would still be calling myself Hutchinson. So you know who I am now?'

'You are Mr Hutchinson's daughter.' I suddenly felt alarmed. 'Is he not well? Is that why he's not here?'

'He is well. Though he still feels the ill-effects of what happened to him in the Travessa do Tronco. Where you so very bravely rescued him, senhor,' she prompted.

'I see.'

'Mostly he feels tired.'

'Then of course he must rest. I quite understand –'

'But if that was the only reason, he would be here. The fact is: I have forbidden him to have dinner with you.'

After a long moment, I said again, 'I see,' though I really didn't.

'He told me he has invited you to this meal, and that you will expect him to pay for it.'

'Well, I –'

'This he cannot do, Mr Hanaway. He is an old man. An old man who has no money. He cannot afford to offer such hospitality. He should not have done it.'

I felt a flush of embarrassment rising to cover my face. I didn't know whether I was more ashamed for Mr Hutchinson or for myself. It seemed when I thought about it to be mostly the latter, as if I had been caught trying to take advantage of a poor and feeble old man.

'Dona Maria Beatriz,' I said to her, as forcefully as I could, 'it is truly of no consequence to me –'

'You must never tell him I said this to you. He would be so hurt. You see – once he was a gentleman, a fine merchant in this city, shipping cargoes from all over the world. But matters went wrong for him . . .' She was silent for a little while. Then she looked up at me, smiled faintly. 'Do you know what he has to do now to earn his living?'

I said that I didn't. I refrained from adding that I rather dreaded to hear whatever it was.

'He sells pictures of the blessed Santo Antônio, and of other saints too, about the streets. He is allowed a few alleys behind the Royal Mint to do this but no more. That is why he was set upon by Tomás Escaravelho yesterday. Because he would not confine himself to the territory he had been given but, finding no customers where he was, had ventured out on to the Rua do Oiro, which is reserved for one of Escaravelho's creatures.'

I struggled for a moment to try and get a grasp on what sounded like a most complicated underworld.

'You know then who committed this assault on your father? Has he been apprehended yet?'

'Of course not,' said Dona Maria Beatriz briskly. 'Escaravelho is under the protection of Dom Jeronymo da Silva.'

I stared at her. I was completely in the dark.

'Dom Jeronymo is a *fidalgo*. A nobleman, you see.'

'A man of importance?'

'Indeed he is. A knight of the Order of Christ. A *familiar* of the Inquisition –'

'And he protects that pack of poxy bravos who set upon your father? But this is monstrous . . . can't this – Jeronymo? – be taken up by the authorities and his gang disbanded?'

'I told you,' the lady said calmly. 'He is a *fidalgo*. Who would take him up? The idea is absurd. But I shall speak to Dom Jeronymo for I am sure Escaravelho was acting without his master's authority. The wretch will be made to suffer for what he did, at least a little. Believe me,' she said, with the same extraordinary calm in her voice, 'it could have been much worse. There are far more dangerous gangs in the Baixa than da Silva's.'

An idea occurred to me. I reached into the pocket of my breeches and withdrew the rumpled bit of paper on which Mr Hutchinson had written for me the address of this tavern. On the other side it showed a woodcut of a sad-looking gentleman wearing a beard, a cloak and, floating above him, a halo. I showed it to Dona Maria Beatriz, and she nodded.

'It is our Santo Antônio,' she agreed. 'It is one of those my father sells. And I –' She seemed a little flustered at this point, and I wondered if her English had let her down at last. But then, bravely: 'I draw them.'

'I congratulate you. In my opinion this is a most creditable performance.'

She shrugged as if it did not matter, but I saw she was pleased at my praise.

'I draw others too. Santa Catarina, Santa Maria Egipcíaca, São Francisco, São José, São Sebastião who can resist death, Santa

Joana Princesa, São Cosme who is the saint of doctors, São Damião of Conceicão Velha, Santo Elói, São Bartolomeu, Santa Rufina, Our Lady of –'

'All these you draw?' I cut in, wanting to put a stop to a list that threatened to become endless.

'I draw them. I take them to the workshop of our friend Tadeu Nunes and trace or copy them on to the wood. He cuts the image into the wood and then runs off as many copies as we think my father can sell. And that is how we live. Barely. For me, it is not so much hardship. I have never known much different, except when I was married to Fonseca who had a good business making furniture. But for my father . . .' She looked mournful. She sighed. Then: 'You see, he has had to give up so much. For he comes from a great family in England.'

While Dona Maria Beatriz gave me details of these illustrious relations – they appeared to be Nottinghamshire people who had made some sort of name for themselves during our civil wars; I had never heard of them – I allowed myself the pleasure of contemplating her person. I guessed in years she might be around fifty, though I wonder now why I thought I had the right to make such a judgement, for I was so hazy about women's ages in those days; the sex appeared to me divided into only two classes: girls, and other women. In any case, she was certainly in the second category and thus not of course at an age that usually recommends itself to the attentions of a fellow as young as I was then. Perhaps though I was in a state of mind to particularly appreciate the maturer female presence in that it awakened in me fond memories of my mother, who was so far from me now and whose state I greatly pitied and desired to alleviate. That may be so, still I cannot say I remember that the attention with which I examined Dona Maria Beatriz from across the table had much of the filial in it.

Purists might have judged her skin a little too swarthy, and I noted that as far as I could tell she had made no attempts to lighten it to any degree, say with the application of ceruse or alabaster. Again while much of her hair appeared excellently black, like a raven's plumage for the most part, the broad streak of grey in the front of it would have been spirited away in a moment by any competent person in London. I could not believe there were not hairdressers here too of sufficient skill to have done the job if it had been called for. Evidently it had not been, and together with her undecorated skin, it showed that she was prepared to face life as she had been made by God, not disguising in the least the years that she had lived. I found myself honouring her for it. It gave her a look of . . . well, in truth, for some moments I was unsure what exact impression she was conveying to me. Independence, I decided in the end it must be; and while one would not usually find that an admirable trait in a woman, in Dona Maria Beatriz it appeared to me both stimulating and pleasing. For it existed side by side with the most feminine of characteristics in both face and form. She was not, in other words, one of those unlucky 'she-men' that, as schoolboys, my friends and I would pursue in the streets with our taunts and the occasional well-aimed stone whenever we discovered one of them at large.

Still, for all her other charms, the most striking ornaments of the woman who sat opposite me were her eyes. With the chance to study them unobserved, as it were, I saw they were truly astonishing. Large and a little slanted, shielded by long, curling lashes, irises of the lightest shade of blue, so light in hue in fact that they appeared almost white. I was so taken up with admiring these splendid orbs that I think I did not realise for some time that their owner had finished speaking. At any rate she was staring at me now in some perplexity. At my silence, I presumed.

I scratched around for something to say, something worthy of those eyes. Sadly all I could think of was to blurt out a question that had been stirring in my brain for several minutes.

'Are you and Mr Hutchinson Catholic?'

The eyes, the wonderful eyes, widened in surprise. 'Yes, we are,' she said. Then with a slightly frigid smile: 'This is a Catholic country, Senhor Hanaway. Have you not noticed that?'

I was once more rendered speechless, this time at my impertinence in asking her such a question . . . Actually, I remember now, that wasn't really how it was, and I am guilty of writing what should have been, rather than what was (which is something I am trying hard to avoid in this account). What was really silencing me just then was that I suddenly became aware within me of the most intense pangs of hunger. It was as if a wild animal was tearing at my gut. As I've said, I'd barely eaten all day. I had to eat soon or die, it felt like – and since I'd been told that dinner was no longer on offer here, I must get myself back out into the street where I could buy something cheaply off a street cart.

At that precise moment, as if lured to the spot by my cravings, one of the little serving-wenches appeared at the side of the table with a tray of food, which she proceeded to set out on the table. Meat, fish, rice, sallad greens, pettitoes, bread – everything I was longing for, and in such abundance. Yet I knew I could not touch it: the little money that was left to me would not possibly pay for this feast. Dona Maria Beatriz was rising to her feet, seemed about to leave. I followed suit, ready to leave too, but she stopped me.

'No. Stay. Eat.'

I hesitated. I looked down at the food, feeling as if I was in mourning, for I knew that poverty must deny me what I wanted so much. Yet I was too foolishly proud to explain the circumstance to Mr Hutchinson's daughter.

'The meal is paid for,' she told me.

'But you said –'

'I said my father could not afford a dinner for both of you. But you were invited here as a guest of my family, and we always meet our obligations. There is enough money for *you* to eat. Please accept this meal as a sign of our gratitude to you for so gallantly rescuing my father.'

Again I cast a lingering look at the food on the table. Though it was a much more positive examination I made of it now. The note of mourning was almost gone, replaced by one of intense antici-pation.

However, I knew what I must say. 'I cannot accept this, when you have told me you are so poor.'

'You would insult us if you did not,' she said simply.

'I don't like to eat alone. Madam, won't you really stay?'

'I'm not hungry. Truly I am not.'

'Please. Not to eat, if you don't wish it. But to be company for me. And perhaps to take a glass of wine . . .?'

I really wanted her to stay. And my sincerity was apparent. Her gaze softened as she watched me. She seemed to reach towards me – or I to her, I wasn't sure – but we were for the moment holding hands. She squeezed mine.

'I cannot stay,' she said at last. 'This is Portugal, Senhor Hanaway.'

'I know it is,' I said, somewhat idiotically, I was so caught up in gazing into her entrancing eyes.

'It is not considered proper for a gentleman and an unmarried lady to be solely in each other's company, even in a public place.'

I tore myself away from her eyes. I must have gaped at her rather, her words only gradually sinking in.

'And this is so,' she went on, gently disengaging her hand from mine as she spoke, 'even when the lady is in such humble circumstances as I am. And even –' she finished, with the beginnings of a smile upon her lips, 'when she is old enough to be the gentleman's mother.'

And yet she did not actually walk away from me. And I do believe that if I had urged her just a little more she would have yielded. Stayed with me for a glass at least. And perhaps under its influence she would have talked. I would have talked . . . But at that moment my attention was distracted by the appearance of the liveried drawer bearing a bottle for our table. Indeed it was not so much his arrival that disturbed me but the fact that, as I glanced indifferently at him, I thought in the instant that I recognised him. That though I had observed him earlier without particular interest in the gloom of the tavern itself, now viewing him out in the open air I was sure I knew who he was.

To explain this I must go back in time a few weeks, to my third day in Lisbon, in fact. Bidden for the first time to appear at my uncle's offices, I had asked directions to where I was to go from my landlord. He had been so kind as to supply me with a guide, a rather surly negro, who I had wittily dubbed (to myself) Wednesday after the day I met him. He took me across town to my uncle's door, after which he immediately disappeared. It was only some minutes later, when I was in my uncle's presence, that I discovered that my purse and the watch my father had given me on my eighteenth birthday had disappeared also. This circumstance did not improve my first interview with my uncle, which was already proving strained and difficult.

Thinking about it on and off since discovering my loss, I had been forced to admit that there were very many people other than Wednesday, perhaps a hundred, probably more, who could have dipped their hands into my pockets as we had walked and jostled through the most crowded parts of town. Nevertheless, the black remained the prime suspect. I had tried to discover his name and current whereabouts from my landlord, Montesinhos, but the fellow seemed oddly reluctant to help me, even after I told him the reason why I wished to find the culprit. In fact, after that he refused to talk on the subject at all, though always couching his refusal in the most polite and respectful of terms so that I could not quite lose my temper with him.

I tried now to make the negro look at me, hoping to see evidence of guilt in his eyes. But he would not look, only bowed and began to leave the table. I said something to him – I can't remember what now – to force him to turn back, but he affected not to hear me and in a moment was gone. All this while Dona Maria Beatriz had been standing, ignored by me, and by the time I was able to deal with her again I found that the gentle look I had been able to engender previously in her lovely eyes had been replaced by one of surprise and almost of hurt at my inattention. I hurried to explain why I had become so distracted, concluding with the words, 'The fellow is a thief, I am almost sure of it.'

'*Who* is a thief?' she demanded, as if not believing she had heard me right.

'Why, him!' I said, and I gestured inelegantly in the direction the drawer had taken. 'The fellow who brought us the wine. I call him Wednesday. After the day I met him . . . *Robinson Crusoe*, you know. The man Friday?'

It was evident she hadn't the faintest idea what I was talking about. Even in the grip of my current agitation, I wondered at it. Mr Defoe's masterpiece, which was my favourite book then in English, had been out in London for two years almost, and had been wildly popular since it first appeared.

'That gentleman's name is Senhor Paulo Reinaldo,' she said.

'Is it so?' I cried out excitedly. 'Yes. That's who I mean. He stole my watch. And my purse.'

'Impossible!' she said. 'The Senhor Reinaldo is *capitão* of the *Irmandade* of Nossa Senhora da Graça.'

'I don't know what that is,' I said at last, feeling my indignation ebb away in spite of myself. 'But –'

'*Capitão* means commander. The *Irmandade* – the Brotherhood – of Nossa Senhora da Graça exists to collect funds to buy the freedom of African slaves in this town. It is a very worthy fraternity, and Senhor Reinaldo's is a position of great dignity. He is respected throughout Lisbon.'

'He is a drawer,' I insisted, getting irritated in my turn by the disdain I heard in her voice. 'A blackamoor drawer at that. And he lifted my watch – the watch my father gave to me. And my purse too, I'm certain of it.'

I am not quite sure what happened next. There appeared to have been a further flurry of activity around the table as the wenches brought yet more food, and at the end of it Dona Maria Beatriz had gone and I was left with the puzzling sensation that I had never actually said goodbye to her. Nor properly thanked her for the feast before me. Nor tried to make amends for what appeared to have been a blunder of some magnitude upon my part concerning this black *capitão* she thought so highly of.

I am sorry to remember that these honourable regrets lasted barely a few seconds before I had thrown my famished being upon the food before me. I ate steadily for twenty-five minutes, and then sank back in my chair, exhausted and content.

That evening was very fine. I was alone in my room, for Bento had been sent out of town on an errand for our landlord and would not return until morning. My window faced roughly towards the west and there was still a glow in the sky so that I did not need to light a candle. The air was as warm almost as it had been during the day, and I had eased myself earlier by undressing down to my drawers. Now I took my chair to the open window. I thought in a little while I might retire to the table, take up an uncompleted letter to my mother and see if I could finish it. Meanwhile, it was very pleasant to sit here and breathe in the soft, scented air. The breeze was blowing from the land that evening and, as I came to learn, often when that happened in the summer the fragrance exuded by the numerous lemon and orange groves outside the city replaced for a time the otherwise characteristic stench of ordure and rot within it.

I heard people in the street below – but they were not this time producing the ugly sounds of dispute and sword-fighting. A group was talking low under my window; I heard a woman's musical laugh from a building across the way; I heard music itself: a few notes plucked from a guitar, and a man's voice, husky and plaintive, raised in song. With all this, and with a full moon beginning to spread its silver upon the roofs and balconies opposite, I was reminded truly of one of those paragraphs inserted in the newspapers at home – usually by those with an interest in vessels that needed passengers – which attempt to prove that the felicities of foreign scenes are worth all the bother and danger of getting to them.

Soothed by such romantic and peaceful images, I let my mind drift again through the events of the afternoon. The encounter with Dona Maria Beatriz, which had started and ended in confusion, but in between had been so pleasing. Then the discovery of the larcenous wine waiter. I had fully expected – once I'd got past the important business of stuffing my belly – that I would go in search of this black senhor who, in spite of Maria Beatriz's avid testimonials, I still regarded as most likely to have taken my purse and watch. But somehow with physical repletion my resolve dwindled. I had seen nothing of the fellow since he'd brought that first bottle to the table. The second had been carried to me by one of the serving girls, and I guessed that the black, seeing that he had been uncovered, was making himself thoroughly scarce. Of course, I could have set about enquiring after him, raising the hue and cry and so on – but truly the idea was fantastic. I was still reduced to communicating with anyone Portuguese in grunts and gestures, and as far as I could tell everyone in this tavern except myself, staff and patrons alike, were of that nation.

So in fact I had done nothing. Only finished my second bottle and then, a little unsteady, and thanking the lady of the house for an excellent dinner – '*Obrigado, obrigado*', I could manage that – had headed through the tavern to the front door.

The wine I had drunk was still at work, making me feel sleepy now. In a little while I was ready for my bed, having given up all thoughts of finishing the letter this night. I left my seat at the window, washed myself and then got under the sheet. Lying there, my thoughts, as they seemed to every night now, went back home to my family. My sisters Sukie and Amelia, younger than me, terrified by what had happened to them, the so-sudden loss of their father above all. I thought of my mother, and of all she had endured since her husband's accident. I vowed that I would by my efforts in this town rescue my relations from their poverty and shame in as short a time as I could manage it. Of course this was a resolution I had made a hundred times before, but there was, I felt, something particularly solemn and resounding in the commitment I made this night.

It would have been appropriate, I suppose, if after such pledges my dreams too had encompassed only serious and honourable matters. I doubt they did, though. Certainly towards the end of the night they revolved wholly around my new acquaintance, Maria Beatriz Fonseca. They were kind enough to allow me to forget the abrupt and ungracious way we had parted, and to let me dwell only on what I had come to admire about her: her face, her smile, her dignity, her eyes . . . But why pretend? It was the body I had sensed beneath her dress – her smooth swarthy skin, her generous breasts – that occupied me mostly in this last passage of sleep. And I imagined too the most copious and lewd of embraces, as we two coupled in the night.

I knew this was what I had dreamed because the memory of it was still strong with me for many minutes after I awoke. My cockstand was, for me, so prodigious that I was fain to measure it. I used my father's rule, which had always lain across the great desk in his office. I had brought it out here in hopes I would find use for it in my own business life. So far I had found none really, other than to measure occasionally my morning erections.

Today I found I had attained a full quarter-inch greater than anything I had achieved before.

3

But as I have said, these separate meetings with the Hutchinsons were only rare diversions in a life that was otherwise almost entirely focused on my existence in the customs house. It was a very dry existence, certainly. When my uncle had first taken me into that great high building that lined one side of the Terreiro do Paço, the immense square that fronted on the Tagus river, I thought I was looking at one of the wonders of civilisation. So many balconies and tiers rising above the great central space, receding from my straining eyes, until they were lost in the hazy blue light that filtered down and across from the stained-glass windows that were let into the roof.

The ground floor itself, I saw, was crammed with assembled merchandise, some resting on the shelves that lined every wall, the remainder distributed in piles and heaps, neat or otherwise, all over the marble floor in an order that must be known, I guessed, to those who worked here, but made no sense at all to the uninformed. Crates of coffee, and rolls of cloth, and sacks of grain and rice, and stacks of hides, and hogsheads of wine and many huge rolls of cured tobacco and, as I was to discover, much else besides that I did not see on this first visit, such as tea and pepper and silks and ambergris, bales of cotton, and stands of ivory from Africa, bananas and indigo and salt and sugar and wood and wax, all of this and more appeared to be mingled in a vast fantastic jumble.

Oh, it was staggering to see it laid out before me. I clearly remember thinking that for the first time in my life I was actually looking upon what might collectively be worth at least a million pounds in sterling. When I had got over my first surprise, I asked my uncle who all this belonged to.

'All this?'

I made a motion of my hand to include everything that was around us. Uncle Felix considered.

'Well, to us, obviously.'

'Us?'

'The English factors here ... Well –' Then grudgingly, 'I suppose you can throw in a few Scotch and Irish too. The British Factory, indeed. Oh, there are a few other countries who have merchants here. Your Dutch, your Germans, the Frogs – but we are certainly top dogs in Lisbon. It is said we do more business here than all other nations combined. Lot more business. We have pretty well the entire export trade, and we're getting hold of the imports too.'

'What of the Portuguese merchants?'

Uncle Felix laughed rudely.

'What Portuguese merchants? The best had Jewish blood in them and the damned Inquisition has so harried and plundered the poor devils that most have gone abroad, taking their fortunes with them – unless the holy fathers got there first. Those that are left we allow a few crumbs from our table, but otherwise . . . Oh, it's us all right. The English. Top dogs, I say!'

He smote a nearby sack of corn pretty hard then, suffering, I supposed, from a sudden excess of patriotism. A cloud of dust rose from the sack, making the already laden air thick to the point of opacity. We both began to cough furiously. My uncle was the first to recover.

'You mustn't mind a bit of dust, Adam,' he gasped at me, streaming-eyed. 'You'll be breathing in worse than this all the blessed day once you start.'

With which proposition I was not thereafter inclined to argue. I breathed in worse by the bucketload in the months I worked in the Alfândega. Time and toil and sweat and the all-pervading dust shortly rendered even that marvellous palace of trade commonplace to me. It was just the place where I worked now, and I had little inclination to stand and marvel at what was only after all a shell for what human beings did within it. In that activity, at least the small part of it that affected me, I stayed very interested indeed. I was becoming increasingly concerned at my relations with my immediate superior, Bartolomeu Gomes. I found him a most difficult man to read. He had seemed very amicable towards me, obsequious even, when my uncle had first introduced us.

The obsequiousness had continued in a fashion. He always spoke to me politely, and called me Senhor Hanaway, once in a while even Dom Adam. Of course I knew by now that this was only an example of the amiable Portuguese custom of elevating everybody in rank by at least two or three degrees when addressing them, but still it gave me a glow of satisfaction whenever Gomes came out with one of these flowery salutations. And this was so even when he was requiring Dom Adam to strip to his waist and fall in beside the assorted snowballs and other ruffians who worked for us and start heaving bales of cloth across the Alfândega's magnificent floor.

However, I was pretty sure by now that Gomes did not like me. I could not think why this was so – except that I suspected he feared my uncle would one day put me over him. Though nothing in Uncle Felix's pretty severe and distant attitude towards me indicated that such a promotion was in the immediate future, I accepted that there was reason in the head clerk's apprehensions. It is the way of the world after all that family ties will always prove superior to the claims of merit and experience. And then there was the fact that I was English and Gomes unquestionably Portuguese. From talking to other English clerks in the Alfândega I had learned that it was considered something of a comedown for my uncle's firm to be headed by a native head clerk. Again it was a powerful argument for his replacement by me, once I was trained.

Which must be the reason, I decided eventually, why he was so loath to actually train me. For instance, he adamantly refused to let me write a word in the Waste Book, the most informal of the firm's accounts. I did not imagine that I would for many months be allowed to touch the more important books, in which the permanent accounts were written: the Day Book and the great Ledger itself, which was always kept in Felix's own office. But it would have made life in the Alfândega much easier if I had been allowed direct access to the Waste Book. As it was, all I was allowed to use were bits of scrap paper, which I had to keep about my person during the day until a convenient opportunity arose when I could turn them over to my superior to be converted by him into an entry in the Waste Book. And my scrap paper, on which I'd worked so hard, ended up as crumpled bits of rubbish on the Alfândega floor. It seemed a fate eloquent enough of my own standing within the firm to this point.

I did not know exactly what to do about this situation. I didn't like to go sneaking to Uncle Felix, though he had said very clearly at the beginning of my employment and before Senhor Gomes too that I was to be trained in all the mysteries of the trade. I should have, I know, taken the matter up boldly with the head clerk himself. But whenever I thought of doing so, something stopped me from doing it. Somebody, rather. The wretched unwelcome presence of Adam Runaway stole into my consciousness and rendered me powerless to act.

And so I continued in my unsatisfactory course of life, and Senhor Gomes continued in his, with his polite smiles and secret deadly glances and with ordering 'Senhor Hanaway' to go and help heft a few more rolls of tobacco from our station in the Alfândega to where my uncle rented space in a ramshackle wooden warehouse behind the Casa da Índia, another of Lisbon's splendid emporiums, which I no longer had the time or desire to marvel at.

One Sunday afternoon, as I was sitting in my room in the Rua do Parreiral, brooding on the 'Gomes situation', I heard a heavy footfall on the landing outside my door. Which was followed immediately by a couple of loud raps upon the door itself. I could not think who it might be. Once in a while my landlord Montesinhos came by to talk about some domestic matter, but he was not in the habit of announcing his arrival in so noisy and peremptory a fashion. I got up off my bed and went to open the door. If it was Montesinhos out there I intended to show by my attitude that I did not like to be startled in such a boorish style.

The door once open, I had to step back precipitately as a moustachioed gentleman of middle years, rather short of stature, in a long sweeping black cloak, marched past me into what had been my room. Having reached the far side of it, he turned, and struck a rather challenging attitude, which caused his cloak to fall away at the side and thus reveal the rapier that he wore descending from his belt. I was certain I had never seen him before. I drifted back towards the open door. I was wondering if I could disembarrass myself of this unwanted visitor by executing a speedy Runaway manoeuvre and dashing away down the stairs – when from out of the gloom of the landing came yet more footsteps, which were immediately followed into the light by the charming person of Mr Allen Hutchinson's daughter.

Dona Maria Beatriz cast a rather amused glance at me as I stood half in and half out of my room staring at her in surprise, and she dropped a curtsey. I remembered my manners at last and answered with a low bow and – since she was heading that way anyway – resolved the arm movement of my genuflection into an invitation that she enter my room. I followed her in and, keeping my eyes as well as I could off the bravo who stood posturing at the window, told her that she was very welcome.

'Thank you,' she said. 'But I'm afraid my visit is not a social one. I come on an errand that causes me much embarrassment to have to carry out.'

I was sorry to hear this. I wondered if the man with the rapier was to play any part of this errand that displeased her. I could not think that I had done anything to either of the Hutchinsons that could warrant an attack on me by a hired bully. I had saved her father's life, for heaven's sake – or very possibly. Had I earned no leniency at all by this?

She must have noticed the frequent furtive glances I was casting at the man in the cloak for she next clicked her teeth in frustration.

'Forgive me,' she said. 'I have been thinking so hard upon my errand that I forgot to introduce my friend. Mr Hanaway – may I present a gentleman who wishes to know you: Dom Jeronymo da Silva.' She turned to the man at the window, said, '*Dom Jeronymo, apresento-lhe um cavalheiro corajoso, Senhor Adam Hanaway.*'

We bowed low to one another. I had the faintest suspicion that I had heard this fellow's name somewhere before, but when and in what context I could not think. But in any case the thought that he had not apparently been brought along to beat or kill me swept all others from my mind. I said to him, and truly meant it, 'Happy to know you, Sir.'

'He doesn't know any English,' Maria Beatriz remarked. 'I

brought Dom Jeronymo with me,' she said then, 'because – well, I have explained the state of things in this country.'

I waited, bemused, for her to enlarge on this. Actually I had no idea what she was talking about.

'Why, yes,' she insisted. 'I explained at the tavern that for a man and a woman to be alone together in public –'

'Ah,' I cried, remembering. 'You are saying then that Dom Jeronymo –'

'And for the lady to be found alone with the man in his own room would be infinitely dangerous to her reputation –'

'– is your chaperon?'

'He is a friend of the family,' she smiled. Her lovely eyes shone upon me. 'He is the guardian of my good name.'

'But,' I argued pedantically, 'as you came up to my room with him were you not at that time a lady alone with a man?'

'He is a *fidalgo*,' she explained simply. 'And his blood has been pure for five generations.'

'Pure?'

'No Jews were among his ancestors. He is a nobleman with the *pureza de sangue* in his veins. More is permitted to him than to ordinary men. Besides, as I have said, he is an old friend of the family.'

I realised to my mortification that she was still standing and made haste to offer her a chair, the only chair at my table. She sat down upon it. There only remained a most rickety three-legged stool, which I offered to the cloaked one. But he bowed and shook his head and indicated that he preferred to stand. I sat down opposite Maria Beatriz, started to say how sorry I was that I could offer her nothing with which to refresh herself. Would she like me to call for the landlord? She shook her head, evidently desiring me to be silent.

'I must say what I have come for,' she said. And then was silent for several moments, until she gave a deep sigh and then felt inside one of the pockets of her mantua. Directly from it she brought out an object that I recognised at once, with a thrill of pleasure.

'My watch!' I cried.

She handed it to me, and I turned it over in my hands. So many emotions coursed through me as I did, so many memories of my poor father, of the day he had given it to me, of the delight in his face at my joy at receiving it. I know there was moisture in my eyes when at last I looked up from the watch to thank her for returning it.

'Senhor Hanaway,' she said, before I could speak, 'I regret very much that at the tavern I was scornful of your suspicions about –'

'It *was* the black,' I cried. 'I knew it! Damn the fellow.'

She closed her splendid eyes and was silent for a moment. Then, opening them, and evidently trying to ignore my lack of refinement, said, 'It was indeed the Senhor Paulo Reinaldo who took your watch. As you had guessed.'

'So the fellow is just a common thief after all.'

'The Senhor Paulo is not a common anything. But the *Irmandade* of Nossa Senhora da Graça, of which you know he is *capitão*, is often short of funds.'

I grunted sceptically at this.

'I told you the important work that it does.'

'Buying freedom for slaves? A worthy ambition. Does it give them the right to steal my watch?'

'No,' she said, 'I believe it does not. And that is what I told Senhor Paulo. And when he heard that it had been a gift from a father to his son, then he agreed to return the property.'

'How kind!' I sneered. 'And will he do the same with the purse he also made off with, damn black scoundrel.'

'Mr Hanaway,' she said, quietly and very coldly, 'I urge you not to abuse the Senhor Paulo Reinaldo in that manner. It displeases me and, what will perhaps be of greater concern to you, Dom Jeronymo, the *fidalgo* who is standing so close to us wearing that great long sword is a good friend of the gentleman you call a "scoundrel".'

There followed a silence between us, composed of injured dignity on my part and, it appeared, contrition on hers, for when next she spoke it was to say, 'I beg your pardon, Sir. I should not have said that. You are a young man of great courage, as my family has every reason to know, and I am sure you would not be unwilling to match swords with Dom Jeronymo da Silva, even though he is known for his skill in all the *bairros*.'

I frowned, not at what she was saying, which indeed was most complimentary to me, but because I could not rid myself of the nagging feeling that I had heard the *fidalgo's* name before.

Then I remembered. Of course!

'Is not this gentleman the protector of the miscreant who attacked your father in that alley?'

'Of Tomás Escaravelho? Yes, he was. You have an excellent memory.'

'He *was* that rogue's protector? But he is no longer?'

'It is Tomás Escaravelho who is no longer. He is dead.'

'Dead?' I gazed at her. I was suddenly cold all over. What had I done? 'I swear I thought I only pinked him, just a scratch –'

'Oh –' She laughed when she caught my meaning. But then sobered quickly as she saw how shocked I was. 'It was because of nothing that you did, Mr Hanaway, I assure you.'

I was looking now from her to the *fidalgo* who, seeing me studying him, again bowed politely from his waist.

'But if this Tomás is – was – Dom Jeronymo's creature –'

'Yes?'

'And Dom Jeronymo is a friend of your family –'

'He is much more my friend than my father's.'

'But all the same –'

'Ah, yes. I see . . . Indeed, Escaravelho allowed a private feud to interfere with his duty to his master. Dom Jeronymo was furious when he found out what had happened.'

'Then was it –?' I glanced a little shyly at the *fidalgo*. 'It was Dom Jeronymo himself who was responsible for the fellow's death?'

'Not him either. Tomás Escaravelho lost his life two weeks ago in a brawl with another band of footpads who are under the protection of Dom Sebastião de Carvalho. I suppose though,' Dona Maria Beatriz mused, 'you could say that in a way both you gentlemen were responsible a little for his death.'

I had much rather she had not said that. I felt the chill return to my face and limbs. 'How is that?' I said glumly.

'Escaravelho lost much reputation by the easy way you dismissed him in that alley. And then because his patron publicly abused him. He was frantic to recover his pride and fame. And so he threw himself into a fight with the Carvalhos, even though his own band was outnumbered three to one.'

Not much else do I remember of this visit by Dona Maria Beatriz and her gentleman friend – whose connexion with her I could not quite interpret, for they often seemed to throw rather languishing glances at each other and she was inclined to break off from speaking to me to exchange long passages with the *fidalgo* in very rapid Portuguese. I complimented her at one point at her mastery of what I had been told was a very difficult language for English people to learn. She seemed surprised by my comment, and confirmed for me what I had already suspected, that she was, as she said, only half-English.

'If that. My mother was Portuguese. I was born here, and have never lived in another country.'

One of these passages with Dom Jeronymo she translated for me thus: 'I was telling him he is the essence of treachery. For when I was young and beautiful and married to Fonseca, he used to come in his great hat and cloak to play his guitar under my window and sing such beautiful songs. But now I am old and ugly and, even worse, free to marry again he has forgot all that. The brute!'

I started to say that she was very far, in my opinion, from being old and – however, she wasn't attending to me, but addressing Dom Jeronymo once more in a tone of mocking raillery. He answered her back, protesting loudly, placing his hand over his heart, giving every evidence that he was wounded to the quick by her words. This went on for quite a while and I watched the nimble exchanges with the uncomprehending fascination of a child at the theatre. At last both at once seemed to abandon themselves to laughter: his loud and booming, hers gentle and musical.

What could all this mean? I pondered the question for quite a while after they had left me, but then concluded sensibly that it was none of my business. Really I was glad that Maria Beatriz had come to see me today, even with her chaperon, and that, as I hoped, the memory of the unsatisfactory way we had parted at our first meeting was now expunged. I was also, you may be sure, prodigiously glad to have got my watch back.

4

After this congenial reunion I had every hope that my acquaintance with the Hutchinsons would be furthered and deepened over the course of subsequent weeks. I anticipated that my loneliness in this city – which I was becoming increasingly aware of as I grew more accustomed to the rigours of my work, so that I was no longer spending almost every hour I was released from the Alfândega in my bed – would be lightened thereby, at least to a small degree. However, it was not to be. Our mutual landlord confided to me one day that Mr Hutchinson was not in the best of health and was keeping to his room. The old gentleman, Montesinhos reported, was in no particular danger but was still feeling the effect of the beating he had received at the hands of the late Tomás Escaravelho.

I supposed I would be meeting up casually about the house with Dona Maria Beatriz before long and could get from her a more exact picture of her father's condition, but the days and then the weeks followed one upon another and I saw nothing of her. Finally, late one Sunday morning, I decided it was time to take the matter in hand and so went down to the Hutchinsons' door on the second floor and knocked upon it. But nobody coming to open it, I stood irresolute for a while on the landing. I did not want to go upstairs again. My room, though adequate for the purposes of undressing and sleeping and then dressing again, which was almost all that I had used it for until now, was not a place where one would wish to spend one's leisure hours. Particularly, to be blunt about it, when as now the chamber pot that I shared with Bento had not been emptied for twenty-four hours at least.

So I went down the stairs instead of up them, and soon was stepping out of Senhor Montesinhos' house into the Rua do Parreiral. In the gap that was left between the tenements that leaned towards each other from either side of the street, I could see that the sky was a beautiful shade of palest blue. The heavy atmosphere of the last two weeks, which had seemed to seal the town off from above, so it made a kind of cauldron of heat and bad air underneath, had blown away overnight. It was the end of July now, and yet it felt more like autumn than the usual Lisbon summer broiling. In short, it was a fine day, and I entered into it in quite a state of exhilaration.

Only one thing marred my pleasure, and that was the fact that the Rua do Parreiral was much used by vehicles. I suppose the street must have provided a convenient passage through this part of the Baixa, and in fact there probably were no other thoroughfares near by that were like it, for it was slightly wider and straighter than almost all the multitude of twisting alleys that surrounded it. Even the very small Lisbon coaches of those days could not go down those constricted tracks. Which left the Rua do Parreiral to take all.

After ten minutes of trying to work my way along between the coach wheels and the sides of the houses, and being very nearly crushed in the endeavour several times, I fled into a side alley. Once more I was back in that labyrinth I had used to stumble through in my first days in this town, before I had learned which streets were safe enough and clean enough to make walking in them other than a hazard and an abomination. The same dank and shadowy surroundings, the same absence of visible life, same dungheaps – and the old melancholy at experiencing them again. I could not endure it, and had made up my mind to retrace my footsteps, gain once more the Rua do Parreiral and, should I be left uncrushed again in crossing it, retreat to my room, stink and all. But at that moment there came to me, borne on some poor lost wind that had strayed into the dismal alley in which I now stood, a faint noise that when I heard it lifted my spirits greatly and made me determined to press on with my expedition. It was the sound of many human voices, of the cries of street-vendors, of music too. I was pretty sure I knew exactly where it was coming from, for I had been to the place once before. And I wondered indeed, as I moved joyfully towards the noise, why I had not thought of going there today, for it made a perfect destination for a Sunday diversion.

The Rossio was the second great square of Lisbon. On the northern edge of the Baixa, the Lower Town – where most of the common people lived, where I lived – it lay more or less opposite to the Terreiro do Paço, which began just beyond the Baixa's southern edge and extended down to the river's edge. It was opposite to that other great space in character too. It had its share of massive and remarkable buildings around it, the Dominican convent for instance, and the palace belonging to the Inquisition, and – surely more blessed in the sight of God – the hospital of Todos os Santos, a sumptuously decorated set of buildings that formed altogether the shape of a prodigious cross. Yet for all these grandeurs, the Rossio had little of that lofty, dispassionate quality that characterised the Terreiro do Paço, which I knew so well from having to cross it almost every day to go to my work.

The Rossio indeed had a human, friendly character to it. Much of it was given over to the stalls of the market folk and it was difficult to become overawed, even by the terrible looming shape of the Paço da Inquisição, when one was treading among piles of oranges and potatoes and bananas and dried fish. Very many beggars disputed one's way across the square, including a veritable army of vigorous cripples, which added to the impression of babble and confusion, as did the raucous presence of many others who tempered their beggary a little by offering some sort of pretext for it, as puppet-masters and street acrobats and fire-eaters and people who offered to tell you fortunes and others who wished to sell you a holy relic or a holy picture – the Hutchinsons' trade in fact, though I think they would never have been allowed by the gangs of bullies who commanded the streets thereabouts to practise it in so favoured a location as the Rossio.

For half an hour I strolled among its pleasures and marvels. I bought some toasted almonds from one vendor and some lemon water from another to wash them down. I wandered towards the north side of the square, where I watched for a little while a prodigiously ugly wild beast that had been captured in the forests of America and brought over to be exhibited in a wooden cage in the Rossio. I gave its keeper a few coppers and hoped earnestly that it would contribute a little to giving the animal a better life, for at the moment it looked deeply dejected by its fate, and only stirred its limbs when its master poked it through the bars with a sharp stick.

I moved on from this spectacle, feeling rather less happy than when I'd begun to watch it. A large fellow with a greasy, shiny face suddenly lurched into my path, clawing at me and uttering the usual beggar's nonsense of 'Heaven prosper your noble excellency, look down with mercy from your eminence upon a poor wretch . . .' Etcetera. All this accompanied by the traditional gusts of mingled garlic and rot. I don't know why, but these familiar proceedings for once struck me not as amusing or, at worst, irritating, but as downright offensive, even sinister. Perhaps it was the effect of watching that sad caged American beast that had made me so prickly. Anyway, I chose to fling an oath at the fellow, one of those I had learned from my fellow-labourers in the Alfândega and which, as was usual, involved placing some saint or other in a peculiarly embarrassing and often disgusting situation.

Unfortunately the particular saint I abused must have had some special relevance for this beggar for he became instantly incensed. Up till now he had been affecting some strange constriction of his limbs in order, I suppose, to arouse pity for his pretended plight. But now he straightened up to a very creditable height, not much less than my own, and displayed before my nose two large fists which, he informed me, he was at the point of smashing into my face. He also called me a fucking *maricão* and a *bosta inglêsa*. A little crowd now began to gather. At first it seemed their sympathies were with me – a well-dressed, presentable young man after all – rather than with the pot-bellied, whiskery bully who menaced me. But when they understood, first that I was English, and second, even worse, the nature of the insult that had brought on the beggar's rage against me, then the mood turned ugly. It was made clear to me that while it was one thing for a true Lisbon Catholic to take the names of the Virgin and the Saints in vain, it was very different when the same was done by an English *herético*.

There were angry cries against me from every side. Somebody suggested that one of the *familiares* of the Inquisition should be called upon to take me into custody. Somebody else cried out that it would be a waste of time to go searching for the authorities. The case against the heretic was perfectly clear, and there were lanterns enough around the square from which he could be expeditiously suspended by the neck. There was a growl of agreement at that piece of common sense from several rough throats.

In this emergency, I did the only thing I could. Adam Hanaway – erstwhile scholar and gentleman, latterly a merchant's clerk – was swiftly sent packing. His brother Runaway stepped forward in his place. First, I apologised very deeply and sincerely to the beggar. Then I gave him all the money I had on me. The beggar took the coins but did not look at all convinced that I had done enough to make amends for my vile behaviour. And around me, the faces of the crowd, fearing to be balked of the ultimate entertainment of watching another human being kicking his life away in mid-air, became not a whit less severe. It was touch and go, I saw. I did the only thing I could. Reached into my waistcoat pocket, and took out my watch and offered it to the beggar.

There was a sigh of admiration as the crowd realised the magnificence of my gift. The beggar accepted it, turned it over in his hands. And I – I took to my heels. I dared not look back but from the start I had the feeling there was no risk of serious pursuit. The watch had done its work; I had found the exact worth of my life in the Rossio. When I did finally look over my shoulder, I found there was no one following me at all.

It might be thought that I would immediately have taken the opportunity to leave this dangerous square and dive back into the anonymity and concealment of the Baixa. But I was so shaken by the encounter with the beggar and his supporters and so troubled by the part I had taken during it that I could not set myself to doing the sensible thing. Instead I continued to wander in the sqaure, though keeping now to the very edges of it, not wishing again to face the rabble in its centre.

In my defence I could say that I was not wearing my hanger that day. Perhaps if I had been, I would have taken a less farcical part in the drama. And, if it had been the beggar alone I'd had to deal with, perhaps it might have been a different story then too. But in both cases I suspected the worst. I knew Runaway, knew his many devices for avoiding conflict and failing to step up to the mark. I wondered wretchedly if I would ever be free of his presence. I was a young, hale, muscular Englishman – and I had fled from a crowd of what the other day in the street I had heard one of my countrymen call 'god-damned Portuguese dwarves'. Worse, before fleeing, I had handed over a possession more precious to me by far than the wealth it represented, though that was considerable. The watch my father had given me. That was stolen from me by the black thief and *capitão* Senhor Reinaldo, restored as in a miracle by Dona Maria Beatriz, and now through my cowardice had been lost again.

It was shameful, utterly so. I did not leave the square now because I could not bear to be alone to contemplate such humiliation. Now I did not even think I had been in any real danger, and therefore there was no need for me to have beaten such a precipitous retreat. For though the mob might have liked to have stretched a heretic's neck to make their holiday, there were enough folk of fashion and rank in the square, plenty of brave *fidalgos* strolling with their wives and families, to have stopped the outrage before it had gone too far. I had only to show for a little while some manly courage and defiance and the mob would have been driven out of countenance. Out of the square too, and I would have been left in sole possession of the ground and of my watch. Oh, shameful!

I was walking now under the arches that lined the sides of the Rossio, where the most luxurious of shops and stalls were situated. The sight of so much excellent merchandise was gradually calming to my spirits, as was that of the many gentle people who were inspecting it, none of whom, I was certain, would even think of calling me a sodomite or an English turd. In a little while I felt much more easy in myself. I stopped by several of these emporia and, showing much assurance, looked over the articles for sale, even though I knew that my pockets now contained not a single penny, *sou*, or *ré*.

At one point I found myself inspecting the wares of a dealer in fine cloths. They had a special interest for me, of course, for so much of my own work was involved in handling such stuff. In a little while the fellow who owned the place was standing at my elbow. He was rubbing his hands in what appeared a rather naked display of optimistic greed. I was about to move on and relieve

47

myself of his presence when my gaze fell upon a bale of serge, which seemed suddenly most familiar to me. The shopkeeper seeing my interest in it sprang forward and unrolled several feet of cloth for my better appreciation. There was no doubt about it. It exactly resembled a number of bales in the latest shipment the firm of Hanaway had taken into the customs house from the wharves. It was of a quite distinctive blue with a grey thread making a pattern in it throughout. I could even name the vessel that had brought it hither, since I'd had to scribble it down several times so that Gomes could make the right entries in the Waste Book: The *Happy Return*, ex-London, Captain Venables commanding.

But here was the thing that baffled me as I studied the opened cloth: I was sure we were the only house that had imported this particular weave of late, and yet our consignment could not have left the Alfândega so soon as this. I knew for certain the customs officers had no plans to even begin clearing it until the middle of next week at the earliest. So how had it got here, on a stall in the Rossio? It was a mystery then, possibly it was a crime. I resolved that I would take it up with my uncle next time I saw him.

'Why, it *is* Mr Hanaway! Large as life. Well met, Sir!'

All thoughts of the baffling presence of blue serge fled from me as I turned to find Mr Hutchinson and his daughter standing behind me, both smiling broadly. Well met indeed! I bowed first to Dona Maria Beatriz, who acknowledged my gesture with perfect condescension. And having saluted the daughter I held out my hand to the father. It was gripped, I was pleased to find, in a clasp that was very emphatic and hearty, and even a little painful to receive. We moved on under the arches, now as a threesome – leaving a disappointed vendor of fine cloths muttering behind us – and were all three chatting animatedly as we walked. It appeared that they too had been merely strolling in the square when they discovered me, having spent a refreshing hour before that listening to the service at the church of Todos os Santos. Maria Beatriz explained that they took especial pleasure in attending that church because it was so cleverly designed that the patients lying in their separate wards were able to hear perfectly the devotions being conducted at the altar and in the choir.

'It is a fine thing, Mr Hanaway,' she said with great solemnity, 'to know that one is sharing one's worship with those poor souls, some of whom are on the very brink of entering Christ's kingdom.'

I suppose I wore on my face the appropriate (and fundamentally impertinent) look of a genteel English Protestant who thinks he hears the approach of Catholic mummery and superstition. That is, I was showing a polite interest in what I heard, but at the same time not disguising by much that scepticism and dislike for fanaticism that seemed to have been bred into the bones of the English of my generation.

'Mr Hanaway does not approve of our devotions, Father,' smiled Maria Beatriz.

I tried to say that this was not quite fair of her. Meanwhile, Mr Hutchinson was blustering away, 'Not approve! What d'yer mean, Sir, not approve?' I repeated that I had no wish in any way to show discourtesy to their religion. Luckily, all this was carried on in quite a good humour; we were still, I think, so pleased to have met up with each other on this cool sunny day in the Rossio.

At that moment Dona Maria Beatriz's name was called and she found herself being embraced by a passing female, evidently a friend. The two ladies fell into an animated conversation, during which Mr Hutchinson and I were reduced to the role of smiling bystanders. And then as men will do during these feminine encounters we drifted off a little to one side and began to talk to each other in low voices. I took the opportunity to say how pleased I was to discover that he had obviously recovered from his recent disorders. He informed me with great good nature that he didn't know what the hell I was talking about. I told him what our mutual landlord had said to me, and he shook his head and gave vent to a rather violent snort.

'Montesinhos is an ass!' he cried. 'A thoroughgoing sawney. He was supposed to tell that to outsiders, strangers who came asking for me. I owe one or two small sums about the town, you see. My hairdresser, my tailor,' he added rather vaguely. 'My lace man . . .'

I was sorry to hear this. I knew that it was quite the custom in

London for impecunious young fops to run up bills with the tradesmen and then have to spend much time and ingenuity avoiding those fellows' attempts to recover what was owing to them. There were many jokes in circulation upon the subject; it seemed to be viewed by the world in the light of mere harmless pranks, the sort of thing that youth will get up to. But it appeared to me almost pitiful that a man of Mr Hutchinson's venerable age should be in an equivalent situation. Moreover, given what I had seen of his everyday appearance – clothes, wig, lace, ribbons, etcetera – it seemed monstrous that anyone who had conveyed to him these shoddy and dated articles should have the impudence to be making a fuss about getting money for them.

'But here's why I say Montesinhos is an ass, Mr Hanaway,' the old man carried on strongly. 'For he should never have given such false information to one of my friends.'

I felt a glow of pleasure at my being described as such and hurried to cover up the emotion. At that moment the ladies kissed one another and separated. Maria Beatriz's friend bobbed a curtsey to Mr Hutchinson and a shallower one to me and, followed by the small and exquisitely dressed negro boy who was her escort in the square, moved on. I was restoring myself after the low bow that I had given the lady – willingly, for she was near as handsome as Mr Hutchinson's daughter – when Maria Beatriz broke out in a stream of rapid Portuguese aimed at her father. I waited patiently for her to finish. At last she realised that in excluding me, as she thought, from her discourse she was being impolite. She put her hand upon my arm and started to apologise. I told her there was no need. I had understood her well enough, and when she looked astonished, I gave her a quick precis of what she had just said.

'Your friend has decided to accept the presence of Antônio Moreira de Mendonça in his great cloak beneath her window, but has told him he had better bring a professional singer with him for if she has to listen to his own voice, which is like that of a sick horse, she will certainly empty her chamber pot upon him.'

I listened, smiling proudly, to their exclamations of wonder at my performance. I told them I had got my knowledge quite informally, mainly just by listening to the chatter of my fellow-workers in the Alfândega. They both said I was doing prodigiously well, much better already than most of the English ever attained, however long they resided in Portugal. Mr Hutchinson was kind enough to offer his opinion that I was 'certainly no nigmenog', by which he meant – well, I didn't know exactly what he meant, but from the tone in which it was said I took it as a compliment, and thanked him for it.

'Although,' said Maria Beatriz then, frowning and using a very clipped voice, and generally imitating for our amusement the person of an aged schooldame, 'I think you got one or two things wrong. Dona Fatima likened Dom Antônio's voice to that of a sick crow not a horse. *Corvo* not *cavalo*, you see?'

I nodded, annoyed with myself at this elementary blunder. We had begun walking again beneath the arches. On my other side Mr Hutchinson emitted a coarse chuckle. 'Also,' he said, 'I rather think when the lady used the word *vaso* she meant she was contemplating emptying the contents of a flower vase on the poor *cavalheiro* beneath, not of her chamber pot!'

I was so mortified to hear this, and I must have looked quite comically dismayed because Maria Beatriz began giggling before I could even bring myself to say anything to them. So kind was her laughter and so infectious that I was grinning too even as I was stammering out my apologies. Mr Hutchinson added his thin bass to our mirth and, to sum up, it was as a very contented friendly group that we at last departed from the Rossio and took our way through the alleys to our shared lodgings.

I found my friends were unwilling to let this pleasing occasion die so soon, just as I was. For Maria Beatriz, who was walking between us men, holding each of us by the arm, enquired as we turned into the Rua do Parreiral whether I was engaged anywhere else tonight, and if not whether I would like to join them in their apartment for the light supper they usually ate together on Sundays. I told her I would be very content to do this. We set a time for me to come downstairs, parted on the second landing, and I continued on my way to the fourth floor with the very great comfort of knowing that this evening at any rate I would not be enduring only my own company.

With an hour to wait before I rejoined them, I lay back upon the mattress so that I could enjoy the prospect ahead more comfortably. After about half a minute of this I fell asleep and did not wake until the morning when Bento, seeing that I had not even begun to stir, apologetically shook me awake and murmured in my ear that it was Monday, the time was *cinco e meia*, and I was due at the Alfândega, to begin my week's labours, within half an hour.

Looking back across a long life, it is hard for me sometimes to make any sense at all of certain of my behaviour when young; in fact, I would say of most of it then, for I am continually struck by some memory of youthful excess or eccentricity. Why did I do these things? I am always asking myself this, as I groan over yet another memory of some piece of poltroonery or folly. What possessed me? What almost drove me to make such a fool of myself?

All this is prefatory to saying that I have hardly any explanation to offer for how I dealt with the situation that had arisen between myself and the two Hutchinsons by my unfortunate failure to keep our appointment for supper. Of course, looking back, I can see that it need have presented me with no more than a momentary embarrassment when I explained to them what had happened. My reason for non-attendance was genuine. The fact that I was tired to my very bones by the labours of the preceding week was excuse surely for my fatal bout of weariness. It might have all ended then in smiles and shrugs, apologies on my part, forgiveness on theirs, and we would have been on as good terms as before in no time. All this, I say, *could* have happened.

What did happen was – nothing. For several days at least. When I was in the house I crept about it, hoping fervently all the while that I would not by accident happen upon one or other of my disappointed hosts. I knew that Mr Hutchinson's disabilities made it unlikely that he would mount the stairs to the fourth floor to demand an explanation. As for Dona Maria Beatriz: I was relying on her advertised concern for her reputation, which would – I hoped sincerely – not permit her to venture alone into a gentleman's chamber. Such a waste of time. Why did I not just do the straightforward thing and go and explain everything to them? Of course, each day, almost each hour that I failed to do this added to the difficulty of ever doing it. Could I not even have sent – by Bento? Or Montesinhos? – a note expressing my deep regrets? Of course I could have, but I didn't.

What I actually did next could not have been better contrived to make things at least fifty times worse than they already were. The Thursday evening after the fatal Sunday, I sent a note via our mutual landlord in which I begged to be forgiven for my forgetfulness but, pray, was the meal we had appointed to eat together *next* Sunday to be dinner or supper? I signed that piece of impertinence with such a flourish, thinking I had devised a perfect solution to my difficulty. I waited for a while in my room in the expectation that Montesinhos would be bringing me a reply, no doubt with an amused reference in it to my faulty memory and a joking revelation that it was *last* Sunday we were meant to have met. But, as I further hoped their note would say, next Sunday would do just as well.

For this reprieve I waited, until it came to me like a stone in my belly that I could wait till the crack of doom and it would never come. It should have been instantly apparent to me then that the Hutchinsons – or indeed any five-year-old child – were not to be deceived by such infantile trickery, and that I had thus changed the small and really unmeant rebuke I had offered them by not turning up for supper into a gross insult to their intelligences that – as it seemed to me then in my ignorance of the world – they would hardly ever wish to forget or forgive. This, I say, is what I should have thought. Instead, I actually grew indignant at their failure to respond to my nonsense, as if what I had wrote to them really was an innocent request for information, instead of a fatuous lie. How dare they, I fumed. How did they find the impudence to ignore me in this way?

Those who have followed my history so far may dismiss this unprecedentedly idiotic course as just another symptom of the Runawayism that, as I have shown, dogged me so close in this period of my life. I certainly can see the family resemblance, but still insist that this was a new departure for me. My brother Runaway in the past had the character of one who, sensing a threat, made immediate and precipitous efforts to get away from it. But my behaviour at this time was not a matter of simple avoidance of danger. I was now entered into realms almost of fantasy. I was denying what was true, I was making things up. I had lost touch more than a little with the reality that brother Runaway had always had a real grasp on in the past.

And so, as I have said, I finally compounded all my previous folly by allowing myself to become angry with those I had offended. I suppose to shield myself from the consequences of having insulted the only two people in the town who had shown the least desire to befriend me, I also endeavoured to persuade myself that they were not worthy of my friendship in the first place. An old superannuated rake of a broken-down, pretended 'gentleman' – how the contemptuous phrases boiled in my brain! – and his elderly papistical daughter, with her dubious Portingale antecedents . . . What a pair! I sneered to myself as I crept downstairs every morning, even more terrified now that I would run into one of them, and repeated the same cowardly journey in reverse each evening. What a couple of beggars! They deserved every insult I could load on their backs. In fact, by being so mean, so negligible, such *scrubs* indeed, they were really the authors of the rift that had grown between us, not I!

In short I was – I thought in my delusion – well rid of this disreputable pair. I turned my attention back to my work and resolved to consider them no more. As for the glimpse of society and friendship – such as it was, I sneered to myself – that they had offered me, I had no need of such from *them* any more. For I was about to be admitted – readmitted rather – into the bosom of what remained of my family. A few days after my excursion to the Rossio, my uncle finally relented. I was invited to spend the Sunday after next at his *quinta* and to dine there with my aunt and my cousins.

Senhor Gomes was standing near us and must have heard my uncle issue this invitation. I thought I detected on his narrow, swarthy brow a sudden frown, of chagrin, I guessed. I fancied that *he* had never been allowed into the Hanaway *quinta* as a guest. I suppose it is further evidence of a certain streak of ill-breeding in my character then that this notion gave me a mean twinge of pleasure.

Felix

He had recognised Marks's small, neat handwriting on the envelope and had taken it into his study and closed and locked the door. He dreaded what the letter inside might contain. He had given up the ghost entirely as far as his South Sea stock was concerned, but still had lingering hopes that the other subscriptions his brother had persuaded him to take up had survived the storm that had been raging in London for the past several months. The London Assurance, English Copper, York Buildings, Orkney Fisheries: surely some value remained in those companies, surely he was not entirely undone?

It was his keenest, most secret shame now to remember that, when he had at last summoned up the courage to read what Solomon Marks had to say, his first emotion when he found that it was purely to inform him of his brother's death was of relief. Thereafter he had begun to feel all the sentiments proper to this catastrophic news, such as shock, desolation, sheer incomprehension that so large a part of his life as his elder brother could be expunged thus in a few lines from Matthew's former head clerk. But still he could not shake off the ravaging memory of that instant when he had thought: It's all right. I'm not yet entirely undone. My London Assurance still stands. My English Copper . . .

Subsequent correspondence from London had revealed that his other shares had gone the same way as the South Sea's. It had been the devil's own job to keep himself afloat. He had managed it – just – by the expedient of cutting his establishment to the bone. For instance, he used to have five under-clerks working in his office and at the Alfândega, good men trained in London and Hamburg. His senior clerk had been apprenticed in a great house in the City and would certainly have made a fine career at home, except that his delicate health had obliged him to remove to the milder climate of Lisbon. All these superior fellows had had to be dismissed. He was reduced to employing a mere Portuguese who, since he was his only employee, could hardly be denied the right to call himself his head clerk too.

A Portuguese as head clerk in the house of Hanaway. It hardly bore thinking of.

But then he felt a revulsion at this mode of thinking. When he thought how much he owed to Bartolomeu Gomes, how the dear fellow had stuck with him through the worst of the storm, had agreed to accept half his previous wage so that the house of Hanaway should not go down, how he had impressed by his energy and his understanding of the business, remarkable in one who had only been employed before, on a casual basis, as a sort of scrivener, translating documents and letters from France and Spain and Italy, all of whose languages he could understand. As well as English and Portuguese, of course. Really Gomes had been a find. Felix did not know what he would have done without him.

Only the other day, for instance, his head clerk had been instrumental in resolving a situation that had arisen out of nephew Adam's inexperience. The boy had come to Felix with some story about a length of cloth he had seen on sale in the Rossio. He was, the boy had said, certain it had once belonged to the stock of fine blue serge that the firm had purchased entire from the *Happy Return*'s cargo, all of which should of course have been still in the customs house where the official rogues who flourished in the place were making particular difficulties about clearing it. Since pilfering from the Alfândega was a persistent problem, Felix had taken his nephew's claims seriously, even given the greenness of the source. He had turned the problem over to Gomes who had made a thorough enquiry. Later he had come to his master to explain that what must have happened was that a sample length of the cloth, which had been sent to one of the wholesale purchasers in the city, had found its way to one of the petty shops in the Rossio. It was not a practice that ought to be encouraged, but still it represented no real loss to Hanaway's. Otherwise Gomes had checked the store of blue serge in the Alfândega and found everything as it should be.

'So there's nothing in Adam's fears?'

'Nothing at all, Sir. It was just a foolish mistake.'

'Yet,' said Felix, not quite happy with his clerk's tone of voice, 'it was an honest mistake after all. Shows he has concern for the firm, I suppose . . . What do you think, Bartolomeu – is it time to bring him on a bit, get him more involved in the business? Something more challenging than – whatever he's doing right now.'

The look of hostile amazement that Gomes gave him persuaded Felix not to pursue the thought just then. Yet he remained indulgent towards Adam's little blunder. It was the recognition that it had been made out of praiseworthy zeal for the firm's best interests that had led him to invite the boy out to the *quinta* at Junquiera to spend a day with his cousins and his Aunt Sarah.

He had left it late, he knew. His brother's son was a good-looking, well-set-up young man, evidently not unintelligent, and in normal circumstances would have been a credit to the firm. He deserved to be encouraged. Yet it was this invitation that had created such problems for Felix from the moment he had told his people that he had issued it. For however much young Adam might have wanted to re-unite with his Lisbon family, it was apparent that a good part of his family did not want to unite with *him*.

Somewhere in the house, a door slammed. Felix winced, and drew deep on his pipe in hopes the smoke would soothe his jangled nerves. It didn't much. He looked across at his wife, who was straightening his shelves on the other side of the study.

'For God's sake, Sarah. This is my brother's own boy. I have been most remiss in keeping him from you and the girls all this time. It cannot go on.'

'Your brother . . .' said Sarah, tight-lipped, bustling about at her domestic foolishness to show him that – reduced in circumstances as she was – she had no time to spare from her duties just to make conversation. 'He was very remiss too in ruining us, don't you think?'

Poor Sarah. As there had once been a half-dozen clerks working in the offices, there had been at least that number of indoor servants at the *quinta*. His wife had used to give herself such airs to be in command of so numerous a staff. Privately, Felix had thought that her manner was rather ridiculous in the mistress of a moderate-sized country house on the less fashionable side of Junquiera, but he had held his peace about that. Now most of the airs and graces were gone along with most of the servants; and most of the horses, dogs, gardeners, and Sarah's beloved yellow phaeton too. Her acting skills were turned in another direction these days, and she lost no occasion to demonstrate before her husband how industriously and unselfishly she was dealing with their new poverty.

'It was not my brother's ambition to ruin us, Sarah. He wanted to make us rich.'

'We were already rich,' his wife snapped. 'We were very satisfied with what we had until he dangled temptation before you.'

His last trip home. He used to go back to London every eighteen months or so to see at first-hand how the parent firm was doing and discuss how the Lisbon branch could be involved in future ventures. His brother had taken him away to his study on that first morning.

'Things are really stirring here, old boy,' Matthew had grinned, when they'd got snug in his deep armchairs, and each had a glass of good French wine before him. (Such a pleasant change for Felix after the everlasting Portuguese stuff.)

'What things? Where are they stirring?'

'Why in 'Change Alley, dear fellow. And what's stirring is Old England herself.'

After which Matthew had proceeded to take him through all the immense changes that had taken place in London since his last visit. He carried him down to Exchange Alley, off Cornhill, to witness the turbulent trading that was going on in the coffee houses there, spilling out into the street itself. The projectors and the speculators and the stock-jobbers, the latter at work at what they called 'selling the bear's skin before they had caught the bear', that is, selling stock that they did not own, betting that the rise in its price would more than cover them when it came time to settle their debt. This was a bet, Matthew told him, that they very rarely lost. The times being what they were.

Of course, even in Lisbon Felix had heard ship-borne rumours of these marvels but it was tremendous to hear Matthew lay them all out before him. They spent some happy hours in the noisy fug of Garroway's coffee house, talking over the merits of all the wonderful companies, dedicated to such a fantastic variety of undertakings, that had sprung up overnight and were making fortunes for their far-sighted backers. Above all, his brother wished to praise the glorious South Sea Company. He showed Felix the company's magnificent new headquarters in Threadneedle Street. He told him of the vastly important men who had become its directors, headed by King George himself. He described how this splendid body of public-spirited notables had even discovered a way of ridding England of its old bugbear, the national debt, by issuing shares to the debt-holders to buy up their claims on the nation's wealth.

'What does this company actually do?' Felix had ventured to ask at one point.

'Do?'

'Yes. Does it for instance trade into the South Seas?'

'Who knows? Who cares? What it does, brother, is make men rich. And you and I will be among those fortunate souls. For I have been promised by Mr Gibbon, who is a director of the company, that I shall certainly be preferred when the second subscription for shares is announced.'

Matthew explained that he was putting all the profits from last year's trading account into the South Sea and had no plans to send out any more ventures this year.

'The thing is, Felix, if we stand still we risk being left behind. There are already fellows in the City who have vaulted ahead of us because they were in the market early. Worthless fellows, some of 'em. I cannot bear to think of being looked down on by such as they.'

His brother had persuaded him to put in all the money he had on deposit in his Lombard Street goldsmith's vault into this South

Sea subscription. Felix would have left to him only what he kept for trading purposes in Lisbon. Matthew also urged him to spread the news of what possibilities were on offer in 'Change Alley among his colleagues in Portugal.

'Start with those you are most fond of,' Matthew had smiled. 'And leave out any you detest. You will be a hero, old boy. Future generations will bless your name as the fellow who brought untold riches to the Lisbon Factory.'

Back in Lisbon, Felix had done what he had been asked. Sent more of his own money home, and a great deal of other men's too, for he had successfully dazzled a number of his oldest and closest friends with the tales he had heard in London: of a footman who had been able to buy a country estate on what he had gained in the market, and a porter who had sold his shares for a £5,000 profit and now drove around in a fine coach and lived in a house he had rented in Leicester Fields; of how even a sober gentleman like the bookseller Mr Guy was said to have made near £200,000 by the South Sea, and Mr Stanhope of the Treasury a quarter of a million. And that Miss Barbier, an actress, had made £8,000 and had quit the stage and bought herself a very pretty fellow who had a title to gift her with too. The list went on and on.

The announcement of the third subscription for South Sea stock reached Lisbon by the Falmouth packet at the end of June. On its return voyage the *Great George* carried a horde of money and bills of exchange as the Factory scrambled to get astride the money-making engine that was spinning away so wonderfully at home. More of Felix's money was aboard the packet too. He now had very little left in his strongbox. But he wasn't worried. Like many others, he used to go down to the wharves when the incoming packet had been sighted to get first news of the rise in the South Sea. In one week in June it went from 508 to 830, by early August it stood at 1,100. Such happy hours Felix spent then computing how rich he had now become. He used to chuckle over it with Sarah, their eyes and cheeks bright with excitement. How fortunate they were that Matthew had brought them sufficiently early into this splendid scheme! Why, the Hanaways would be among the first families in Lisbon soon. In fact, said Felix, reckoning up precisely what the stock trading at 1,100 meant for them, they already were.

The packet that arrived at the end of August brought the news that the South Sea had fallen back to 800. There was no panic among the Lisbon Factory. A temporary adjustment in the market, it was universally agreed. Some indeed, to show their confidence, sent more bills of exchange and orders to buy by the returning packet. Felix was not one of these. He discussed with Sarah whether it was time to sell, at least some of his shares. She persuaded him it was best to wait to hear from Matthew, 'who is so much better placed than us to know what is going on'.

By the next packet, in September, the waiting factors learned that the price had slipped below 600. After that the grim news came in ship after ship: 500, then 370, then 300, 190, 180 . . . From Matthew there came nothing. Everything was silent, silent as the –

'Are we ruined?' Sarah had asked him as he was poring over his accounts, his share certificates, all the numbers and the small print that blurred and trembled before his aching eyes.

'I don't know. I had money in other companies too. Perhaps they are still sound. London Assurance, the Orkney Fisheries, at least they have some real business that they do, unlike that damned –'

Another door now slammed in the recesses of the house. Felix grimaced, looked at his wife.

'Betty?'

'Of course, Betty. She has no more liking for this occasion than I do.'

'What of Nancy?'

'Oh, who knows what that girl is thinking, she is so closed in on herself. She doesn't confide in *me*. But Betty does, you may be sure. She asked me why should she pretend to be glad to receive her horrible cousin after his hateful father has ruined us. What was I to say to her?'

Felix sighed. He supposed he couldn't entirely blame his oldest child for her attitude. Two things she valued above all others had been taken away from her by the catastrophe: first, her beloved little mare, Poppy; second, apparently, any prospects that she might have had of marrying Dick Johnson, son to Sir Harry Johnson who headed one of the wealthiest houses in Lisbon. At any rate the boy had not been seen in Junquiera since Felix's financial woes could no longer be concealed. He was not quite sure which of the two – the horse or the heir – Miss Betty most regretted losing, but it was hard luck that both should be removed from her by the same stroke of fate.

'You will tell the girl that Adam comes as a guest to our house and she will behave properly towards him or will answer to me afterwards.'

For a moment Sarah held his gaze as if she would defy him, but then her eyes dropped away, she shrugged.

'For God's sake, Sarah, it's not the boy's fault. We agreed that, didn't we? And he has suffered by what happened just as we have. Can we not be charitable? Aren't we a family?'

Sarah was silent for a time. Then, reluctantly, she nodded. Felix drew out his watch.

'He will be here within the hour.'

'Then I'd better go and make sure everything is ready for our distinguished guest.'

Felix sighed. He thought that petty piece of irony was unworthy of his wife. Still, he relied on her not to let him down this afternoon. He watched her as she made her way to the door. Her anger had given her cheeks quite a glow, he saw, and her breast had been heaving as she had stood before him just then, controlling her irritation. He had felt a little stir of lust within him, which was not something that happened much lately. Not since the South Sea stock touched 300, in fact. He reflected sadly that he could think of much better things to do with the afternoon than spend it giving dinner to his late brother's son.

'Sarah,' he said.

She looked around.

'You know he still believes the story of how Matthew met his death.'

'What,' she said, surprised, 'that nonsense about cleaning his guns? Why, the coroner had to be bribed to bring in Accidental Death. The boy must be a simpleton if he still believes that story.'

'Nevertheless, please: don't say anything today to undeceive him.'

She came forward, touched his arm, looked into his eyes. 'I will be discreet, my love. You can be sure of that . . . But something else is bothering you, isn't it?'

'It's nothing.'

'What is it?'

'It's really nothing . . . Except that we've lost another of those wretched girls. Doroteia has gone.'

'The servant? When was this?'

'Yesterday. Gomes told me about it yesterday anyway. It's a shame. She was a funny little thing, but I had grown quite fond of her. I wonder that she never came to me if she was unhappy in our service . . . Well, never mind. There are always new girls to be had.'

'Leave it to Gomes. He will sort it out.'

'Of course he will. Yes, we can depend on Gomes. He is my rock.'

Adam

1

After so much eager anticipation, the actual circumstances of my reunion with the full complement of my Lisbon family were something of a disappointment. Though Uncle Felix was obviously trying to make the day go well – I remember him blustering a great deal and there was much rather false-sounding laughter too from him – yet I felt a good deal of what I can only call resentment towards me on the part of other relations. My Aunt Sarah offered to hug me when I first appeared before her, but thereafter kept herself pretty much away from me, and passed the time with much tight-lipped smiling, and some rather intrusive questions about my own people's circumstances back home. I was sorry to see she appeared to derive a certain discreet but genuine pleasure at hearing how my mother and sisters were reduced to living in a dank cottage in the country, without servants, all sleeping together in one room, without even possession of a proper close stool for easement and the necessity to use a mere pewter pot.

If my aunt was distinguished by her significant reserve, I must say that at least one of her daughters was plain rude to me. I refer to Betty. Almost as soon as I got over the shock of finding that the jolly little fair girl that I remembered had grown at sixteen into a great, looming, breasted hoyden, I found she was assaulting me with all sorts of noisy though indistinct exclamations, expressive of disdain, irritation, and general anger at my presence. Indeed she was so unpleasant that my uncle twice had to reprove her before the covers had been lifted from the dinner dishes. She improved a little after that, but only because – to the accompaniment of further angry, though necessarily muffled snorts – she was so busy shovelling food past her discontented red lips.

I do except my other cousin from these censures. I could not quite work out what Nancy was thinking, whether she was particularly happy to see me or not, but still I did feel a certain sympathy towards me emanating from her. At least, I thought, she did not actively resent my presence. She too had changed greatly in the years since I had last seen her, though she was always a quiet, reserved little thing. She was still quiet, but certainly not little any more. As we moved towards the dining room she towered over her sister and mother, and was only a foot or so below my own height.

At fourteen, she was a pretty girl, dark and brown-eyed in contrast to the rest of the family who were fair and pale-complex-ioned, like all the Hanaways, like myself. There was no mystery about Nancy's singularity, however, for she was not related by blood to any of us. Her real father was an old schoolfriend of Uncle Felix, also a merchant, who had married a Christian woman whom he had met on a trading voyage to Aleppo. Not long after Nancy was born, this woman had accompanied her husband on another voyage, to Holland this time, where my uncle's friend had profitable contacts in the supply department of our army there during the late wars. Nancy was left behind in the care of my uncle and aunt. On the way home the ship her parents were on was sunk by a French privateer and all aboard were lost. Nancy's stay in our family became permanent, my aunt and uncle legally adopted the baby girl, and she was given our name. I hardly ever remembered that she was only by accident and law my cousin except when, as now, I was suddenly struck by her so-different colouring and look.

As to why – except for Nancy, and blustering Felix – I was received so in the bosom of my Lisbon family: I came to the unhappy conclusion that it was because of lingering bad feeling over the distress that my father's folly and collapse had caused them too. It seemed extraordinary to me when I compared these people's living arrangements with those endured by my mother and sisters, but they evidently felt hard done by, and I, as the sole available representative of my father, was made to feel the brunt of it. At least no one spoke his name with scorn, or at all, in fact. I do not think I could have kept my temper if they had. It was already sorely tried, especially when Aunt Sarah sent one of her disapproving, accusing glances at me down the table, or cousin Betty indulged herself in another noisy, baleful grunt.

My uncle was returning to town that evening and had the kindness to offer to carry me there with him in a carriage he had rented for the day. Nothing much occurred on the journey back. The road was pretty crowded with people returning from their Sunday excursions, and our progress was slow. My uncle and I sat in silence for most of the way, though when we were stopped in the long line of carriages that waited to pass through the Alcântara gate, he had the kindness to ask me about my life in Lisbon, and whether I had made many friends here. Having no one else to talk about, I mentioned the Hutchinsons – describing the father, more or less truthfully, as a retired English gentleman, and his daughter as his sole companion and protector. I did not think it worth mentioning that I had no expectations of ever being in my 'friends" company again, and yet it might not have hurt me if I had, for on hearing all this my uncle frowned.

'Allen Hutchinson,' he mused. 'I do believe I know the name. There are some rather distasteful stories connected with that gentleman, I think – but I don't recall what they might be.'

I repeated that Mr Hutchinson certainly was a gentleman, and that both he and his daughter, as far as I knew, were thoroughly respectable. My uncle shrugged and only said that there were many 'odd fish' that came out to Lisbon from England and I should always be wary of new acquaintance. And after that we relapsed again into silence.

Just before he set me down in the Terreiro do Paço, Felix told me that there was to be an assembly in the Factory meeting hall in two weeks' time, and if I wanted he could get me a ticket for it. I told him I would like that excessively, and did not add, but felt it keenly, that I was even more delighted to think that, together with my somewhat ambiguous acceptance today at his country home, this benevolent invitation represented a real turning-point in my uncle's hitherto sometimes prickly attitude towards me. That he had seen what I could do in the Alfândega, how very hard I was ready to work and that I did not hesitate to engage even in the meanest of employment to serve the interests of his firm – whoever's son I was.

Somewhat perversely, I suppose, I then took certain steps to curtail my involvement with the meaner side of my business. For I decided that very night that I could not do all that I might on my uncle's behalf unless I removed myself decisively from the condition of common labourer. It seemed evident to me that what was needed above all in a firm like Uncle Felix's – after such financial blows as it had suffered of late – was an infusion of authority and direction at or near the head of it. As a Hanaway myself, of the blood royal, as it were, it was something I ought to be capable of furnishing to some degree at least. And yet as long as I was spending much of my time in a thoroughly menial state of being – no better than anyone else who laboured for the firm, not even the most casual and occasional of the snowballs – it was also something I found myself unable to supply.

I had been turning the matter over even before my day in Junquiera, but had done nothing about it. In fact I had got rather diverted from the straightest course of action by worrying over the reasons why I was so passive. I feared the ever-present threat of Runaway had something to do with it. For I would have to confront Gomes about this matter in the first instance, and, as I've said, I was never easy with that man.

But after the visit to the *quinta*, I was resolved to command my fears and have the matter out with Senhor Gomes. On the Monday morning when I came into the great dim customs building my fists were clenched as if I expected to come to blows at any moment with my adversary (as I now viewed my superior). I rehearsed my arguments. I told myself I would not yield and, if he would not satisfy me, I would vow to him that I would take my case to my Uncle Felix.

I was practising saying just that under my breath, with the emphasis greatly on the 'my' before the 'Uncle Felix', as I rounded the great stack of hides behind which was my firm's allotted space.

Gomes was already there. He did not in fact immediately attempt to send me to labour with the other men, but I told him anyway the things I had decided. I found it hard. I know I gabbled and stumbled in passages. My heart was pounding throughout my speech. But I got it all out at last, and then waited for him to respond. It didn't take long. He seemed to think for a moment, and then he said:

That he was glad I had spoken like this. That he had been thinking there was something not right about what had been happening. That though it had been necessary for a time that I should add the labour of my own arms and back to that of the others, yet it was neither fair to myself nor good for the firm's reputation that someone who shared the name and blood of its principal should be seen in such a condition for too long. That he agreed therefore that I should consider myself as no longer available for physical work, and instead he hoped to be able to draw me into the more complex and demanding side of the firm's activities. Indeed, he said, he had urged Mr Felix not long before that it was time his nephew moved on to better things. Felix had seemed reluctant, Gomes added sadly, but he was sure he could persuade his employer to do the right thing in the end. He was so confident of this that, he said, we might as well start now at improving my lot.

He then bunched up a sheaf of papers that was lying on the little lectern where he used to prop the Waste Book when he wanted to make entries in it. He handed them to me, told me he had to go and talk to 'that confounded *guarda-mor*' again, and asked if I would mind finishing what he had been doing and transferring the information in the papers into the Waste Book.

I took the bits of paper with a full and joyous heart. 'I will,' I said. And then, deciding that this was not a time for holding back, I added, 'Senhor Bartolomeu.'

Gomes levelled a pretty keen stare at me, and I decided fast that I had gone a bit too far.

'Right away, Senhor Gomes,' I cried out then, quite the brave little midshipman to his first mate. 'I'll see to it then.'

*   *   *

There is one other matter that I might as well place here, though for no better reason than that it occurred at about this time. Certainly I had no thought then of it having any particular significance or importance. It happened on the Friday after the visit to my uncle's *quinta*. I had been at the Alfândega since early morning and now, in the evening, as I needed to obtain something from my landlord – I cannot now remember what, perhaps more candles or to borrow a plate or a cup for my supper – I came down to the ground floor where I knew I would be most likely to find him. He was not in his living room, nor in the kitchen, and so I went to the corridor at the end of which was his little parlour. I had been in it a couple of times to pay my rent and to see the fact acknowledged in his ledger, and so I knew that Montesinhos used it for an office as well as for his recreation.

The door of this room was open and walking towards it I could see beyond to where there was a table covered with a fine lace cloth, and on it were some tall tapers burning in golden candle-sticks, which even at a distance looked to be more elaborate and costly than I would have thought the landlord of a shabby house in the Baixa would ever own. Certainly I had never noticed these on my previous visits to the parlour and it made me curious to see them closer. Still walking, I caught a glimpse then of Montesinhos. In a moment he was gone again. It was my impression there were other people in the room too. And then, to my shock, Maria Beatriz Fonseca-Hutchinson appeared in the doorway, smiling – it looked as if at something that had just been said to her. I came to a stop, a few yards from her. She happened to look up, saw me watching. Then she turned her head and I saw her speaking to someone. She moved out of my sight. Nothing happened for a moment, and then an unseen hand – perhaps hers, perhaps another's – closed the door firmly against me.

I thought of going to it, rapping on it, and demanding to speak to Montesinhos. But the knowledge that Maria Beatriz was also behind that door held me back. I waited for a bit in the gloom of the hall, gazing at the closed door. I felt shut out – and no wonder, for shut out I exactly was. I imagined the sociable company in Montesinhos' little parlour. No doubt the handsome candlesticks had been brought out to mark some special occasion. A birthday? A betrothal? Anyway, something cheerful. I strained to hear their talk and their laughter. I wished so much at that moment that my folly towards the Hutchinsons – which I painfully recollected in this moment – had not prevented me from being a welcome part of this gathering. For a moment, I felt my aloneness again like a knife-thrust in the breast. Then I just felt numb and sad. In the end, I gave up on my quest for whatever it was I had wanted from Montesinhos, and went back up to my room.

2

The place I was bidden to that night was in an elegant quarter of town, more recently built than the rest of it, which was called the Bairro Alto, and which adjoined and looked down upon my own slovenly and plebeian Baixa. The roads up to it were confoundedly steep and by the time I got to where I wanted to be I was sweating prodigiously with the effort. I resolved to spend a few minutes lingering among the crowd that hung about the Factory meeting house's open front doors in order to cool myself in the soft night air. The last thing I wanted to do was to make my first appearance in the general English society here with face shining and every other part of me leaking uncomfortably into my costume. I wished now I had spent a shilling to take a chaise to where I had to go. On the other hand, I recalled that the shilling I hadn't spent was all I had to feed me for the next two days until I was paid my wages.

At last I felt sufficiently composed to make my entrance. I prepared to show my ticket to whoever wanted it, but one of the liveried major-domos or doormen who stood at the open entrance waved me onwards without bothering to look carefully at it, which gave me a pretty good idea of the effect the fine costume I was wearing must have upon the vulgar, until it occurred to me that the fellows at the door probably couldn't read, certainly not English, which is what the tickets were written in. As long as I had something that was roughly the same size and shape of the official invitation then it might have had an advertisement on it for corn-plasters or false teeth, it would have gained me admission just as well as the genuine article.

In any event, I found myself being carried into the building inside an eager, clamorous crowd, every one of whose members seemed to be buzzing with anticipation for the evening ahead. The strains of distant music tempted me on from the lobby or ante-room I first found myself in and, apologising as I went, I pushed myself through the crowd towards them. I saw to my satisfaction that my progress was observed by several of the ladies, who cast an inquisitive and, as I believed, appreciative eye upon me as I went by. Less happily, I also caught the attention of several pretty truculent old fellows who at first I thought were scowling at me in defence of their ladies' honours, but became aware in a while from all the 'Have a care, Sir's and other such warnings that the scabbard of my sword was swinging too freely behind me and wreaking painful havoc upon the gentlemen's calves.

Understanding my mistake, I sought to remedy it by grasping the sword-handle tight in my right hand, and it was in this posture that my Uncle Felix discovered me. I had just penetrated into the room beyond the lobby, and found I still had not yet reached the source of the music. However, since by its metre I could tell it was presently being played for the pleasure the sounds might give the guests, rather than to inspire them to dancing, I decided there was no need to hurry on towards it, for I could hear it perfectly well where I was. Too, the crush of bodies in this new area was much less oppressive than in the lobby, so that all in all I was happy to linger here for a while. I was turning on my heel to survey the room, and wondering if I might, without introduction, approach any of the animated little groups I saw, and attempt to become part of one of them, when I heard behind me a, 'Well, nephew, I had thought to see you here before now.'

I turned and was glad to see someone I knew, though to be sure Uncle Felix did not look so pleased to be viewing me.

'Your invitation said for seven o'clock, did it not?'

'It did, Uncle. But in London, y'know –'

'We are not in London, sirrah. Not a part of your *beau monde*. Here when we are bidden somewhere we appear when asked; not before, and certainly never after.'

'But, Uncle –' I reached for my watch, remembered I'd had to surrender it to a beggar in the Rossio, pointed instead to the fine big wall-clock above the great fireplace. 'See, it is only twenty minutes past the hour. And you know, there were many other people arriving at the same time I did.'

I was really quite disheartened to find I was already in some sort of piddling dispute with my uncle before we had hardly greeted one another tonight. And I think he too suddenly felt the smallness of our proceedings, for he sighed gustily and shook his head and said he had not meant to quarrel with me.

'It's these occasions, you know, Adam. I find them such a trial –' He had taken me by the arm, was leading me across the room. 'Before I arrive, I'm dreading them. Can't wait for the time when I can reasonably leave. And everything in between is pretty much ashes to me . . . Ah, Mr Tolliver, how d'ye do?'

This to a thick-set, rumpled-faced character of fifty or so who, spying Felix and myself approaching, had held out his arms to my uncle and then, when they had embraced, turned to me and smiled and said, 'Your servant, Sir.'

I gripped my sword a little tighter and bowed over low. When I straightened up, the gentleman had turned to my uncle with an enquiring glance.

'And who is this handsome young man, Felix?'

'He is my nephew, Adam,' Felix explained, and I do wish there had been a little more enthusiasm in his voice when he spoke of me. 'Adam, this gentleman is Mr Tolliver who has just been elected Treasurer to our Factory, and so is of great consequence in this town.'

'Consequence, pish,' Mr Tolliver scoffed. He beamed at me then, a smile so wide and ingenuous and, as it felt to me, meaningless that I was hardly to see its like again until years later when I lived in America and found my vote being courted by certain Philadelphia politicians during one or other of the numerous elections to the colonial assembly. 'Mr Adam Hanaway, is it?' Mr Tolliver cried out gladly.

'It is, Sir.'

'Excellent!' cheered the Treasurer.

'Adam has come to Lisbon to learn the trade,' my uncle commented morosely.

'Has he, though? In your own firm, of course, Felix?'

Felix nodded. Mr Tolliver looked me over. 'You could not have done better, Mr Hanaway,' he assured me. 'Your uncle is a – a well-respected colleague,' he insisted with peculiar emphasis. 'You will benefit greatly by studying his example. And of course Lisbon is of all places – I do not except even London itself – the one where a young man can best make his mark and grow an ample fortune if he is industrious, and lucky.'

'It is what I so much hope to do, Mr Tolliver,' I assured him very genuinely. 'I mean to make my way.'

'Well –' said the Treasurer, seeming taken aback a little by my earnestness. He looked me over once again. Then twinkled merrily. 'You have certainly come armed for the struggle. Gracious, Felix . . .' He turned to my uncle and I saw for the first time just a glimpse of scorn in the way he regarded him. 'Your nephew is quite a Mohock, I see!'

'Merely ignorant, Jacob,' my uncle grunted, and I was glad to see that, though I understood his stock had sunk very low in the past few months among the Factory, he still had spirit enough to resent being teased by anyone in a family matter, even by its treasurer. He looked at me and tried to smile. 'We don't think it quite the thing, you see, to carry swords into these assemblies, Adam. Being plain merchant folk, you know, and not cavaliers.'

A lady went by then with her hair built high and white, in which were enfolded diamonds and pearls which, at a glance, could not have cost less than £10,000. I forbore though to point her out as an example of my uncle's 'plain folk'. I was feeling much too embarrassed to have made such a *faux pas* as to come armed to a sociable evening. After my previous fashionable blunder at his town house, I had taken care to ask my uncle how I should dress myself for the assembly. He had told me with, I think, a faint inflection of irony in his voice, that the pretty costume I had worn on the day I had come to dine with his friends would do very well. Unhappily I had neglected to enquire specifically about the sword – whether to wear it or not. I started to apologise now for making the wrong choice, but my uncle shushed me, said it was all right, I was not to know. I could think of nothing better to do with myself than to grip my sword-handle even harder, so much so that I actually pulled a few inches of the blade clear from its nest.

'I do believe he's going to run us through, Felix!' giggled Jacob Tolliver, who, I was starting to think, for all of his weathered masculine exterior, had something of feminine spite in him too.

'No, he's not,' Felix grunted, and held me quite gently by the arm. 'I'll take him to the negro fellow. He can leave the damned thing with him.'

'No need,' called out the Treasurer. 'My son will be glad to assist.' And he beckoned to somebody behind me. I looked around and saw a big young fellow in a turquoise suit of clothes pressing towards us through the crowd, a broad grin upon his florid countenance.

'What is it, Father?'

Mr Tolliver senior explained that I needed to be shown where I could leave my sword.

'Certainly!' cried the young man. Before we set off, he stuck out his hand to me, and said, 'Ralph Tolliver.' I shook hands and told him my own name. Looking at him close like this, I reckoned that he was older than me by a few years, being twenty-seven, say, or twenty-eight.

'Good to meet you, Mr Hanaway,' he shouted above a surrounding din, which was growing all the time. He put his hand familiarly upon my shoulder, and turned me into the crowd. After much pushing and apologising, we got out into the lobby. At least by now, with people passing from it all the time and fewer arriving, it had become comparatively empty. We both I think relaxed a little at having removed ourselves from the worst crush of bodies. Ralph Tolliver smiled at me. I decided that it was as empty a grimace as I had seen just now on his father's face, and it was not hard at all to see the son, twenty or twenty-five years from now, raised by means of this meaningless smile to his father's present eminence.

'Here we are, Mr Hanaway,' Tolliver said then. 'Augustus will look after you. Mind now, Augustus,' he called. 'I want you to take especial care of Mr Hanaway's hanger, for you see it's a damned fine one.'

We were in front of a cubicle or alcove, just off the lobby, rather like those they have in theatres or at the Opera House. There were lines of coats and cloaks hanging up in there, a few hats, a few cases, many pairs of heavy outdoor shoes and, I could see as I peered around inside this space, a couple of swords and many more canes hanging there too. The whole collection was presided over by a black man in a smart livery – who I immediately recognised. I had no idea why Tolliver was calling him Augustus, though. In fact his name was Pedro (though he was called more usually Pedrito, that is, 'Little Peter', because of course he was so tall), and he was one of the Alfândega snowballs who worked most often for our firm. Indeed, I recalled suddenly, with a stir of embarrassment, that it was only two or at most three weeks ago that, both of us stripped to the waist, I had worked and sweated alongside him, clearing a consignment of rice that had come in the day before from Carolina.

I held my breath, expecting Pedrito at any moment to recognise me and claim my acquaintance. I intended of course to hotly reject his assertion of a connexion between us, and if he persisted in it in front of Ralph Tolliver to use the sword that I was presently removing from my waist to threaten him into silence. However, there proved no need of such exertions. After a first quick glance at my face, Pedrito kept his eyes lowered thereafter. I handed over the sword and scabbard and he gave me a little numbered ticket in exchange. Tolliver leaned towards me and muttered pretty loud, 'It's usual to give him a few *reis*, you know.' I nodded my thanks for the hint and pretended to fumble in my pocket for some coppers. My hand closed over the single solitary shilling it contained. As I have said, it was all I had to last me until next Tuesday. And yet I must take it out and hand it over or else look ridiculous.

Ralph Tolliver gave me a hearty pat on my shoulder before I could.

'I must leave you, Mr Hanaway, for there are some people I have engaged myself to for supper. Will you be all right now?'

I indicated that I would be, and he left after blessing me with another of his warm and empty smiles. I watched him go. Then I removed my hand from my pocket. It was empty. Not by the twitching of a muscle did Pedrito betray either chagrin or disappointment. I wanted to tell him that I would be sure to make it up to him next time I saw him in the Alfândega. But he would not look at me and, some other people arriving to deposit their cloaks and boots, I took the opportunity to sneak away and lose myself in the crowd.

What happened to me over the next half-hour or so is somewhat hazy in my memory. This certainly has much to do with the fact, which I do recall, that not long after leaving Pedrito I took the opportunity to help myself to three full bumpers of very strong punch. Swaying a little now probably, I went back into the assembly rooms and, I suppose, mingled or tried to mingle with other guests. At some point I penetrated all the way to where a little orchestra sawed its way through a selection of tunes from the Italian opera. In an adjoining room, equally spacious, supper was laid out upon long tables, and I am sure I visited those tables at least once for I do distinctly remember that at the moment when I set eyes on the first woman that I ever desired to make my wife I was balancing upon my lap a plate heaped pretty high with several excellent slices of brawn.

She was sitting with two or three other people, almost directly opposite my own chair, on the other side of the room. She appeared to me the most attractive young woman I had ever seen. I doubt I have the ability to describe her so well as to make this claim indisputable. In any case it might reasonably be argued that, as my acquaintance with womankind at this date was not at all extensive, for me to call someone the most attractive of her gender I had seen might not be a compliment so very high after all. But I can only repeat this is how she seemed to me. She was fair, she was full of smiles as she talked with her friends. Her head was small, and balanced upon a long and graceful neck. The hair was worn down, as was proper for a girl who seemed still quite young. On her brow it was arranged in a cluster of those fetching little curls that were called then, I think, *favorites*. In colour it was light-brown, but with glints of dull gold within it; actually it looked like fresh honey. As for her figure: even sitting as she was, she seemed admirably formed. My gaze travelled appreciatively over all that I could see of her. My only regret was that the fine silken stole that hung from her shoulders concealed what I was certain must be a most lovely and shapely bosom.

She turned her head to speak to the old gentleman – her father? – who sat on one side of her. I was enchanted by the appearance of one perfect little ear beneath her curls. She turned to her other side to talk to a gallumphing boy of about sixteen – her brother? If so he was sorely lacking his sister's grace and charm – thus showing me the equally charming second of the pair. How I wished I could hear her voice; I was certain it would be musical – musical and kind. Then I saw that the motion of her turning had displaced the stole from across her breast. I caught my breath. I leaned forward to claim the opportunity to see, at least half unclothed, what I doubted not at least approached a wonder of nature. Need I say that the brawn in my lap was quite forgotten now?

The next moment a groan of despair fell from my lips. Followed immediately by: 'Supper not agreeing with you, coz? Poor you!'

I looked up to see my youngest cousin's sharp and teazing little face looking down at me.

'Oh, hello, Nan,' I said, pretty gloomily. 'Are you here?'

My gaze returned to the beauty across the room. She had re-adjusted her stole so that once again it covered her bosom, but I could not forget what I had seen the moment after that bit of silk had fallen from her.

Out of politeness perhaps, or more likely because I could not bear to gaze on what seemed now to be conclusively denied to me, I shifted my attention a little to my cousin, who had just settled on the empty chair next to mine. She had a bit of cake on her plate, and began to consume it with what can only be described as gusto. It ill accorded with my present distraught emotions.

'Is Betty here too?' I asked without having much interest in the answer.

'Somewhere,' Nancy nodded. 'I expect she's with Dick Johnson. They've probably gone to the churchyard down the street. That's where all the sparking couples go when there's a party here. Unless he's avoiding her,' the child went on, with significant emphasis.

'Why do you say that?' I asked, not much interested in the answer.

'She was supposed to marry Dick Johnson. At least that's what she told me. And I know Mama liked the idea too. Dick's a bit of an ass but his father's awfully well off. But he hasn't been seen at the house at all since –' She hesitated. Then, in a muffled voice: 'Since we became poor.'

I thought back to my day at the *quinta*. Betty's scowls and angry stares. No wonder she had received me so if she blamed my father, and through him me for throwing her romantic hopes and plans into disarray. Would there ever be an end to the mischief that damned Bubble had caused?

Nancy ate a few more mouthfuls of cake. She licked her fingers.

'I saw you staring at Gabby Lowther just then,' she said.

I looked at her curiously.

'Gabby?'

She nodded at the source of all my current grief across the room.

'Gabriella. Her mother was Italian, you know. Everybody calls her Gabby.'

I made a vow to myself that I never should.

'I suppose I can't blame you. All the men make fools of themselves over her. Do you think her beautiful?'

'Perhaps I do,' I said grudgingly.

'You must do, for you were ogling her so.'

'Oh, Nan,' I scoffed, with rather more heat than I had intended. 'And what would *you* know about "ogling"?'

Perhaps annoyed at the scorn in my voice, Nancy chose to rub salt upon the wound. 'Why don't you go over and talk to her if you like her so much?'

I reminded myself then that she could not know what pangs of hurt and disappointment I was concealing, so I only replied as mildly as I could that I did not wish to be stepping on the heels of other gentlemen.

'Particularly one other,' I said, with heavy emphasis.

My cousin looked mystified. 'What do you mean by that? Gabby Lowther has no special sweetheart.'

'Of course she does,' I said, speaking again more sharply than I had intended. 'And look,' I cried out in despair, 'there he is!'

Nancy's gaze followed mine to where Ralph Tolliver had evidently just finished some witty story or other, for Gabriella had put her lovely head back and was laughing very freely, disclosing at the same time a glimpse of perfect little teeth. It was the first sight of Tolliver, looming over Miss Lowther as she had adjusted her stole, that had plunged me from joy to despair moments before. It was impossible to mistake his commanding proprietorial air as he bent over her, nor to ignore her familiar responding gestures. These two were lovers, I guessed that immediately.

'There he is,' I repeated gloomily now. 'Her sweetheart.'

'Ralph Tolliver?' Nancy wondered. Then she laughed. 'I don't think so. How can Mr Tolliver be her sweetheart when he is married?'

'*Married*?'

Nancy shrank back a little from the glare I threw at her.

'Ralph Tolliver is married?'

'Well, yes – he is.'

'Are you sure?'

'Am I sure? He married Sarah Dunn last summer. Who was a friend of Betty's. *She* went to the wedding in church,' Nancy grumped. 'I was only allowed to the supper after. It was a very good match, everyone said. Sarah was worth ten thousand.'

I turned back to look across the room. I saw my 'rival' was gone now. Miss Lowther was sipping the tea he had brought her. My thoughts were in a whirl and I did not know whether my luck was improved by this new information or the opposite. I had been certain that there was some sort of amorous bond between the two. Miss Lowther could not be, in any decent sense, attached to Ralph Tolliver – but this might mean that she was vicious. She raised her cup to her pretty lips again. I resolved that, even if she had fallen, still I would lift her up. I would help her to turn away from her past.

After taking this vow, I decided it would be well to know by how far she had sunk, how far I must raise her up.

'Would Miss Lowther know that Tolliver is married?'

'Why do you go on so about Ralph Tolliver?' frowned Nancy. Then: 'I suppose she would. Sarah wasn't hidden away or anything. She used to come to these assemblies quite a lot.'

'Used to? Do you mean she is –?'

'In London.'

'She lives apart from her husband?'

'No, silly!' Nancy grinned. 'Her father was ailing and she took him back home, that's all. I daresay,' she went on cheerfully, 'she's waiting for the old gentleman to die before she comes back here. I believe when he does she and Ralph will be disgustingly rich.'

I didn't know what to think. I stared glumly at my shoes. But it was no good. I had to look at her. I raised my gaze. She was talking and smiling now to some new young man who stood by her chair, leaning towards her in a manner that I decided to find both familiar and offensive. Good God, I ground away to myself, is she completely without discrimination? Can any plausible young fellow engage her interest, and no doubt in short order her person? How lucky I was to discover her true nature before I had advanced an inch in our acquaintance. How fortunate that –

'Do you want to be introduced to her?' Nancy said casually.

'Yes!' I said, and sprang to my feet. Unluckily I had forgot the brawn in my lap and as the plate fell to the floor a trace of meat jelly got on to the front of my breeches. I was trying to wipe it off, under my cousin's curious gaze, as I asked her, 'But do you know her well enough, Nan?'

'Of course I do.' And, as I still looked dubious, she laughed, a little sourly perhaps. 'Gabby is Papa's godchild. Oh, don't look so surprised,' she went on. 'Everybody's mixed up together in the Factory, you know.'

And at that she got up and took my arm and started across the room. I must admit to a slight but definite attack of the Runaways as I prepared to meet this ravishing and enigmatic creature – myself in stained breeches, damn it – and Nancy had to keep pulling on my arm all the way across to her. But at last the short journey was accomplished.

'Hello, Gabs,' my cousin said.

'Sweet little Nancy!'

Nancy made a face at that, but bent and kissed the lovely cheek Miss Lowther offered her. Then she made a somewhat inelegant gesture at me. Miss Lowther, I saw, with a heart that both sank and rejoiced at the same time, was looking up at me with what I convinced myself was a certain interest.

'My cousin Adam is desperate to meet you,' said the wicked child.

'Fancy that!' smiled Miss Lowther.

I bowed as I had been taught in dancing class at my school.

'Adam Hanaway,' I murmured. 'At your service.'

'And I am Gabriella Lowther.'

'Yes. I know.'

We smiled at one another, she still sitting, I standing above her, very conscious that the unfortunate marks on my breeches were only inches from her eyes. Seconds passed away. I was truly lost for a while gazing into her face. From my perch across the room, I had not seen half her beauty. No doubt I have made her appear when first I spoke of her – and perhaps I saw her like this at first too – as something like a doll, a blue-eyed, golden-haired doll, and very wonderful as that. But what was truly spellbinding was to look into her eyes, which were set wide apart in her face, and see in them so much character, such life, and such amusement and interest now as she looked back at me.

I don't know how the spell would have ever been broken if, at last, another voice had not claimed our attention.

'Adam Hanaway, did he say? Is this Felix's relation?'

It was the old fellow sitting at her left that she had been speaking to before. Reluctantly I removed my gaze from Miss Lowther.

'Yes, Sir. I am his nephew.'

'I had heard somewhere that you was come to join us.'

Nancy, I noticed, was no longer with us. For a moment I wondered if she had been hurt by my entire concentration on Miss Lowther. It was rather ridiculous if so, considering that she was but a little girl, and my cousin to boot, but I knew enough at least about women then to know that any of 'em, any age and condition, can become restive and dissatisfied when another female engrosses all of a man's attention.

However, the old fellow was staring up at me, evidently waiting for me to speak, and I let thoughts of Nancy go in the instant. He was not actually all that old, I noticed. My uncle's age perhaps, and with a vigorous, decided-looking face under his periwig. I had a sudden dreadful thought that this might be yet another suitor for Miss Lowther's hand, a mature but still dangerous rival.

'Uncle Felix,' I told him, 'has been kind enough to take me into his business.'

'Has he? Good for him. You will learn much from him, I am sure.' He held out his hand. 'I am an old friend to your uncle. Phillip Lowther.' He made an affectionate gesture at my unsuspecting inamorata. 'I am this minx's father.'

We shook hands, and then he shifted himself across to the chair next to him and patted the one he had vacated, beside his daughter's.

'Here. Sit, young man. We must become acquainted.'

I was quick to obey him. As I sat I found my thighs inevitably became pressed against Miss Lowther's. I apologised, and tried to withdraw myself a little from the delightful contact. She said I was not to worry about it, and so I didn't. How much I would have liked to have proceeded from there to a long and deep conversation with her. But it was not to be. Her father wished, it seemed, to hold exactly one of those with me. He had a score of questions and I was hard put to keep up with him. Only once in a while he broke into the interrogation by tossing a word or two at his daughter, and thus bringing her into the conversation. I would have wished to have kept her there. I found her ever more fascinating. The purity and honesty of her gaze and smile, the hint of lasciviousness in her full red lips. The combination met the natural combustibility of a young man's constitution and set me on fire almost.

I no longer feared Tolliver. Indeed I wondered why I had ever bothered with him. Actually I wonder even now, and can only say that my acquaintance with the world of women and girls was so very limited then. Whenever I got close to one who particularly drew me to her I was inclined to let my imagination, my fears, hopes, doubts all run riot together and turn me into a being who was not far off being at least half mad.

I saw the fellow once or twice out of the corner of my eye. He hovered for a while at the edge of our group, then went away, as nobody took any notice of him. I was delighted to see this. In fact I exulted at how easy it appeared to have been to unsaddle this dangerous rival. Except that I had no sooner ceased congratulating myself than Miss Lowther – with an apologetic squeeze of my arm – got up and, as I followed her with tragic eyes, walked across the room to join the infamous Ralph, where he stood chatting to two other young women. I forgot how a moment before I had been wondering at my terror of Tolliver. I watched him turn to her and smile and say something and saw her laugh back at him and could have cried out in my jealous rage . . . when I realised suddenly that Mr Lowther had asked me yet another of his damned questions – possibly asked it twice without getting a response – and I had to deal with him.

'I'm sorry, Sir,' I said morosely. 'I did not exactly hear what you said then. Pray, repeat it.'

Mr Lowther, who certainly at no time that I knew him ever had a reputation for being a fool, looked across at his daughter – still making merry with Tolliver – and then back at me, and nodded and said gently, 'Perhaps it was not so important after all.'

I was stricken suddenly by how impolite I had been and faced him and said as sincerely as I could, 'I assure you, Sir, I should like to know what you said.'

And so we went along for a quarter of an hour or twenty minutes more, and I must admit that I grew at least a little interested in our conversation. For as I've implied, Mr Lowther was a clever man, and having lived in Lisbon for twenty-five years at least, had much in the way of information that it was needful for me to know.

There was one other matter that I remember from this time with him, which I could not exactly understand when it was happening. For at one moment, out of the corner of my eye, I saw my uncle Felix standing near. I turned to him. He was looking fixedly at Mr Lowther. I thought for certain he intended to join us, and was getting ready to rise from my seat so he could be accommodated next to his friend. But then, a curious thing: I saw Mr Lowther look up, seem to stare at Felix – and then quite deliberately, as it appeared to me, look away from him. And when I next looked Uncle Felix had disappeared back into the crowd.

I dismissed the matter, reserving it for later reflection, as Mr Lowther resumed his interesting descriptions of life in Lisbon and within the Factory. At last though his daughter came back to us, and made a funny little face at him, and he slapped his thighs and sighed, 'I know, I know. Time for us to go.' He heaved himself to his feet. Again he held out his hand to me, and we shook with much more real warmth than before. I believed he had come to like me a little; as for myself, I had found in him a most agreeable and knowledgeable gentleman, and have always been sorry that my acquaintance with Mr Lowther was not destined to be a long, nor a very happy one.

'I am pleased to have met you, Adam – do you mind me calling you that?'

I said I didn't. He looked me over approvingly.

'It's good to see the Hanaways are still coming forward, after –'

He stopped, hesitated. 'After such ghastly disasters,' I half expected him to say. Or, 'After your father had gone so wrong.' But in fact he never finished his comment, but reached out and held my arm in a most amiable gesture. 'We should like to see more of you. Shouldn't we, Gabs?'

Miss Lowther smiled and indicated that 'we' should.

'Sunday fortnight. My fond mother, abetted by my dear daughter here, has provoked me into giving what she is pleased to call a "tea". It is a modern invention of the ladies to lure the gentlemen into sharing their particular pastime. But so as not to entirely oppress and repulse the masculine half of the company, I can say that for my part I shall be offering some rather good wine too, and also true British ale just landed from Falmouth. Ha'past two in the afternoon is the starting time. Will you come?'

I hesitated, but only because I could not seem to get my tongue around the word 'Yes'. Miss Lowther seemed to interpret my silence as reluctance and made a little pout of regret most flattering to me.

'Oh, do, Mr Hanaway. It will be great fun. Won't you really come?'

'I will,' I said, as solemnly as if I was saying it to the clergyman and we – oh, happy thought! – exchanging our marriage vows.

'Good! Excellent!' beamed worthy Mr Lowther. 'You'll have no difficulty finding us. We're not far from here. Rua Formosa. Ask for the house called Os Dois Pinheiros.'

He gave me a friendly nod and took his daughter's arm. She just had time to throw me a smile before they had gone from me. I watched after them. My heart soaring, my eyes – I cannot conceal the fact – feasting upon the rear-view of her. It was as charming as I could have wished, and as stirring of my venereal desires. It achieved what many years later a fellow-enthusiast for the female posterior would tell me was the highest state that wonder of nature could aspire to, which was 'a life of its own'.

<h1 align="center">3</h1>

With the Lowthers gone, it came to me that there was no reason why I should not go now too. And so, after giving them time to clear the building, I made for the lobby. Floated, I should say, for I was still so borne up by thoughts of Miss Gabriella Lowther, and of how I intended to lay siege to her heart and so drive from her mind all memories of her possible infatuation with the hateful – and illegal – Ralph Tolliver. The fact that at this very moment I was possessed only of one shilling of ready money in the world with which to back up my suit did not bother me in the least. Indeed I was so far above such petty considerations that, as I approached the counter where Pedrito was stationed, my main thought was that it would be a pretty gesture indeed to tip him with the very same shilling. 'And to the devil with the consequences!' I thought to myself most bravely.

I am at least grateful that I was saved from that great bit of foolishness, and so was able to eat for the next couple of days. It was not exactly my good sense that prevented this folly, but rather an unexpected encounter with an old friend that distracted me from my generous impulse. At first though all I was aware of was a huddle of backs belonging to some fellows who were leaning against Pedrito's counter and, as it sounded to me, abusing him in a rather coarse fashion. My snowball fellow-labourer appeared immune to their taunts. At least his features moved not at all, but I could see by a certain flicker in his eyes that he was not completely deaf to the vulgarities that were being thrown at him. I guessed he was only being restrained by his livery from serving these oafs as they ought to be, and I also guessed that the time might not be far off when the bonds of employment would not be sufficient to protect them from his anger.

Having seen Pedrito lift a chest of Seville oranges by himself and chuck it across the Alfândega floor as if it were an empty crate, I thought it for the good of the English abusers as much as for their African victim that I try to interrupt the proceedings as soon as I could.

'Excuse me, gentlemen!' I called out.

Nobody seemed to hear me. They kept on chaffing poor Pedrito.

'I say,' I said. 'Will you let me through here, please?'

'Your arse,' came the ready response.

I had not seen who had said it. I was faced with the same implacable row of backs. I would have to make them turn to me, and demand that the one who had insulted me should own up to it. And then . . . ? To end such an evening as this with a brawl seemed suddenly a desperate sad thing. As a measure of how far the beautiful Miss Lowther had penetrated my sensibilities, I may say that it was this that was uppermost in my thoughts; for once Adam Runaway was not pushing himself forward, and so I was not particularly concerned for my personal safety. Gabriella had made me – if not brave, then at least for the time being a little indifferent to danger.

'Who said that?' I cried out in a higher voice than I had meant. Then when I still got no response: 'Damn it! I demand to know – which of you scrubs said that?'

I saw over their heads that Pedrito had glanced up at me. As I watched him, he gave a great slow wink in my direction. It was a wink that said, as clearly as if he had spoken: 'Good luck, you fool.' It also occurred to me that my hanger was still within his possession. In other words I was unarmed and was on my own and

I had just called a party of noisy young bullies 'scrubs'. Simple as that.

The row of backs had stiffened at my last remark. Slowly, as one, they turned. Four flushed drunken faces staring at me. There was one who looked particularly dangerous – average height and build, but with a face that might have been made for jeering or any other kind of mischief. His lips curled extravagantly, his features were sharp, his eyes in contrast had a strangely flat and lifeless quality.

He spoke first. 'What did you say, you son-of-a-bitch?'

Silence. I tried to find the spit to moisten my throat. I had to say it again. No backing down was possible. There were witnesses. I opened my mouth . . .

'Why, Adam!' cried the fellow on the left of the line, who I had not really studied much, being so taken up with the satanic aspect of his friend in the centre. 'Is it really you?'

I turned to look. And then what I had managed to assemble of fighting spirit melted all away.

'Oh, hello, Harry,' I said weakly.

Harry Bennett and I had become acquainted on the packet boat that had brought us to Lisbon. There was not much in the way of opportunity for social mingling on board the *Hanover*. The naval persons among the passengers all hung together behind their screen of nautical jargon, and were clearly too proud to wish to mix with anyone else. Most of the other men were of the merchant class, middle-aged or elderly factors, and though I might have appreciated gaining from them some foreknowledge of the life I was about to embark upon, they made it pretty clear they had not much use for me. I suppose that, in spite of all my resolutions of turning my back on my old life, I still bore for them too many offensive signs of the fashionable beau and Oxford gentleman-commoner, of all in fact that I had so recently been torn from.

So I was left mostly with the company of the ordinary young Englishmen that accompany practically every packet sailing to and from Lisbon. Almost all of them were junior clerks or servants of an even less exalted kind, and to Oxford-nurtured senses appeared a most noisy, uncouth and, I must say, stinking crowd of boys. From among their number I chose to be my shipboard companion the one who appeared least to exhibit these unattractive qualities – Mr Harry Bennett, a gangling young man with a countenance much marked with pubescent pox, and a shock of bright-red hair. After a short visit home, he was returning to Lisbon, where he had already spent eighteen months as a junior clerk. At least in comparison with his riotous fellows Harry was a fairly quiet and sober sort of chap. He also had the attribute – very attractive to me in my then rather sorry state of mind – of evincing from the first a marked inclination in my favour. It almost amounted to hero-worship. And, as I was forced to admit when I looked back on the voyage, I encouraged this admiration shamefully, managing to convey to my new acquaintance very well the glories of my former state – the country house, the horses, the fine clothes, the hanger in its jewelled scabbard, Oxford, the rich and titled friends I had made there, etcetera *ad nauseam* – without bothering him much with the poverty and uncertainty of my present one.

As I say, Harry and I made reasonably good companions on-board ship, and certainly his kindness and deference towards me did much to soothe my spirit, which was still greatly troubled by the bruising experiences of the last few months in England. On land, however, I thought we could never be friends. Though he shone in comparison with the rest of his kind, what I perceived to be his unmistakable mediocrity and ill-breeding still made that impossible. As often as I told myself I had to forget the world I had been raised for, my upbringing, particularly the last few years of it, still fought in the other direction.

The last day and night, after we entered the mouth of the Tagus river, I made sure that I barely saw him. And on the wharf where we docked had literally and cruelly turned my back on my shipboard pal. I had been standing wondering where I should go, when a husky native fellow had first beckoned to me persuasively, and then, without my exactly agreeing to anything, had hefted my two trunks on to a little wheeled cart and then started pushing the contraption away from the river's edge.

Which was how I had ended up at the Rua do Parreiral. It had turned out well enough for me – but of course it need not have. I might have been lured into a dark alley and knocked over the head and all my possessions stolen. It was very imprudent of me to have let this stranger take over so. From behind me had come a cry from Harry Bennett – possibly of warning. But I didn't heed him except – with my back still turned – to give a wave of farewell. I had no fear that he would try to catch me up. I knew he was already immersed again in his business duties, making sure that his employer's goods (which had been loaded on to the packet at Falmouth and had only just begun the process of passing from ship to shore) were directed to the customs house with the minimum of pilfering by the host of dirty, sly-looking beasts that had gathered on the wharf to greet the ship's arrival.

And so until this evening at the assembly, Harry Bennett had been lost to me. I ought to say straight off that I found before long that I had seriously underestimated my shipboard companion. Found that he was, for all his unprepossessing exterior, a young man of parts. He was to demonstrate them to me in Lisbon, and thereafter decidedly to the world at large. Many years later, to my astonishment, I read in a New York newspaper that a 'Sir Harold Bennett' had been elected Lord Mayor of London. The news was followed by a biographical account of the new Mayor, and it showed me it was my own Harry who had been thus honoured for it spoke among much else of his early residence in Lisbon, the firm he had worked for there, and everything matched. I did wonder – if he had made such a distinguished career for himself – why in the course of my own fairly extensive dealings with London and Lisbon merchants I had never heard his name spoken. But the article cleared that up too, explaining that for many years Sir Harold had been engaged solely in the Baltic trade – indeed his name was apparently almost synonymous with that important department of England's far-flung trading empire – and so his interests and mine would hardly have coincided.

Just now the future Lord Mayor was still the same gawky, red-haired, modest boy that I had known on the *Hanover* and deserted on the wharf. After pumping my hand very vigorously he made it clear that he would not let me go so easily this time. Would not listen to my explanations that he had caught me on my way out and I really ought to keep to my path, nor to my advice to him that it was so late he and his friends had quite missed the party, for everybody had either gone home or, like me, were in the process of going.

'Oh, not at all,' he smiled at me pretty tipsily. He had now draped his arm about my shoulders. 'This is the best time to come to one of these brawls, for there are always a few jolly girls left over and ready for a bit of fun.'

I told him I believed he would not find any of that sort in here, but then looking up I noticed several young ladies standing about who might answer the description. They all looked pretty flushed and were inclined to clutch hold of each other and emit great loud giggles. They also were glancing with sly interest in our group's direction.

'Look at those nice little whores,' sneered the evil-looking fellow at my other side. 'We'll have 'em up at the churchyard and bent over a slab in no time.'

'Adam,' said Harry joyfully, ignoring his salacious friend. 'You will certainly share a bumper with us before you go.' His arm against my shoulder was very insistent and I felt myself almost driven into a small room off the lobby. I had not been into it before, and I saw before me a number of tables and chairs, all unoccupied. From the stained and bedraggled cloths that were upon these tables and the several empty bottles scattered on the floor, I surmised that this had served as a retreat during the evening for those gentlemen who had been fetched to the assembly by their partners, but were disinclined to actually take part in the social side of it: the dancing, the chit-chat, and so on. Harry Bennett stopped at one of the tables and picked up an overturned chair from the floor, and dusted it down for me.

'There, Adam . . . Sit!' he beseeched me, and in the end I did what he asked. The other fellows were also at finding chairs and sitting on them around the table. I was trying to hold on to remaining thoughts of Miss Gabriella Lowther – but it was hard enough with these specimens staring at me with a concentration that I found rather disconcerting.

'Now then!' beamed Harry. 'Here are the very chaps I should most like to be known to one another. This is Adam – my particular friend, Mr Adam Hanaway – we came over on the packet together, had tremendous fun on it, didn't we, Adam? . . . and this gentleman' – he indicated the black, jeering fellow – 'is my other particular friend, Mr Evan Williams, late of Wales, currently an ornament of our great Factory here.'

Mr Williams and I regarded each other. We did not attempt to touch hands. The Welshman gave a brief nod at last, and muttered, 'Your servant, Sir,' and I followed suit.

'A rather lesser ornament of the same noble institution,' Harry went on, turning to the sandy-haired ruffian upon his right. 'Mr John Fosdyke who has the misfortune to hail from Yorkshire.'

'Oh go and fuck yourself, Bennett,' Mr Fosdyke said amiably and then turned to me and said, 'Your servant,' and I reciprocated as politely as I could.

'And last and definitely least . . .' Harry waved a hand at a rather dreamy-eyed individual with yellow hair and a face that still retained the roundness of adolescence. 'Here's our young Billy Ward, who's from nowhere in particular, are you, Billy?'

'Servant, Mr Hanaway,' said Billy Ward. He held out his hand to me. 'Any friend of Harry's is certainly one of mine.'

'Oh "hear-him" to that,' Evan Williams drawled.

When I had finished shaking hands with Mr Ward, Harry called for the waiter. Fosdyke and Billy Ward began talking to each other, some loud jeering nonsense about whether a bottle of Madeira or one of Porto could get you drunkest fastest. Mr Evan Williams sat entirely silent, until the first serving of wine arrived at the table – and the waiter who had brought it been roundly abused and had gone away – when at last he spoke up.

'Han-a-way,' he said, slowly but very clearly. Then there seemed to be a rush of excitement in his voice. 'By God, I know who you are. You are the Englishman who works as a labourer in the Alfândega. Aren't you?'

There was silence around the table. Harry Bennett, suddenly sober, broke it at last.

'Now come on, Evan,' he said. 'That's a hell of a thing to say about a chap.'

'Am I right, Mr Hanaway?' Williams nodded cheerfully. 'You are a labourer, are you not?'

'No, Sir,' I said, very frigidly. 'I am a clerk in my uncle's employ.'

'Oh that too, I daresay. But all the same you work beside the scum of Lisbon, hauling the goods about, don't you? The damned Portingales in our firm are always talking of you, the new *inglês* in the Alfândega who's not ashamed to work with his hands. And –' His glance swept the table, inviting the others to share in his disgust. 'They say he has his shirt off while he's doing it!'

And so it had come at last. Words had been spoken that demanded from me only one response. I had waited for this moment for so long. As I suppose has every young man with pretensions to gentility and self-respect. Certainly in my case you may be sure that dread and an anxiety that I would not rise to the occasion formed a great part of my waiting. But I suddenly knew, with a decided lurch in my stomach, that I would not fail now. With whatever reluctance, I would take the field against my calumniator. Some patch of ground at dawn. Swords or pistols, which would it be? It would be my opponent's choice as the challenged party. Would it be pistols then?

'Gentlemen, take your mark . . .'

Johnny Fosdyke yawned. 'Oh for Christ's sake, Evan,' he drawled, 'I've done that myself. When the work gets too much at our warehouse, the governor makes me strip down and pitch in. It'd be a kick in the arse for me if I did not do it.'

'And I've done the same thing many times too,' sighed Billy Ward. 'It's been that, or lose my position.'

'Oh, you've done every damn silly thing, haven't you?' snapped Williams, his gaze for the first time shifting from me and looking with irritation upon Ward.

'But so have you, Evan,' Billy protested. 'I saw you with my own eyes heaving casks into the cellar when I called at your factor's house the other day. You had your shirt on, but definitely not your coat.'

'That was in-house,' Mr Williams gritted. 'Not in the Alfândega. Not in public where anyone can see it.'

'Oh who cares,' Harry Bennett shrugged. 'We all have to pitch in and use our hands sometimes. I don't see it makes any difference whether it's in the Alfândega or anywhere else.'

'The difference is – the natives see it in the Alfândega. And it's very bad for the reputation of we British that they do.'

'Come off it, Evan,' Fosdyke scoffed. 'There are plenty of British whores in town too, and I don't see the reputation of the old country suffers by it much.'

Now I was not sure who I should resent the most: Mr Williams for being disrespectful to me in the first place – or Mr Fosdyke for comparing me, apparently, to a whore. I decided on the former. My heart was very much lighter now. For I knew that I was not the only English – or Welsh – clerk who had lowered himself to do manual work in this city, no longer the solitary scrub who had let his country down. Also I had a pretty good instinct now that I could press my anger with Williams almost as far as I liked and the man would not retaliate by much, if at all. Mr Williams was all show and menace and Welsh gammon, like somebody in a play. No question of real-live swords or pistols at any rate, and that was good enough for me.

'Mr Williams,' I said in a slow and, I hoped, impressive voice when I found a gap in the clerks' bickering, 'you have used words towards me such as can only be answered by a gentleman in one way. You will be pleased to tell me the name of your second. I shall ask a friend of mine to call upon him . . .'

Now who could that 'friend' be, I wondered. My landlord? Mr Hutchinson? Harry Bennett? Pedrito?

I looked around the table, showing, I hoped, the same dignified exasperation as I had tried to put into my voice. There was a moment of shocked silence – actually many moments of it, as I remember. And then, first Billy Ward started to giggle, and then Fosdyke followed and soon afterwards Harry Bennett. Soon they were roaring with laughter, slapping their breeches and generally rolling around in their mirth. Even Mr Williams wore a faint smile upon a face which, a few moments before, I'd had the gratification of seeing grow white with fear. Now it was returning to its normal sallow complexion, but the memory of its previous state was still sweet.

'Oh, come on, Adam,' cried Harry Bennett at last, wiping his eyes. 'Don't take on so. Evan didn't mean anything. He was just smoking you, don't you see? Weren't you, Evan?'

Mr Williams offered an uneasy smile.

'As he says, Mr Hanaway. Just smoking you. We're a rowdy sort of club, we are, and don't mind what we say to each other to raise a laugh. But I should not have attempted to teaze you, Sir, in that way. No offence intended.'

'And none taken,' insisted Fosdyke. He looked around. 'Hey, waiter, here!' he bawled. 'More of the old *tinto*, for Christ's sake. Drink and make up, I say!'

I still had not yet really decided to accept Williams' apology. But somehow, in a little while, the whole incident seemed rather ridiculous, and certainly unimportant. I joined quite enthusiastically in the new bout of drinking Mr Fosdyke had launched our company upon. It seemed that everybody else who had attended at this house tonight had gone home by now. Only we were left, and our waiter, and a couple of the jolly girls I had noticed before who joined us at some point and started to lay themselves pretty indiscriminately across our laps.

I began to quite enjoy the company of Harry and his friends, perceiving their ludicrous and, in one way of thinking, offensive manner of speech to be no more than the harmless banter of a quartet of young 'prentices out on a spree. Even Mr Williams – though I knew I could never love him, however many drinking bouts we shared – was essentially harmless, I decided, just a thoughtless rattle after all, and his efforts at raillery, and even impudence, designed not so much to wound as to raise a cheap laugh among his companions.

So I resolved to change my attitude forthwith, and had so far succeeded in it before the end of the evening that I distinctly remember myself at one point pledging bawdy bumpers with Mr Williams: the usual thing at low revelries such as these – 'May your purse and prick ne'er fail you' and 'To the best cunt in Christendom', and so on. Another time I was linking arms with Billy Ward on one side and a big busty girl called Dora or Nora on the other as we sang through the interminable stanzas of 'Barbara Allen'.

Whether these performances were greatly appreciated by anyone but the actual performers I do not know, but I was sure that my altered attitude was at least welcomed by my companions and their feelings towards me were much improved by the end of the evening. I took the firmest evidence of their goodwill to be that, as I started at last to make somewhat slurred farewells and ready myself to leave them, I was implored to be one of a party they were getting up to attend, or at least to inspect a forthcoming religious festival or procession or something of the sort that was due to be held shortly in the town.

'We have,' said Mr Williams (who it was that had issued the invitation), 'secured a very good window from which to watch it. We won't miss a thing – will we, lads?' he appealed to his fellows.

I noticed that Messrs Bennett and Fosdyke were exchanging rather strange glances. (Billy Ward was too far gone in drink for any such ambitious exertions.)

'What is it?' I asked Harry.

'Well, you know,' Evan Williams interposed smoothly, 'the religion of this people is Catholic and, I don't know, a good Protestant such as yourself, Mr Hanaway – you are a Protestant, I suppose?'

'I am,' I said, with something of a return to my earlier spirit. Then, recollecting that we were all friends now, I added, 'But that doesn't mean I can't appreciate the customs of other nations – even the religious customs.'

'Excellent!' cried Williams. 'Then can we count on you?'

'Look, Adam,' Harry spoke up. 'It's pretty – well, it's pretty rough, this particular festival. Why don't we wait till next year and try for the Corpo de Cristo procession instead? We can get good seats for that too, and it's a prodigiously colourful show, most amusing –'

'Oh, my arse to your Corpo de Cristo,' Mr Williams scoffed. 'That's just a crowd of dirty, garlick-stinking tradesmen, dressed up in stupid old costumes and wagging tattered banners around and all that tame nonsense. Besides, you'll have to wait ages for it, whereas *my* festival, Mr Hanaway, is only next month. And you'll be amused by it, I promise you.'

I supposed the show he was inviting me to – and which simple Harry thought would offend me – was something of the nature of the low sports and entertainments to be found at the yearly Bartholomew's Fair in London. Female acrobats and strong men and whiskered ladies and the exhibition of exotick animals and the like. All before an audience of thieves, whores, footpads, pick-pockets and, of course, a hundred thousand ordinary Londoners. It was true that as a young child I had been kept from the Fair, in order I suppose to protect my infant morals, but in my early teens my father even started to take me to it himself. I was made wildly excited by all the show and the smells and the crowds, but not in the least disturbed or ever more than pleasurably frightened by anything I saw or did there.

'Very well,' I said. 'I should be glad to see it with you.'

'Excellent!' cried Mr Williams once again, clapping me rather harder on the shoulder than I would have wished him to, and turning back to the others launched into a deafening rendition of 'Lillibullero'.

As I was leaving at last, Harry came with me a few steps. His expression was most serious.

'I do entreat you,' he said, 'to avoid this outing Evan has proposed. You will not enjoy it, I'm almost sure you won't.'

For a moment I took it very ill that Mr Bennett should intrude himself in this way, and seek to play some sort of nurse or governess towards me. My God, I was old enough, and had seen enough sorrow in the last few months that I had no need for anybody else's protection. Particularly when that 'anybody' was a good two years younger than myself – and spoke with an un-regenerate cockney accent besides!

But then seeing the concern behind his earnest, beseeching gaze, I softened. Though clumsy, his entreaties were no doubt kindly meant. And I supposed there might be something unexpected on display at this festival, something that Harry might well believe I would take offence to, probably some papist show or nastiness peculiar to the day. I put my hand on his shoulder, pulled him a little towards me. It was as much for my support as to show him affection that I did this, for I felt confoundedly unsteady, as far gone as Billy Ward at that moment.

'It's all right, Harry,' I said. 'I don't suppose I shall be able to come to the blessed thing anyway. My uncle keeps me pretty close to the grindstone, you know. And I think he has plans to use up my leisure time too for he has spoken of having me out to his *quinta* again before long.'

4

I arrived back at my lodgement just after midnight, having spent the journey very happily in remembering all the many allurements of the wondrous Gabriella. And that was practically the last occasion that I thought of her for many days. Not that my ardour had dimmed at all in the meantime, but that I was so confoundedly busy at my work. Having offered myself as a proper person to take on responsibility in the firm, I could not of course refuse the extra duties that such a promotion brought with it. Nor did I want to refuse them. My ambition had never faltered. I wanted to make something of myself, and most of all I wanted to elevate my people back in England from their present miserable condition.

Yet I did not even find the time to write to my mother the good news of the progress I was making. The moment I appeared in the Alfândega on Monday, Gomes was before me, with a request – a request now! – that I check again the cargo off the *Fortune* (Captain Hawes commanding) that I remembered having helped inspect only last week. I must have looked surprised, for Gomes then, as one responsible clerk to another, explained to me that there were rumours the thieves had been very busy in the customs house over the weekend. I was charmed to hear this. Not of course about the thievery, but that I was now to be trusted to hear this sort of important intelligence at first hand. I set to checking the cargo again with enthusiasm.

Thereafter I was required – asked, I should say – to enter my findings direct into the Waste Book, both my computations of quantities and those of values too, in pounds sterling. Here I began to discover a distinct weakness in my composition as a merchant that was to rather plague my whole career. The fact was I had no gift at all for the science of mental arithmetic. Adding, subtracting, dividing, multiplying – these make up the very bedrock of a merchant's vocation, and without ease of performance in them one is always at a disadvantage, even when one has a dozen clerks under one who have been hired to do just these mundane calculations. Simply put, I know that though I have found some success in business in my life – indeed at times I have grown rich by it – I would have been much more successful and much richer too if I'd been fortunate enough to be a mathematical man.

In the days of which I speak I had no assistance at all. Nor did I feel it right to ask for any. I resolved that hard work and concentration must replace what aptitude had failed to give me. From then on, my working days, already long, grew to a prodigious extent. I went home every night by starlight. I seriously contemplated making my bed in the Alfândega, for the interval between stopping work and starting it again had grown so brief. My eyes became weary and began to hurt from the hours I worked by candlelight. I was so exhausted that I fell asleep sometimes, standing up, during the day, trying to unravel a knotty sum, or else when bending over the Waste Book to write in my calculations.

At last Uncle Felix put a stop to this immoderation. I'm not sure who alerted him to the situation. Perhaps it was Gomes – I thought it was then, and half resented, half appreciated my senior's kindness. But I soon came to believe that some other factor in the Alfândega had seen what I was up to and had spoken to Felix about it. No, it would not have been Gomes; kindness was not part of his make-up as far as I could ever tell, and if it was, I was about the last person who could expect to receive it from him.

Whoever had tipped him off, Felix was concerned to put me back on to the path of sensible endeavour. When I protested that I could not do my duties properly within the ordinary hours of business, he said that I only had to ask Senhor Gomes and he was sure that my senior colleague would help out. Senhor Gomes himself, who had been brought into this discussion, agreed most effusively that he would be delighted to do just that. He had only held off because he had thought that Senhor Adam had made it a point of pride to do everything himself.

'Come now, Bartolomeu, we can't drive the poor fellow into distraction, can we? I should think you could see your way to lending him a hand once in a while, couldn't you?'

It was the mildest of reproofs, but I could see by a flash in his eye and a tightening of his lips that Gomes was not pleased to receive it. However, he agreed to lighten the load from my shoulders if that was what my uncle wanted. Whether I wanted it, I was not certain at first, but in a short time became very grateful for the assistance Gomes was giving me. And of course I trusted him and did not think at all to check the calculations he thereafter brought to me, but just entered them with my own into the Waste Book, where they lay undifferentiated and in my own handwriting, of course.

I remember that, after he had instructed Gomes to help me in the future, and the head clerk had gone away, my uncle lingered beside me for a little while, as if he desired to prolong our discussion. I thought that I detected a certain softening in his usual rather formal attitude towards me. I suspected that, though he deprecated the extravagant style of working I had got myself into, he was somewhat impressed by it too. But in any case, I shortly found that he had other reasons to feel kindly towards me, for he said at last, 'Well, young man, I understand that you have made a successful entry into our society here.'

'Uncle?'

'Haven't you been invited to take tea at Phil Lowther's house?'

'Phil? – *Mister* Lowther. Yes, Uncle, I have.'

Felix stuck his hand then in his coat and brought out a sheet of paper and unfolded it. 'So he informs me in this letter. It's well for you, Adam. The Lowthers have many friends here, in and out of the Factory. It is a good acquaintanceship for you to make. And you will find a rather more exclusive set of guests at this "tea-time" than you did at that assembly.'

'Yes, Uncle.'

He was silent for a little while. Then, almost reluctantly: 'He also requests that your aunt and I attend at his house on this occasion. Betty and Nancy too.'

I studied my uncle. I could not think what he was about. His face was screwed up in a fashion expressive of the greatest resentment. He looked up again, caught me staring at him. He smiled a little sadly, then shook his head.

'Phil Lowther and I were good friends once. For twenty years this was so. I am godfather to his only daughter, you know.'

'Yes. Nancy told me.'

'Did she? Did she also tell you that when the disaster happened last year he dropped me as if I was dirt?'

I knew now it wasn't resentment exactly I had seen on his face. It was anger. My uncle was furious.

'The godfather of his own child and he cuts me and Sarah off as if . . .' Words seemed to fail him. He screwed up the letter in his hand. Looked as if he would hurl it from him. Though in the end he did nothing more ferocious than stick it back in the pocket he had taken it from.

'We shan't go to this tea, none of us will. I suppose Phil has heard that the firm will survive after all, and so I am receivable again. Damn him, though. Am I to be insulted so by him and then, when he feels like taking me back, be expected to turn up at his damned house as if nothing had happened?'

I felt very proud of my uncle at that moment. It seemed to me he was showing exactly the proper spirit – telling the world, as embodied in Phillip Lowther, that though he had been unfortunate he still was not to be trifled with.

'I shan't go either, Uncle,' I cried out impetuously.

Long after these incidents were in the grave – along with my uncle, my aunt, and Mr Lowther too – I came to believe that Felix had not been in the right here after all. Though he might have satisfied his gnawing rancour for the moment, he had not really served his own interest by being so proud. Mr Phillip Lowther, as I had cause to know in time, was too important a man within the Factory, too influential in this city, to insult upon a whim. My uncle would have been better off swallowing his pride and accepting the invitation. He should have seen it as an olive branch, not as a stick with which to beat an old friend, who might well be feeling remorse for his previous behaviour and could be encouraged to earn forgiveness by doing what was in his power to help the still-precarious fortunes of the firm of Hanaway.

But that was for later, wiser reflection. Just now, as I say, I was all fired up by my uncle's defiance. At the same time I was becoming horribly aware that I had just said a most stupid thing. I had actually volunteered to deprive myself of the best hope of seeing Mr Lowther's enchanting daughter again any time soon. Luckily for my sanity, Felix took little time to decline my impulsive offer. Yet I could see he was pleased by it. He crossed the short space between us and shook my hand.

'No, Adam,' he said. 'You must go. It's time you started to be known in the Factory. It would be good for our family if you were.'

Apart from this conversation, not much remains to me of that period when I was so heavily engaged with my duties in the Alfândega. Now that Gomes was – as I thought – assisting me in my work, I had a little time also to spend in looking forward with longing and apprehension to my next meeting with Miss Lowther. But this was still in the future, and otherwise I had no contact at all with anyone I could call a friend, let alone an unsuspecting sweetheart. My dealings with the Hutchinsons, who I'd once thought might have been my friends, were close to non-existent. In all the time since our initial breach – whose cause by now I had almost forgotten – I had not seen Mr Hutchinson at all, and his daughter only that once, at a distance, in the candle-glow of Montesinhos' parlour. It was not a memory I cherished, only seeming to emphasise how friendless I still was in this town.

I had then an indelible sense of my own aloneness – and it must have been the reason why, one afternoon in the Alfândega, I felt a positive stab of pleasure when I looked up from whatever I was doing and saw Mr Evan Williams, my semi-adversary from the Factory assembly house, lounging not far off and directing a very searching gaze at me. Seeing me looking, he laughed and straightened up and walked towards me, holding out his hand as he did. I was, as I say, so pleased by this unexpected visit that I took his hand gladly, though really, as I recalled in the same instant, I had found the young man essentially disgusting at our first meeting.

'So this is your little corner of the world,' said Evan Williams. He walked among our store of goods. He bent over and rubbed his fingers along the edge of a bale of worsted. 'Not bad,' he commented authoritatively.

'It's my uncle's corner of the world, certainly.'

'Ah.' Mr Williams straightened up. 'Old Felix! Is he here? I should much like to say hello to him.'

I told him that he wasn't here, wondering at the same time if 'Old Felix' would be particularly keen to be saluted by this young man. I looked him over, noted the same sallow countenance, the same lethargic black eyes, same sneer on his face, an expression placed between scorn and devilry.

'Now then, Adam,' he drawled at me. 'You'll ask yourself what brings me round. Has Harry Bennett been in to see you lately?'

'Bennett?' I said. 'Why no. I haven't seen him since –'

Mr Williams was clicking his tongue in irritation. And shaking his head, I supposed from the same cause.

'Not since the assembly? I knew it. He was positively instructed by Johnny and Billy and me last week to attend you here and remind you of your engagement with us for next Saturday. Really, Harry is such a numbskull. I despair of him sometimes.'

He looked at me with a grin on his lips and I guessed I was being invited to laugh too at Harry's witlessness. I had no particular reason to want to defend Mr Bennett, but still I shrank from joining with Williams to make fun of him in his absence.

'I daresay Harry planned to come round between now and then,' I muttered. 'After all, there's still two whole days until Saturday.'

Evan Williams seemed about to dispute this kindly view of Bennett's conduct. But then he checked himself, and shrugged.

'Perhaps you're right. But no harm in my raising the matter with you too. You are still planning to join us?'

I hesitated. Truly I had hardly considered this proposition since it had been made to me, my thoughts being of course entirely preoccupied with the other much more promising invitation to the

Lowthers' tea party, an occasion now still a week and a half away. Williams saw by my face that I hadn't much enthusiasm for his own plan. His mouth dropped into one of its most formidable sneers and his black eyes, which, as I have said, had been until now almost without animation, began to glitter quite dangerously.

'I suppose Bennett managed to scare you off.'

'I beg your pardon.'

'All that shite he was giving you about how you will hate this festival, that it's too rough, etcetera. He has certainly affrighted you, Mr Hanaway, hasn't he?'

I was so incensed by this insulting accusation that I could do nothing for the moment except stammer. I wanted to tell him to go to hell, that I was not in the habit of being 'affrighted' by anyone, let alone by Harry Bennett – but I could not utter the words. Williams took advantage of my incapacity to come near me and place a hand upon my arm. I wanted to shake him off but seemed to be transfixed by the sincerity and urgency of his black gaze.

'Oh look, Adam, I'll confess: there *are* going to be one or two pretty odd goings-on at this procession. Perhaps you will find them offensive. Harry was right, I should have been frank about them. But I am such a coxcomb, you know. I do love to surprise people.'

'Odd goings-on?'

'There'll be a few flagellants at this affair. That's what I meant.'

'Flagellants?'

'Mmm. Or "*penitentes*", if you like. They are the chaps who walk bare-backed in the procession and thrash themselves with leather thongs.'

I was about to say, 'Leather thongs?' but realised I'd done nothing for the past few moments except repeat Williams' words back at him.

'Why do they do this?'

'Scourge the flesh, save the soul, I suppose. Oh, and these thongs are pretty formidable items, I can promise you. They're tipped with balls of wax in which broken glass has been stuck, and they draw the blood like anything. It's damnably diverting. You'll laugh yourself silly at it.'

'Why should I laugh at such a thing? It sounds . . .'

Actually, it struck me that it sounded rather interesting. Certainly it was something quite outside my past experience. The streets of London, to be sure, sometimes resounded mightily with hard blows given and taken, but you would not see anyone so distracted as to be wielding the lash upon themselves, and if ever a man was caught in such a situation he would doubtless be placed under restraint and conducted to Bedlam forthwith. I really thought that perhaps I should witness this exotic pastime. One came abroad to experience the strangeness of life in foreign parts – and yet the damnable thing is that, when one is condemned, as I was, to repeat the same essential round of work and sleep day after day after day, then only a few weeks of this suffice to make any place seem ordinary and familiar. Such was my present perception of the great and remarkable city of Lisbon, at least of the small bit of it that I knew well. It would do me good, I thought, to revive my feelings of wonder at its particularity.

Williams, sensing that I was moving towards a decision, threw in his reserves.

'But what really makes it so fucking laughable, Adam,' he said, laughing himself as he spoke, 'are the baggages at the window. The *women*!' he cried out, as I gazed at him in confusion. 'You don't know which to look at most. The silly fools thrashing themselves in the streets or their whores and mistresses at the windows waving at them and shouting at them to hit harder, make the blood flow stronger. And showing off their bubs all the while for anyone to look at!'

I felt a mixture of nausea and excitement at the picture Evan Williams had painted. I was certain now this was something I should not miss, and assured him that I would join him and his friends on the Saturday, 'Unless my uncle wishes me to work that day.'

'Oh, tell the old prick on the Friday evening that you're not feeling well. Then he won't blame you if you don't turn up here next day.'

I knew I ought to resent him calling my uncle by such a name, but I had become in a manner intoxicated by his impudent, daring style. My blood seemed to run hotter in my veins, and it felt like a fine swaggering thing to be young and bold and hurling about words like 'whore' and 'prick' and –

'God damn it!' I cried. 'You are right, Evan. I'll be with you, come what may.'

We shook hands, even more warmly than before, and he told me the place where I was to go on Saturday morning. He warned me to come early if I wanted a good view for there would be many others wanting to see this diverting spectacle. And with that, and a last wicked grin, he took himself off.

5

Saturday dawned clear and much cooler than of late, for which I was grateful. Once washed, dressed, breakfasted and out in the Rua do Parreiral, I prepared myself for a day of merriment and novelty and company. The place I was aiming for lay in a street that began behind the Rossio. I now knew enough of the town's geography to be able to approach my destination without having to go through the square itself which, I could hear from the cacophony of voices that rose from it, must be pretty crowded by now, even this early in the day. As I ducked down various alleys and crossed little malodorous patches of ground, which it would have been too flattering to have denominated as squares, I tried to remember if anyone had told me what particular Romish festival this day was meant to commemorate. I really knew so little of the rites of that church. Except that it seemed to have an extraordinary fondness for sending its adherents out on to the streets. Often as I moved about the city I met with one of these noisy and colourful processions honouring some saint or other, who sometimes I think were quite unknown outside this country.

One thing I was certain was that today's event was not the great Corpo de Cristo festival, for I knew that had already taken place back in June. Even though I'd arrived in the city by then, I had managed to miss it – and been chided for the fact at my uncle's *quinta*, for it is supposed to be a very fine show that no curious visitor should miss. I remember mostly the emptiness of the town on that day as I walked about in the Terreiro do Paço and that at a certain point I had been startled at hearing sudden great bursts of artillery fire, coming, as I ascertained, from the direction both of the castle of St George on the hill and downriver towards Belém. The echoes rolled around and along the river banks on either side and distantly from the centre of town came a great cry from a multitude of throats and I guessed that whichever part of Christ's body or His apparel that the city was in possession of was now being revealed to His adoring followers in the Rossio.

Today another great crowd was filling the square. I heard their clamour rising all the time as I came close to my destination, and I quickened my step, not wanting to miss anything of the entertainment. I reached the proper street and saw straight away I would have no problem finding the exact address, for there was a knot of lively young fellows lounging about by the door of one particular house, who by their dress and, as I got closer, their speech were evidently English. None of them though was known to me and, after making only a bare nod in response to some rather cocking stares that were thrown at me, I pressed in through the door and then up the stairway that was situated directly ahead of me, for I heard by the noise and laughter beyond the top step that this was where the main party was concentrated.

Reaching that step, I found the press of bodies in the main room was so close that quite a number of people had been unable to get into it and were milling about on the landing. I really wondered whether it was worth trying to gain admission, and thought perhaps it would be better to try my chances with the crowd in the Rossio. However, I thought I would at least make an effort here, for I had been told by Evan Williams that this would be a particularly fine vantage point to watch these native extravagances and it would be a pity to miss the chance. So I joined the back of the group that was trying to force its way into the room and did my best to push and pull and wriggle my way to the front. In the same cause, I also did a fair amount of kicking out at various neighbouring ankles and calves.

I had got nearly to the front row when all forward progress was stopped and I could see no way of advancing myself any further.

The people near me had not been made happy by my exertions, and were beginning to resist me strongly. I had numerous elbows shoved into my stomach and heard cries of 'It's all the fault of that damned scrub in the red coat', which could only have meant me (though the coat I wore was really burgundy rather than red). And I heard worse curses too flung at my head, several of them, I was shocked to note, coming from a large, red-faced young woman in a green dress, Irish by her accent, who at one point told me, 'I'm going to put my fist into your fucking face, mister, if you step on my heels again.'

I had almost decided to give up and go away – when a hand reached through the press and caught my sleeve and tugged on me with a great heave. At the same time some sort of altercation or battery seemed to be taking place in front of me, for I heard sharp cries of pain. The crowd I was in became suddenly fluid and I found myself being drawn through it. The Irish girl let out a shriek of dismay at seeing me pass through the ranks of the excluded. But she could do nothing to hold me back. I was beyond those people now and safe inside the room.

And I was now gazing into the black eyes of Mr Evan Williams, who it was had rescued me from oblivion.

'I was looking out for you,' he yelled into my ear. 'Why did you arrive so confounded late?'

I yelled back – I don't remember what I yelled. The noise of humanity, loud even out on the landing, was prodigious in here. Evan shook his head to show he hadn't heard me, and then gave me a glass of wine, which I think had been his own. I thanked him and, as he went in search of another glass for himself, looked around at my surroundings. There must have been several hundred people crammed into this room which, though pretty big, was almost certainly not designed to hold so many. At the borders of my consciousness appeared certain incipient Runaway fears that at any moment the floor would give way and we would all be plunged to our dooms. However, I made myself master of those unworthy apprehensions and concentrated on studying the plan of the room I was in.

Its most notable feature comprised the two large windows at either end. They were each nearly from floor to ceiling in their dimensions and occupied too most of the width of the walls they were set in. Between them they let in a blaze of light that made the burning candles in the chandeliers quite superfluous. They also, being wide open, admitted the sounds of the streets and square below, as I could hear now even above the roar of my fellow-guests. Most of these latter were now congregated near the window at the – I believe – eastern end of the room, and it was in that direction that Evan Williams, when he found me again, directed that we should go. On my way through the room I discovered Johnny Fosdyke leaning against a long table on which were piled great stores of food and very many bottles. He appeared to be sparking with two young ladies, one of whom I saw was my Irish adversary who had lately declared her wish to punch me in the face.

Johnny, when he saw me looking at him, waved in a most friendly fashion – and I felt quite a ridiculous degree of pleasure at being recognised and greeted thus. More certainly than Evan Williams' ambiguous affability, it made me feel I had a place and a welcome in this gathering. And then to reinforce the impression, there appeared the familiar person of Billy Ward before me. He had a large bit of chicken or goose or some other fowl in his right hand, which he transferred immediately to his left and after a cursory wipe of the other hand upon his waistcoat used it to grip my own.

'Well, Adam –!' he shouted. 'Here's sport! You are just in time. All their plaguey guilds and confraternities have almost all gone by now.'

'The tradesmen,' Evan Williams explained into my ear. I felt his spittle strike my skin. 'Not worth watching. After them come the *cavalheiros* – the gentlemen on horseback.'

'The military orders,' Billy Ward nodded. 'There's the Order of Avis and then of Santiago and of St John and – help me, Evan.'

'And of Christ. Founded in the old days to defend the faith and do charitable works and so on. But that's all behind them and what they are mainly now is rich as hell. Every jack of them has to be at least a *fidalgo simple*, and these are the fellows who really run this country. Under the King, of course.'

There was some sort of restraining ironwork or low balcony at the furthest edges of the window, otherwise I doubt not but our front ranks would have been sent soaring into the air, so great was the shove of bodies as people strained to get a look at the show. Eventually, after much angry shouting from those in front and a certain reluctant lessening of effort from those behind, we settled down into some sort of equilibrium. I was just able to catch a glimpse of the street between the large head of a short young lady, who complained loudly and often that she couldn't see a 'single bloody thing', and the shoulder of a red-headed giant who, by his incomprehensible speech, revealed that he had the misfortune to be a Scot. As advertised by my friends Ward and Williams, many ranks of horsemen were now passing under review. They made an impressive sight – but perhaps after more than five hundred had gone by, rank upon rank, no longer a particularly exciting one. The crowd at the window calmed considerably as the procession went on and on. A few, out of boredom presumably, broke away from it and I was enabled because of that to squeeze myself into a much more advantageous situation.

Now I had an entire view of the scene below me. Beside the *fidalgos* marched their 'pages', presumably fellows in their service, each carrying his master's banner. Truly, watching them, one could imagine oneself in an earlier, more romantic century. I played with the fantasy for a little while, though it was not easy with the modern smells of tobacco all about me, and the extremely modern conversations I was forced to overhear.

'Look at those poor bloody horses. Spavined beasts every one; you'd be ashamed to be seen on 'em in the Strand. What do you say, Sammy? Would you give me five guineas for any of 'em?'

'Give you less than that for the fellows who are on top of 'em. They ride so deuced proud, but most of 'em I daresay you could knock down the entire estate for under twenty quid . . . Boo! Boo!' This yelled by 'Sammy' very suddenly, almost into my left ear. 'Papist shite! Boo!'

Growing a little fatigued myself by the unvarying procession below, I let my gaze drift upwards to look at the windows in the buildings lining the opposite side of the street. They too, I saw, were crammed with people, Portuguese, I thought, and most of them women. They seemed much more active and vivacious than what one saw generally in the women of this country. They were also, I saw even at this distance, highly painted and elaborately coiffed for the occasion. The sound of their excited chatter reached even across the road to my ears. I remembered that Harry Bennett had told me once on the packet that the Portuguese male was such a jealous beggar that he would not allow his womenfolk to be seen by any other men.

'It's said,' had said Harry, 'that the poor souls leave their houses only three times in their lives: to be baptised, to be married, and to be buried.'

It was pleasing therefore to see so many ladies now crammed at the windows, and waving at the passing *cavalheiros*. Presumably the jealousy of their masters had been for one day set aside in the cause of 'true religion'. Certainly any man who wanted could look into their bright faces, as I was doing, and, given the fashion of the day for low-cut bodices, when they leaned over the windowsills for a better view of the procession, one could catch sight of even more alluring portions of their anatomy.

But at last even this vision palled and I began to grow restive, and then to consider that I was feeling rather hungry. What an urgent and insatiable appetite I had when I was young! It was only an hour or two since I had made a pretty good breakfast at my lodgings and already I was thinking earnestly of the long table I had seen Johnny Fosdyke standing by a while ago, and how it had been so loaded with good food and drink. And I was made suddenly alarmed that all this excellent fare would be eaten up by my fellow-guests before I could get to it. I thought this wasn't at all unlikely. That Irishwoman had looked as if she could easily eat her own weight in a sitting. As for the Scottish giant . . .

In a state of mild panic, I began to move away from the window, quite ready to abandon my excellent position. I felt an iron grip upon my upper arm, which prevented me from moving a step further. 'Oh this isn't the time to leave, Adam.' I heard the voice of Evan Williams behind me. 'Not when the fun is just about to begin.'

I looked round to see him gazing at me, with the familiar crooked smile upon his lips – and at that precise moment there came from outside a great roar, louder than anything I had heard before, and in which the notes of ecstatic female squealing were dominant. No, I couldn't leave at this moment. Even Williams' smile, growing in width and mischief all the while, showed he knew I must stay. And then in any case the decision was taken out of my hands as a rush of people back to the window carried me too with it so that once again I was standing pressed against the railing.

At least those damned horsemen have gone, was my first thought. The second was that the huge silver Cross that was being slowly advanced down the street towards my building was quite the largest such device that I had ever seen. It took four shaven-headed friars to carry it, and all the time one expected them to slip and the emblem of Christ's suffering to be pitched into the Lisbon mud. Behind the Cross was a troupe of drummers, who set up a prodigious rat-a-tatting as they went beneath us. Then, as the shrill clamour from the windows opposite grew into a quite unearthly shrieking, I saw the first of the day's *penitentes* pass under review. This was a bald fellow in, I should think, his late forties. He was undressed to the waist – a fact which, since he was markedly corpulent in physique, caused an explosion of mirth from across the street. He was carrying a whip that was composed of several long leather tails, with which he was, at widely spaced intervals, lightly flogging himself over his shoulder. I could see that the ends of the tails were not, as I had been promised, tipped with anything likely to do damage and indeed after repeated strokes of this whip the *penitente*'s plump back was hardly even reddened.

The lack of true suffering was also noted in the windows opposite. Applause turned to scorn. The fellow was dismissed to the unkind attentions of other windows further down the street and we, in our place, turned to review the next candidates. These were much more to our liking. Some bared to the waist, others clad only in flimsy shirts, these fellows were set on doing at least a bit of damage to themselves. The spiked tips rose and fell, blood dripped from backs and shoulders. The wailing from the windows grew so that it sounded as if the women had turned almost demented. I felt

Mr Williams nudge me from behind, felt his lips come close to my ear. I shuddered at his approach. Yet I would not have moved from my spot. The spectacle was truly so amazing, like nothing I could have imagined even in the wildest dream.

'Look at the ribbons on those fellows' wrists,' Evan Williams instructed.

I tried to find what he was after – and there indeed, on the wrists above several of the hands that wielded the whips, were tied bright-coloured ribbons, each one a different colour, as far as I could tell.

'They wear them so their mistresses can pick them out in the crowd,' Williams murmured. 'Ain't it a sport?'

I studied the *penitentes* even more carefully. Saw that, even as they cried out in their pain, they were looking upwards all the while – though not to Heaven, I was sure, but to the gay and colourful windows above them. And then, looking over there, I saw women pointing at a particular *penitente* and blowing kisses, which had the clear effect of making the flagellant thus singled out redouble his efforts, scar his naked flesh even more terribly, cause the blood to flow in rivers.

'I expect there's a few wet little cunnies across the way just now,' sighed Evan Williams into my ear. 'Shouldn't you like to get over there and diddle with a couple of 'em? Eh, Mr Hanaway?'

I shook my head to make him desist, and he stepped promptly away from me. But his beastly words of course lingered in my ear. The moans and shrieks from across the way, the sight of the women's faces flushed beyond the capability of paint, their lips contorted and teeth bared – all of it spoke of a passion beyond that of simple mirth and wonder at what they were seeing. And I was reminded too well of the secret I had heard whispered around my school, and had only half believed then, that women too were capable of experiencing the extremes of sexual transport. I felt myself getting out of breath. The sight of the flagellants threshing at themselves, the sound of the women urging them on, the blood that seemed to make a river between the two – it was all overwhelming, stirring, inflaming to my own carnal appetite too.

Except that I do remember there was one moment when our

noise fell away, and I think even the women across the street had the grace to be silent. It was at the sight of one particular *penitente* who walked by himself. I don't know exactly what calmed us so. He was a young man, about my own age, I think. He too was naked to the waist and his body seen thus to be thin almost to the point of emaciation. He had a good face though, a high clear forehead, strong bones and a pale complexion: the sort of features that make one inevitably think of words like 'well born' or 'noble'. Perhaps he was; or perhaps he was nothing like this, a baker's son or a porter's, it doesn't matter. What I remember of him, as well as the crimson stripes that criss-crossed the white skin of his back, was an air he had of such deep and devout preoccupation. It was apparent that he at least was subjecting himself to this scourging not in order to win a woman's hand, or the applause of the crowd. It was done out of reverence, in some intricate way it belonged to his own personal Faith, and however absurd and vain his conduct appeared in the cold light of reason, as he thrashed intently at his own body, still I – and many others there, I think – could not withhold from him our admiration at his single-minded piety. I almost wished for a moment I too thought like him, and that the road to Heaven, however painful, was so straightforward that anyone could walk along it confidently all the way, as long as one had sufficient courage.

But then he passed from our view and with his going the spell he had laid upon so many of us was broken. We returned to our cheering and jeering, and the women across the way to their fervid screaming. The show ended with a final eruption of absurdity as the last group of flagellants chose to perform their exercises in pairs, taking turns to whip one another. The temptation to lay the strokes rather harder on a partner's back than one might have wished for one's own was not always resisted. There were angry altercations down in the street as the paired *penitentes* rounded on each other. And, to a veritable din of cat-calls and huzzahs, one couple even descended into a fist-fight that had to be stopped by some of the ill-dressed soldiers who were lining the route. Truly it was farcical, beyond anything one could see in a playhouse.

Put in great good humour by these antics, our crowd turned

away from the window and went straightway upon the serious business of pouring as much drink and shovelling as much food inside itself as it could manage. I saw, as I let myself be borne unresisting towards the long table, that my fears had been quite groundless. There was still plenty to eat – or more likely, I guess, what I had seen before had long since been consumed and now I was looking at the replenishments, perhaps the latest of several since I had been here last.

It did make me wonder, as soon as the pangs of hunger had a little diminished, how such a feast could be paid for when the guests, as far as I had seen, were without exception only junior clerks and apprentices and their girls. Even collectively I thought it would be a stretch for them to pay for the hire of this room and such splendid and apparently inexhaustible supplies of grub. But I could not think how else it was managed – which thought in turn led me to consider whether I too was not to be laid under some sort of tribute. I had not been asked ahead of time certainly to pay my way here, and I would take it as a pretty unfriendly act on the part of Evan Williams and his friends if they had invited me to this occasion without telling me I was expected to help fund it.

Worries on the score led me to raise the question of who was paying for our fun with Mr Fosdyke, who at that moment had reappeared at the table. He quickly set my mind at rest, explaining that the food and drink and the hire of the hall were at the charge of several of the richest senior factors in the town, who did this every year to honour their juniors and apprentices.

'It's very good of them,' I said reaching out, without hesitation – now I knew it would cost me nothing at all – to help myself to a dish of roast veal. I retrieved then a bottle of Canary from across the table, denying by a second or two other hands that were clutching at it. I filled Johnny Fosdyke's glass, then my own, and we gave a toast to that splendid set of gentlemen who were placed in authority over us.

When I was able to look up at last from my feasting, I observed that the atmosphere in the room had in the meantime 'got a bit ripe' – in the words of my friend Billy Ward, into whom the person of Mr Fosdyke appeared mysteriously to have been transmuted. The young men and ladies, having like me satisfied their bellies, were now feeding other appetites. In couples and threes and fours, they were hugging and bussing and rubbing themselves against one another. I saw that my old Irish enemy in the green dress was well to the fore in these sports and was presently holding to her bosom, as a hawk rises with a mouse in its talons, a very pretty young fellow who could not have been above seventeen. Yet it would be prejudiced of me not to report that there were very many other young ladies, English by their accents, who were behaving with equal vigour and abandon. Including an extremely pretty girl in a pink-and-white dress, who first I spied kissing the Scotch giant I had rubbed shoulders with at the window. She had, I saw with amusement, to stand on the points of her shoes to reach him, though he bent down to meet her very willingly. Then she was lost to me in the crowd for a time and when next I saw her she was standing with three other young ladies who were laughing immoderately among themselves, and breaking off from that occupation from time to time to rather gently repel the advances of a party of young men who were standing near to them.

At one moment, she saw me looking at her. She stopped what she was doing, considered me carefully, and then gave me a most charming smile before turning back to resume shrieking with her girlfriends. I was at a loss what to do. The invitation in her smile was quite evident, and certainly flattering to me. And yet I considered myself under a certain obligation to Miss Gabriella Lowther, whose fervent admirer I owned myself to be. However, on the somewhat specious persuasion that Miss Lowther did not actually know of my devotion, and so that a brief holiday from her service would not be noticed and would hardly matter much therefore, I had about made up my mind to go across to Miss Pink-and-White and ask her what she meant by that intriguing smile, and indeed had taken the first couple of steps towards her – when a hand laid upon my arm made me lose my impetus. I looked round to see Harry Bennett looking somewhat wryly at me.

'Why, Harry,' I said, not with much enthusiasm. Turning back towards the crowd I saw that my young lady was now talking in a most lively fashion with a young gentleman who, I saw with regret, was very good-looking and, by the casual smile he wore as he replied to her, very easy and confident with the ladies too.

I gave up Miss Pink-and-White with a sigh and turned back to Harry. I noted he seemed rather more subdued than when I had last seen him.

'How are you, Harry?' I asked.

He shrugged. 'Feeling a little poorly. Headache, you know. Think I might go outside.'

'Do you want me to go with you?'

I dreaded that he would say he did, and I would be drawn away from this party, which had now turned out to be so entertaining – and full of promise too, for I had not entirely surrendered my hopes of Pink-and-White and, fortified with all the wine and cock-ale I had drunk, felt ready to challenge the prettiest of gentlemen for her favours. To my relief, Harry shook his head, thanked me for my kind offer, and said it wouldn't be necessary. After that, I couldn't think we had much more to say to one another, parti-cularly as he was really beginning to look quite ill. However, he lingered on, and so I felt I ought to scratch around to find something to say.

'Well, Harry,' I said, adopting a tone of smart raillery, 'you see how your fears all came to nought?'

'Pardon?'

'All your warnings to me. That I should find the goings-on at this party to be so offensive. But I'm made of stronger stuff than that. Don't you see?'

He nodded, but still seemed to hesitate before agreeing with me.

'Are you sure?' he said. 'Do you really know the worst of it?'

I thought of the flagellants in the street, myself in the very front row of spectators. It was true that I had felt a variety of emotions while I watched. It would not be right to say simply that I had enjoyed the show. It was more complicated than that. But to reassure Harry that I had received no deep or lasting hurt from it I said only, and as calmly as I could, 'I know the worst, Harry. It disgusts me a little but it don't really trouble me.'

'I was wrong then,' said Harry. 'It surprises me. I thought it would upset you. But if you say you know the worst and are still willing to stay here . . . then I have nothing more to say. Except I find it does trouble me, more than I thought it would. I shouldn't have come here.'

I felt, obscurely, that I had disappointed him by my refusal to balk at what had frightened him. But I could not see that I should pretend to an abhorrence that I really did not feel. If men wanted to flog each other – well, what else was there to do but stare and laugh at them? We now gazed at one another mutely for a little while, and then he shrugged and held out his hand.

'I'll go and get some air. Perhaps I'll go home. In either case: goodbye Adam, and truly I am glad that you care about these things so little. No nightmares will pursue you after today.'

'No nightmares,' I repeated as if it was the catch-phrase of some secret club we both belonged to, and so we shook hands and I watched his red head weaving through the crowd towards the doors. I did not quite see why he should choose to go now, when what he evidently considered to be the repulsive part of the day was behind us. Better, I thought, if he had elected to make his first appearance now, so that he could have enjoyed the party without being assailed by memories of those poor fools whipping themselves, and making their blood flow on to the cobbles. Anyway, hardier than poor Mr Bennett, I certainly did not intend to allow such recollections to prevent *my* enjoyment and, dismissing both him and his over-nice conscience, I turned back to the table.

I was glad to see that a number of desserts had arrived. Not being able to decide between an almond pudding and an apple tart handsomely dressed with whipped cream, I took a good portion of each, and then retired a step or two from the table in order to consume them with less danger of having my arm and elbow jogged by the other diners. Vaguely, I noticed, as I ate, that the noise in the room which, as so many were preoccupied with the food, had settled for a while into the relative calm of mere conversation, in which nothing louder than the occasional excited female scream was heard, had now risen again to the prodigious pitch that had prevailed while the *penitentes* were at their work. I noted that the major source of this renewed clamour was at the far end of the room, that is, where the other great set of windows was located. I wondered whether the flagellants had made their way round to that side of our building and were reaping fresh applause by their efforts. I felt no inclination to go and see them again. The first sight had certainly been spectacular and I did not want to dull my memory of it by repetition.

Moreover, there were enough amusing sights to enjoy without having to go to the windows. As I was sipping at some brandy punch, I noted Billy Ward standing near by. He was showing a little black-eyed girl in a yellow dress how he could touch the tip of his nose with his tongue. She, in the meantime, under the pretence of fondling him, had got her hand around his back and was attaching to his coat a sign that read 'Kick Me Please'. I found myself laughing very hard as if at the funniest joke in the world. I concluded when I had caught my breath that my mirth had mostly to do with the effect of the punch. Just in order to test this hypothesis – in a scientifick fashion, as I assured myself – I turned back to the bowl and helped myself to another glass.

As I was doing so, I found my nostrils were assaulted suddenly with a very strong scent of roasting meat, presumably rising from the kitchens, which – again presumably – must be on the ground floor or basement of this building. It was something that was quite unexpected for I had followed devotedly the course of this feast so far, and yet here it seemed we were about to start it all over again. At first the idea quite repelled me. It put me in mind of a young gentleman of my College, who out of a rather leaden affectation chose for the space of a term to begin all his meals from what should have been their end. Thus a gooseberry pie, followed by cheese, followed by a plate of beef and carrots, then a bit of fish, and concluding with a bowl of soup. This mode of eating recommended itself to no one else, and indeed by the next term he too had had resumed the orthodox style, confessing what everybody had already guessed, that he had only acted as he did in the feeble hope of earning some sort of reputation thereby. So remembering him, I considered now that I would have nothing to do with these fresh supplies, whose arrival at our table would be so oddly timed.

However . . . I have said my appetite when young was so keen that it was hardly capable of being sated. The aromas that were passing over me put me so in mind of the sizzling juice of a good roast beef – or was it lamb? I wasn't quite certain. In any case these rich odours discovered certain pockets and crannies in my stomach that could still just accommodate a little extra food. I had about resolved indeed to try a little of these fragrant new meats, whenever they should arrive – when my arms were seized suddenly on either side. I was so startled that I struck out in a sort of panic at the assailant on my right hand, and was immediately thereafter shocked to find that I had landed a glancing blow to the cheek of a young lady. Who, on closer inspection, revealed herself to be the very same Miss Pink-and-White that I had been ogling – and she me, I insist – just twenty minutes or so before. On my other side, her confederate, who I discovered was Mr Evan Williams, was laughing like a fool at my error. I ignored him as best I could and made profuse apologies to the girl. Who shook her head, grinned at me bravely, and in accents purely redolent of Whitechapel and Bethnal Green informed me that it was nothing, that 'Pa used to hit me worse than that when he was drunk', and she didn't mind him much either.

'Hooray for that!' cried Mr Williams in a sneering way that I thought gave little credit to the girl's spirited air. 'Now then, Adam, you must know that this young lady – Miss Jennifer Tripp – desires very much that you and she should become most intimately connected –'

'Oh go on with you!' shouted Miss Tripp, 'I said no such thing.' But she smiled at me significantly as she said it.

'So to start the ball: Miss Tripp – Mr Hanaway – Mr Hanaway – Miss Tripp. There, I have done it. But I did not think, Adam, that you would make such a decided impression upon our Jenny so very soon. A palpable hit, eh?'

We all three chortled at that bit of wit, though I still felt very guilty for what I had done. Particularly when I could see that my hand had brought a red flush to one side of Miss Tripp's pretty face. I wanted to ask if I might escort her to some place where her face might be bathed, and where we could perhaps find a salve that would soothe her pain – but before I could put the suggestion to her, Evan Williams was talking again, in his peculiar jeering manner.

'Well, Mr Hanaway, now why are you standing here alone and missing all the fun?'

I told him rather briskly that indeed I had already seen the 'fun', as he would have known for he had been standing near me at the window when the *penitentes* had passed by. He shook his head, impatiently.

'Why, that was nothing. That was just some silly clowning. No, we have come to take you to see the real show.'

And with a glance at the girl, in which for a moment I saw – and I am sure this is not just the fancy of recollection – a true gleam of satanic malice, he took me by my arm again, and the girl seized my other, and together, ignoring my protests, they almost ran me towards the crowd at the far window. The people there, who had seemed before as crammed together and spikily de-fended as a bramble bush, appeared to magically part before our charge. I saw laughing faces turning to me; there were other hands placed on my back to urge me on. I felt like a small child on a Christmas excursion, wondering where I was to go. I may even have shouted out that question, though if I had certainly none could have heard me, for the baying of the mob, both within and without this room, was so extremely loud now. Ahead I could see only the hard clear sky of a late-summer Lisbon day. For a moment I thought I was likely to be hurled into the empyrean – and yet for once, rendered giddy as I was by the velocity of our approach, I was not afraid. It seemed to me I would fly above the danger, above the rooftops and the trees and the palaces and all the towers and monuments of this great city, and I would find myself, without effort, back in my room in the house on the Rua do Parreiral, in bed, just waking up after one of my frequent dreams of flying.

And then we three slammed to a stop at the railing. We could go no further. Evan Williams pointed where I was to look, and I did as I was bid, and after that everything that had puzzled me today – Harry Bennett's glum qualms and scruples, the excitement at loose among my fellow-guests that had often seemed to come close to madness, the smell of roasting meat, the devil's grin on Williams' face, and the empty naughty laughter of Miss Jennifer Tripp – all of it became suddenly clear, for I found myself staring into the very mouth of Hell.

6

Later I was told, by one of the fellows at the Alfândega who had also been present, that 'only' five unfortunates had suffered in that day's *auto-da-fé*, and that two of the party, a man and a woman, had been strangled at the stake so that they were already dead by the time the flames touched their bodies. I could not have made so critical an assessment at the time. I did not see how many victims there were, nor of what gender, nor who was already dead or who still alive. Only a moment's horrific vision in which everything I saw seemed melted together and I could hardly distinguish the seared flesh from the hungry fire, or the poor folk below me who screamed and suffered from those many wretches who cheered at their agonies.

And then I fainted. Fainted clean away. I remember nothing else that happened in that upstairs room, except I believe I heard through my swoon the sounds of surprise and consternation as people gathered around my fallen frame – disturbed by the trivial accident before them, and yet only entertained by the horrors happening in the courtyard of the Dominican friars, a few yards beneath them. And from beyond the circle of those who bent over me, I believe I heard too the harsh sound of Mr Evan Williams laughing, of course at my discomfiture.

How I got home from this scene was for a while a mystery to me. I regained full consciousness in my own bed in the Rua do Parreiral. For all I knew I might have grown wings and flown here. And yet I spent little time considering the question. I was too much occupied with another mystery. Bento, my friend and room-mate, was standing at the foot of my bed, watching me in quite an agony of despair. But the real shock was to find that, sitting beside me on the bed, bathing my forehead with a cool damp cloth, was Maria Beatriz Hutchinson-Fonseca. I thought of all the obvious things to explain her presence to my fuddled mind. That she was an angel – or else a dream conjured up in my sleep, and still somehow managing to remain corporeal for a time after my waking. Any moment she would shimmer and disappear, and leave me with Bento, a reassuring presence but no angel or dream, certainly.

But she did not disappear. She kept stroking my forehead. And when Bento cried out in pleasure at seeing me awake, she too smiled to find it so. I tried to push myself upwards but her hand urged me back upon my pillow.

'Rest,' she said.

I didn't want to rest. I wanted to – I scarcely knew what. Remember, this was the first time I had set eyes on Maria Beatriz in several weeks. Excepting for that single enigmatic sighting of her in Montesinhos' parlour. It was sheer pleasure to see her again. I wanted to tell her that. At the same time there arose within me, like a great oncoming wave, the remembrance of why we had become estranged, and that it had all been my fault, and that I needed before anything else to confess to my guilt.

I was just selecting the words to convey all this, and to add my remorse at my folly, when I did what it seemed I had wanted to do all along. I reached up and touched her hand, and then began to weep uncontrollably. I hardly knew what was happening to me. It did not seem that even my memories of the breach between myself and the Hutchinsons had been so upsetting as to cause this cataract of tears. Without letting go of Maria Beatriz' hand, I fell back upon the pillow. Bento, in his alarm, had got a little closer to the bed. Looking up through the blear of tears I saw him bending towards me. The expression on his face seemed suddenly comical to me. And I began to laugh – without ceasing also to cry.

Some time after, I fell asleep again. Or rather into a doze in which I could still hear the hushed sounds made by the good people who ministered to me, and could feel the gentle disturbances in the air as they moved about my bed. Maria Beatriz was there often, and Bento, and I know that my landlord Montesinhos made at least one appearance. I believe I was like this, sleeping and waking and sometimes crying, for all the rest of that day and through the night and into the next day too. Bento was good enough to set out from our room an hour earlier than he usually did in order to take word to the Alfândega that I was indisposed and could not be in today. He came back with a verbal message from Gomes – which he now repeated to me – to say that I should not concern myself with the work, but direct all my efforts to getting better. My senior's concern and consideration moved me greatly. The tears welled up in me once more. I told Bento what an excellent colleague I had in Gomes. What a good man he was, how lucky I was to have him over me.

Towards the end of that day I had a visitor from outside the house. Montesinhos had climbed up to my room, carrying a dish of tea for me. He mentioned that a Mr Bennett waited below and would like to call on me if it was convenient. I told the landlord that I would much rather receive him downstairs if I might be allowed the use of one of his reception rooms. I tried to get up from where I lay on top of my bedclothes – I was dressed by now – but the effort sent my head swimming around and I fell back upon the pillow. Montesinhos was of the opinion that I was still too weak to receive company. I insisted that I could, but would have to entertain my guest in my room after all. I did ask that the chamber pot be removed before the gentleman was brought up. Though I did not think that Harry Bennett was so nice as to object to the presence of such a customary and necessary article of furniture, yet the day was warm and the pot pretty full and I was certain we would be more comfortable in its absence.

A short delay brought the little negro girl who belonged to the house, and usually performed this office, to fetch away the offending article and then I heard the clump of heavier feet upon the stairs. There was a muttered conversation at the door. I heard such phrases as 'Still very weak, senhor' and 'Dona Maria Beatriz asks that you do not strain him', and I raised my head and called out, 'Don't listen to him, Harry! I'm fit as a fiddle.' There followed a brief silence in which I could imagine Montesinhos shrugging to show the responsibility was off his shoulders anyway and then Harry's red poll poked round the door. I beckoned him to come across to me. He did so, breaking into a broad relieved grin when he saw that I was not, as he'd evidently feared, at death's door. Indeed, by now I felt perfectly well, only a little tired. This confounded tendency to burst into tears was still with me though, and betrayed the fact that I was not quite right. I hoped to keep the weakness hidden from Harry.

'No, don't get up!' he cried.

I had no intention of doing so. The vigorous pumping he gave my hand when he reached me was all the exercise I wanted just now. When he let me go at last I indicated the nearest chair and he dragged it across so he could position himself near to where I sat on the edge of the bed. We exchanged a few pleasantries, and then I asked him if it was the case, as I had already guessed, that it was he who had brought me back to my lodgings on that day – only yesterday! It seemed as if at least a week had passed since then.

Harry said it was indeed he. That he'd still been pacing in the road outside the house where the party was, and Billy Ward had come flying out of it to say that I had collapsed unconscious, and nobody knew what to do with me, or where to take me.

'We hired a chaise. There were a few lined up at the door, waiting to take the people away. When the entertainment was finished.' Harry made a grimace at that. 'So a lot of people helped you down the stairs. You were still out to the world. We put you into the back seat and I got in after you. Billy had a mind to come too but he'd just made the acquaintance of a likely girl and didn't quite want to leave her.'

I had a sudden clear vision of a little black-eyed urchin in a yellow dress and Billy Ward showing her how he could touch his nose with his tongue.

'How did you know where to bring me, Harry?'

'But you had told me where you lived,' Harry said. 'Don't you remember? At the assembly hall that night? When we were all singing and carrying on? . . . I shouldn't wonder at it,' Harry said reassuringly, when it was clear that I didn't remember anything much. 'You were jolly drunk that night. Well, we all were.'

We talked a little about yesterday, the beastliness of it all. My reaction. The fact that I had been so unprepared.

'I tried to warn you,' Harry said. 'You said you knew the worst and you weren't bothered by it.'

'I thought you were talking about the flagellants. I had no idea. I would never have come to that filthy party if I'd known.'

'Yes,' Harry said sadly. 'I knew and yet I came. I had run away from it last year, but this time I told myself I would stay and see it. Evan had ribbed me so all year long, and I was determined to show him. But I couldn't in the end. I couldn't watch that horrible thing.'

'Evan Williams is a wicked man,' I told Harry solemnly. 'I think you should avoid him, Harry. I really do.'

'Yes.' Harry was quiet for a moment. Then: 'I went round to see him last night to ask why he had forced that spectacle upon you. He told me that it was your fault. That you had made him look foolish when you challenged him at the assembly. And he thought he would try how far *your* courage ran. I told him I didn't think a man needed courage to face the sight of burning people, but hardness of heart and cruelty of nature, which I knew my friend Adam Hanaway did not possess. Unlike certain other people . . . Mr Williams then told me,' ended Harry with a wry grin, 'that I should no longer consider myself as his friend.'

I was rendered quite sober by this further evidence of Harry's decency and kindness. I also acknowledged – though only to myself – that I had deserved Evan Williams' hatred by my behaviour in the assembly hall. I told Harry I was sorry to have been the cause of this break with his friend.

'But you said it were best I avoid him.'

'Still . . .'

'I'm not sorry. I believe I must change my ways, and it might as well start with Williams. Yesterday convinced me of that. I've had enough of racketing about with other young fools, doing low things just to keep them as my friends. I really want to be a serious man, Adam. Perhaps I shall have to leave this town to become one. I've spoken to my factor and he has told me he can find a place for me at our London office, if I want it.'

'Go home?'

'I mean it. What happened to you yesterday has shocked me.'

'But I'm *much* better. It was just a turn.'

'No. You were the only one who behaved as the occasion merited. Can you believe it? The boys and girls of the British Factory assembled together to stuff our guts and make merry while those . . . poor people were destroyed for our entertainment.'

'Not for our entertainment, Harry. It was for their damnable religion they did it. We were only bystanders. And even there, you cannot exactly blame us for it. It were the senior Factors who paid for the feast and encouraged us to make merry at it.'

'And so I should want to grow into such as they? No, Adam, it won't do. Perhaps it's the heat or the religion or the strangeness of the place and the people – but there's something not right about this town, at least for Englishmen.' He broke into a sudden shy grin then, I suppose at the portentousness of his words. 'At least for this Englishman. It's time I went home for good. And I do believe that lady was the one who convinced me of it.'

'Lady?'

'I mean the lady . . . I think she lives in this house. Your landlord called her up here when we had got you on to the bed. The look she gave me when I explained what had brought on your fit – such contempt as I hope never to see again, not directed at me at least.'

'I'm sorry. She should not have done that. You were owed thanks for bringing me home. My thanks at any rate.'

And I clasped Harry's hand again.

'She did thank me,' Harry said, seeming – though he held my hand tightly still – to be in some other place just now. 'When she took me down to the front door to show me out, she thanked me. Really I thought at that moment I would have done anything on earth to deserve her thanks again. Or just to be allowed to look into those eyes . . . I so much hoped I would see her again today.'

Harry was beginning to babble a little, I decided, and I steered the conversation away from Maria Beatriz and her fascinating eyes. We talked for at least an hour, and became quite close. 'I should be very sorry to see you leave Lisbon, Harry,' I said at last, and meant it. I could hardly say that our friendship had ever been intimate, but I had learned to respect him as a decent young fellow who wanted strongly to improve himself, and I was heartily sorry that my foolish pride had precluded me from getting to know him much better than I had.

*   *   *

127

In that period when I was keeping to my room, Harry Bennett was like a solitary comet that wanders into our corner of the heavens and then is gone. My bright eternal star at this time was Maria Beatriz. I longed to hear her footstep on the stair, was alive and happy all the time she was with me, was wretched when at last she left me, though she never did so without a promise to return at such-and-such an exact time, promises that she never broke. As to what we said and did while she was with me – I remember talk and laughter, serious moments too for the incident that had felled me and brought me to this bed was still livid in my thoughts and I had to talk to someone about it. She listened, her face grave and her eyes filled with understanding. Listened until I was beginning to become repetitive, and then, without my hardly being aware of what she was doing, she nudged me towards other, happier topics, so that a short while after talking of my horror – at the angry flames, at the stench of roasting flesh – I was giggling at her account of the antics of the Lourenços, a warring couple who lived in one room on the third floor. Lately, they had been taking it in turns to lock each other out of their apartment. Twice Montesinhos had had to threaten to break down the door, which of course was not something he wanted to do in his own house.

'He has given them notice to leave now. Poor things. Where will they go?'

I advised her that this should not be the first of her concerns. The main thing was that she would be getting rid of some detestable neighbours. She could look forward to some peace and quiet at last.

'Yes. But sometimes they are very sweet together,' Maria Beatriz sighed. 'When I lie in my bed, I can hear them making love just above me. And then afterwards they talk fondly together half the night.'

She was not really an English lady and so I did not condemn her as I might have done for such a casual mention of 'making love' and its aftermath. But still I had conceived such a great respect for her that I did not quite like to hear her sullying her lips in this way, and in my turn steered the conversation to safer topics. I asked how her father did and was sorry to hear that he was a little out-of-sorts. I asked what it was that ailed him and she said she thought it was mainly that autumn was almost here, and winter would be following it close, and her father hated the winter.

'It makes him think of death,' she said. 'The cold.'

'Does it ever get cold in this town?' I wondered, genuinely curious, for I had never known the air here to vary much between burning hot and pleasantly warm.

'It gets cold enough,' she said.

Finally, I brought up the subject that, in my mind anyway, lay like a heavy boulder between us. In fits and starts I rehearsed that unlucky occasion when I had failed to keep my appointment with the Hutchinsons for supper and then had compounded my error by sending a silly mendacious note to them. I told her – I insisted – that I had not meant to insult either her or her father. It was an accident, I swore. I had simply fallen asleep that afternoon.

'That's what we guessed had happened.'

'You guessed?' I stared at her. 'You knew what had happened?'

'Well . . . we didn't *know*. I thought of coming up to see how you were. But then my father said that perhaps you had decided to avoid us, and that it would be presumptuous to pursue you to your room.'

'Why on earth would you think I wanted to avoid you?'

'Well . . .' Maria Beatriz looked uncomfortable. 'When you think what we are. Street-sellers. Peddlers. And you – a gentleman after all –'

I groaned at that and hid my face for a moment.

'But you knew I was poor. You know how little money I pay for this room.'

'You have prospects, Adam. That's what we knew. And we guessed that it would not improve them if you were seen to be associating with people like us. And we supposed you had come to that conclusion too.'

'You must have been very angry with me.'

'Not really.'

'And then – that note.'

'A little angry when I read that.'

'But if you were only a little angry – why did you avoid me for so many weeks?'

'Who avoided who?' said Maria Beatriz spiritedly.

I thought it over. Nodded. It was true. I had put my best efforts into hiding from the Hutchinsons.

'It was not we who had offended, after all, and so we did not think it was our responsibility to mend matters.'

'You could not even have smiled at me when I saw you in Montesinhos' parlour that day?'

After I'd said that, she regarded me quite seriously. My words seemed to have left a greater impression on her than I had intended. At last she shrugged and said, 'I was busy that day in the parlour. I'm sorry if you were insulted. It was our fault. We should have kept the door closed, but it was so hot and the room has no windows. We could scarcely breathe if the door was shut.'

I spent three full days and nights in my room. I really did not want to leave it. I had discovered that the world beyond was a crueller place than I had believed possible, even after the calamities of the previous twelve months. I had seen human beings, blackened and burning. For two seconds before my swoon released me I had stood there with the taste of apple tart and brandy punch in my mouth and the stink of seared meat in my nostrils and had seen this, and – I thought I could not go back to sorting serges and worsteds and counting sacks of sugar. Maria Beatriz became quite worried for me. Also, she let me know, without anger, that in order to spend as much time with me as she had she had been neglecting her own work, and her other duties. I tended to forget, what she never could, that in this time she was serving two demanding invalids. A sick old man on the second floor and on the fourth – I don't know what to call myself: a lethargic, lachrymose younger one?

Even if I wasn't ready to change my present mode of existence, she made it clear she could no longer play her part in it to the same extent. The thought of lying on my bed all day without the hope of regularly seeing her certainly took much of the attraction out of that prospect. And too, as she delicately hinted then, I had to consider the financial aspect. My uncle might be the most kind and indulgent of relations – which he hardly was – but he would not probably want to keep paying a salary to any employee, even me, if I did not turn up to do some work once in a while.

These arguments made me determine to rouse myself at last and take up again the reins of industry. I told my decision to Maria Beatriz on the Thursday when she came up with my midday meal. It would take effect on the morrow, I told her. She was delighted to hear it, and not only I do believe because it would release her from the chore of attending on me. Maria Beatriz always wanted what was best for me, and she could see that lying on his back, brooding or yawning or weeping, was not a fit existence for a healthy young man. She brought the bad news, however, that she would not be able to visit me further this afternoon for she had an appointment to see her printer and go over with him her latest batch of drawings, and what she required to be done with each. However, she had a suggestion to offer that she thought might appeal to me, which was that – 'If you feel you are able to' – I should get up off my bed and descend the stairs to the Hutchinsons' rooms where the old gentleman would be very happy indeed to spend an hour or so with me.

I thought it was a good notion, and when she had left me, I tidied myself up as well as I could, and put on a plain coat and went downstairs. I spent a couple of hours with Mr Hutchinson that afternoon and we entertained each other very much. I think Maria Beatriz had left instructions with him that he should keep away from all sad or heavy things when he spoke with me. He obeyed her to the letter. I only remember our laughter and ease that afternoon, though nothing exactly of what we talked about remains. Except that at one point, when I had been delivering myself of a pretty lengthy and glowing encomium upon his daughter's excellence as a nurse, he broke in to ask if she had administered to me a certain 'most efficacious specific for almost any kind of complaint. Except broken bones and so on, of course'.

'Tell me what it is, Sir. I'll endeavour to remember.'

'Soup made from a fresh-killed cock,' said Mr Hutchinson promptly. 'It must be whipped to death just before it goes into the pot and preferably in the same room with the patient. And then the broth must be eaten the day the fowl is killed – it will have more life in it then, you see.'

I told Mr Hutchinson that I was almost certain that no cocks had been whipped to death in my room, though indeed Dona Maria Beatriz had fed me several bowls of excellent chicken soup. And that is really all I remember of our talk, except that I am sure I must have told him what I had said to his daughter before – that I was heartily sorry that I had behaved so foolishly in the matter of the missed appointment for supper and the subsequent folly of the letter I had wrote to try and shift the blame off myself. No doubt he was gracious in hearing this tale; Mr Hutchinson, who could be brusque and even violent in his language at times, would always discover the utmost consideration when his gentlemanly instincts were appealed to.

I felt so well restored by this visit to the Hutchinsons', together with the days of rest that had preceded it, that I did not hesitate, when I heard Bento stirring from his bed at dawn the next morning, to get up myself and dress for business. Bento recommended caution, another day or two of idleness, but I brushed aside his advice. I set off for the Alfândega with quite a complacent glow in my breast. I thought I was a fine, conscientious fellow to be doing this, even though for all I knew I was not yet entirely well.

Nobody at the Alfândega seemed to notice my sacrifice, however. There were a few cursory nods from some of our regular labourers. Gomes appeared about five minutes after I got to our place on the floor. He seemed rather distracted, told me that the Falmouth packet had been seen off Cascais this morning, would probably be at the wharf today, and included in its cargo was a quantity of the stuff called haberdashery-ware, that is, thread and gimps and bone-lace and so on, which we were taking off a Bristol merchant for sale in Lisbon, or else to be sent on to Spain. In addition a lighter from the Setubal mines was due in at about the same time with a cargo of salt in which we had an interest. Room must be found for both consignments before evening. He himself would go down to the river to prepare for the ships' arrival. It was left to me to make sure everything would be arranged in the customs house for the reception of our goods.

I thought I might have counted on at least a brief enquiry as to how I did, and whether I was quite recovered from my illness. However, there was nothing like this. Gomes gave me directions as to how many labourers I could hire for the day, added that my uncle had gone to Almada across the river to inspect some vineyards where the vintage this year was said to be promising. He was not expected in the Alfândega again before Monday.

My senior then left me without another word. However, I was still in such a buoyant state of mind that I did not let this neglect of my well-being bother me by much, but set upon my tasks with a will. Actually my enthusiasm to be doing these commonplace duties made me realise how weary I had become of lounging around in my room for the past few days. I organised my little troop of labourers, gave clear instructions, put them to work, and would by no means let them slacken off as the day wore on. I even got them to work through the sacred hour of *sesta* using a combination of bribes and threats that the firm would never employ them again if they failed me now. By the time Gomes returned with the news that the packet was at anchor and ready to be unloaded, all the goods that had been cluttering our bit of floor were neatly stacked away and the floor itself bare and ready to receive. He had the grace to mutter as he came up to me that I had done well.

This cheered me up. The next thing he said though cast me down utterly. The customs officers were insisting that each of our haberdashery chests would have to be opened and the contents minutely examined. It was also likely that they would make some trouble about the salt, for though this should have been the easiest of items to clear yet, as with all the products of their native earth, to their irrational way of thinking we foreigners were purloining from the national patrimony in engaging in their export. In fact, the officers always discovered an absurd proprietary interest in the salt, and it was almost more trouble than it was worth to get it out of their grasp. All of which, said Gomes, added up to the fact that we would have to work right through the morrow, which was Saturday.

This news was a great shock to me, for Saturday was the day of the Lowthers' 'tea'. I told him directly that I could not work beyond noon, and when he started to object said that I was bidden to the home of important people in the afternoon, that my uncle knew of it and approved, that it would be good for the firm for it to be represented at this superior social gathering, and it would have to be me that was doing the representing as my uncle had declined his own invitation and, as Gomes had told me, gone out of town.

This did not please Senhor Gomes one bit, but as I showed I was adamant in my intention and since no higher authority could be appealed to with my uncle safely across the river, he was forced to accept my terms. Even so, when the morrow came, it was more difficult than I thought it would be to extricate myself from my labours. The work was at a critical point, and we really did not have enough labourers to do the job within the day's span that Gomes and my uncle had allotted for it. Still, I hardened my heart and defying the stares of my fellow-labourers – for I had once more, as an exception, doffed my jacket and worked alongside them with my hands – and the almost open scorn of Gomes, I took myself away from the Alfândega, not at twelve o'clock as I had hoped but within a half-hour after that.

7

At my request the coachman stopped his ramshackle equipage at the entrance to the Rua Formosa. It was exactly the sort of road where my – I almost said beloved, but I knew I had not the right to call her that yet – where my Gabriella would live. The houses on either side were large and handsome, and the grounds they sat in spacious and well-wooded for city dwellings. After feasting my eyes on them and wondering which was *hers*, I stepped down from my seat and paid the driver the sum we had agreed.

The two pine trees, Os Dois Pinheiros, in fact, that were guarding the gate of one particular property, gave me a pretty good clue to discovering the location of the Lowthers' home. Even more helpful were the several handsome carriages that were lined up in the half-moon drive outside the front doors and the little crowds of gaily dressed ladies and gentlemen who were seeking entrance through them. I hurried up the drive and managed to insinuate myself into one of these groups and soon nobody would have been able to tell in what manner of equipage I had arrived at the house, for it looked as if I'd descended like the rest from one or other of those fine coaches. (One of which, I saw with a thrill, even had a coat of arms upon its side.)

And now I was in the very place wherein she dwelled! Still with the herd of strangers among whom I had arrived, I passed through another crowd composed of footmen and curtseying maids, all Portuguese as far as I could tell, one of whom relieved me of my hat. Beyond this melee, I found myself in a prodigiously extensive kind of drawing room, a space so vast that it almost rivalled that room near the Rossio that I had visited a week before and which, I remembered, had managed to contain a couple of hundred people in it and furniture too. There was not nearly that number of folk present in this room, of course; even so it was a fair-sized crowd and we new arrivals swelled it appreciably. I smiled and bowed at various passing people but none seemed inclined to stop and converse with me, and so I kept moving too.

At the far end of the room I saw a set of great windows, which extended from floor to ceiling. This too put me in mind of that other, that fateful room. But I saw as I walked towards them that, far from looking upon scenes of folly and cruelty, these windows gave out on a most agreeable view of an extensive and well-planted garden, and beyond that of piney hills rolling down to a distant vision of glinting river.

I was standing, admiring this prospect, when a well-remembered voice broke into my reverie.

'Mr Adam Hanaway,' it said. And, 'I was hoping you would come.'

I turned in delight and apprehension to meet the smiling gaze of Miss Gabriella Lowther. I had determined before I got here that I would have to search for her high and low, that, as every lover has his challenges and difficulties to overcome, my first one would be to discover her whereabouts and manage the still more perplexing task of getting her away from other people, so I could talk to her face to face and, as it were, alone.

Yet here she was, standing before me, smiling up at me – and only me! I just had the wit to remember to bow to her. When I got steady again, I shot a quick glance above her head and then at each side of her. I discovered there was nobody else at all within hearing distance.

'Are you looking for someone?' enquired Miss Lowther. 'Is there somebody you would like me to introduce to you?'

'Not at all,' I vowed earnestly. 'I should not like that one bit, Miss Lowther.'

'Have you not come to our house to be sociable then?' she smiled.

I was ravished by the sight of her little white teeth, but did not forget to open my own mouth in order to deliver a graceful response to her question. Unhappily nothing whatsoever came into my mind to say, and so I was reduced to gazing at her, and shaking my head and, until I thought to close my mouth, gaping at her too, like a fish.

After giving me ample time to display my wit and elegance, Miss Lowther evidently concluded that neither was going to appear just now, for she gave a little shrug and said, 'I am under orders from my father to tell all the gentlemen that he is holding court in the drawing room. And if you do not care to take tea' – she nodded towards where several servants were bowed over some seated lady guests and handing them china cups and saucers – 'then he can promise you something more fortifying if you will join him there.'

'Is this not the drawing room then?'

'No, sir. It is the ballroom. But my grandmama has commandeered it today for her tea. The drawing room is through that door there.'

'But I would much rather stay and talk to you, Miss Lowther,' I blurted out.

Her first response was to put on an air of conventional coquetry as if I had just said something charming but unmeant, the usual thing I suppose at these gatherings. But then, hearing at last the blunt sincerity in my voice, her little artificial smile dropped away. She gazed up at me curiously. And then a real frank grin curved her lips.

'I should like to talk to you too, Mr Hanaway.'

'You would?' I murmured, thrilled.

'Indeed I would.' She laughed lightly, a most enchanting sound. 'Why wouldn't I?'

We stood gazing at each other. Rather, on my part it was a kind of feasting I was engaged in, as I took in again the beauty of her face and form. She was wearing a casual dress of palest blue today and, as it was the afternoon, a little linen cap upon her fair curls. Her skin in the pure light that flowed in from the windows was – I can only repeat the word: it was pure, pure white except for a blush like dawn where the blood rose closest to the surface.

It seemed to be rising rather fast now in her cheeks as I continued to stare at her with barely disguised yearning. At the time I put down this change of colour to her maidenly response to what she may have feared was my predatory maleness. On the other hand, in the time I was to know her Gabriella always struck me as a fairly cool customer when it came to dealing with men, and so I have concluded since that the alteration was as likely to have been connected with the changing light at the window as anything else.

Anyway she gave me a hurried little bob of a curtsey then and turned away. I stood cursing myself for what I perceived had been my repellent oafishness. She had gone just two or three steps from me when she looked back.

'I must see to our other guests,' she said. 'But I really should like to talk to you, Mr Hanaway.' And again she showed me her perfect little teeth as she smiled. 'I hope you will not leave before we can do that.'

I wandered over towards the door that led into the drawing room in a kind of happy daze. It did not leave me even when in my inattention I almost bumped into another guest as we were both endeavouring to open the door. The fellow smiled and backed politely away to let me do the honours. It was only as I, striving for equal politeness, held the door open for him to go through that I realised that the gentleman was none other than Ralph Tolliver. He favoured me with a complacent smile as he passed me. It was clear he did not recognise me. I told myself there was no real reason why he should have. Nevertheless my failure to have made an impression on him at the assembly, as well as his actual presence, put something of a dent in my previous happy mood. I could not but remember the jealous pangs I had felt when I had first seen him at the assembly house, bending over my soon-to-be-beloved with such an insolent air of possession.

In this rather incoherent state of mind, I followed my 'rival' into a room that was certainly spacious though not so large as the one I had left. There were about twenty men already in there, standing about near the fireplace (which held no fire of course on this mild day, but a great vase of ornamental grass), or lounging on chairs and settees. I saw that Gabriella's father was presiding over the room, having taken up a position near a long table on which was a snow-white cloth and on that many bottles of wine, some in ice-buckets, and glasses, and also a couple of oaken barrels. I watched him put out his hand to greet Ralph Tolliver. I saw them shake, saw Mr Lowther laugh at something Tolliver said to him. I waited until the two had finished their exchanges and Tolliver had taken his bumper of wine and gone away, and then myself approached the long table and my host.

Mr Lowther appeared pleased to see me, though not of course to the extent by which he had shown his favour to Ralph Tolliver. Still he remembered who I was, and professed himself delighted that I was able to do him the honour of calling at his house. He asked then if I had found the journey up here from the lower city a trial and I said that I was fortunate in my choice of conveyance, managing to imply that the equipage that had brought me here was at least a well-turned-out coach and four, rather than a dilapidated cart dragged by two decrepit mules and driven by an equally broken-down old man. We turned then to the important matter of what I would take to drink. And though I was sure that any wine that came from Mr Lowther's cellars was bound to be of superior merit – on another planet for instance from that which I had just managed to swallow at the Hutchinsons' the other day – yet I had a sudden desire to drink ale again.

'Very good choice, Mr Hanaway – or may I call you Adam? I feel that my old friend's nephew is quite one of the family. This is something I import from my own home county: Sleeford's Lincolnshire Particular.'

I signified my approval of being served this Sleeford's brew. Lowther nodded to the Portuguese fellow who stood behind the table. At his master's signal, he stepped forward and drew me off a tankard. I sipped at it a little apprehensively. Often these local beers were recommended by their champions more for reasons of patriotism than discernment. However, Sleeford's Particular turned out to be very acceptable. Its taste was almost like that of porter, though not quite so dark to the sight. There was something flowery in it too, something added which I could not quite discover. Certainly it was a powerful brew and after the first swallow I resolved to observe my consumption of it very carefully. I had in mind the promise of a further talk with Miss Lowther. Having already appeared before her today as a lustful mute, I did not want to complete my downfall by showing up next as a sot.

I congratulated Mr Lowther on the excellence of his – I almost said 'daughter' but at the last moment managed to substitute the word 'ale'. He seemed pleased at my approbation, and spoke a little of the mysteries of the manufacture. The flowery taste I had noticed was that of elderberries, which were added in the last stages of the fermentation. He said the resultant mixture was exported in bottles as well as barrels and he would be glad to send a half-dozen of the former to my lodgings if I truly liked it. I just had time to assure him that I did, very much, and would be most gratified to receive such a gift, when a party composed of several noisy gentlemen appeared before the table, clamouring for wine, and I left Mr Lowther and his servant to deal with them.

I took a turn around the room. There was nobody that I recognised, except for the offensive Ralph Tolliver, who I saw, to my chagrin, was apparently being made much of by the group of factors clustered before the fireplace. Certainly they appeared to be hanging on his words, and as I watched they put back their heads as one and brayed with laughter at his latest quip. I could not bear to watch the spectacle of easy Tolliver triumphs any more, and turned and slowly, in a stop-and-start fashion, retraced my steps.

Eventually I knew I would be brought face-to-face again with Mr Lowther at the table and, though our last encounter had been most cordial, I surmised that we had concluded our business for the time being at any rate, and guessed that he would be as uncertain what to say now to me as I would be to answer him. Moreover there was the danger that he might suspect that I could not, for reasons of gross appetite, bear to stay away for long from the table where the drinks were kept. Yet I did not know where else to go.

Without much enthusiasm, I attached myself at last rather loosely to the gang near the fireplace. They appeared to be in the throes of a very lively discussion, to which I listened for a time. It seemed to consist mostly of various complaints against the Portuguese nation, particularly that portion of it that served the King's customs. Another, separate battery was also firing away steadily at the archaic Portuguese legislation upon which the whole rickety structure of business and trade operated here. In particular we were invited to condemn a law – dating from 1325, as one young factor kept repeating, as if the fact disposed of any and all arguments in its favour – that made the taking of bullion out of the country a crime punishable even by death. Since the Portuguese had a great need for foreign imports, and since their principal means of paying for them was by the gold that flooded in from their colonial mines it was easy to see that this prohibition operated mainly to create a vast system of smuggling and official corruption.

'And it is all so unnecessary,' the young factor complained. 'For don't you see – it belongs to the year 1325 when things were quite different.'

In other words it was the sort of stuff one could hear any time of the day in one or other of those coffee houses in the Rua Nova dos Ferros that the English patronised. Pretty soon I got very bored by it. Somebody – was it Ralph Tolliver? I could not see from the back of the crowd – was now boasting of how the whole hateful confusion could be sorted out in a trice if the government at home would only send a couple of ships of the line into the Tagus and then inform the scurvy ministers of João V that, unless they dealt harshly with their creatures who worked in the customs house, and fairly with the decent British merchants who had only come to their paltry country to bring enlightenment and the benefits of trade to the benighted natives, then their famous capital would be cannonaded into a smoking ruin.

This savage, though certainly meaningless threat brought forth a full-throated roar of approbation from the other merchants, and I took the opportunity during it to slip away from their company and then from the room itself. I was now anxious to take up Miss Lowther's promise of an interview. As before I supposed that the importance of the prize I sought guaranteed that the quest after it would be long and arduous. Yet also as before I was to be pleasantly surprised to find it was not so. Miss Lowther was standing at the ballroom windows in about the same spot where we had first met today. It was almost as if she had not moved from it in the twenty minutes or so since we parted. She was talking to a young lady, about her own age. She looked up as I bore down on her, and I flattered myself that the smile of welcome she offered me was perfectly genuine.

'This is Miss Mills,' she told me after we had greeted one another. She turned to display her friend to me. I bowed to Miss Mills. She was quite a pretty girl, yet I urgently wished she would go away as soon as possible. I desired to speak to Miss Lowther alone, and could not bear to think of the little time we would have together being wasted in the polite chit-chat that the presence of another would enforce. Luckily, Miss Mills almost immediately discovered that she wanted to talk to another young woman who was sitting some way off. (I say 'luckily' – I think I'm not flattering myself overmuch if I suggest it was most probable that Miss Mills' early departure was something that had been arranged between the girls to occur as soon as I appeared.)

And so there were just the two of us. I had so much I wanted to say. My Gabriella. I could not find the words immediately, but it didn't bother me much. I felt a sense of peace, I felt I would get the words out in time, and I believed we would have that time, if not today then on another day, another occasion. I could see a whole succession of days like this, entertainments, tête-à-têtes, teas and parties. I knew her father liked me. I hoped she liked me; she was smiling at me now as if she did. I thought I would become a frequent visitor to her dear house. This house. One of the family, yes, and in this unfolding drama Ralph Tolliver, the definitively married Ralph Tolliver, would be a meaningless unthought-of nullity.

'You are sweating, Sir,' said my fair companion then. 'You are sweating something prodigious.'

This, as an entry on the remarkable, or at least polite and charming conversation I hoped to have with Miss Lowther, was so far from what I had expected – that I decided to act as if I had not heard it. I gestured gracefully at the window, what lay beyond.

'Miss Lowther, I think I have not seen a more fetching prospect than this,' I said, 'in all the time I have been in Lisbon.'

'Thank you. But still – I must say it: you are sweating very badly, Mr Hanaway. You alarm me. Are you unwell?'

I put up my hand and touched my forehead. As I knew it would be, it was covered in a thick and strangely oily liquid film. I examined my palm when I had lowered it, as if I could by all the force of my detestation wish the affliction away from me. A little hand with a little handkerchief in it appeared under my gaze. I started to push it away, but she insisted and I took the bit of silk at last and mopped my brow with it. Even as I disposed of the original perspiration, I knew that more moisture was streaming down not only from my forehead, but my neck too. At least the offence of that was hidden under my wig. But there was no disguising the state of my face.

'I am not ill,' I promised her. 'It is just that I find the climate here very trying.'

'But it's not hot today.'

'Not to you perhaps who have lived here a long time. But for me –' I shook my head. Unhappily that motion caused several drops of sweat to fly from my forehead and land on Miss Lowther's sleeve and naked arm. Horrified, I seized her hand and vigorously applied the handkerchief to her arm. Several moments passed like this, until I realised that I was holding hands in public with my host's daughter and – and I flung the poor girl's hand from me almost as if it was on fire, and instead started dabbing again at my brow where yet another river of sweat had begun to trickle down from under my wig.

At last, having repaired myself as best I could, I offered to hand the kerchief back to Miss Lowther. She took it, though at the last moment it had occurred to me that the state it was now in must be fairly disgusting and I had tried to hold it back from her. But she tucked it away in the pocket of her apron without apparent distaste.

'If you find it hot here,' said Miss Lowther, 'why do you dress so warm? That coat is velvet, is it not?'

'It is,' I said, preening myself a little under her gaze. Today, having dressed in my best suit, I had the satisfaction of knowing that my appearance at least could not be faulted. Except for the sweating, of course. And that, as I had noticed when I'd first come into the house, I had done wrong in not bringing my sword today, for every other gentleman was wearing his.

'Why do you wear velvet? It is a very heavy material. Look at me. My dress is made of muslin. I find it delightfully cool.'

'I would not think,' I smirked, rather indulgently, I suppose, and probably irritatingly too, 'that muslin would be quite the thing for a gentleman's –'

'My father in hot weather only wears suits of silk or cotton. Would it not have been more sensible to have dressed in one of those today?'

Indeed it would have, and if I had such a choice of costume as Mr Lowther obviously had, silk or cotton is what I should have certainly preferred. But owning only one good suit in the whole universe, I'd had the choice of arriving here in a sweat or staying away completely. I was thinking how I could put this to her without betraying completely the depths of my poverty, when she spoke again:

'And your wig, Mr Hanaway. It is so high and full, and I'm sure must be very heavy. Anybody would be warm under that.'

'It is warm,' I admitted. 'But what am I to do? Every other gentleman you will see is wearing one too.'

'But none so vast as yours, Sir. See –' She nodded towards where Ralph Tolliver was crossing the room to talk to Miss Mills and her new companion. 'Mr Tolliver's is not even half the size of yours.'

How little I enjoyed hearing my beloved hold up my rival as something I should emulate. But I had to concede, even in my rage, that she had a point. If Monsieur Baye of Oxford had a fault it was that he adamantly set his face against the new fashion for shorter, lighter wigs for gentlemen's wear. It may have been that now, a year after I had employed his services, he had been forced to bow to the current, for it was well-nigh irresistible, but when he was making my wig he was still quite stubborn. And so here I was, wearing something that I knew was already unfashionable, even in this unfashionable city, and though it did not date me so badly as, say, the extraordinary creations that Mr Hutchinson sometimes wore upon his head, yet it definitely said that I was not quite in the mode.

It was also, as Miss Lowther had pointed out, confoundedly hot to wear.

'You should take it off,' the enchanting girl nodded. 'Your coat too. And drink something cool. You know we have some bottles of Rhenish brought up from the cellar.'

'Thank you. A cool drink would be most agreeable.'

'It will make little difference if you are still wearing that heavy coat.'

'But, Miss Lowther, while I don't deny what you say, how can I take off my coat in here –?'

'And your wig.'

'But –' I gave a quick, uncertain glance at all the crowd around us. 'I cannot do that. Not in such a place as this. With so many people watching.'

'I know a place where you can do it. And nobody will see you, except me.' She regarded me out of frank blue eyes. 'Will you trust me, Sir?'

'Of course I will,' I murmured, entranced under her gaze.

'Then come with me.'

And with that she turned and, as if in a fairy story, walked right through the window, her body seeming to dissolve the panes of glass in its graceful motion. For a second I did indeed think we had entered a world of enchantment and she had done this amazing thing. Then I noticed that of course there were no longer panes or lead to impede her, that since I'd last been here the windows had been opened wide to allow in a breeze to cool the air within the room. I went after her. Her slim young form wavered in the light before me. We were high up, and the dress she was wearing seemed to merge sometimes with the pale-blue of the sky. Then we passed beside some trees. The white of her cap and her neck and arms became startling against the darker hues. She turned and smiled back at me. Her finger beckoned me on. I plunged after her gladly. I would have followed her as far as the distant River Tagus and into its waters and under them too if she had still been beckoning me.

We had left the formal part of the garden now and Miss Lowther had plunged into a sort of wood or copse. I had caught up with her and she had taken my hand in hers. Still she led me on. It was dark here in the woods, but ahead I could see what appeared to be the light of a clearing.

'Here we are,' she said.

We broke free of the woods. Ahead of us, in this clearing, stood a most extraordinary structure. It was a tiny house. Topped with a tiled roof, with gables at either end, and a little chimney in the middle. The walls were of brick, the windows of glass with white frames. There was a front door, fresh-painted in red, with a little boot-scraper on one side of it and on the other a lamp depending from a wooden pole. It was all neat and bright and tidy and tiny. What on earth was it doing here? I walked all the way around it marvelling at its diminutive perfection. I came back to where Miss Lowther still stood in the place from which I had started out. There was a gratified smile on her face as she watched my amazement.

'My father had it made for me when I was a little girl. I used to entertain my friends here. The servants would bring us tea and so on, and we'd have great times playing at being the adults.' She turned from me to survey her small estate. I watched her delectable profile. She was staring at the house in a way that suggested she was looking fondly back through great swathes of time, but I supposed it was not really so.

'When did you last play here?'

'Oh . . . when I was twelve, perhaps.'

So. Perhaps four years ago.

'When he saw I no longer came here any more, my father said he would have it pulled down. But when it came to it, he could not do it. He said it reminded him too well of when I was little, and my mother still alive, and how I would send them both invitations inviting them to dine with me here or take tea or chocolate. So it was left standing. And I am glad now it was. It's a pretty sight, don't you think?'

We were silent for a moment. Miss Lowther presumably contemplating the memory of her deceased parent, and I – well, not doing anything more profound than wondering what was going to happen next. My companion solved the mystery by then advancing to the red front door and turning the handle so as to open it. She looked back at me and I saw her eyes were twinkling.

'Won't you step inside, Sir?' she asked.

I found the interior to be just as tastefully succinct and dainty as the outside. We were in a parlour, about eight feet by ten. The ceiling had just enough height to clear my wig. There was a little grate, two little armchairs, a table beside each, all perfectly in proportion. On the floor was a square of Oriental carpet which, though worn, looked to be of excellent quality. Another door was at the far end of the room. Miss Lowther seeing me glancing at it told me that it led to a room where she had used to put her dolls to bed and get them out of it five minutes later and generally fuss about with their care, cleanliness and education.

'What do you think of my house?' asked Miss Lowther then.

I assured her that I admired it excessively. And truly I did. When I thought about it later, I realised that there must be very many whole families back in England who occupied areas that were no greater than this one. And the Irish in their kennels certainly found themselves even more confined and immured. But there was something so pert and pretty about this bright little home, and it was marvellous to consider that it and everything in it was made not for a horde of bawling paupers but for one rich little girl and her favoured playmates. It gave me too while I was in it a feeling of privilege and security such as I had once used to know, but not for a long time now.

'Won't you sit, Mr Hanaway?'

I chose my chair, and found it to be, though a pretty tight fit, capable of receiving me. She lowered herself into the chair opposite sitting as far forward as she might to allow her hoops enough room, and so we sat on either side of the grate, like a long-married couple, smiling at each other.

'And so, Sir?'

'And so, Miss?'

'Are you not going to do what I brought you here for? You are not in public any more. So why do you not take off that great wig?'

Really, as I considered the matter, there was no reason why I shouldn't. It was true that the atmosphere in this room was rather cooler than on the outside, yet it was still mild enough to make my scalp feel pretty warm under the mountain of strangers' hair that I wore. And there would be no real impropriety in exposing my own hair to Miss Lowther. After all, if I were to come calling at her father's house in the future without the inducement of an invitation to a particular function, I might well choose to wear only my own hair, and nobody would think me barbarous for leaving off Monsieur Baye's creation.

'Well, Mr Hanaway?'

I made up my mind. Raised both my hands and lifted off the peruke and set it on the miniature table beside me. Miss Lowther clapped her hands in delight.

'You are fair,' she cried. 'Just like me.'

I put my hand up to my head to smooth my hair down. Without thinking what I was doing, I began to give my scalp a good scratch for the removal of my wig seemed to have released a great fund of itching in what it had covered.

'Do you have fleas, Sir?'

'No!' I snatched away my hand.

'Really? I used to suffer from them always in this house. When I was little my mother would wash my hair in vinegar-water if I had played in here for a long time. But,' she reflected, 'as you have only just come into it, I don't see how it could be blamed for infesting you so soon.'

'But I assure you, Miss Lowther, that I am quite free from fleas.'

It was, I considered, another example of the kind of curious side roads that I seemed to find myself on when conversing with Miss Lowther. After sweat, fleas, for heaven's sake! However, I let the matter go, stretched forth my limbs as I settled back in my little armchair. It really was very pleasant not to have that great hot wig crouched upon my head like some horrid hairy beast. If not for fashion, for the mode, I truly thought I would be quite happy to appear *sans perruque* almost all of the time.

'Now, Sir, that great heavy coat.'

I looked into her eyes. They were expectant; even, I thought, a little impatient.

'I believe I will keep it on,' I ventured.

'Nonsense. I have brought you here so that you may get comfortable at last. It will be a poor reward for my trouble if you don't take advantage of it. And see – you are still sweating.'

It could not be denied. That wretched film had reappeared on my brow, even bare-headed as I was. Miss Lowther produced again from her pocket the little handkerchief. It had got dry once more in her possession and had too, I noticed as I brought it up to my face, taken on the scent of its owner. Which was – well, I could not place it at all. Not orange-water, nor lavender, nor anything that I could exactly identify. It was only later in life, when I was first married, and afterwards when I was intimate with other women, that I knew it for what it was: the precious fragrance of healthy young female.

I attempted to return the handkerchief. She told me I should keep it. I was certain to have need of it again if I persisted in wearing that foolish great coat. We continued to gaze at one another. I saw she was implacable. It was also, I realised, something that I suddenly wished to do very much. I got to my feet. Removed my coat and laid it next to my wig. Again she clapped her hands as I sat down again. I was blessing my good fortune that I had thought to put on a clean shirt today, and hoping that the inevitable dark stains under my arms would not disgust her too much.

How often in the long years that followed this episode did I return to it and speculate as to exactly what this lovely girl was doing when she brought a young man into an empty house and proceeded once they were alone to make him undress himself. Of course the obvious answer – certainly the most flattering to me – was that she did it out of concupiscence. That, consciously or no, she wanted me – and then herself too, no doubt, to strip off our clothes and let our animal instincts take their course.

But I do not think this was really so. For there was something oddly innocent about Gabriella when a girl, and something child-ish too. I felt that overpoweringly of course sitting with her in this toy house. I think it as likely, in other words, that she wanted to play as to flirt with me. That I was like one of her dolls, her poppets, that she could at her will dress and undress in what manner of costume she cared. Even if there was a sensual ingre-dient in her researches, yet still I think it was on this level of childishness. For I remember I had sometimes seen my sister Amelia when she was little take off the breeches of a boy doll of hers called William (in honour of the late King) and examine the undifferentiated bump between his legs with warm unguarded curiosity. Gabriella this afternoon reminded me a little of that.

I think she simply wanted to see me in a state of undress. Partly for my benefit, partly for hers. And, if it was not beyond all the bounds of propriety, I believe she would have been happy to see me remove my waistcoat, breeches, stockings, drawers, every-thing. Just to see how I looked. It was an essentially meaningless curiosity and I suppose for that reason did not fire up my own passions by very much.

'Are we not easy and comfortable now?' Gabriella said. 'And aren't you glad you came with me, Mr Hanaway?'

Well, she was right. Easy and comfortable was just how I felt. A hand to my forehead showed that the wretched perspiration had dried up almost completely.

'I would always be happy to go anywhere with you, Miss Lowther,' I said with what I hoped was a rather effective stab at gallantry – and was sorry then to see a little frown appear on her clear white brow.

'Do you know, I think it is rather odd that we sit here like this calling each other Mr Hanaway and Miss Lowther. Don't you? I should like to call you Adam. And for you to call me Gabriella. Oh, I don't mean,' she said, acknowledging the rather worried look that must have appeared on my face, 'that we should do it when we are with others. It is too soon for that. But just while we are in this house. For you know – Adam – that we are like an old married couple sitting here, and married folk don't stand on ceremony much, do they?'

Had she any idea what she was saying? It was true that she was echoing certain stray thoughts that had already passed through my mind too. Nevertheless, to bring them out into the open, as it were, to speak of them aloud, suggested either great sophistication, or an artlessness that was almost dangerous in a girl of marriageable age.

'Well, I shall call you Gabriella then,' I said.

'Good, but only in this house. D'you promise?'

I nodded, and she smiled at me brightly.

'Well, Adam,' she said, 'I wish you would tell me something of yourself.'

'I would much rather – Gabriella – hear you speak of yourself.'

'Oh, you would not if I did. My life is so very dull. I live here –'

My gaze went involuntarily around the little room. She laughed.

'I mean I live in the big house, of course. I get up every morning. I see my father. Madame Corréade comes to give me French lessons, and I am instructed in Italian by Signora Brunetti in memory of my mother –'

'Do you learn Portuguese too?'

'Portuguese? No. Why should I? I've picked it up a little, from the servants and so on . . . Miss Graveney comes to the house once a week to instruct me on the harpsichord, and I take drawing lessons from Senhor José every Tuesday. I go out for a drive in the phaeton each afternoon. On Sundays I usually visit my grand-mama's *quinta* . . . and that is my life. I did warn you – Adam – that it was a dull one.'

After this complete though, as she said, rather dry account of her existence, I could not withhold from her my own story. And so it all came out – or rather as much of it as I thought fit to tell. The

Alfândega – Uncle Felix – Aunt Sarah – cousins Betty and Nancy – more of the Alfândega – my mother and sisters back home – my servant (as I dubbed him) Bento – my lodgings in the Rua do Parreiral, which in the telling metamorphosed somehow from a cramped fourth-floor room into a set of rather commodious *quartos* on the first floor – my multitudinous wanderings about the streets and alleys of the Baixa, and in the Rossio and along the river shore. I concluded with a final volley touching on my life in the Alfândega and then fell silent, hoping I had not wearied her over much.

'You seem to spend a great deal of time in this – Alfândega, do you call it?'

'It is my business,' I said. 'I hope it will be my career.'

'You work with your uncle?'

'Uncle Felix. Yes.'

'You hope to make your fortune with him?'

'Certainly I hope to *start* making my fortune in his service.'

'But I have heard that he is a fool.'

Now this was a most outrageous thing for her to say to me, the nephew. Only a very innocent or a very malicious person could have said it. Miss Lowther certainly looked the picture of innocence as she waited for me to respond. It was only at the very moment when I turned away from her to consider what I should say that I thought I caught just a hint of naughty glee in her eyes. I looked back at her quickly, but her gaze now was as open and transparent as before.

What should I say? Perhaps I ought to just deny the accusation and leave it at that. But I really wanted to discover what she meant by it. Loyalty to my uncle, in other words, struggled against sheer curiosity.

Curiosity won. 'Who do you hear that from?'

'My father. He said it at supper here one night to Mr Tolliver.'

The thought of the detested Ralph Tolliver being a party to a conversation in which *any* Hanaway was abused and slandered enraged me greatly and I was about to burst out with some malediction upon his name when Gabriella, who perhaps had that species of intuition given to young and artless girls, remarked, 'I don't mean *Ralph* Tolliver, of course. I mean his father, Jacob.'

This calmed me considerably, but I still found myself resentful because of her words.

'I thought your father was a friend of Uncle Felix.'

'You can be friends with someone surely and think them a fool too.'

'Can you?'

'I am. With Mary Mills, for instance. But tell me if I have been spreading a false report. If your uncle is not a fool, I should be glad to hear it.'

I took a moment or two before replying, and in that period I realised that there was indeed a part of me that thought my uncle sometimes was a bit of a fool. Yet I knew I could not admit to it to anyone outside the family, even to so enchanting a stranger as Gabriella Lowther.

'My uncle has been unfortunate in some financial dealings. And when that happens to a gentleman' – I said this soberly, thinking very hard upon the fate of my poor father – 'then there will always be other men willing to call him fool and knave.'

'In that case,' said Gabriella brightly, 'they would have to call my father by those names too, for I know he has lost a great deal of money this year.'

'In the South Sea stock?'

'I don't know how exactly. But I heard him complaining of it to my grandmama the other day.'

We both sat in melancholy contemplation of our relatives' folly – until Miss Lowther roused herself and looked around her.

'I wish I had something to offer you, Adam,' she said.

I asked the question mutely of her. She giggled.

'I mean refreshments, of course. Wouldn't it be nice if I had a rope in here that I could pull on and summon a servant to wait on us?'

I agreed that it would be prodigiously nice. But added that I was quite comfortable in here as it was, and would be happy to remain so – unless Gabriella wished to leave.

'Not at all,' she said. 'I think we still have business here. For I do not believe I have heard your story entire. For instance, you have not told me who your friends are in this town.'

In my mind I went over a rough jumble of fellows I was acquainted with, some of the snowballs in the customs house, a fellow with one leg, who claimed to be an old soldier, from whose stall next to the slaughterhouse I used to buy a cup of wine sometimes on my way home and exchange a few friendly insults with him. Senhor Gomes. Bento. Montesinhos. The muster was not impressive.

'Surely you must have friends.'

And then like rescuing cavalry galloping into view came thoughts of the Hutchinsons. Of course! Who else should I talk about? For they were indeed my only friends in Lisbon. And who could be more appropriate to the task for a young man seeking to intrigue a young woman and pique her interest in his doings than this couple? For were they not by turns amusing, pitiful, brave, colourful, unusual? There was also the added benefit – which I was not slow to take advantage of – that the manner of my meeting them had details in it that certainly reflected on myself in a flattering way.

So it came out. The sight of poor Mr Hutchinson in the alley, set upon by a band of bullies. My instantaneous decision to go to his help. Modestly I allowed that if I'd time for reflection I might have been slower in offering my aid.

'For there were half a dozen of them, at least,' I reported to Miss Gabriella. 'And of all them big, brutal fellows you would not like to meet up with on a moonless night. Though it was not so dark as that, certainly.'

Gabriella clapped her hands in her admiration quite as energetically as I could have wished. I went on to detail less exciting but still, I thought, entertaining episodes in my friendship with the Hutchinsons. The dinner I had almost ate with Dona Maria Beatriz – the negro robber and philanthropist Senhor Reinaldo – Dom Jeronymo – the return of the stolen watch – the stroll in the Rossio – Maria Beatriz's kindness in nursing me when I was 'temporarily disabled', as I phrased it.

'This lady seems to be a very excellent person altogether,' remarked Gabriella rather coolly. 'Is she beautiful?'

I hesitated. 'She is past forty,' I said carefully at last. 'She may be fifty or near it.'

'Oh, *old*,' said my companion, and nodded her head in complete satisfaction.

All through my narrative, Gabriella showed the most flattering degree of attention and signified by many little nods and sighs and smiles and glances that she was fascinated by what I told her. And, I suppose, in comparison to the dull round she had described her own life to be, my paltry adventures with and without the Hutchinsons were the stuff of romance. At least of some novelty. In any event she seemed to have an appetite for them that I still had not yet slaked.

'Tell me more about the Hutchinsons,' she cried out.

I was a little sorry to hear her say that. I had rather exhausted what I could say about my friends. It was also the case that all the pretty sighing, nodding and smiling that had greeted my narrative had rather aroused me. Indeed, I was wondering, even as I told my history, whether I had the courage to attempt to get a little closer to the lovely young person opposite and, if I had the least encouragement, to kiss her. It would not be an easy manoeuvre, I saw. We seemed so thoroughly rooted to our armchairs and there was a good yard of ground that separated us. And beyond, that her hoops offered a further defence against my ardour.

Nevertheless I was game to try. Had already leaned towards her as far as I could without falling over. Was ready to get to my feet – when her renewed request stopped me in my tracks. I was inclined to dismiss it, admit that I had used up all I knew, but her gaze was so importunate that I knew I had to try to think of something else interesting to tell her. I scratched around therefore in my brain and at last came up with what I thought might entertain her for a little while. And after that, I decided, there would be no more delays. I wanted to kiss her. I would kiss her . . . I certainly hoped I would have the courage to try to.

'You know I told you that Mr Hutchinson is the most old-fashioned of gentlemen?'

'So you did,' cried Gabriella happily.

'Well, it even extends to his speech. He has a whole miscellany of strange words in his vocabulary, that I think must date back to Queen Elizabeth's time at least and which I have not the least idea what they mean when he says 'em.'

'Such words as which?' cried Gabriella, her eyes willing me to make her laugh. 'Pray tell me, Adam.'

'Well . . . well . . .' Now I had to come up with something. I tried so hard to drag something up from memory. It was peculiarly difficult. I certainly had not lied. Mr Hutchinson was a treasure-trove of arcane and ridiculous words and phrases, yet I could not think of any of them. Until:

'Slubberdegullion!' I brought forth triumphantly.

'What?'

'I assure you. Slubberdegullion. He says that a lot.'

'Slubber-de-gullion,' repeated Gabriella wonderingly. 'But what does he mean by it?'

'I have never liked to ask. But given the context in which he says it, when he is usually abusing some fellow, I think it means something like "rogue" or "brute".'

Well, I came up with a few more of old Hutchinson's sayings after that. I gave interpretations of them too, though most of them I invented myself for I certainly did not know what 'sawney' or 'jack pudding' or 'singleton' or 'pipkin vent' or 'nockandro' might really mean. Of course I avoided all words that discovered some obviously offensive meaning. Thus I suppressed the phrase 'farting crackers', by which I had heard Mr Hutchinson once refer to his own breeches, and the word 'strunt', which I did not know at all what it meant but which sounded perfectly disgusting. On the other hand I did not hesitate to offer up 'rump-sticker', which I explained as an implement of use either in agricultural pursuits, some sort of goad, for instance, or at the butcher's shop, rather like a skewer. Again I was actually quite in ignorance of its true meaning, but I thought that 'rump-sticker', though no doubt inoffensive in reality, had an earthy, vulgar sound that would nicely set the stage for the modestly wanton scene I hoped soon to play with Miss Gabriella.

At any rate she heard them all with apparent delight, which though finally showed signs of running out. And that was fortunate for I had also pretty much exhausted by now my fund of old Hutchinson's silly words. Now at last the moment had really come when I must make my attempt on the cheek – or lips? – of the divine Gabriella, or consider myself what Mr Hutchinson would have undoubtedly called a 'pilgarlic', a poor, pitiful creature, in fact.

'Gabriella . . .' I murmured.

'Yes, Sir?' the lovely girl said demurely.

'Oh, Gabriella . . .'

'What is it, Adam?'

I stood up so that I might cross the short distance that lay between us . . .

And was thus already in perfect position to greet the new arrival when she came through the door, which she did a moment after I had risen, being closely followed into the room by her escort.

'I guessed you had come here, Gabby!' cried Miss Mills. 'I told Ralph this is where you would have taken Mr Hanaway to be alone with him. Didn't I tell you that, Ralph?'

I am pretty sure that neither I nor Gabriella looked very happy to find that our promising tête-à-tête had been broken in upon. Miss Mills, who had entered with a bright smile, as one who knows she will be welcomed, began to falter somewhat as she read the expressions on our faces. As for Ralph Tolliver: he could not seem to shift his stare from my coatless upper portion. I tried to engage him boldly with my eyes, but could never find a way to meet them for his own were always roving upon my shirt-sleeves and the ruffles of my chest.

'Oh, hello, Mary,' said Gabriella sombrely. Then, like the well-schooled girl she was, she pulled herself together. She looked around the little room, which had certainly grown even smaller with so many of us crowding into it, and then flashed a smile at her friend. 'Remember how we used to play in here?'

'Oh, I do,' said Mary Mills fervently. Then she tried to drag us gentlemen into the discussion. 'We were always here when we were little girls, serving tea to each other –'

'And to our poppets.'

'Indeed, the babies. The little dolls. Do you still have them, Gabs?'

'In the next room,' promised my Gabriella.

Miss Mills gave what sounded like a rather forced scream of delight and demanded to see them. Gabriella shrugged and led her from the room. Ralph Tolliver, after a conventional gesture at their leaving, turned again to me. His gaze now was quite ferocious, but I didn't care much. I was still so chagrined that my interview with my beloved had been disturbed.

'You are not wearing your coat, Sir,' young Mr Tolliver remarked.

I forbore to utter the obvious sneering compliments on his powers of observation.

'I was warm. Miss Lowther gave me permission to remove the garment.'

'And your wig too, I see.'

'For the same reason.'

'I did not know you were on such familiar terms with *Gabriella* as would persuade you to behave in such a casual manner, even with her permission.'

The proprietary accent he had put upon my beloved's Christian name was impossible to miss. I had strayed inside a circle that he thought he had erected around her and we were two snarling dogs facing each other across it.

'Oh, don't be so tedious, Ralph,' said Gabriella marching back into the room as she spoke. I thought it certain that she had lingered near the door in the other room and heard what had passed between Tolliver and me. She was carrying a wooden stool. Both us men leaped to take it from her. Being a little closer to her when we started, I was able to win the race.

'Put it over there,' Gabriella instructed, pointing to a spot between the armchairs, 'then we can all sit and be comfortable. Mary will bring out the other chair.'

I took this as my cue – or at least as another chance to show my breeding as compared with Ralph's – and made for the door. As I went out I heard him muttering, 'I am thinking only of your reputation, my dear,' and on the other side of the door – so tiny, as

I repeat, was this house – I could hear her quite clearly answering, 'Oh for heaven's sake, Ralph. He was very hot under that coat. It was my idea.'

I found myself in a room that was almost the twin of the one I had left, although in this case furnished very like one would see in a nursery, with bright colours on the walls and many pretty silk hangings and scarves descending from the ceiling. There were three or four little cribs in the centre of the floor, each containing a doll, and on one side a sofa on which sat many more of these homunculi, some made of wool or rag or some other common stuff, but most of wax or of alabaster and looking, if not exactly lifelike, then close enough to make me feel for the moment that I was under the watchful eyes of a host of little persons. Their eyes invariably were blue and their cheeks flushed so rosily as to seem almost feverish. Mary Mills was standing before this sofa and staring at her small charges in a rather distracted manner.

Clearly from the other room came Ralph Tolliver's growl. 'You have never told me about this place, Gabby.'

'Haven't I?' I heard my beloved carelessly reply.

'And yet you show it to this – this Hanaway – who you do not know from Adam.'

He paused as Gabriella giggled, I suppose at the fact that my name indeed *was* Adam.

'Who nobody knows – whose only connection is that blackguard uncle of his.'

How I boiled to hear this slander. I was only stopped from going out and confronting the fellow by the indisputable fact that he was armed and I was not. To which I immediately joined the other argument that if I went out and upbraided him for his insults upon myself and my family I would have to reveal before Gabriella that I had been guilty of the shabby practice of eavesdropping.

To do nothing was the best, certainly the safest, course of action. That and to get back into the room where surely Tolliver would have the decency to rein in his animosity in my presence. Yet I vowed that I would not forget these affronts, and that if ever it was within my power I would pay him back for them.

I turned to Miss Mills. She was looking quite stricken – of course she too had heard everything that was said in the other room.

'I'm so sorry,' she whispered to me, her hand at her throat. 'I'm sorry for interrupting you – '

'There was nothing to interrupt,' I said loudly, certain that my words too would carry from room to room. '*You* certainly are very welcome to join us, Miss Mills.'

And with that I seized a stool, companion to the one Gabriella had already brought into the drawing room, and with a polite nod to Mary Mills indicated she should lead the way. Ralph Tolliver was looking rather flushed, I saw. I hoped very much it was because he had overheard my last remark. He had the civility at least to get off his posterior when Miss Mills came in. I put my stool on the other side of the armchair, so as to have at least one girl and one substantial piece of furniture between myself and my rival.

Miss Mills took the chair I had earlier vacated. Ralph Tolliver was gazing at Gabriella in what I imagine he thought was an enticing and soulful fashion. Gabriella did not seem to be paying much attention to him. I took the opportunity to put my coat back on. I would never have done it while he was watching me, but this way it appeared as if it was upon my own volition, and certainly not on his. My wig remained where I had left it, and in my opinion sat there like a rebuke to Tolliver to say I would only move it back to my head when it suited me.

'We were having such a gay time, Mr Hanaway and I,' sighed dear Gabriella. 'He was making me laugh so much.'

We were back to being Mr and Miss, I saw. I did not really mind. The intimacy we had enjoyed was not for sharing with other people.

'Oh, pray,' begged Miss Mills, 'do tell me, Mr Hanaway, what you were talking about. I love to laugh so much.'

Ignoring various sceptical grunts and snorts from Tolliver, I smiled at the girl next to me. Of course she did not aspire to the perfection of my beloved, but she was certainly a pretty little person. Bright as a button, as they say. I remembered Gabriella had called her a fool. I did not see much evidence of that, but then how can one tell with young unmarried girls? Even then I knew that the cleverest of them will often affect a kind of light-headed silliness in their behaviour because they are convinced it will recommend them to the men.

'Why, Miss Mills, it wasn't much, you know. I was only talking of a friend of mine. A Mr Hutchinson, an elderly gentleman who has some amusing ways of carrying on.'

Miss Mills' smile, which I thought was becoming a little stiff, willed me to entertain her. I was about to proceed, though reluctantly, for I had been over all this ground already with Miss Lowther, when Tolliver's voice cut in.

'I know this Hutchinson,' he said. 'My father told me about him once. He is a scoundrel. I wonder, Sir, that he should be a friend of yours.'

I let my gaze travel quite slowly from the pink-and-white countenance of Miss Mills to the empurpled one of Ralph Tolliver, as if it had only dawned upon me gradually that he had just spoken, so little – as I hoped he would gather – did I care what he said.

'My father says that when he first came here and set up as a merchant he was a strutting, brawling sort of fellow. He got into very many fights, and though he was usually at fault he was always the first to draw. Indeed, he may have killed a man in one of these affrays.'

' "Got into very many fights," I repeated contemptuously. "May have killed a man"! And when did these pretended incidents take place? Very long ago, of course, and no credible witnesses to them still alive . . . And besides, what does it matter if he *was* free with his blade or his pistol? The young men of Mr Hutchinson's day were very spirited gentlemen and took their manners from the best people in the land. They were not, as we are, confined and harried by the morals of a bunch of scrubby trades-people and cowardly merchant riff-raff.'

I have no idea why, in taking this high-flown line against the merchant class, I did not see that I was in a way abusing myself, who at least aspired to that rank. Nor why I did not notice that I was disparaging my own father and almost making a mockery of a career in which, until just before the end, he had taken such justified pride. Nor indeed not remember that, as I had been informed more than once, Mr Hutchinson had been some time a merchant himself. But there it was, I was all froth and guts that afternoon, I was a knight in armour trampling down the scurvy varlets and cits, and Mr Hutchinson – the Hutchinson of fifty years ago – was my boon companion riding at my side.

Ralph Tolliver certainly had no doubt who I was aiming at: young merchant extraordinaire, embryonic Treasurer to the great Lisbon Factory. Himself indeed. He sneered at me, but was silent for a moment or two, and I was congratulating myself that I had drawn his fangs entirely – and in front of Gabriella too. But then he proved he was not quite ready to abandon the field to me.

'That isn't all. Do you know your friend is an unregenerate Catholic?'

'Of course I do,' I said loftily. 'He makes no secret of it. And where's the harm? He has removed himself to a Catholic country, and here he lives and follows his faith without offence to anyone English or Portuguese.'

'He has offended very many English here, I assure you. The Factory washed its hands of him long ago. Also' – Ralph's gaze swept over the two girls as if he was confident he was winning their support – 'there is worse: the fellow is nothing more than a street-peddler. An Englishman, a common peddler. It doesn't bear thinking of.'

'Perhaps,' I said, with all the scorn in my voice that I could muster, 'if the Factory had not "washed its hands of him", Mr Hutchinson would not have been reduced to making his living in the way he does.'

'I am sure he glories in it,' my rival sneered. Again his gaze encompassed the two girls before returning to concentrate on me. 'For what he sells in the streets are beastly images of the saints and so on. Catholic mummery and superstition. What do you say to that, Mr Hanaway? D'you still ambition to defend the scrub?'

The scabbard of Ralph Tolliver's sword clanked menacingly against the stool leg as he moved his knees. His gaze met mine so fiercely that I longed to look away from it. I had to think of something tremendous to say to distract him from whatever belligerent purposes were forming in his mind.

However, I could not.

'My mother was a Catholic,' Miss Lowther remarked suddenly. 'Do you include her in your disdain, Ralph?'

Which nicely took the wind out of the offensive Ralph's sails. He started on a confused semi-apology in which he tried to demonstrate that he had meant no offence to such as the late Madam Lowther, who had been born a Catholic in a Catholic country and so could not really help herself – but, before he could get to the end of this rather feeble explanation, Gabriella had put her little hands on the rests of her armchair and pushed herself out of it.

'I want to go,' she said. 'You gentlemen are not being at all amusing.'

Ralph and I vied with each other both to be first to our feet and with apologies for our conduct.

'Oh, Gabby,' complained Miss Mills, who had also had to get up. 'I wanted to hear Mr Hanaway speak of this funny old friend of his.'

'I'll tell you all about it,' Miss Lowther promised. 'It is most diverting, his amusing sayings, and if Mr Hanaway had not been distracted from his task' – this with a stern look at Ralph Tolliver – 'he would probably have made us laugh and laugh.'

With that she swept from the room, Miss Mills following after her. Tolliver and I glared at each other. Each of us probably blamed the other for the collapse of this afternoon's entertainment. But since it was apparent that Gabriella blamed Tolliver, I could not help but feel that I had come out of the contest the winner. I snatched up my wig and put it back on my head under Ralph's unforgiving stare. There followed an intense little struggle as we fought to see which of us could show the most parts by letting the other out of the door first. Again I was the victor. Ralph at last flung out of the house, uttering as he went what I took to be a muffled curse, certainly directed at myself.

Outside he and I walked towards the house, not so much side by side as one a foot or two behind the other. Ahead of us the slim forms of the girls glided over the grass. I heard Mary Mills laughing from time to time and I surmised that Gabriella was regaling her with some of Mr Hutchinson's funny old words. At that moment I thanked God I had kept such as 'strunt' and 'farting crackers' in my locker. As we broke from the trees and saw the big house before us, Miss Lowther left her friend and came back to walk beside me. She made it pretty clear she expected Ralph Tolliver to take her vacated place beside Miss Mills, who was all alone now, but Ralph was such a boor that he would not leave us until we were within a few yards of the house. And so Miss Lowther only had a moment or two to murmur that she was going to ask her father if I might be allowed to join the family next Sunday when they went out to visit her grandmama's *quinta*, which, she said, was in a neighbourhood called Buenos Ayres.

'If you would like that – Adam?'

Oh, no need to say how I responded.

Once back in the house Gabriella was swallowed up in a crowd of her other guests and I, seeing there was nothing more for me to do here, nothing more certainly that I wished to do, retrieved my hat and found my way to the front door. I walked back down from the heights of the Bairro Alto to the depths of my Baixa in almost a delirium of joy, as I remembered the enchanted hour I had spent with my darling girl this afternoon and looked forward to the still more perfect meetings with her that were certain to come, and the first of them very soon, only a week away.

Lowther

It was the time of day, and season of year that he liked above all.
Five o'clock in the morning, and the weather could not make
up its mind whether it belonged to the end of summer or the
beginning of autumn. Soon the sun would appear above the castle
of São Jorge. Its first rays would touch the Bairro Alto and start to
burn away the river mist that had gathered above it in the night,
even while it still lay thick and undisturbed upon the Lower Town.
Just now though the air was cool and grey as Lowther drank a cup
of chocolate in the kitchen, nodded his thanks to the serving-girl
who had made it for him, and then let himself out into the
courtyard. His dogs, Vitor and Pero, were waiting for him. They
got noiselessly to their feet, came to him so that he could ruffle
their ears. Then the little pack, Lowther in the lead, crossed the
cobbled yard, passed through the arch into the stables beyond.

One of the hands had left a bucket full of apples and carrots for
him at the side of the archway. Mr Lowther stooped to fill his
hands. Straightening up, he felt a spasm of pain in his lower back.
He hoped to God this wasn't going to be one of his bad days. It
always seemed to him a particular insult on the part of the Deity to
make him suffer with his blasted back on a day as pretty, as
sublime as this one promised to be.

The horses all had their heads out of their stall doors, waiting for
him. The big strawberry roan Excalibur that Lowther usually rode
on his infrequent excursions on horseback whinnied in a friendly
sort of way. He went to her first and gave her a couple of sweet
apples. The other animals soon grew restive at this blatant piece of
favouritism and started kicking their doors and stamping their
hooves. He moved along the row. They pushed their large soft
mouths into his hand, extracted the titbits he held out to them.

As they were eating, Lowther looked closely into their eyes, at their muzzles, the state of their ears, their teeth, looking for any sign of strain or injury or disease. It would have to be a pretty conspicuous sign. The truth was he had never been much of a judge of horseflesh, hale or infirm. It didn't concern him. There was only one sphere of life in which he felt himself truly an expert: the making of money. And, as if the Lord had ordered everything just to suit Phillip Lowther, it happened to be the one competency that he could use to make up for all his deficiencies.

Nevertheless, it would give him pleasure to be able to remark casually to his head groom when he saw him later this morning that 'Excalibur seemed a little peaked this morning' or 'I don't like the look in Rainha's eye'. He was perfectly well aware that the groom had no sort of belief in his employer's ability to know how his horses did. On the other hand the fellow was not fool enough to ignore what he said and, with every appearance of gravity and concern, would subject the horse that had caught Lowther's attention to a thorough examination this very day.

However, his careful though inexpert inspection failed to discover the least blemish on any of the half-dozen animals that stood looking out of their stalls, greeting him and his apples and the fine morning too. For which Mr Lowther sensibly knew he should be thankful. He kept feeding the beasts, and let his mind wander casually as he did. What a wonderful thing money was, he thought. There was not much novelty in the sentiment, he knew, but still he thought it would be churlish not to often acknowledge it, considering all that his money had brought him. Such as respect, attention, the services of experts, the obedience of other, possibly cleverer, but certainly poorer men. Money had secured to him too this house, these grounds, these horses, the continuance of the distinguished firm of Lowther & Robbins that supplied the means to sustain all the others. (He had kept the name on, even after his late partner had passed on in the spring of 1719, knocked down by a coach and four when he was crossing the Terreiro do Paço on a morning much like this one, cool and beautiful, a hint of autumn in the air.)

Death for Daniel Robbins then. But for Phillip Lowther still – a comfortable and assured future. How much he would hate to see it go, and be reduced to an impecunious failure, like his one-time friend Felix Hanaway, for instance. It had almost happened. Lowther too had been burned in the market last year, but only by a little. He had first heard of the excitement over the South Sea in London with cautious interest. He had listened too to the boasts and urgings of men like Hanaway, with their promises that it was impossible to avoid making a fortune, and then another fortune on top of that, if only one would show a little boldness and foresight and buy in all the stock one could. In the end, unable to resist these arguments, and more to the point, dazzled by the rise in the prices for stock as spring that year moved towards summer and each fresh packet brought news of unbelievable further increases, he could hold back no longer. He bought £5,000 of the stock from a friend who had plunged heavily on the second South Sea subscription and now wanted to realise on a little of what he had bought, though as he had told Lowther plaintively he would by no means have let the paper go except that he had to meet a note due at the end of the month and must raise some ready money.

Thereafter, Lowther had the pleasure of seeing his new-bought stock almost double its price over the next month. It was a mixed pleasure, though. Half the time he was cursing himself that he had bought such a paltry amount of it when he'd had the chance. He resolved that he would cease this miserly sort of approach. He had never been a coward in business before, but always keen and aggressive. He was not going to change now, when the chance to put his fortune on a permanently lofty footing was within his grasp. He sent a note to his banker in London instructing him to put almost all of the great sum of money deposited in his name into a purchase of the next subscription. A week after he had despatched that letter, a new-arriving packet in Lisbon brought news that the South Sea had fallen 150 points. The next one carried what seemed to Lowther the announcement of his personal doom: the stock was fallen 200 from its peak, and according to the Captain, who found himself surrounded by anxious British merchants as he stepped on to the quay, everybody at home was saying the bubble was exploded.

He had gone home after that. He had locked himself in his room. He had thought of his pistols and whether it were best to make a quick exit from this life that had turned so sour or stay and face the appalling consequences of his folly. He had thought of his daughter. He had promised his wife when she lay dying that their child's happiness would be always his first concern. How could he face Gabriella now? With her beauty and his money, he had believed that there might be almost no eminence she could not aspire to when she married at last. It had become almost an obsession with him, as if by making Gabby a countess or a marchioness he could have shown visible proof to his dead wife that he had not failed in his promise.

But now? Who would marry her now, lovely as she was? Not even a younger son would have her now. He was ruined. Ruined – he tasted the word in his mouth. It was like wormwood. He looked at the pistols again.

He didn't kill himself that day. He left the matter in abeyance. Perhaps he lacked courage for it. Perhaps he would do it tomorrow, or the next day. But he didn't. And on the day after that another packet boat brought a letter from his banker. It was a timid sort of letter from one who had never displayed such weakness to Lowther before. It started by begging his pardon, then went on to say that it was the first time he had ever declined the prompt performance of a client's clear instructions but that 'the feeling in Exchange Alley has turned so decidedly against the South Sea' that he must ask for further instructions before he did what Mr Lowther had asked him to. Meanwhile, his client's money still lay in his account and, the banker pointed out, continued to attract an excellent rate of interest.

Lowther took the good news that he was saved, and need not put a bullet through his temple after all, quite temperately. For a while, he thought the whole experience had been a godsend. It had cleared out a number of foolish schemes and notions that had been cluttering up his brain. In particular it gave him a better understanding of what he owed in love to his daughter. It horrified him that he had even contemplated leaving her alone in life, both parents dead, and the fortune that might have protected her a little lost as he had thought. And then too, he saw in the light of the redemption that had been offered him by his faithful, disobedient banker that he had been very wrong to think that a great marriage would somehow earn him forgiveness at last from his dead wife, forgiveness he stood much in need of. He had tried her gentle spirit greatly in the years of their marriage. On the very night of her death he had not been beside her; instead he was entertaining two whores at once down in the Baixa, in one of the brothels on the Rua Suja. (It was useless to tell himself, as he sometimes did, that he had been assured by his incompetent doctor that her time to die was still at least a week away.) He had come back to the Bairro Alto in the early morning, when it was still dark. Lights were burning in the house. His doctor had come down the stairs to meet him. His face was full of grief. 'Ah, Senhor Lowther . . .' was all he could say. Lowther ran up the stairs past him, taking the steps two at a time. But it was too late.

Well, he was not going to seek forgiveness any more by bartering their daughter's happiness for a title. She would, Phillip Lowther resolved – turning away from the horses, walking towards the trough in the middle of the courtyard so he could wash his hands – marry who she wanted. Within reason. And there would be love there, or he would not insist that she marry anyone. Ever. But he hoped she would, of course. And, he couldn't help thinking now, it would be agreeable to him if she should happen to find that love with at least a baronet.

Or an ordinary decent merchant, Lowther thought, impatient with himself. He splashed water on to his face. Saved. He had been saved last year. At least had lost only what he could afford to. He made no secret among the Factory of the fact that he had bought £5,000 of the South Sea and had as little hope of recovering it as anyone else struck by the disaster. That was only good business. He had long ago noted that a confession of disaster – as long as it was not too large and did not make one appear a fool for having suffered it – served to deflect other men's envy, which could be dangerous. Moreover, everyone also knew that he had prudently kept most of his fortune out of the hands of the stock-jobbers and for this he got great credit, not seeing it necessary to explain that his 'prudence' had been due to his banker, and not at all to himself.

When he heard of the crashes of other men, he sent up a silent prayer of thanks that he had just missed the rocks himself. Superstitiously he tended to avoid those men. He had avoided his old friend Felix Hanaway in particular. It was as if he did not want to besmirch his own good luck by associating with someone who the fates had not reprieved. And when he heard of Felix's brother's suicide – which is what it was, however a bribed coroner had dressed it up – it made him all the more anxious to keep away from that unlucky family.

Shot himself through the temple – the very same doom as he had contemplated for himself. No, he could not face Felix after that for many months, for all that they had known each other for nearly twenty-five years, since they both started out as junior clerks, fresh arrived in Lisbon. Long ago he had understood that Felix was not his equal, either intellectually or in business. Nevertheless, he had been very fond of him – and yet for months he never spoke to him. Only the other week he had seen his old friend staring at him across the room through the crowd at the assembly house. He had deliberately turned away from him.

But not long after that night he had come to see at last that this behaviour was not worthy of him. Besides, Felix had not, as he'd expected, folded up after the crash and gone home to England. Perhaps Lowther would have wished that had happened; his conscience would have tested him less if the Hanaways were hundreds of miles away, instead of just over the hills at Junquiera. But he'd stayed. Somehow he had kept himself going. Now there was a new Hanaway come to join him. The old firm was putting out new growth. It was admirable really. Lowther decided to make an end of this unfortunate separation. He had sent Felix an invitation to yesterday's 'tea'. He wasn't much surprised by Felix's refusal to appear, indeed he rather esteemed him for it, that he wouldn't come running when a finger was crooked at him, after so long a separation. But at least he had sent the nephew. Mr Lowther thought there was every possibility that another invitation would fetch the uncle in too. Perhaps to dinner one afternoon? Gabby's birthday was coming up. Seventeen. That was worth celebrating with a small, select dinner party. A mixture of young and old guests, he thought.

Presumably one of the other guests would be Adam Hanaway. He would ask Gabby about this, but he was pretty sure that she would agree to it. He turned away from the fountain, smiling as he thought this. He had noticed towards the end of the tea that his daughter and the young man were in some sort of deep conversation. It was just before Adam had gone home. She had been laughing happily when she turned away from him, and in the boy's eyes Mr Lowther had read a most languishing and devoted look as he had watched after his daughter.

Well, there's a thought, Lowther mused as he dried his hands on a towel one of the stable boys had brought to him. Adam Hanaway and his daughter. Yet the boy is such a beggar. The father broke, the uncle almost did. It was all very well to want Gabby to marry for love, but there were limits surely. And yet . . . he had liked the fellow, the little he knew him. He reminded him – not of Felix when he was young, but rather of himself. Intelligent, nervous, every emotion revealed on his face. And very handsome, of course!

Phillip Lowther chuckled to himself. He felt in his pocket and came up with a few bits of biscuit, which he threw to the dogs who had been following him all around the yard. One person who would not be invited to her birthday party, he thought, would be the young Tolliver. Nor the old one either, though he had no particular animus against Jacob, except that he rather disliked him. But the egregious Ralph needed to be discouraged and it might help in this if he was made to understand that the entire house of Tolliver risked Phillip Lowther's disfavour if he did not cease dancing attendance on his daughter. Lowther did not think that matters had progressed beyond the borders of decency yet, but he had seen what he had seen and was resolved to put a stop to things before they did. His daughter still had to make her match, and it would do her reputation and her chances no good at all for it to be widely known that the entirely married Ralph Tolliver had been making love to her, under her father's nose.

He frowned then, wanting to jog his memory. There was something about young Hanaway, not at all to his credit, and it was Ralph Tolliver who had told him about it yesterday, after the tea had ended. Something peculiar . . .

Yes! Adam had been talking smut to his daughter. Was that to be credited? Or was Ralph slandering someone he disliked and who he saw had found favour with Mr Lowther's daughter? He would have to ask Gabriella about this when he saw her. If it was true it was all very odd. Was this a method of courting, hitherto unknown to him? If so, he didn't think his daughter would be much impressed by it. Having secretly overheard one or two of her arguments with her girlfriends, he knew she had possession of a pretty ripe vocabulary of curses and insults herself. So it was unlikely that Adam Hanaway could do much to amaze her by his foul utterances (always supposing that Tolliver had been speaking the truth). Still, it was not a gentlemanly thing for him to be doing, and it ought to stop.

With a sigh, Phillip Lowther turned back towards the house. The sun was up; it was going to be a hotter day than he had first thought when he'd got out of bed. He would have liked to have spent it restfully. Perhaps have Excalibur saddled up and go riding over the Santa Catarina hills. Gabby could come with him, if she liked. She could ride the grey, which needed the exercise. For one day he would give her dispensation from her lessons, and he might take the opportunity as they rode to investigate discreetly what she thought about this young Hanaway.

For a moment it was as if this was really what was going to happen. But then he dismissed the fantasy. No riding in the hills for him. He had to go down to the Alfândega this morning and join a deputation of his colleagues which, by prior arrangement, would call upon the exalted fellow in charge of the customs house, the *ouvidor da alfândega*, in fact, and remind the son-of-a-bitch that England's privileges in Lisbon were not a result of the whims of whichever Portuguese official or politician was currently in the saddle, but belonged to the Factory as of right and by a treaty made between Cromwell's government and the Portuguese crown back in 1654. And in sum, the endless difficulties that were being made for the Factory at this time in the courts and by the officials of every level in the Alfândega must stop immediately or . . . or . . .

Or what? The bastards in Whitehall would do nothing much but hum and haw and after six months there would come a message from the Secretary of State to Burnett, the Consul here, to say it was all very regrettable, and the Minister was most distressed to hear of the merchants' grievances, but on the other hand maintenance of friendly relations with the Crown of Portugal was of paramount . . . etcetera, etcetera, ad nauseam.

For just a moment, Mr Lowther entertained a pleasing daydream in which Oliver Cromwell, old Copper-nose himself, still held power in London. Not that he was against the monarchy: no man who coveted a title as much as he did could be that. But to think what the old monster would have done to these Portuguese rascals if he knew with what contempt they observed the treaty he had rammed down their throats sixty-six years ago . . . Ah, that was a thought to cheer a man, to put stiffening in the spine of any English factor worth his –

At that point Mr Lowther found that his daydream was being broken into. There were shouts – screams more like, coming from the house. His first thought was that fire had broken out inside. Oh, Gabby, he thought, my darling. He ran towards the open kitchen door. Made his way through to the staircase in the hall. Gabriella's maid was standing at the foot of it, bawling her head off. He took her by the shoulders and shook her. He couldn't smell smoke in the air, nothing appeared out of place. Except this girl screaming.

'What is it? What is it?'

She said the words he dreaded to hear. Dona Gabriella. She was – what was it? She was in trouble. In pain. '*Tem uma dor de cabeça!*' He ran up the stairs. He remembered doing just this, and with the same dread clutching at his heart the morning he had come home to find his wife had died. He ran along the landing. Flung open the door of her room, not pausing to knock on it. The room was half in darkness. The maid had only finished opening one of the shutters. Gabriella was sitting up in bed. Her hands were covering her face. He went to sit beside her. Tried to prise her hands away. She wouldn't let him.

'Oh, Papa,' he heard her murmur behind her fingers, 'it hurts so much. I'm on fire . . .'

Adam

1

T he afterglow of that happy afternoon I had spent at the
Lowthers' house was still with me when I reached the
Alfândega on the Monday morning. I entered on my work with
almost feverish enthusiasm, and everything seemed so clear and
easy for me now. Where I used to stand for many minutes, even
hours, puzzling over my accounts, now the complicated sums
seemed to solve themselves in a trice. I finished what Senhor
Gomes had asked me to do for the day even before the hour of
sesta arrived, and went to him to ask for more work. He gave it to
me, and thereafter I caught him looking at me from time to time.
Poor fool: I thought they were looks of admiration, and felt myself
very puffed up by what I saw as his silent praise.

Later that afternoon, my uncle finally made an appearance in
the Alfândega. I was standing near Pedrito with some lading bills
in my hand. It must have appeared as if I was carefully comparing the figures on them with those my snowball friend was
counting out loud. But my spate of furious energy had slackened
somewhat in the past half-hour – the sleepless night had caught
up with me at last – and I was actually engaged in remembering
the way Miss Lowther's precious little mouth would sometimes
turn down at the corners just before she laughed. My uncle
beckoned me to walk with him, and I gladly abandoned the
lading bills. Felix took me a little way off and stopped there and
turned to me. He seemed to be having some difficulty coming to
what he wanted to say, so to help him out I began the conversation by asking him how he had enjoyed his visit to the
vineyards over the weekend, not forgetting to enquire, with

appropriately serious mien, whether he thought there was any business to be done with their owners.

Of course both of us knew that this trip had been undertaken mainly to give colour to his explanation for his non-attendance at an old friend's levee. Nevertheless, he gave me a conscientious account of his tour, and finished by saying he thought we could do business with one of these vineyards, at least to the extent of taking twenty or thirty pipes from them. As he spoke I nodded and shook my head at moments I hoped were appropriate and generally tried to look much more interested than I felt. Thoughts of Gabriella would keep breaking in, though, and it was hard indeed to concentrate on pipes of wine. I remembered she had offered me a glass of cool Rhenish at one point in our discourse. How beautiful, how merciful, and almost religious that sweet proposal seemed to me now.

I became aware that my uncle had finished speaking, and concentrated upon him again. I thought he seemed to be looking at me with a clear show of approbation. I had half an idea that he might have spoken to Gomes before coming to me, and that the senior clerk had told him how exceptionally hard I had been working today. But this, it turned out, was not at all the source of that benevolent smile that was on his lips.

'Well, Adam, did you enjoy yourself at Mr Lowther's yesterday?'

'I did, Sir.'

I gave him then as full an account as I could of the occasion, somewhat hampered by the fact that I was keen to keep the most important part of it hidden from him. My connection with Gabriella was still so new, its exact nature still too uncertain to be exposed yet to the public view, and I did not think I could give an account of my time in her presence without betraying the ardour I felt for her. So I concentrated mostly on the period I had spent in Mr Lowther's drawing room, and hardly even touched on the hour and more I passed with his daughter on either side of it.

When I finished my account, he told me he thought I had done well for the family by showing myself to advantage before the Factory, especially before Mr Lowther.

'I also spoke with Miss Lowther,' I could not help myself saying then, mostly I think for the pleasure of saying her name.

'Ah, little Gabby!' said my uncle sentimentally. 'She is a dear little thing, is she not?'

I agreed that she was. I tried to keep the fervour from my voice when I said that, but probably with indifferent success for my uncle threw me quite a thoughtful glance. I imagine it had occurred to him suddenly that Mr Lowther's daughter had perhaps grown beyond the stage where she could be exactly described as a 'dear little thing'.

'You must be careful, Adam,' he said. 'Fathers and their daughters – well, I know myself how precious they are to a man. And Phil Lowther particularly dotes on his child – ever since his wife died.'

'I assure you, Uncle –'

'I know, I know. I only say – be careful. Treat her just as you would the Virgin Mary and you cannot go wrong with Phil.'

I stared at this, to find Felix chuckling at his little joke. And that was all he wished to say to me that day. My hard work, not just today but for many weeks previous, appeared to have made no impact on him. All of that seemed to count for nothing compared to the spectacle of me moving in circles that he esteemed, in which it would be well for the family to have an entrée, and from which he had become estranged during the past year of financial turmoil.

For the next few days I waited for the invitation from the Lowthers to arrive at my lodgings or else at Uncle Felix's offices. I scarcely doubted that it would appear. As my uncle had confirmed, Mr Lowther doted on his daughter, a fact that convinced me that he was bound to accede to her modest request that I should join their party on Sunday. Besides, he liked me of his own accord, he had made it clear he did, or otherwise why would he have told me I was like a member of his family?

On the Tuesday I laid out much of my small store of money on the purchase of a pair of silver buckles at a most reputable shop in the Rua da Prata where this particular trade congregated. I thought happily of the show I would make with them on Sunday. My confidence that the invitation would be forthcoming was so high that I felt perfectly comfortable engaging in such an extravagant purchase. Now I think about it, though, it may be that it was not so much a sign of confidence as a rather desperate and expensive gesture on my part to will into life what I wanted so much to happen. But this was for later reflection. As I say, insofar as I was aware of it at the time, much of that week passed without apprehension on my part.

During it, I fell into a pleasing habit of calling in at the Hutchinsons' after work. Mr Hutchinson was always at home, and usually Maria Beatriz too. I would ask how they did and they would invite me to take a glass of something. For about thirty minutes or an hour we would entertain ourselves in conversation – at least Mr Hutchinson and I would, sitting comfortably in the armchairs on either side of the still-barren grate, making each other merry, while Maria Beatriz sat by the window, sewing and darning, or looking through her most recent drawings, and listening to us with a half-smile on her lips.

Once in a while, usually when her father had grown too exaggerated in telling his stories, she would put in a gently chiding word or two to rein him in. Or she would ask me a question about my home and my family. My mother, my sisters would live and flourish before me for a little while as I spoke of them. It was good to remember them thus, and really high time that I did, for in the rush of my Lisbon life I had certainly neglected of late to think of my nearest surviving relations as much as I ought.

On the Wednesday of that week when I was waiting for the invitation to arrive, I brought my own bottle of wine downstairs with me, and I think the Hutchinsons were pretty pleased to see it, for even the small amount of their supplies that I had drunk so far had somewhat taxed their resources. That evening I spent nearly two hours with them, and at one point we called up the little African girl and sent her out to buy a few specimens of a certain pastry, a local delicacy that all three of us had discovered was our particular passion. It was a confection of spun sugar and chocolate that went under the name of 'nun's tresses' (though Mr Hutchinson, when Maria Beatriz had left the room temporarily, intimated to me, with the accompaniment of various winks and snickers, that it was more usually called after another growth of hair that was invariably kept hidden from men's view by nuns, and indeed, except on intimate occasions, by all other sorts of ladies).

As to what we talked about on those evenings, I really cannot remember in any detail. Through Wednesday it was all casual, amicable, unimportant stuff. The Thursday evening was somewhat different, however. Shown into the living room as usual by a smiling Maria Beatriz, I found lounging in my usual chair a gentleman who, after he had politely risen to acknowledge me, discovered himself to be a small, rather fierce-looking fellow with elaborately curled moustachios who I immediately recognised as the person Maria Beatriz had once spoken of as a dear friend to her family, and had introduced me to him in my room as such – in fact the *fidalgo* Dom Jeronymo da Silva.

It appeared that, like me, he had come calling on the Hutchinsons in a casual fashion and had been prevailed on by them to stay for a meal. Of course I immediately proposed that I should take myself off and leave my friends to the uninterrupted enjoyment of their guest – but they would have none of it and Dom Jeronymo too, once it had been explained to him why I was making such a fuss about sitting down at the fire with the rest of them, added his prayers that I should stay. And though I must believe that it mattered much less to him than to the others that I should – indeed I doubted whether he cared at all – in the Portuguese style his entreaties were even more ardent and certainly couched in much more flowery language than theirs.

In the end I did what I had wanted to all along and stayed, and the four of us proceeded to make up a very congenial party, starting around the fire – lit for the first time since I'd begun visiting the Hutchinsons – then at the dining table where with the considerable assistance of a ham bone that Dom Jeronymo had considerately brought with him, Maria Beatriz was able to serve a very adequate sort of ragout with rice. Once again I had thought to bring wine with me, and with that and with what the Hutchinsons could offer we found ourselves drinking pretty deep before the evening was half over.

Which must have been why I was so imprudent as to venture at one point on matters that would certainly have been better left alone. For Mr Hutchinson – who appeared to discover an ever greater admiration for the *fidalgo* the longer the evening lasted and the more we drank – had enunciated for my benefit the many honours and titles that Dom Jeronymo had won during his illustrious existence: high officer of the military Order of Christ, *capitão* of the confraternity of Almas dos Martires, distinguished graduate of Coimbra University ('which, as you know, Adam, is elevated above all other seats of learning in Europe, certainly above your own poor Oxford') . . . the list went on and on, and in time, particularly when Mr Hutchinson forgot he had already reeled it off and started on it again, I grew somewhat restive at having to hear it. My mood was not much improved by the fact that Dom Jeronymo listened to both recitations of his dignities with visible pride and pleasure and indeed seemed to want to exult in them in an open, vainglorious fashion, which I was sure that any Englishman of like elevation would have found thoroughly distasteful.

The honour that Dom Jeronymo seemed to be most proud of was his position as a *familiar* of the Inquisition. He referred to it several times, and when Mr Hutchinson forgot to include it in his second report he reminded him of it pretty sharply. My experiences had of course made me into a very decided opponent of certain practices of this infamous and bloody institution. I began to make sharp comments about these activities and to wonder aloud what sort of religion was being served by the excesses of the so-called 'Holy Office'. Dom Jeronymo began to look a little puzzled, and then more than a little annoyed, but still as if he was trusting it was because of my inadequate command of his language that I was, without knowing it, uttering pernicious absurdities.

Had I bothered to look around me I am sure I would have found that the Hutchinsons – certainly *one* of them – would have been casting at me glances of concern and warning. But I did not bother; I was staring steadily at Dom Jeronymo and enjoying my sport at the expense of this *familiar*, whose other important honours also included, I reminded myself, though unmentioned tonight by Mr Hutchinson, his position as protector of a violent street gang, one of whose bravos had attacked in the Travessa do Tronco the old man at whose table we sat.

I was just embarking on a very pretty piece of sarcasm in which I was asking Dom Jeronymo ('as a distinguished servant of the Holy Office') if he would do me the favour to explain how the burning of fellow-creatures at the stake in the midst of a civilised European capital differed in any material respect from the human sacrifices that were demanded and performed by priests who served the primitive and hideous religions of the jungles of Africa and America – when I felt a most tremendous kick upon the lower part of my leg. I looked up, speechless with agony and surprise. Mr Hutchinson appeared to be looking at me with somewhat fuddled incomprehension. I didn't think he was sufficiently in possession of himself to have been the author of the assault on me. Dom Jeronymo at the other end of the table was simply too far away to have done it. It must have been Maria Beatriz who was the culprit, even though she was presently engaged in carefully spooning ham stew into her mouth, her eyes lowered to her task.

At any rate her action had the effect desired by her. I was almost too tormented by pain to say anything more to the *fidalgo*, however innocuous. Besides, when the agony had subsided just a little, I was able to consider the warning she wanted to convey, and I did begin to see that I had been speaking unwisely, and certainly impertinently, to an old friend of her family who was tonight an honoured guest in her home.

And so I sat in silence, even when Dom Jeronymo offered his opinion that 'like so many English heretics' I did not truly understand the nature of the *autos-da-fé* that I had seemed to be hinting at. He proceeded, while I fumed inwardly but wordlessly, to favour me with his own account of those blessed 'Acts of the Faith', which were not, he insisted, about killing people, but instead were celebrations of the return of so many lost souls to the embrace of the One True Church. Not lawless orgies of murder, 'as Senhor Hanaway seems to think', but solemn and legal procedures, first called into life by Pope Gregory IX five hundred years ago, and conducted ever since under the light and grace of Heaven. During them, only 'a trifling handful' of those who showed themselves absolutely unshakable in their pact with the Devil might be put at last into the fires, and never, he emphasised, by the holy fathers, who, at that point, forced by the heretics' inflexibility to give up all hopes of saving them from Hell, turned them over to the civil authorities to do the unhappy but necessary work of ridding the world of such contagion.

The *fidalgo* took himself off not long after the meal was concluded. I noted – and did not really blame him for it – that his farewell to me was markedly less affable than his greeting had been. When Maria Beatriz came back into the living room from seeing him out, I expected we would have some sort of discussion in which both my rash speaking and her grave assault upon my leg would be considered and apologised for. But at the sight of her it was clear to me that she was in no mood to apologise. Her eyes were flashing, her chin was up.

'Are you mad, Adam?' she cried, sounding as if she quite despaired of me. 'Are you truly insane? Were you not told what Dom Jeronymo is?'

I defied her blazing eyes. It was on my tongue to ask her what she meant by that. Did she mean he was a nobleman? Loyal subject of King João? Brigand? Bully? Luckily I said none of this.

'You were told he is a *familiar* of the Inquisition.'

I shrugged to show both that of course I knew it – it had been impossible not to have known it tonight – and that it didn't matter a damn to me.

'It is his duty to discover those who are guilty of heresy. And to inform the authorities of those who he discovers. You saw what happens to such people. Have you learned nothing at all about this country?'

I gazed at her blankly.

'But I am an Englishman,' was all I could think of saying.

Maria Beatriz produced then a most expressive sound from the back of her throat. It said everything she might have wished to say about my idiocy, my imprudence, folly, ignorance, much else. After that she sank down on the chair the *fidalgo* had used during an earlier, happier phase in the evening. She closed her eyes, shook her head, breathed deeply.

Mr Hutchinson and I exchanged glances. We sat down on either side of her. I rubbed my leg, which still was shooting darts of pain up to my knee. Mr Hutchinson elected to play the peace-maker.

'Come now, daughter. Adam has nothing to fear from the likes of Dom Jeronymo. I know these fellows,' he trumpeted. 'All brag and bluster. It just needed somebody to give him a sharp rap on the mazzard and he would have climbed down very fast, I assure you.'

Maria Beatriz instantly repudiated this assertion and accompanied her response with quite a jeering laugh, unexpected from one who always showed her father at least the semblance of daughterly respect. I had to admit – though only to myself – that I agreed with her, at least to the point that I thought it was unprovable what the *fidalgo* would have done if he had been rapped on this mysterious 'mazzard' or any other part of him, especially since neither Mr Hutchinson nor I was seriously up to that job.

After drinking a pretty full glass of wine with us, however, Maria Beatriz retreated a little from her stance. She admitted, to the accompaniment of surprisingly girlish giggles, that Dom Jeronymo was usually more dreadful in his boasts and threats than in his performance. She also acknowledged under her father's pressure that the position of *familiar* of the Inquisition – with which she had so alarmed me – though prestigious, was really more of an honorary title than an actual occupation. At least among those *fidalgos* whose notion of their own importance was as high as Dom Jeronymo's, the exercise of their office rarely amounted to more than an occasional visit to a distracted old lady who had set up as a cunning woman, or some idle fellow whose neighbours had denounced him for being slothful in his church attendance, and warning them to mend their ways.

'Then I was in no danger at all!' I cried out, a little indignant now, as if I had been imposed upon.

Maria Beatriz frowned and shook her head, and even Mr Hutchinson looked doubtful.

'With this nation,' she explained, 'particularly with those of high birth, one can never be absolutely certain. They are so mild and kind for so long and then suddenly, if they feel their honour has been touched, or their Faith, they can turn into the cruellest people on earth.'

I stayed on at the Hutchinsons throughout the rest of the evening, and our intercourse was by no means confined to such gloomy topics as *familiares* and *autos-da-fé*. I remember fragments of our talk – Mr Hutchinson's reminiscences of his young days in London, some friends of Maria Beatriz that she thought I would like to meet, the view of the city from the convent of São Pedro de Alcântara, which they both positively recommended to me – but nothing remarkable.

At some time Maria Beatriz went off to her bed. I talked a little longer with Mr Hutchinson, intending at any moment to take myself and my still sore lower leg upstairs to my own room. I had the grace to apologise at last for having so teazed his other guest tonight. He said I was not to mind it, he was only sorry that I had seemed to show such scorn towards the Faith that both he and Dom Jeronymo were proud to serve.

I must have fallen asleep in my chair soon after that for I never saw Mr Hutchinson leave the room to go to his bed. When next I was conscious, I was alone and the thin light of dawn was falling through the window. Maria Beatriz moved into my vision. She looked down at me. Her face seemed solemn and suddenly old, and I remember thinking rather sadly that it was not so surprising she should seem this way, for indeed she *was* old, probably fifty at least, though somehow I rarely thought of it when I was with her, for her manner, her form, her face: none of them spoke of age to me. Only now when she was utterly still, watching me.

And then she saw me looking up at her and she broke into a smile and the years and many cares seemed to fall away from her in a moment.

I suppose I have spoken at such length about that evening at the Hutchinsons' because it was – at least the end of it was – the last truly contented time I was to know for many a week. It certainly provided a contrast to what was to follow. The simplest of these calamities to tell is that the longed-for, the golden invitation never arrived. On Sunday morning I was so certain that its non-appearance was a result of some mistake – a feckless servant sent to deliver it and losing it along his way was my most likely guess – that I was prepared to go up to the Bairro Alto, to sacred Os Dois Pinheiros, and explain what had happened.

'Of course they meant to invite me,' I argued with Bento, who I had requested to help me dress for the occasion. 'They will discover not the least surprise when I appear. As far as they know, I received the invitation the day it was sent. The servant was probably too scared to reveal to them that he had lost it.'

Bento dissuaded me from this course for a time, but only after a very long discussion, which often became heated. He watched me for an hour or two thereafter, but at last his vigilance lapsed and I made my escape. I flew like a bird up the towering slopes to the Bairro Alto – truly I do not remember my feet ever touching the earth as I climbed. Then I was in the Rua Formosa, my own Via Sacra. I hurried to Gabriella's front door. Beat upon it. A servant of some sort of elevated quality, Portuguese, opened it after a long delay. I told him I was come to see his master. I also told him, when that news did not appear to impress him much, that I was here by invitation. I added as he continued to stare at me stolidly, what I should have said in the first place, that I was 'Mr Hanaway'. Mr Adam Hanaway. A friend to Mr Lowther.

He said that nobody was at home. I turned to look where in the driveway were standing several carriages. From beyond the open door I heard the tinkling of a harpsichord. Gabriella was at her lessons, I was sure of it. With Miss Graveney. And Madame Corréade instructed her in French and Senhor José in drawing. Oh, all of this was burned into my brain then, you may be sure, so I can remember it now, almost sixty years later.

I pointed out to this doorkeeper, or major-domo, whatever he was, that what he had said was manifestly impossible. Somebody was clearly at home – unless the servants had become mutinous and were using the house to their own advantage in their master's absence. In which case, I invented wildly, he ought to open the door to me so that I could bang a few heads – I waved my fist in the air at this point to show what I would do – and restore order in the name of my good friend Mr Lowther.

The fellow appeared to consider my demonstration of what I intended against the servants as some sort of physical threat to him, for he gave a cry of alarm, which brought two other servants quickly to his side. Both of them were pretty robust-looking fellows, certainly for Portuguese. I looked them over. In the house whoever had been playing the harpsichord had stopped. It was as if they – *she* – were listening to the altercation at the front door. Perhaps dear Miss Lowther was at this moment waiting to see if I would be bold enough to hurl myself at these louts and burst through to where she was being held incommunicado.

On the other hand, she might not be there at all. Insofar as I retained a few shreds of sanity at this point, I really knew I could not plunge into a degrading fight with a set of servants in order to find out. Had I thought to bring my sword with me, I might have imposed myself on them with a flick of my wrist. But this would be an affair of fists and boots and sticks, in which I might well not emerge the victor. If there was anything less calculated to enhance my reputation in the eyes of Mr Lowther and his daughter than a successful affray upon their doorstep, it would be one where I was soundly beaten by their churls and ejected from the premises.

I uttered several loud grunts and 'pshaws', indicative I hoped of my extreme displeasure at their behaviour and of the condign punishment that no doubt waited for them when Mr Lowther heard how they had treated me. They received these ejaculations with marked indifference, and then their leader closed the door, virtually in my face. I thought of pounding on it once again but even if it was opened I was certain I would get no better treatment than I had the first time. Through the shut door I heard, very faintly, the notes of the harpsichord once again. Oh Gabriella, I moaned, heartbroken – though not by half as much as I would grow over the next few days. I retreated to the Rua Formosa. I walked under the two pine trees and waited out there the rest of the day and into the night. Lights came on in the house windows. I saw dim shapes pass across them. And then the curtains were drawn, and there was nothing at all, except for the trees and for a chill wind that got up about three hours after nightfall. It was the first true harbinger of the Lisbon autumn, but I did not think of that. Only that it corresponded with the coldness I felt in my stomach, my heart, everywhere. Somehow I knew, even in these first few hours, that my dream was over. It was dead.

It may be wondered why I did not, on Monday morning, cleave to my wretched room in my sorrow. But I did go that unhappy morn to the Alfândega, indeed rather earlier than was my habit of late. I think some sort of frayed defiance was at work here. One way of dealing with my hurt was to pretend that it did not exist, that Gabriella meant only a little to me after all, and so her loss troubled me correspondingly little.

This experiment had pretty much collapsed by the time I found myself at my old station on the Alfândega floor. The pain was back, it was overwhelming. However, there was work to be done. Senhor Gomes told me what it was; there were snowballs and others waiting for me to take the lead. But I could do nothing. I crept into a sort of cave formed by several thick rolls of tobacco. It was dark in there, and I curled up at the far end of the space. It was in this posture that my Uncle Felix found me, about a half-hour later.

He was furious with me. I supposed it was because of the condition he had found me in, and because of what it said of my lack of attention to the work. Without much interest in whether he believed me or not, I attempted to defend myself. I said I was suffering from a deep pain in my gut – which was true – and had lain down in an attempt to recover from it. The alternative, I explained, was to leave the Alfândega immediately, and retire to my lodgings, in which case the firm would certainly be deprived of my assistance for the whole day. Whereas by staying on, there was at least a chance – should I recover – that I could attend to my duties in the time remaining.

Felix said he didn't give a damn about all that. He was not here to talk about that. He was obviously so wound up that even in my misery over Gabriella I wondered what it was that had brought him to this pitch. It was only a brief curiosity. In a moment, the waves of sorrow for my lost love were breaking again over my suffering head.

'I received a letter from Mr Lowther this morning,' Felix announced – or rather gritted out. 'It was such a letter as I would have hoped never to have received from one who was once my friend and whose opinion I still value. He asks me to tell you that you are never to attempt to make contact with either himself or his daughter again. In view of your disgraceful conduct last Sunday week at his house.'

No doubt Felix would have expected me – once I'd recovered from the shock his announcement had evidently caused me – to demand a further explanation from him, or to give him explanations for the offence I must know I had caused. But I had no time to spare on such trifles. I waited for a few seconds for his words to entirely sink in, and for me to comprehend that he had actually said them. And then I turned on my heel and headed for the nearest exit. I heard my uncle call after me, 'Adam!' It only served to urge me on. I broke into a run. Other merchants were shouting at me in anger as I stepped over and often enough upon their wares. I didn't pay any of them the least attention.

The path up to the plateau where both the Factory assembly rooms and Gabriella's house were situated was now so familiar to me that it seemed as if I trod it in a dream. Yet as in some dreams everything had become the appalling obverse of real life. The happy, optimistic mood in which I had climbed this hill on previous occasions had turned into dread. Indeed, where once I had hoped for great things, now I was only furiously concerned to drive away whatever lies and misrepresentation had soured my excellent relations with the Lowthers. They would not, I told myself, let me be lost by them without even giving me the chance to explain – whatever it was. Gabriella would insist upon it. She would threaten terrible things if Mr Lowther would not hear me. Even to kill herself . . .

At which point, what remained of my common sense took over. Gabriella would do no such thing. Even in the transports of threatened love, I knew that at bottom she was a rich, well-brought-up girl who no doubt thoroughly enjoyed the luxurious surroundings that had cosseted her all her life. She would do nothing to imperil that state, she would certainly not balk at anything her father seriously required of her, not on my account whose company she had shared for what amounted to barely an hour altogether.

In other words I had to speak to Mr Lowther direct, and clear up this muddle. Somehow I suspected the jealous Ralph Tolliver was at the bottom of it. In any case, his misrepresentations – if that was what had caused this muddle – could be easily refuted. My conscience was clear. I had behaved with utmost propriety at the tea. And even if the report of those unorthodox few minutes in the little toy house when I had divested myself of my coat and wig had reached Mr Lowther, surely that could not have offended him so much as to cause him to ban me for ever from his and Gabriella's presence, particularly when it was she who had persuaded me to take them off. And though I excused her from being obliged to commit self-murder on my account, I did rely on her sense of honour that she would tell him this.

Still feeling as if I was in a recurring dream, I presented myself at the Lowthers' front door. I knocked, the door opened. Just as happened yesterday, a servant, though not the same one, stood there barring my entrance. This was a rather formidable, intelligent-looking man who, when I demanded to know who I was speaking to, said that he acted as Mr Lowther's steward and secretary. In near-perfect English, he asked me what I wanted. I gave him my name and said that I desired to speak to his employer. He told me that the family was away, that they had gone into the country and would not return for many weeks. He declined to give me the whereabouts of this country retreat, and I was about to use his refusal to argue that he was making the whole thing up. But there was something in the atmosphere of the house, as I read it, craning to see above his head, that said to me he was not lying. Unlike yesterday, it was the air of an empty house I was seeing, hearing, breathing.

I told him then that I would like at least to send a letter to Mr Lowther. I would write it now if he could give me the pen and paper with which to do it. Would he agree to put it before Mr Lowther when he could? He said that he had received specific orders that no communications should be received from Mr Adam Hanaway. He went on to say that he had been further commanded to inform Mr Hanaway that, if he persisted in coming to the house, he would be reported to both the British Consul-General and the *desembargador do paço* (Lisbon's chief magistrate, in fact) as being an unruly and contumacious Briton who well deserved expulsion from the peaceful realm of King João V.

The shock that I felt, and certainly would have shown as I listened to this pronouncement, must have been evident to this steward as he watched me. His manner became a little less harsh, his gaze rather more lenient as he studied me. I told him, when I could find my tongue again, that I did not understand this, that I had done nothing to deserve it. He replied that he had now said all he'd been instructed to.

'What have I done?' I cried out in despair, as he stepped back into the house and the door started to close.

He looked out at me through the little gap that remained, seemed to consider his position for a moment, then said, 'It is all in the letter Mr Lowther sent to your uncle. I wrote it myself at his dictation.'

'Then tell me what you wrote.'

But it was no good. The door was shut. I stepped back a few paces. Looked the house over, like some old-time knight besieging a castle who searches its battlements for its weakest points. But as this was modern times and not the twelfth century, my search led to nothing. In any case, what was the point of capturing a castle in which all that had been of value to me was gone from it? Now my uncle – that was a quarry worth pursuing. He had all the details of my supposed iniquity in that letter – how I cursed myself now for running out of the Alfândega before he'd had a chance to tell me what they were. Never mind. I would get to the truth now. And once I had dispelled the cloud of malice and lies – for I *knew* that I was innocent – then he at least would be able to get word to Mr Lowther. And this whole bizarre and hateful episode would be in the past.

I had to find my uncle. The day was quite advanced. I guessed by now he would have quitted the Alfândega certainly, and probably left his office in town too. He would be now, or very soon, in his carriage, on the road to his *quinta*. Thither, I decided, I would go too. This meant that for once I would not be returning the way I had come by descending from the plateau down to the

Baixa. I turned instead in the other direction and began to cross the hills of Santa Catarina, heading west and south, aiming to join the highway along the river as it wended its way to Junquiera.

Soon I had left the streets of the Bairro Alto behind me. There were only occasional houses now, interspersed with fields and groves of olive trees, sheep on distant hillsides. And then there were no houses at all. The path I was on was no longer paved. I threw up clouds of dust as I marched along it. I met very few other travellers along the way. Really, it was like being out in a wilderness almost. At one point I thought I heard the scuffling of a large animal in the woods near by, and I imagined wild boar, even wolves. To my left I could see still the great white and rosy city gleaming beneath me. It would be, I thought, a cruel fate to be brought down by a pack of wolves when still in sight of that.

Descending now all the while, sometimes almost at a run, I reached the highway at last. Again I had to put behind me memories of the light-hearted spirit in which I'd last made such a journey. I was all grim determination now. I must have been. Not even the threat – however slim – of attacking wolves had deterred me from my course. My love, my anger had driven every trace of Runaway out of me. I had no uneasy thoughts about my forthcoming encounter with my uncle either; I was longing for it. Somebody would pay for the agonies I had been put through. It might as well start with Felix. Mr Lowther would have to suffer too. And the great prize at the end of my quest would be that lying toad, Ralph Tolliver, who *must* be at the bottom of this. I was hungry to get even with him. I scurried along the road, still heading west, never bothering to look away from my goal, not even at the vast shimmering river at my left side, and all the ships upon it.

2

My uncle was not at home. So said the servant – yet another damned servant – who opened the door of the *quinta* to me. He could not say where he was, or when he would arrive, or whether he ever would tonight. I asked then if my aunt was in the house.

He said she was. I said that I would come in then and speak to her. He said that she was indisposed and that he had firm orders to admit no one. I asked him if he knew who I was. He said he did. He remembered me perfectly. He added that he had particular orders not to admit Mr Adam Hanaway. And he closed the door upon me.

I need not describe the absolute pain and confusion this treatment plunged me into. To be sent away from the door of a man who I had barely known was one thing. To be refused at the house of one's own relatives something hideously other. I wandered about outside my uncle's gate, truly in a daze. I was finally rescued from this state by the most commonplace of emergencies. So wound up had I been by the twin keys of love and fear that in all the time since I'd left the Alfândega I had forgotten to empty my bladder. This fact was suddenly borne upon me in the most pressing fashion. I had half a notion of using the occasion to scornfully direct the stream at the house, at least at the gate of my perfidious relations. They deserved it and I felt angry enough to do it. But the laws of habit and convention held me in their thrall, no matter how angry I was. I stepped behind the single great elm tree that stood outside the property and there, sheltered from the gaze of the house, unbuttoned my breeches and exposed myself.

I was halfway through a most gratifying piss when I heard a female voice, very close and getting closer, calling my name. I was in such haste to stuff away my member that I was doing it before I was able to entirely suppress my stream, and consequently got my hands and the front of my breeches well wetted. I was still buttoning up the latter when my cousin Nancy came round the trunk of the tree. She gazed at my confusion. Luckily the evening was coming on fast, as it does in that country, and my breeches were a dull colour anyway so probably she could not see the most embarrassing clues to my difficulty.

'What are you doing, Adam?' she said.

I brushed aside the question with an angry gesture and used the same hand to finish buttoning myself up. 'What is it, Nan?' I said. I did not disguise the anger that was washing about inside me. She might be only a child but even so my fury at her parents' behaviour was strong enough to include her too. Also, I resented the fact that my bladder was still only half emptied. I wished she would go away so I could finish the task.

'What have you done, Adam?'

What was I doing? What had I done? I was about to tell the provoking child to go back inside the *quinta* and stop bothering me with these foolish questions, when she shook her head and said, 'My mother is in such a passion. It is something to do with you and Gabby Lowther. Yet they won't tell me what it is. And my sister don't know either.'

I was silent, dumb; I could not believe what a web I was trapped inside. I suppose Nancy took my silence to mean that I was having difficulty getting out the terrible story of my transgression, whatever it was. She stepped forward and tried to take my hand. Mindful of the state it was in, I did not let her. Her hand fell upon my sleeve instead.

'You can tell me, Adam,' she sighed. Her eyes were large and sincere as she gazed up at me. I searched for a hint of glee in them too – which would have been natural, for other people's disasters are usually entertaining, even a cousin's – but did not find it. 'Did you violate poor Gabby?'

'No!' I was almost as shocked that little Nancy should know such a word as I was at her accusation. 'Damn it, I have done nothing!'

I had shouted this so loud that Nancy glanced towards the house, fearful that I had been overheard. When she returned her gaze to me, it had changed its flavour. Now she looked puzzled and, I was certain now, a little disappointed.

'You can't have done *nothing*,' she said. 'Otherwise my mother wouldn't be crying all the time. And this morning my father said you were beneath contempt and that me and Betty must never speak to you again. And all because of something that happened at Gabby's father's house, he said that much to us.'

'Oh, Nan,' I said. 'It's so unfair. That my own aunt should not receive me!'

'I know. It's wicked. I hate her!'

I started walking up and down in my passion. Nancy kept up

with me. I described to her as best I remembered – which was pretty well – everything that had transpired during my visit to the Lowthers' house. Nancy listened carefully, trying with me to hit upon the moment when, without my knowing it, I had caused this mortal offence for which apparently I must now be banned from the presence of all decent, right-thinking people.

At one point, when I was telling her how Gabriella had led me to the little dolls' house, she said, 'She took you to that house? She used to always be taking boys into that house, but I thought she had grown beyond that.'

But, even though she spoke of this little habit of Gabriella's with some scorn, she acknowledged that this was not anything that should have caused the universal revulsion I was now struggling against.

'I suppose *they* could have thought that her reputation was compromised by your being in the house alone with her. But since that had happened so often with other boys I don't see what reputation she has left to compromise.'

This, I thought, was rather severe, and at any other time I would have reproved Nancy for her speech, but I was so upset by this point that my heart was even beginning to harden a little against my beloved. Nancy listened to my tale of what had gone on inside the house. Though she looked a little odd at my description of how I had removed my wig and coat for a time, she conceded that not even this could have made my name stink so much as it did now.

'What else, Adam?'

I shrugged. 'Nothing. Miss Mills and Ralph Tolliver came into the house then. We all talked some nonsense . . .' I stopped. Thought for a moment. 'Tolliver and I had a bit of an argument, I remember.'

'What about?'

'An old fellow I know. Mr Hutchinson. Tolliver said he was a rascal and I defended him.'

'And then?'

'And then we all went back to the house. I left it a few minutes later. Just after Gabriella –' Here I indulged myself in what I thought was a fond smile, but may have come over to Nancy as a rather foolish simper, for she knit her brows pretty irritably at the sight of it. 'Just after she said that she would have her father invite me to join the family on an expedition the next weekend. Last weekend, that is,' I added sadly. 'The invitation never came.'

We went over the same ground a couple more times trying to work out why this apparently innocuous visit had turned out so disastrously for me. The only fresh thing I remembered was that I had entertained Gabriella with some of old Hutchinson's comical sayings. But that, we both agreed, could hardly have any relevance here. In the end, it was growing so dark, Nancy said she had best go inside, and added what she said she had really come out in the first place to tell me, that there was no use me waiting near the *quinta* for her father was not expected there tonight. He had sent word that he would be staying at the house in town. Wishing rather that she had got this information out first thing instead of last, but still grateful to her for her concern and kindness, I thanked her with a kiss upon her lips. She stood for a moment staring at me, and then said it was the first time I had ever done that to her.

I protested. 'I am sure it is not. I have often kissed you, Nan.'

'But always there,' she said, touching both her cheeks. 'Never here.' And she placed two of her fingers upon her mouth. Then she turned and ran away towards the house.

I did not see her go in through the gate. I was already heading for a nearby grove of cork oaks, on the first stage of my walk back to town. Actually the first stage ended *in* the oak grove, for I was forced almost immediately to complete the task I had begun twenty minutes earlier against the great elm tree.

Having taken care to wipe my hands upon some tufts of grass, I set out anew to walk the several miles back into the town. Night was fallen now, and such a night as seemed designed to impress a lonely traveller with the dangers – wild animals, highwaymen, etcetera – that might lie in his path. High scudding clouds raced across a yellow hazy moon. The wind blew off the river in forceful gusts that sometimes threw bursts of rain or spray into my face as I marched along. The trees above me groaned and cracked and swayed their branches in a most ominous fashion. Actually the journey was entirely without incident, and I for my part was still so concentrated upon the task ahead of me, and so angry still that I had been driven to this pass, that in the first half of my expedition I scarcely thought of the perils that might be about me, and in the second I found myself in the protective company of a set of hefty road-menders who were going by in their wagon and kindly offered me a ride into town.

They put me down in Remolares, near the wharves. If I had thought about it, I was probably in more danger of attack in this district, which was home to a chaotic population of free negroes, foreign seamen, and domestic whores, than I had ever been upon the highway. But I did not think of it. My righteous indignation carried me along the filthy, water-logged streets, past the dark silent houses and the demented roaring taverns, and I felt not a qualm. I reached the Terreiro do Paço at last, and if I'd had my wits about me would have breathed easier now, for the activities of the footpads were seriously discouraged in the great square, though they were not entirely unknown. But the King himself had one of his palaces here, and it would not look well if distinguished foreign visitors – I don't mean myself – were regularly knocked on the head in front of it, and so a desultory patrol of soldiers was kept up in the square.

At last I presented myself at my uncle's front door. This time, I resolved, I would not allow myself to be turned away by some servant. If I was told that Felix was not at home, or that he would not see me, I would use my strength to push past whoever stood in my way, and once inside the house I would refuse to leave until I had been granted my interview. I had been insulted, I had been lied about – and also I had walked many miles since I had left the Alfândega; it seemed like a week ago at least. I was tired and filthy, my shoes were cut and scuffed so that they were near the point of dissolution. And how could I afford a new pair? I thought I would insist that Uncle Felix supply me with that, in return for all the bother he had caused me.

While I was thinking all these militant, vengeful thoughts, I assumed that whenever the door was finally opened – I had now rapped on it three times, each time louder than the one before – I would find one of the under-servants holding up a candle and blinking out at me. But it was Senhor Gomes who opened the door to me at last. Gomes with a candle, true, but also bearing a cudgel in his other hand. The cudgel I had not reckoned with. Nevertheless, I determined to make my voice strong and steady when I told him that I believed my uncle was spending the night here and that I – expected? Desired? – no, *required* to see him.

There was the smallest of pauses as Gomes seemed to consider what he would say to me. I thought he was going to refuse me and in that event I had no doubt, inside my shell of rage and hurt as I was, I would rush upon him and take my chances against the cudgel. If it led to my suffering a savage beating at Gomes' hands then this would just be one more injury against me to lay upon Uncle Felix's conscience.

Senhor Gomes shrugged and turned from me and went inside, leaving the door open and the decision up to me whether I would follow him in or not. I did follow, and closed the door behind me. I expected that he would go up first to acquaint my uncle that I was here but, when I paused at the foot of the stairs, he turned and asked me what I did down there. And so I climbed after him. I had never been in this house at night before. It was never a particularly bright house: shadows lay upon the landings and the staircase even in the middle of the day. But at night the gloom was complete. Gomes' candle was a mere point in the black. I could not see his form at all unless I came up right behind him. I wondered that my uncle did not set out more – or any – lights along the stairs in his house. But did not wonder for long. It was poverty, the price of a candle or two, that was the reason. Poverty, which had become somehow inseparable from the notion of my family.

On the second landing Gomes held up the candle so I could see both his face and, when I looked towards where he was nodding, a door at the end of the passage. Looking back at Gomes, I found he was already starting up the stairs, I supposed towards his own lodgement. Anxious not to lose the last vestiges of light till I had got where I wished to go, I hurried down the landing towards the door. Knocked at it and then, because I did not want to waste a trace of the righteous anger that had brought me here, I opened it without waiting for a response. Uncle Felix was sitting beside the fire, which was a pretty feeble, low-burning affair, not much less wretched than the Hutchinsons were able to maintain in their rooms. He did not look up as I came in and I saw he had fallen into what looked like an uneasy doze. I closed the door behind me, careful not to make a noise when doing so. I stood irresolute a little distance away from where he sat, looking down on him. At his ease, he was not of course wearing his wig. I studied the naked skull, the few strands of orange hair, which seemed to have grown fewer still since the last time I'd seen him in this *déshabillé*. Bald, his clothes dishevelled as they were now, his mouth sunk in because so many of his teeth were missing, he looked like nothing more than a poor old man.

And yet I remembered him so different, and that not many years ago. I remembered how in my little bed I used to hear my father come into the house with my uncle, dear 'Nun-nun', after an evening spent in the coffee house or at a tavern, both of them laughing and talking so loud and vigorous. My mother would come out of her parlour to take their cloaks and reprove them for making so much noise, and to remember the children sleeping above their heads. My father used to call his brother 'the Young One' and said that nobody in the world could make him laugh so hard as Felix.

Well, all this was useless stuff, I decided impatiently. Those days were gone, and for certain could never return. My father was dead, and Nun-nun, the Young One, turned into this pathetic old man. I reflected on the fact that I was not here to turn over the ancient runes of my family but to seek explanation and redress for the very current difficulty I was in. I also concluded now that I had been wrong in closing the door in a way that did not disturb my dozing uncle. I should have slammed it hard and made the fellow sit up and take notice of me.

I did the next best thing. Picked up an old, stout volume from the table before my uncle's chair, noted that it contained some of the works of John Milton, who I did not care for, and dropped it heavily upon the floor. My uncle sat up with a great jerk, and stared at me. I thought I had never seen so frightened an expression as was in his eyes now, and I began to feel a little guilty at having put it there. At that moment he saw who it was standing over him, and the fear dropped away, to be replaced by a kind of querulous relief.

'Good God, Adam, I thought you were a burglar come to rob me. It is very bad in this town for house-breaking, you know, as bad as London almost.'

He sat up straight in his chair, and yawned and smacked his lips together a few times. Then he looked around him rather keenly. I guessed he was looking for some wine to moisten his throat, or for somebody who would fetch it for him. I did not intend to be that person. I had more important business with him.

'How did you get into the house, Adam?' he asked then, somewhat peevishly, I thought.

'Gomes admitted me.'

'*Senhor* Gomes,' he corrected me, as if without thinking. He frowned. 'Then why did he not come to tell me you were here?'

I shook my head. I didn't know why.

'It's all most peculiar. And unsatisfactory.'

He had a shawl or a blanket about his shoulders. At this point he drew it close to him and shivered profoundly. He did look like a woebegone as well as an ancient party at this moment. But I hardened my heart against him.

'Uncle,' I said, 'I have been wretchedly treated. I demand an explanation. And an apology.'

'*You* demand an explanation.' There was a blaze of anger now in his eyes, which at least had the effect of shedding a few years from his countenance. 'You think it is *you* who should be apologised to?'

Unbidden, I pulled a hard-backed chair away from its place against the book-shelves and set it opposite Uncle Felix's. Seated, I told him that I had no idea what he meant when he informed me in the Alfândega that Mr Lowther was so angry with me. That I had gone out to his house – information that produced a grunt of irate incredulity – but could not find any of the Lowthers there, only a kind of servant who had told me that everything that was laid against me was to be found in a letter Mr Lowther had written, or at least signed, which had gone to Mr Felix Hanaway. I added – without betraying that it was Nancy who was the source of the information – that I understood the cause of complaint had something to do with my very brief and entirely innocent connection with Miss Gabriella Lowther, but that what specifically it was alleged I had done wrong was the completest mystery to me.

My uncle continued to gaze upon me for some time after the conclusion of this speech. Then he leaned forward and took up a poker from the hearth and began to stir about the few remaining brands. I supposed he was considering what he should say. I hoped he would be frank with me. I felt very tired suddenly. The passions and the exertions of the day had caught up with me. Yet I knew there could be no rest for me, nor would I leave this house until I had found out what I needed to know.

'And so, Sir,' said my uncle, 'you think it is innocent, do you, to waylay a young girl and talk filthy things into her untainted ear?'

My absolute shock at hearing this astonishing accusation was so evident to him that for the first time Felix grew a little uncertain in his manner towards me.

'Now, Adam, see here . . . There cannot have been a mistake. The testimony to your shocking behaviour came to Mr Lowther from the most unimpeachable source –'

'Ralph Tolliver.' The name was ground out of me, and my uncle's countenance lost a little of its former unease as it seemed I had confirmed there was some substance at least in the story.

'Indeed, Sir. Ralph Tolliver. Whose father is an old and dear friend of the Lowthers, and who himself has always taken a brotherly interest in little Gabriella's welfare . . .'

It was on the tip of my tongue to tell him of the decidedly unbrotherly interest that I suspected the loathsome, the *married* Ralph had been taking in 'little Gabriella' of late. But I threw this away as unimportant beside the great need I was in to find how and in what manner Tolliver had libelled me. My eyes must have been burning into my poor uncle's for he tripped over his tongue a little as he hurried on.

'Young Toll-toll-tolliver reported to Phil Lowther that you had taken Gabby-Gabriella into a se-secluded spot, and there regaled her with a string of disgusting utterances such as that only after Mr Lowther's repeated entreaties could he bring himself to s-say exactly what they were. And to compound the offence – Felix's voice was growing stronger as he felt his outrage to be on firm foundations now – 'it transpires that these dirty things that were flung at the poor girl were got by you from that wicked old reprobate Allen Hutchinson, who I warned you against, Adam, you surely remember that.'

Now I was in a peculiar state. I knew I was entirely innocent of wanting to talk dirt to Gabriella, but now I had been told what the grounds of these infamous accusations were, and I found that my conscience was not entirely, one hundred per cent clear. Ninety-eight per cent, I could vouch for that, but I remembered now that, even as I was telling Gabriella Mr Hutchinson's silly old sayings, I knew that I did not know what half of them meant. I thought they were inoffensive – I hoped they were – but the thing was, knowing that neither she nor I had a clue as to the real meanings, I was not quite as scrupulous as I might have been in avoiding all cause of offence.

No, that is making too much of a meal of it. I talked nonsense to Gabriella. She enjoyed it as such, and it was only now, looking back, after the intervention of Ralph Tolliver, that things took on an ever so slightly dubious cast.

What I said then was, 'But Ralph wasn't even present when I was telling Miss Lowther.'

'Aha!' Felix's countenance now wore a look of rather sour triumph. 'So you admit it, do you, Sir?'

'I admit that I told Gabriella of some foolish old sayings that I had heard from Mr Hutchinson. I hoped to make her laugh at them. She did laugh, for they were all just nonsense. I had no idea at all that any of them were nasty or vulgar. Indeed, I still cannot think any of them were so bad. Mr Hutchinson is a gentleman after all.'

'A gentleman of the last century, perhaps,' said my uncle gloomily. 'When manners were not so correct as now.'

We were both, I guessed, thinking of my Grandfather Jack, who before his last illness silenced him certainly had one of the foulest tongues in the City of London. On the other hand, Old Jack could never have been described as a gentleman.

'Also,' I went on, 'I heard many of those words when Mr Hutchinson was speaking in the presence of his own daughter. Surely he would not have said anything so very bad before her?'

'I would put nothing,' Felix grunted, 'past that particular man.'

We were silent for a little while. Then after a minute or so Uncle Felix shifted himself about in his seat and again cast a hungry look around him. I thought once more that he was trying to locate his wine bottle, and almost volunteered to get it for him. But then the thought that – our relations being now what they were – if I did he would actually refuse to drink with me froze me to my seat. And by this time he was talking again.

'Can you remember any of these "foolish old sayings" of Hutchinson's?'

'Did Mr Lowther not say what they were in his letter?'

'No, Sir. He wrote that he could not make his pen to write them down, so vile and disgraceful they were.'

'But this is most unfair,' I fretted. 'I am being condemned and yet the evidence is withheld from me.'

'Try to remember them, Adam. Perhaps indeed there has been some misunderstanding here.'

It was as if I was plunged back into that room in the toy house, scratching my head, trying to come up with the right response. Only this time my interlocutor was far uglier and much less indulgent towards me than my Gabriella had been.

' "Slubberdegullion." '

'I beg your pardon?'

' "Slubberdegullion". That was one of them.'

' "Slubberdegullion",' repeated my uncle thoughtfully. 'I think I know the word. The old men used to say it when I was a boy. It means . . . "Fool". Or "knave". Silly old fellows. Why could they not use proper English?'

'But it is not a very offensive word is it, Uncle? And remember that neither of us really knew what it meant.'

'I suppose not,' Felix conceded. 'It is hardly a word one would wish to hear a young gentleman employing before a young lady.

But I don't see Phil Lowther getting as angry as he is over "slubberdegullion". What else was there?'

And so as I had with Gabriella I went through the list of what I had remembered of Mr Hutchinson's rich repertoire. Felix listened carefully, and to most of these odd-sounding words he was able to give some sort of explanation. Almost all belonged to the species of mild insult or curse and meant 'fool' or 'clown' or 'boor' or 'damn me' or something of the ilk. He did frown a couple of times at a word which, as he explained, seemed to cast doubt on the legitimate parentage of those it was used to describe, and he was quite bothered at some others that appeared to refer to women in a disrespectful fashion – such as 'blowse' and 'gixie' and, most mysteriously, 'cooler'. But it was only when we got to 'rump-sticker' that he really sat up and stared.

'You said what?'

' "Rump-sticker . . ." ' My voice had become suddenly unsteady. I hastened to add, 'I don't know what that means either. I told her –' I was clawing at my memory now, striving to make it yield up any and all justification that was available. 'I made it up, I said I thought it was something to do with agriculture –'

'Agriculture!'

'Yes. It was a sort of pike or probe. Used by the labourer to move his beasts along, by striking and sticking with it upon their flanks. Or rumps . . .'

My uncle stared at me in such horror I felt myself almost shrinking bodily where I sat. He flung his hand out towards the mantelpiece and cried, 'Get me that bottle!'

I got up, fetched it and the glass that was beside it. I set it on the table before my uncle. As I had feared, he had no desire to drink with me, but only filled his glass and then threw half of it down in one swallow. It was certainly a great insult he had offered me by refusing all duties as a host and leaving me dry while he drank. But I suppose the peculiar nature of my visit here meant that he could absolve himself of any blame for his incivility. And even parched as I was after my tramping about the countryside, I now wanted explanations even more than I did wine.

'What does it mean, Sir? This "rump-sticker"?'

Felix shook his head.

'I refuse to tell you,' he said, through teeth that appeared clenched as tight as they could be and still allow intelligible words to escape from between them. 'I will say though that if I ever heard that you had used the expression before Betty or Nancy, I would knock you down, Sir, I would beat you so with my cane that you would never forget it . . . Oh, for heaven's sake!' he cried out, driven it seemed into a passion by the dumb horror I must have been showing as I listened to these shocking threats. 'A "rump-sticker" is what all men carry between their legs. Even you, you poor stupid boy. It's a prick, Sir. A yard, a jockum, a tool. Damn it, Adam, it's a cock!'

We brooded for a while over the disaster. My uncle relented towards me so far as to let me go find a glass of my own and fill it with his wine. I too drank deep, as to the ruin of all my hopes. Yet my very obvious ignorance of what I had said to Miss Lowther, and my concern over it, must have worked with Uncle Felix on my behalf. Gradually, the thing appeared to take on a less horrendous aspect in his eyes. Once or twice, as he was speaking of the shock that must have been occasioned to Gabriella's father, I even caught him smiling a little. But he quickly pulled himself together and retrieved the appropriate melancholy frown with which to meet this emergency.

'What must have happened,' I said, 'is that Miss Lowther innocently mentioned the words to Ralph Tolliver. Or else it was Miss Mills who was the source –'

'Good God, you spake filth to another girl too?'

'No, Sir. She must have got it from Gabriella. And that paltry Ralph,' I hurried on, not wanting to open up this new chasm, 'knowing how greatly it would injure me if it was known what I'd said, went and told Mr Lowther as soon as he could. What surprises me,' I said, after a moment's silence, 'is that Tolliver should know what these old words meant when I did not.'

'Is he not older than you by several years?'

'Only by ten at the most, I think.'

'It's enough. Words – especially that description of word – go in and out of fashion like periwigs or my lady's garters. Ten years ago, I remember, we were all using the word "biter" for any malicious witty person. He was a "biter", she was a worse one – for there were females of the "biting" species too – and pray, what do you think of the next one's latest "bite"? You never hear the word any more, yet I am sure there are just as many spiteful wits about as there were back then.'

I shook off my uncle's etymological discourse as soon as was polite, though I think in his essentially gentle soul he would have much preferred a scholarly discussion of the roots of every – decent – word that we could imagine rather than having to face the crisis presently before us. I wanted to know indeed how serious a crisis was it. Given my honest ignorance of what I was talking about to Gabriella, would Mr Lowther ever be persuaded that I was not a vicious fellow but only a blunderer and as such amenable to correction and improvement? Uncle Felix, when he had truly focused at last on the problem, hummed and hawed very considerably, but at last gave his opinion that though the Phil Lowther he had once known – 'a lively young spark with a pretty taste for bawdy' – was no more, surely there must be enough memory in him of what he had once been that he might be persuaded at last to look indulgently upon the mistakes of what my uncle was pleased to call 'a harmless young fool'.

I did not mind him calling me that, at least not very much. And whatever chagrin I might have felt was soon dispelled by a glow of hope when he pronounced that tentative verdict. So perhaps dear Gabriella might not yet be lost to me. I think I must have been grinning then like a fool indeed, for my uncle threw me a very cautionary look. But then he too could not help smiling a little and, when I held out my hand to him, he hardly hesitated before grasping it.

'Perhaps we can get you out of this muddle,' he said. 'But it will take time.'

'I know, Uncle. And I know you will do your best for me.'

'I shan't like having to pay court to Phil Lowther after the way he has treated me. But then again,' said Felix, brightening, 'it was time we made up our differences and maybe this is the means by which we shall do it.'

'So perhaps some good will come of it?'

'But mind, Adam: all this is upon the understanding that your offence went no further than what you have told me. That it was confined to the one word only –'

' "Rump-sticker"?'

'No need to say it so loud, boy, as if you were proud of it . . . Yes, that word. Only that one. Can you assure me it is so?'

Could I? Could I? I strained to remember. My uncle watched me keenly all the time. I wanted so much to have done with this, but I dared not deliberately conceal anything that might be counted against me. I told him everything else I could remember. It wasn't much, nor apparently was it very bad. 'Cuffin', 'grinders', 'ogles', 'roarers' – they were all apparertly too innocuous to bother about or too obscure for my uncle, or anyone else under Mr Hutchinson's age to know what they meant. 'Buffer', 'canary', 'quod', 'sawney': nothing to worry about there either.

'Then there is only one other of his sayings that I can remember telling Miss Lowther' – I felt such relief now, knowing that I was at last at the end of a wearying and rather degrading task, and that still my offence was confined to the one unlucky word – 'and that was once when Mr Hutchinson said to me he gave no more attention to what the English Factory thought of him – pardon me, Uncle, but these were his words – than he did to a "pipkin vent". And that, Sir,' I said, with a humorous shrug to accompany my fun, 'is the end of my sorry lading bill.'

I liked that last touch mightily, conveying as I hoped it did an acknowledgement of our mutual good fortune in being worthy English merchants, no matter what that wretched old Hutchinson might say of the noble Factory. I glanced at my uncle to see if he had appreciated the stroke – only to find that he appeared to have plunged into some sort of appalling seizure. His face was almost as purple as our wine, and he was having the utmost difficulty breathing. I was quickly out of my chair to go to his rescue, but he flung my willing hands from his body and accompanied the gesture with an oath of extraordinary violence.

When he recovered his breath, he told me to get out of his house. He wished to see me no more; whether no more this night or for all eternity, he did not specify. He was in a towering passion. I think he might not have avoided that trusty old catchphrase of the playhouses back home and told me never to darken his doorstep again if he had thought of it. But it was clear that this was the meaning of the dark imprecations he flung at me. Looking back it all seems very comic: my uncle in his dishevelled undress, his bald pate gleaming in the candlelight, not dulled at all by the few unfortunate strands of hair that straggled across it, and the spit flying from his lips as he struggled to give release to his rage. And myself, who had engendered this passion, listening in utmost horror to his words, my stomach working so that I thought I was bound to have to void it from one orifice or the other.

Yet for certain it was not comical at the time. I left the room, my uncle still shouting after me. I went back across the square and into the alleys of the Baixa. In the dark night the gangs were out. I could hear near to me harsh shouts, running feet, the clash of swords, the cries of the wounded. In my present mood I did not care about any of them. Indeed I thought it would be a kindness to me if some bravo would knock me over the head. But I walked through the danger without it ever coming upon me. I reached my lodging. I went straight up to the second floor and knocked on the Hutchinsons' door. The old man opened it after a while. I pushed past him. I stood in the parlour. He asked if I wanted to go through into the sitting room. I said I only wanted to ask him some questions and that this room would do as well as another. He said then that Maria Beatriz was in another apartment in the building, sitting with a neighbour who was poorly. He said he could fetch her if I wanted; he was sure she would like to see me too and hear my news. I said that wasn't necessary.

It would be a weary task to describe how I went again through my account of what had transpired between Gabriella and me on that fateful afternoon in the toy house. Mr Hutchinson looked somewhat vexed to hear that his characteristic sayings had been served up by me for Miss Lowther's entertainment. But I was too focused on my own distress to care much about his. I said that it appeared most of the words I had told her were innocent, but that a couple had got me into great trouble when it was reported that I had spoken them. I mentioned 'rump-sticker' and was about to press on to what appeared to be my much greater blunder, when he stopped me.

'You used the word "rump-sticker" to a young lady?'

'Yes. It was a mistake. I did not know what it meant.'

'It means a –'

'I know *now* what it means. My uncle was kind enough to inform me.'

'You should never have said that word before a lady. Has she not a brother? A father? I would have called you out, Sir, if you had ever uttered such an expression in the hearing of my daughter or my sister. I would have killed you without mercy!'

Ridiculous old man. He was actually almost shaking with indignation against me, and no doubt imagining himself spitting me on his trusty sword. Yet he could hardly stand up any more unaided.

'Mr Hutchinson, I tell you it was a mistake. I thought it meant . . . it doesn't matter what I thought. The thing is, I said it. And it was not the worst. Apparently.'

I then told him the phrase that, when my uncle heard it, had sent him into almost a paroxysm of shock and rage. Mr Hutchinson's response was not quite so monumental, but he stared at me in silence for at least a minute before he could speak, and when he first tried to he had to clear his throat several times before the words could come out.

'You said *that* to the girl? To a decent, young –'

'Yes. I know. It must be very bad. But –'

'You actually said "*pipkin vent*" to her?'

'What does it mean, Sir? I must know. It is intolerable. I have done something very wrong yet I don't know what it is.'

Mr Hutchinson turned and walked from me into the living room. I seemed to have been left to make my own choice whether to follow him or not. When I did, I found him sitting in his usual chair and, as my uncle had been doing a half-hour before, taking deep restorative gulps of wine. He looked up at me at last as I lingered in the doorway.

'I don't wish to tell you what it means,' he said. And when I attempted to argue with him, 'The reason mankind makes up these nonsensical cant words for things is because it were too shameful to have to say out loud the proper words for them.'

I came and sank down into the chair opposite.

'Was it truly so very disgusting what I said?' I asked him. My head was bowed as I waited for the answer. In fact, I hardly knew whether I wished to hear it. I suspected it might seal my fate – at least that I would know it was sealed when it was revealed to me how wicked I had been.

Mr Hutchinson did not answer me. And when I looked up to see what the matter was I found to my surprise that there was a kind of smile upon his lips, an expression on his face too which pointed to an emotion that in another context I might have said could best be described in a Portuguese word I had lately learned: saudade, which means a kind of fond, sad longing for things far away or long ago, a yearning for something very sweet and dear that has been lost. What exactly Mr Hutchinson might be experiencing this emotion for at the present moment I could not tell, unless indeed it was for this mysterious 'pipkin vent'. At last he stirred in his seat.

'I suppose,' he said, 'you have a right to know in exactly what manner you have made a complete nigit of yourself. And since what it was you heard from me on an unlucky day . . . Well then, "pipkin vent" –' He stopped again there, with me hanging as it were upon his lips. 'Damn it, Adam, you make it very difficult. I don't know where to start.'

'Start with "pipkin".'

'A pipkin. A pipkin. All right . . . Well, don't you know what a pipkin is?'

'I think – I think it is an old word for a jug, is it not?'

'We're not talking about confounded jugs . . . Oh, look, if you must know, it was a word we young fellows of the time of Charles II would use for a female's part. You know?'

'Part?' said I.

'Yes, damn it, part. What they have down there. The opposite to a rump-sticker. The ring, the bite, the cunny, the passarinha, the buceta, the pussy – whatever you call it. God damn it, boy, the *vagina*! Well, don't look like that,' he hurried on angrily, trying, I think, to cover his embarrassment with a show of spleen. 'Whenever you have to spell out a joke or anything humorous by way of an aside it's bound to sound pretty foolish . . . As for "vent". Well, you must know what that is.'

'I don't, though.'

'Lord, it's plain English. "Vent", man. It means a wind.'

'I don't understand,' I said miserably, after cogitating this riddle for a minute and more.

Mr Hutchinson sighed once again. 'How many winds to you know of?' he asked patiently.

'Soft winds, strong winds, cold winds –'

'I am not talking meteorologically, damn it. I am speaking of the kind of winds that . . . that the body may emit. Good God, do I have to say it all? I'm talking about farts, Sir. Farts from the pipkin. Pussy farts, there, you have made me say it.'

I stared at the old man, whose features seemed to be struggling with annoyance at my own slowness and the effort to stop himself from laughing at the ridiculous matter that had been introduced into our discussion. For my part, I was beginning to feel quite incensed at the levity with which he was treating something that for me at least had almost life-and-death significance. I also had a rising sense that I was being seriously imposed upon. For little as I knew of sensuality, the physical attributes of womankind and so on, one thing I was sure of was that such an effect as he had just described could not be produced from the organ he had named. A pipkin, to use his own antique terminology, simply could not vent. It was not built to do so.

Having expressed this opinion in forthright terms, and having had to endure it while Mr Hutchinson finished tittering at my ignorance, I was then led down an instructional path during which this hardened beau of the age of Nellie Gwynn and my Lady Castelmaine showed me just how the inexplicable could be explained. I was horrified, nauseated, shamed – I have no idea why I felt any of those now. In my time as a lover of women, now sadly as long distant to me as Mr Hutchinson's then was to him, I came rather to feel affection for the dear old 'pipkin vent' when I heard it, as a sweetly human reminder of the comedy of coition. I would likely burst out laughing at those moments, and thought a little less of my partner if she did not join me in mirth but acted dour or embarrassed or with the pretence that nothing had happened.

But that was when I was older and less ignorant by far. Have attitudes generally changed by so much? I don't know. I suppose that in this reasonable age the whole matter might be investigated scientifically, would exercise the ingenious and practical talents of such a man as, say, Doctor Franklin of Pennsylvania, who I was once proud to call my friend and who currently and remarkably is serving as envoy from the American rebels at the Court of Versailles. I daresay that great man has little time now for philosophical speculations of this nature, but he has a multitude of epigones, in both the Old and New Worlds. Perhaps the scholars of the college he founded in Philadelphia (and in whose birth I too played a small part as a member of its fund-raising committee) could be encouraged to take up the task. The angle of penetration, the co-efficiency of friction, the size of the male part, the narrowness of the female: all of which combine on occasion during intercourse to force out air from the latter organ with a sound that exactly mimics the conventional fart – all this, I say, may be considered abstractly, scientifically, any way you like, so dispassionate and mechanical we have grown.

But back then in the dark ages, at least to a boy who had never got further in love than pecking a few girls on the lips at parties and running away from the whores in Drury Lane, the matter seemed so wickedly arcane, so very foul, spoke of such loathsome and almost Devil-deduced knowledge about matters that should ever be concealed that I trembled for my own soul. But not half as much as I was to quiver at the closely following thought that it was this beastly abomination that I had served up as a treat to Gabriella Lowther. And it was *known* I had done this. Ralph Tolliver knew it. Mr Lowther knew it. My uncle too. Soon the whole Factory would be made aware of it – Tolliver would make sure of that. I knew I was finished in this city. The man who had spoken of 'pipkin vents' to a virgin, and a wealthy and well-born virgin at that? Doomed. Finished. No question about it.

*   *   *

I was gone from Mr Hutchinson's rooms before his daughter came home. For the rest of that week I was in a kind of daze. I went to the Alfândega every day, and performed my duties and I believe I performed them as well as ever. At least labour dulled a little the ache in my heart. Senhor Gomes watched me throughout the week. I think there must have been something defeated about my countenance and posture that decided him at the end of it that now was the time for him to strike at me. Also he probably knew of my disgrace and, if he was not informed of the exact reason for it, knew that the one certain thing that had protected me up till now – my uncle's belief that I was making my way in Factory society – need no longer be considered.

I wonder still why Gomes decided to get rid of me then. I certainly was not much of a threat to his present criminality, nor to his future plans. It is possible that it was done out of simple hatred for me. Or perhaps he feared that at some point I might stumble by accident across some of the accounting distortions that were now littering the firm's Waste Book, the ledger that was nominally under my command. Or perhaps it was done from even slighter motives or none at all. The labourers who worked for us, and who knew him much better than I did, used to call him 'o escorpião' behind his back, which means the scorpion. I think it just as likely that he struck at me simply because he could, because it was in his nature to strike, like a scorpion.

On the Friday then, Felix came down to the Alfândega and asked me to take a walk with him outside. I had in fact spoken to him, very briefly, once or twice since that terrible evening when he had ordered me from his house. On those occasions he had never caught my eye when he spoke to me, but gazed to one side of my head or the other, as if my face was too loathsome an object for him to contemplate straight on. He affected the same oblique manner of speaking to me this time too.

We walked down to the river's edge and then alongside it, beside the quays and between the parties of sailors and porters who were carrying the goods up from the waterfront and the clerks from the various factors who were endeavouring to keep an eye on them and try to ensure that as little thievery as possible took place. One of these latter I noticed suddenly was my erstwhile adversary Mr Evan Williams. It was the first time I had set eyes on him since the afternoon in the room with the great windows, and I suppose I might have expected to have been badly affected by the sighting. In fact I felt quite indifferent. I didn't know why. I hoped it wasn't that I had discovered that the sufferings of burning people meant much less to me than my being rejected by a girl – at least by her father. But there it was. My main thought at the sight of Evan Williams was that I hoped he would not notice me. It seemed unlikely that he would. Currently he was engaged in shouting at a pair of snowballs. The effort was making even his sallow complexion take on a purplish shade. I sent a wish winging over towards him that it would result in a seizure of more or less mortal proportions, and kept plodding on beside my uncle, whose shortness of leg meant that our pace was pretty slow.

(I might mention here that this curse I had flighted towards Mr Williams on this occasion was, of course, not seriously meant, or not very seriously anyway. Though this did not prevent me from experiencing a guilty pang when, a couple of years later in London, at Buttons coffee house in Russell Street, I happened to meet up with an old Lisbon acquaintance, Billy Ward of the yellow hair and the sprightly girlfriend, who mentioned at one point that Evan Williams – 'who you might remember' – had died not long before while being cut for a stone in his bladder, which he had waited too long before having removed.

'They said it was as big as a pigeon's egg,' Billy said. 'He must have been in pain for years, poor old fellow.')

'I'm going to let you go, Adam,' my uncle said.

At first I thought he was just dismissing me from his presence, wanting to end our walk together; when I understood what he truly meant, I mumbled something about it being hard to be punished so for an error of taste I had never meant to commit. He said it was not for that he was expelling me from the firm. But the reason he wanted me out now was that he had spent the past two evenings going over the firm's books with Senhor Gomes – at the latter's request – with a particular concentration on the Waste Book, which had become my responsibility. This study had proved to him, without possibility of error, that I had behaved in a fashion so negligent that it amounted almost to the criminal. I had at least the self-respect to try and object to that description of me, but he held up his hand and soon silenced me.

'I said "almost". I must believe it was only sheer idleness, ignorance and slovenliness that guided your work, and not an actual desire to commit fraud against me. But the result is the same. Gomes has proved to me that very great losses and pilfering have been concealed by your blundering. Very great,' repeated Felix solemnly. 'And I will say this to you, whether you like to hear it or not: while your father brought me to the brink of ruin almost, you, Adam, have very nearly sent me over it. You will leave my employment, Sir, and you will go this very day.'

Let me mention that in time I was to adjust my thinking towards what I may call 'the pipkin-vent incident'. For I came to see it at last as only a humorous accident, in which I was really very little to blame. But while I came to have a relaxed attitude at last to one of my youthful follies, I never could help but be mortified when I looked back at this other one: on my conduct when I worked for my uncle. For I had indeed taken charge of the Waste Book and, though I knew that the many gross errors that were in it were a result of my too-trusting acceptance of what Gomes told me, still it was my responsibility and my fault in the end that it had become such a disgraceful repository for error and fraud. I thought in fact that my uncle was right to be angry with me, right to let me go.

I could have tried, I supposed, to point out how hard I had worked for him for so many months, but I was not sure indeed that he had ever really noticed the fact, and I was certain by now that Gomes would never have mentioned it to him. All I could do – not in my defence, but in order to do something at last that might help my uncle and not harm him – was to mumble a warning that Gomes should be watched for I had come to believe that the head clerk might be thoroughly dishonest. I was going on to describe to Felix how many of the entries I had written in the Waste Book and which he now found to be so erroneous had been dictated to me by Gomes, and that he had certainly reviewed all of them – when I found that my uncle had closed his eyes tight, and actually placed both hands against the buckles of his wig, as if to block out from his ears what I was telling him.

Naturally I stopped speaking. He told me then that he always hated it when an Englishman tried to blame his own shortcomings upon a native.

'I do certainly blame Gomes,' he added, 'but only because he did not come to me with his suspicions about you when he first entertained them. But he has explained that he felt the situation was so delicate, you being my relation, that he could not alert me until he was absolutely sure that if your behaviour continued as it had been you would fatally harm the firm. He is a good and loyal servant, I won't hear him being traduced by you, Sirrah.'

And that really was that. He offered me twenty pounds to pay for my passage back to England, but I said I had no need of it – which was a lie – and that anyway I did not think I should take any more money from an uncle who clearly despised me, which was true. He said he would not trouble my mother with his opinion of me, but would leave it up to my conscience whether I would tell her honestly of my behaviour. Then he quitted me without another word, leaving me to walk alone beside the Tagus, or to drown myself in it if I wanted, or any other thing I cared to do. For himself, he had made it quite clear he was indifferent to whatever course I chose.

BOOK TWO

Gomes

B artolomeu Vincente Rufino Gomes. Born in a village in the central Alentejo province, thirty-one years ago. The fifth son of Rufino Joaquim Gomes, who held his bit of land from the local *fidalgo*. To Dom José Almeida the peasant owed three-quarters of what he produced before he could start to feed his own family, and when the harvests were poor – which they usually were in those years – the family came very close to starving. From this situation Bartolomeu had escaped at the age of fourteen to follow a body of English troops that had been encamped in the neighbourhood. After some initial confusion caused by his appearance out of the darkness around the camp fire – during which, he was to learn afterwards, some of the soldiers had wanted to hang him for a French spy – he was taken on by a Captain Merriweather to be his personal body servant, to clean his boots and walk his horse and untangle his wig and empty his chamber pot and do all the myriad things that had to be done to render an English officer and gentle-man presentable in the camp and on parade. It was only on the third night after entering the Captain's service that he was summoned to join his new master on the trestle bed in his tent, and learned that his terms of employment included other, even more personal duties.

Bartolomeu remained in Captain Merriweather's service for almost three years. In that time he learned much and travelled far. He soon learned, for instance, that the regiment he was now part of was called Farquharson's Dragoons, being named after its colonel, Sir Michael Farquharson, a gentleman who was not, it turned out, anywhere near his troops' present location, having applied for leave on health grounds at about the time the regiment was ordered to Portugal. Presently 'Old Micky', which is what the men called him, was in residence at an English town named Bath, from where he kept up a languid correspondence with his second-in-command, a Lieutenant Colonel Maurice who, confusingly to Bartolomeu, turned out to be a Frenchman.

'I thought we fight against fucking French?' he wondered to Dragoon Smart one afternoon.

'This is a different sort of fucking Frenchman, Bart. He's the Protestant kind. Good. Catholic Frenchman – no good. Have you got it?'

Bartolomeu pretended that he had. In fact, at this point in his grasp of English he hardly understood two sentences of the language strung together. It took him minutes to work out how he should put whatever he wanted to say, let alone how he might comprehend an answer. Besides, this good-and-bad Frenchman business was really too advanced for him even to come near. He was still stuck on such elementary tasks as how to pronounce words like 'Bath' and 'Dragoon' and, worst of all, 'Farquharson'.

Captain Merriweather proved hardly active in helping to advance Bartolomeu's language skills. The only English instruction his new master ever essayed was to confine all his orders to him in that language, which indeed were almost the only occasions when he spoke to his servant, except in bed when his ecstatic utterances came really too fast and incoherent for Bartolomeu to have a hope of understanding. Still, it was probably the best way forward for the young servant. He heard only English in Captain Merriweather's tent, and when he ventured outside it on his duties he heard only English from the men. It was a deep immersion in the language, and after a few weeks he surfaced speaking a variety of it that, he was assured, could be tolerably well understood.

'Except that I'm afraid you have learned to curse and talk filth most horribly, poor lad.'

'I'm fucking sorry for that, Mr Baxter,' said Bartolomeu contritely.

And Dragoon Baxter, Bartolomeu's best friend in the regiment, sighed and shook his head and went back to the book he was reading, the book he was always to be found reading, and which Bartolomeu, with a shock of dismay, had discovered not long before was actually a portion of the Holy Bible, a sacred thing that he could never have imagined being in the hands, not of a priest or friar, but of a common soldier.

Bartolomeu came to love Farquharson's Dragoons, loved especially to watch the regiment on parade. The hundreds of men in their scarlet coats, moving this way and that upon their fine horses as if they were one, with the regiment's banners and guidons snapping above their heads, gave him a vision of perfect harmony and power and grace that he knew he would always remember. Every morning he would watch them at their exercises, hearing the words of command, and, as his English grew stronger, repeating them under his breath:

'Dragoons, sling your muskets.'

'Make ready your links.'

'Clear your right foot of the stirrups.'

'Dismount and stand at your horses' heads.'

And:

'Dragoons, handle your daggers.'

'Draw forth your daggers.'

'Clear your pan . . .'

And so on, and so thrilling for Bartolomeu. He came to understand the special nature of the dragoon service. 'For we are not infantry chaps exactly,' Baxter explained to him one evening, 'nor cavalry either exactly, though it seems we are heading that way. What we are is mounted infantry. We ride to the battle, then we get off our mounts and fight upon the ground. The horses' bridles are linked, and one man is detailed to hold them while his comrades are fighting. Then when it's over we get up on our horses and move off again.'

'Why d'you bother to learn the little fucker, Baxter?' Corporal Norris remarked, as he was passing by. 'All he needs to know is how to clean the shite off the Captain's boots. And to bend over when the officer fancies his arse.'

'Shut your mouth, Norris,' Baxter said. And Bartolomeu was afraid for him, for he knew that the Corporal out-ranked his friend and might well resent such an insult. For a moment it seemed indeed that Norris would make trouble. But then, perhaps reflecting that in order to have Baxter disciplined he would need to explain to Captain Merriweather the grounds of the dispute, he chose only to snarl, 'Watch it, Dragoon,' and go on his way.

Month after month, then year after year, marching behind Farquharson's Dragoons, all over the frontier region between Portugal and Spain. In this time he learned to speak and read English well, mainly under the tuition of the heretic dragoon Baxter. Another matter that took up a lot of his time was the avoiding, and then, when it was absolutely necessary to keep his employment, the succumbing to the carnal attentions of his master, Captain Merriweather. One grey and dripping afternoon in camp, when the regiment had moved back to Belem, within a few miles of the capital, Dragoon Baxter had urged him seriously to escape from the Captain's clutches, telling him that what he was being forced to do with him was 'an abomination in the sight of God'.

'Go on, Bart. Lisbon is just down the road. You can be there in a few hours and he'll never find you again.'

Bartolomeu promised he would do it. By this time Baxter was almost dead from a fever epidemic that was spreading through the camp and Bartolomeu saw no harm in promising him anything. He had already assured his friend that he would turn his back on what Baxter was pleased to call 'the beastly whore of Rome', and seek his true salvation in ardent study of the New Testament, which, the dying dragoon revealed, was the true reason he had been so assiduous in teaching Bartolomeu his English letters. Baxter proposed to leave the volume to him upon his death, and Bartolomeu swore that indeed he would wear out his eyes reading it, if he must, in order to discover the true way to Christ. One more promise that he had no intention of keeping would not hurt, he decided, and it had the merit of soothing Baxter's last hours. When the time came, and the poor wasted English body had been committed to the Portuguese earth, Bartolomeu sold the New Testament the same evening to a Dutch soldier, another heretic, and wished him joy of it.

It did linger in his mind though that Baxter had spoken the truth when he'd said that with Lisbon so near he had the best opportunity he was ever likely to get to escape from his master. The town was so close that on a clear day, when he stood on the shore, looking downriver, it seemed as if he could reach out and touch it.

Merriweather would never catch up with him in that great labyrinth. And if he did – Bartolomeu touched the dagger he always wore now at his side – he supposed the throat of an English officer would be as easy to cut as anyone else's.

Yet in the end he did not go. In the spring, the regiment marched off again, back to the war, and Bartolomeu went with them. When he thought about it, he only allowed himself a mercenary reason for the decision. He had served Captain Merriweather for nearly three years now and, though nothing had ever been said between them, Bartolomeu had made himself believe that when the time came – the war over, the British forces no longer needed by the new Portuguese king Dom João V, the regiment ordered back to England – then his master would not forget his trusty servant. Hazily, the idea of some superior leaving-present formed in Bartolomeu's mind. He had heard the dragoons talking sometimes of what the future held for them. The greatest desire any of them had was to lay their hands upon some exceptional piece of loot that when converted into cash would, as they said, set them up for life. Enough, say, to buy a tavern in their home village back in England or Ireland, or a stable-yard, or a grog shop. That is what Bartolomeu decided he wanted from the Captain, an amount that would set him up for life. He did not see how he could be denied it. There was no difficulty about the money, for he knew he served a rich man. Bartolomeu had once heard Merriweather's brother-officers speculating on whether he would offer to buy a troop of his own to command when his immediate superior, Captain Stephenson, decided to sell up. Hearing the amount this transfer would cost made Bartolomeu gasp. To make *him* satisfied would cost infinitely less. The price of a Portuguese tavern or vineyard would touch the Captain's brimming purse hardly at all, and Bartolomeu would be mad to leave his service before he had claimed his well-earned prize.

The regiment, having marched all the way around the capital to a bay about ten miles south of it, found ships waiting there to take it and its horses and all its equipment on board. There followed several weeks on the water, a situation Bartolomeu had never expected to find himself in when he had linked his fate with

Farquharson's Dragoons. Two big storms and several lesser blows battered the convoy as it beat along the Atlantic coast. At last it turned towards the milder waters of the Mediterranean. Soon it was sailing past the great fortress of Gibraltar, just newly captured by the British and their allies. The fort saluted the fleet with gunfire and the ships responded each in turn. The weather, which had been heavy and lowering in Portuguese waters, now turned balmy. The soldiers basked in the sunshine, most of them stripped to the waist. They played card games and drank the wine they had smuggled aboard. There were fiddlers in the evening and some of the men danced for the appreciation of their comrades. There were singers too, and one man who could do stunning feats of acrobatics. Several among his audience called out that he was good enough for Bartholomew's Fair, which confused the Portuguese servant for a while until he found out what it meant.

At night the moon gleamed on the waters, by day dolphins and tunny pursued the ships and flying fish rose and fell on the waves. Flocks of birds, so dense they darkened the sky, passed constantly overhead, crossing from Africa to their breeding homes in Europe. But of all the wonders Bartolomeu saw or heard on the voyage what most impressed him was a conversation he overheard one afternoon when he had taken the Captain's best uniform on to the officer's deck to brush and sponge it. The rumour was that the ship would make landfall the following day and Merriweather wanted to look his best at the head of his newly acquired troop. As Bartolomeu sheltered from the midday sun against an overturned rowing-boat, one of those that sheltered the ship's supply of vegetables against the salt spray, two officers who were standing on the other side of it began to talk. One of them he recognised straight away was his master, the other he decided was Major Evans, an officer popular among the men for his reputed humanity. For a while they discussed matters pertaining to the regiment's efficiency – whether this voyage would have made the men slack, the need to institute some parade drill as soon as they got ashore, whether adequate supplies would have been collected at the Spanish town of Alicante where they would soon land – none of which was of much interest to Bartolomeu. He was wondering whether he oughtn't to try and steal away unobserved for it would not be in his interest to be found concealed, apparently listening to his superiors' conversation – when he heard something that made him sit up and take real notice, and lose all thoughts of leaving.

Merriweather told his brother-officer that this campaign would be his last. He intended to sell up and quit the regiment when it was over.

'But you've just bought Stephenson's troop.'

'Can't be helped. The parents have summoned me home to take up my duties on the estate. Brother Harry has died. Perhaps you knew?'

'I didn't. Sorry about that, Merriweather.'

'Yes, well . . .'

The two men talked of various practicalities connected to Merriweather's planned departure. And then, just as it seemed they would finish their conversation and part, Major Evans said casually, 'By the way, Jack, what will you do about the lad?'

'The lad?'

'Yes. Your body-servant. What's his confounded name?'

'You mean Bartolomeu?' said Merriweather.

'That's the one.'

'Why, I shan't be doing anything about him. How odd that you should mention the rogue . . . Do you want him, Major? After I have gone?'

'Oh, I have no need of a servant like that,' Evans said, without – as far as Bartolomeu could hear – a trace of sarcasm in his voice. 'But will you just let him go when you leave? In the middle of Spain?'

Bartolomeu heard a muffled sound, which he took to be an expression of agreement from his master.

'But you'll give him a decent present, at least?' the Major suggested.

'I shouldn't think so.'

'Seems a bit harsh.'

'Oh, don't worry about him, Major. He's the sort that always lands on his feet. Perhaps I'll give him enough to get him back to his own poxy country. But I have to practise economy now, you know, for between them Father and Harry have got the estate into a confoundedly mazy condition.'

The day after Bartolomeu had overheard this conversation, Farquharson's Dragoons landed with the rest of the little English army on the Spanish shore. It was joined by Portuguese and other foreign contingents and the combined force soon headed north with the ambition of entering the capital Madrid and placing the Allied candidate upon the Spanish throne. Experienced now in the ways of modern war, it did not puzzle Bartolomeu to be told that the commander of the force he marched with against the French was actually a Frenchman himself, Henri de Massue Ruvigny, a Protestant heretic who had been created Earl of Galway by the English King William (who had been a Dutchman). In any case Bartolomeu had no time to waste on such trivial matters. His mind was entirely filled with rage at his master's planned abandonment of his servant, a design of the highest treachery which, he learned the very night the regiment had set up camp again on dry land, did not cause the Captain sufficient shame to prevent him insisting that Bartolomeu join him once again in his bed.

The Earl of Galway, Bartolomeu discovered on the march, had a high reputation as a general. Which made it something of a puzzle that his manoeuvres in this campaign had the result at last of bringing his small force face-to-face to with a French and Spanish army, twice as large as his own, on a broad plain outside the little town of Almanza. The Allied force was clearly not going to be allowed to proceed to Madrid without a battle. The preliminaries of the contest were soon begun, and the opposing artillery were banging away at each other across the bare plateau. Bartolomeu, as was always his habit when an engagement threatened, was preparing to retire with the spare horse far to the rear – when Captain Merriweather rode up to him in a great state. His eyes were glazed over, his lips were trembling, snot dribbled from his nose. Bartolomeu had never seen his master in such a condition.

'Listen, Bart,' the Captain gasped, and he laid his hand upon his servant's sleeve. 'The Portuguese have run away again and we have been ordered to charge across that bloody open piece of ground to cover their desertion –' He released Bartolomeu's arm here, so that he could gesture at the plateau before them. On the far side of it were the enemy masses. Great flashes of fire and balls of smoke rose from their gun batteries. So far their shot was falling short, but even at this distance the noise of its descent was terrifyingly loud.

'Bart, I know I'm not going to survive this charge. I want you to ride with me, lad. And when I have fallen, I want you to take me back and ask Major Evans – if he survives – or any other of the officers to see that I am buried in a decent grave. With the chaplain saying a few kindly words, you know?'

Bartolomeu was almost overwhelmed. He had never been allowed to take part in any of the regiment's martial duties, not on parade, certainly not in action. He was so proud now to be summoned thus that he almost forgot his new hatred for the Captain. He definitely forgot about the danger to himself if he should be so foolish as to listen to his master's words and charge with him against the enemy. He said nothing, he only nodded, and after the Captain turned his horse and galloped towards the front, he actually went after him. The regiment was lined up in ranks. The Captain rode to the front of his troop. Bartolomeu took a position just behind him. Nobody objected, nobody even seemed to notice him. The dragoons were all staring towards the front. All were waiting for the bugle to call them to advance.

Just before it did, the Captain turned in his saddle. He held out something to Bartolomeu, who took it, scarcely noticing at first what it was. He turned it over upon his thigh. It was the Captain's favourite pistol, primed and cocked. Fear must have made his master tender-hearted; he had not wanted his servant to go into battle unarmed.

The bugles sounded. The dragoons started off. Soon they were under fire. Plumes of smoke grew from the earth before them. Horses and riders were falling in struggling heaps. The pace quickened. The dragoons, as so often on parade, drew their swords. They were galloping now. The smoke was so thick that only in patches could each man see his fellows. Bartolomeu had a job to keep in touch with his master. With every pace the volume of fire from the enemy seemed to double. The regiment was dissolving within its fury. Bartolomeu had lost sight of the Captain. With difficulty he reined in his maddened horse. He searched in the thick haze. There were no dragoons riding past him to the charge any more. Only the heaps of bodies on the ground, and the noise of conflict up ahead. At one point, the smoke cleared. Bartolomeu had a clear view of Merriweather – not at the head of his gallant troop charging at the French guns, but abjectly riding to the rear. He was about ten yards from Bartolomeu, though he did not see his servant for his head was bowed, in shame presumably. Bartolomeu rode forward, raised the Captain's pistol and when, perhaps because of some premonition, its owner looked around at him, shot him in the face.

After that, he dismounted and – in pursuance of his late master's instructions – loaded the body on to his own horse and on foot led it and its burden back through the fire of the victorious enemy to the English positions. The beaten army retreated for fifty miles towards the coast until it was deemed by its general to be at last out of reach of the pursuing French. The first evening in camp Bartolomeu got word that his conduct during the disaster of Almanza had been observed and that the officers of the regiment – those who had survived the battle – desired to speak to him. The command was brought to him by Corporal Norris, who had never been his friend, and Bartolomeu knew it was useless to beg that he would turn a blind eye and let him escape. So, knowing he was going to his death, and only wondering what particular diabolical punishment awaited a lowly Portuguese slayer of an English officer, Bartolomeu followed the corporal towards the command tent where the officers awaited him.

When he got through the entrance he found them all drawn up in a semi-circle. At first sight of him, they broke into applause, pounding the palms of their hands together and calling out his name. Then Lieutenant Colonel Maurice stepped forward. Bartolomeu had never had the pleasure of even being noticed before by this august personage. But now he was actually beaming at him.

'Well done, Bartholomew, lad!' he said. 'Several of us saw your gallant and faithful action in bringing poor brave Jack Merriweather's body back from the inferno. Of course' – the Lieutenant Colonel allowed a smile of mock-reproof to play upon his lips – 'you should not really have been taking part in that charge at all –'

'It was by the officer's orders, Sir,' Bartolomeu ventured to interrupt.

'I know, lad. Captain Merriweather told Major Evans he was going to order you to do this. Still, it was a fine loyal thing what you did. Staying with your master into the teeth of the French guns, and then to bring him back. Splendid!'

Again the officers broke into applause, even Captain Whitby, who had lost an arm in some other war years ago, did his best to make a noise, while Bartolomeu stood with his head bowed modestly, thanking Nossa Senhora in Heaven that the huge black clouds of cannon-smoke that had rolled intermittently across the battlefield had left exposed his meritorious deeds while concealing his murderous one. When the applause died away, the Colonel nodded to one of his young cornets, the Lord Denborough, who stepped forward and handed Bartolomeu a leather purse. 'There you are, Bart,' my lord said. 'In recognition of your great services.'

'Well done, lad!' cried out Major Evans and, 'Hear him, hear him!' all the other officers chorused, and then Norris was showing him out of the tent before he had a chance to thank them for their applause and their gift.

Back in his quarters he found the purse contained one hundred golden guineas, truly a little fortune. He lay on his bed for hours just staring at the purse and, from time to time, feeling its hard bulges. The next day Captain Whitby stopped by to enquire if he was ready now to take up service under him. I have no desire at all to be buggered by a one-armed man, thought Bartolomeu who, though Captain Whitby had never given any indications of sharing the *maricão* tendencies of the late Merriweather, was no longer willing to take his chances with the officers of Farquharson's Dragoons. In any case, he'd had enough of campaigning. He left the regiment that afternoon without saying farewell to anyone, and made his way to Alicante, which was still in the hands of the Allies. There he found the captain of a Portuguese supply ship returning to Lisbon, who for ten of his guineas would take Bartolomeu along as passenger.

The sound of a heavy foot-tread startled Gomes out of his reverie, jerking him from the heaving deck of *O Rei Escondido* fourteen years ago to the unshakable floor of the Alfândega today. He straightened up, then nodded as the man came into view around some crates of nectarines that marked the beginning of another merchant's holdings. The smell of the fruit was heavy in the air. Gomes reckoned their owner would have to shift them on to the market by noon tomorrow at the latest or risk losing the lot. He knew the merchant was resisting the extra-high price he was being asked to pay to have his crates cleared; Gomes guessed he would crumble first thing tomorrow when he smelled the taint of over-ripeness.

The man stopped before him, looked him over. The light was very dim, it was nearly nine o'clock at night, hardly anybody was left in the building.

'Well, then, Gomes?'

'*Como está, Senhor Porteiro?*' asked Gomes politely.

'Well enough,' the doorkeeper grunted. He didn't ask after Gomes' health. Gomes didn't expect him to. In spite of the modesty of his title, the doorkeeper's was a prodigiously impor-tant post in the customs house. He had the responsibility for seeing to the safety of and proper assignment of customs dues for every article of trade that passed through the building. God knows, thought Gomes, how much he had paid to get this job.

The doorkeeper leaned back against the bale of cloth, which was also supporting Gomes. He folded his arms, yawned, gave a visible shudder.

'Cold,' he said.

'It's October,' Gomes pointed out.

'Thank you. I know it's October. All right, what do you have for me?'

Straight to business as usual. On the whole Gomes approved, though he would have liked a little more in the way of casual conversation from the doorkeeper, if only to show they were partners in this enterprise, albeit of very different stature. Still, he cleared his mind, concentrated on what he planned to say.

'Harkins are bringing in a cargo of plates and pewter pans.'

'How much?'

'I only have the value. They say five thousand *moedas*.'

'Well, enough, I can place it. Tavares shall handle it,' the doorkeeper decided. (Gomes was already scribbling a note for himself. He could have written it up even before he had consulted the doorkeeper. Álvaro José Tavares disposed of most of the household goods and furniture that were stolen from the Alfândega.) 'Yet it's a damned finicky article, Bartolemeu. Haven't you got anything easier to handle for me?'

'What say you to a few bales of French silk? Best quality.'

'I say excellent.'

'Davis and Tunbridge have them on order from St Nazaire. They expect to land them soon. The ship has been seen off the Rock.'

'My God, we'll have to move fast. Tell Costa – no, second thoughts, I was disappointed in the last job he did for us.'

'What about Carlos Sampaio? He's very keen to work with us. He'll do it for next to nothing.'

'All right. But your responsibility if it goes wrong. What else?'

And so Gomes went through the information he had picked up in the preceding week. What cargoes, which ships, which merchants. It was important to have early warning of what was on its way to the Alfândega. Plans had to be in place even before the goods started lining the shelves. Such matters had to be decided as, for instance, whether it was necessary to go extra slow in assessing the customs due so that the men who were to dispose of the goods once stolen were ready for the job – and that the best men were available, of course. Then the timing of the theft had to be right. It would be best of all if the job could be done before an agreed accounting had taken place between the factor and the customs officer. In that event there was no independent evidence for how much of an article had originally been brought into the Alfândega (and so of how much of it had been stolen either). Then again it had to be agreed as to what proportion of a cargo should be purloined and what left in the hands of the *herético* merchant. This was a delicate decision, political really, and almost entirely the responsibility of the doorkeeper, though he also consulted on occasion with representatives of his superior, the *ouvidor da alfândega*, who in turn sometimes spoke with the agents of the *conservador*, the Portuguese magistrate who was charged with deciding in all legal cases that involved English subjects.

Put bluntly, the knotty question always at issue was: how much could the officers of the Alfândega steal without enraging the English Factory so much that it would appeal above their heads to the court of Dom João itself, and also, through the British Ambassador, bring the weight of its detestable, heretical but, unfortunately, powerful country to bear upon this issue? At the very least such interference from London would annoy the courtiers and statesmen in the royal palace, which might make them decide to replace the officers of the Alfândega who had made life temporarily difficult for them.

Everybody above a certain rank in the customs house had an interest in this danger, as indeed all had a share in the proceeds of the thievery. Not one of them, Gomes knew, felt the least twinge of conscience about what they were doing. And why should they? After all, the accursed English had come across the sea uninvited and had used their money and the threat of their military might to steal the wealth of poor Portugal; it was only right and fair that a few Portuguese should take advantage of their positions to steal a little of it back from the oppressors.

Gomes came at last to the end of his list. Most of what he had found out came from overhearing the casual conversation of his English fellow-clerks over the previous week. As a Portuguese he was not permitted to join in the social activities of his colleagues, of course: no rowdy drinking sessions after-hours in the taverns around the Alfândega, no hilarious weekend excursions to the *hortas*, the gardens beyond the city, where the Lisbon people liked to go in the hot weather. Gomes didn't mind about that. He'd had his fill of dirt and plants growing up. Nor was he much concerned about missing the disgusting exhibitions of drunkenness that the English conceived to be the height of pleasure. He got what he wanted out of his position in that he was allowed, in working hours, to join groups of his fellow-clerks and, as long as he kept himself back and did not try to impose himself in any way, listen to what was being said.

'All right, Bartolemeu,' the doorkeeper grunted now. 'Here's for your trouble.'

He passed over a few coins. Gomes did not bother to look at them. It was the same every week, and always disappointing. What the doorkeeper gave him just barely doubled the meagre salary that Felix Hanaway paid him.

'You didn't mention your own firm,' the other man said, heaving himself away from his resting place, preparing to go. 'Treasure of the Indies expected at Hanaway's next week, is it?'

Gomes smiled to show he understood the doorkeeper was making a little joke. It was the same little joke that he made almost every week. Actually Gomes found it slightly annoying to hear his firm so regularly belittled. He couldn't have said exactly why. The failing fortunes of Felix Hanaway ought not to bother him in the least. Nevertheless it did annoy him, and was one reason, though by far the lesser, why he kept quiet about the fact that, after many months of indifferent imports, hardly even worth stealing, the firm of Hanaway was indeed poised to handle something rather impressive.

He had begun to make his plans as soon as he had heard what was afoot. It was why he'd got rid of Adam Hanaway when he had, even though the job was still months in the future. His uncle's faith in his head clerk, Gomes well knew, was bottomless. The Hanaway cub too suffered from the family vice of being over-trusting. But he was not stupid, as Felix essentially was, and if he was given enough time, Gomes feared, he might perceive what a labyrinth of fraud the head clerk had built in the heart of the firm, with connecting tunnels through much of the Alfândega. It was not a risk that Gomes wished to take. He wanted Adam out, and Felix the Trusting had been happy to oblige him, even acting against his own family to do this.

But why, after all this care and foresight, should he tell the doorkeeper what was coming so slowly to the boil at Hanaway's? When he could dispose of the whole business by himself, and keep all the money too? Of course, after he did that, he would never work again in the Alfândega – or in Lisbon, or Portugal even – but never mind, it was time to move on. Once he had made his modest fortune. He didn't require much, he wasn't greedy. All that Senhor Hanaway possessed would be enough for him.

He shook his head. 'Nothing's on its way to us,' he said. 'Nothing you'd be interested in, Excellency.'

Adam

1

I passed under the Acro dos Pregos and walked along the Rua Nova dos Ferros until I reached the Rua do Oiro. Along my way I attempted to shift some of my merchandise into the hands of passers-by but had no better luck than during the three-quarters of an hour I had wasted trying to do the same in the Terreiro do Paço. It was a blowy, wet, late-winter day and in the square the wind had come off the Tagus in great clammy gusts, which made people stagger as they tried to push across its centre, or more sensibly cling to its edges and duck under the covered walks that lined it between the Paço do Ribeiro and the Alfândega.

At least the rising wind had blown away the last of the fog in which the city had lain enshrouded for the past couple of days. For which the population – the law-abiding part of it – had heaved a great collective sigh of relief, for the depredations of the criminals and the mischief-makers were made that much more difficult. Dom Sebastião de Carvalho's gang had been rioting in the Baixa on consecutive nights and the deaths of at least three innocent and defenceless citizens were laid to their account. And other malefactors had been out in the same streets, sheltering their depravity under the cloak of murk and invisibility.

Nevertheless, the new weather was no more helpful to my own, honest business than the fog had been. Few people were about and those that were had little inclination to stand in the drizzle while I showed them my wares, having to shield these at the same time from the elements that also disturbed and drove away my customers. On the other hand, it was just because the weather was so menacing that I had decided to try my luck in the square today.

For I thought correctly that it would keep away for once the well-protected rogues who had permanent rights to the lucrative trade within it. Only on a day like this might I hope to work without risk of harassment – and yet on a day like this my chances of making any sales were minimal. It was a gamble. So far today I was losing.

At the corner of the Rua do Oiro it came on to rain pretty hard and I took shelter under the awning of the first of the goldsmiths' shops that lined that street. Even though I was thus nominally out of the rain, the air was so thick with vapour that my coat and my clothing under it were becoming saturated with moisture. I stared out at the falling drops. They were coming on heavier than before. I wondered whether it made sense to keep on with my task today. Maria Beatriz had advised me against going out, said that there were some days when the effort of trying to make a sale was so great and the outcome so doubtful that one might as well stay at home and conserve one's energies for a better occasion. But I was cocky – I still had a tendency to that, in spite of all the recent setbacks and plain disasters that should have made me otherwise – and decided I would show her that for a prodigy like myself no days could be judged as utterly without hope.

It seemed though I had found at least one that was just that. Yes, I would go home. Back to the Rua do Parreiral. Tomorrow I would try twice as hard, sell twice as much as on an ordinary day. I would have to. This weather was very hard on Mr Hutchinson's arthritis. He could barely walk some days. Today had been one of those, and I doubted myself whether he would be up and about within the week. Which made me the sole breadwinner of our little 'family'.

Just as I had decided to gather my coat around me and make a run for it and not stop till I was back at my lodging, I found I had a companion in my shelter. A broad, short man, quite well-dressed, breathing hard, having it seemed been running along the street to get where he was going before plunging under my awning. We exchanged rueful glances. He was brushing off the largest of the raindrops that were clinging to his cloak. I wondered if he was a foreigner, which was not unlikely for many visiting merchants found their way to the Rua do Oiro to pick up a few gold trinkets to take home. It was one of the few legitimate ways of getting the metal out of the country.

'*Chuva de merda,*' the man commented when he'd done what he could with his cloak.

So no foreigner here, though I guessed from his accent he was not a native of Lisbon. From Porto probably, or Viana – somewhere to the north. I agreed with him. The rain was shitty, and showed no sign of stopping. Even now I could feel that the feet of my stockings and my toes within them were beginning to turn moist and cold. Yet only yesterday I had inspected the soles of my shoes most carefully and had found nothing much amiss.

'I think it's set in for the day,' I said, more to take my mind off my poor feet than anything else. 'The wind's coming in steady from the ocean.'

On hearing this, the man glanced curiously at me. He could no doubt hear by my accent that I was not a native, yet my command of his language was pretty much perfect now. It was not a combination often to be found in Lisbon, where most foreigners decided they only needed a few words of Portuguese with which to get by. However, if he had wanted to pursue the matter, find out why I was different from the others, he was suddenly prevented as he fell victim to an enormous sneeze. And then to another.

'God damn it!' he spluttered, when the fit had passed. And then, '*Desculpeme, senhor*! My profoundest apologies.'

'*De nada*. Not a day to be out, is it?'

'Can't help it. Business, you know. A meeting I could not avoid. It would have cost me quite a few *cruzados* if I had, I can assure you.' The fellow said all this with a certain pride, and I didn't wonder at it. Portuguese of the better sort were usually good for nothing more useful than careers in such undemanding institutions as the Church or the Army or the Court. They made a great fuss about how they couldn't possibly stoop to the menial tasks required by trade, but I had long since decided that the truth was that most of them knew their faulty upbringing meant they hadn't the capacity for any occupation that required actual performance rather than mere show and posturing.

I would have liked to ask what business indeed this gentleman was in, but another great bout of sneezing from him effectively prevented all communication for a while. During it I moved discreetly a few paces further from him. I could not afford to go down with what he had. With me laid up and Mr Hutchinson likewise, we could not possibly meet our landlord Montesinhos' weekly exactions, even though they were not unreasonable. Maria Beatriz was doing what she could, working with her pen and brush long into the night to turn out extra drawings for our printer Tadeu Nunes. These were intended not so much for our own use but to be sold on in bulk to other families of street-hawkers.

I asked her once why she needed to keep up this constant supply of fresh drawings since I had thought it was the essence of the printing process that a great number of copies of the same image could be produced by it. She said that was true, but that the capricious spirit of the Lisbon folk, our customers, required that they always be offered something new and different before they would part with their money. It was not enough to have a copy of last year's drawing to show them; it had to be fresh, changed, better: a different background or foreground, a new tilt to the halo, a new beard or a wound, hitherto unsuspected, even a whole new-discovered saint who would offer holy assistance in the case of distempers that nobody had even heard of before.

'I cannot afford to be ill,' the man beside me lamented, echoing my own thoughts. He considered the matter for a moment, then seemed to brighten up a bit. 'I shall say a prayer to Santo Antônio when I reach home. I have his image set up on the wall in my bedroom.'

'The Blessed Antônio is a most efficacious saint,' I said slowly. The very dawn of a hope was beginning to steal over me.

'Yes,' said the man, rather smugly. 'He has been good to me . . . And when he is not good to me, he knows he will be punished.'

'Punished?'

'Yes,' said the man again, very firmly. 'He knows I will not hesitate to take him down to the cellar again. Oh yes, I've done it before, and shall do it again if I have to. Let him lie in blackness, looking at nothing for a few hours. Then, you'll see, he'll be ready to do any favour I require of him.'

I actually closed my eyes for a moment, as I sent up a silent prayer of thanks for the absurd credulity and religiosity of the Portuguese. When I had opened them again, I nodded and said, 'Santo Antônio is certainly a powerful intercessor with the Lord upon our behalf. But I wonder, senhor – is he a sure specific for what may be ailing you?'

'How do you mean?' asked the businessman, puzzled.

'Well, look at it this way,' I argued blandly, 'as well as having the entire city of Lisbon under his protection, he also offers his help in mending broken bones –'

'And jugs, as they say, and vases. And plates . . .'

'Doesn't it sound as if the poor dear man had quite enough *on his own plate*?' I smirked then. The Portuguese always love playing with their language – as I suppose do we English with our incorrigible and universal habit of punning.

The man laughed appreciatively at my stroke. I pressed home my advantage.

'But nowhere do I think it is said or writ that the Blessed Antônio has any particular interest in dealing with such symptoms as your excellency is displaying. Whereas –'

Here, with a practised sweep of arm and hand, I in the same movement unfastened the lock on my oilskin bag, opened it, and took out one of the sheets of paper that was inside. Offering a silent prayer of thanks that the rain did not appear to have penetrated to it, I presented it to my new friend with a flourish.

'Whereas São Damião sits in Heaven, very close to the right hand of Almighty God, and intercedes precisely for all those who suffer from bodily ills. Except that of broken limbs for which, I agree, it would certainly be better to apply to the Blessed Antônio.'

'São Damião?' said the Portuguese thoughtfully.

He was inspecting the image I was holding up for him. Just at that moment it struck me that I had probably got it wrong. It was always difficult for me to keep in order the preposterous Catholic table of saints and their specific attributes. Why it was necessary to pray to São Cristóvão if one was going on a journey, and quite useless to apply to São José or São Cosme for the same assistance, why Santo Elói is the saint who has taken the goldsmiths under his protection, and São Benedito is the one that must be courted by those who lack bread, and why on earth one should pray to Santo Alexis if one is affected by bed-lice. And much, much else. Who could remember all that tangle of nonsense?

It was the strongest contrary argument I had to make when the Hutchinsons first put to me the idea that I should join them in their own trade of street-selling. I was at a pretty low point then. Many fruitless applications had shown me that I was unemployable in the world of the English Factory, for my reputation as fraudster, with a pretty sideline in speaking filth to young girls, had preceded me everywhere I went. Still I could not for some time seriously consider the Hutchinsons' proposition, and it truly was not, as Maria Beatriz later told me she had suspected, because I believed I was too good for their trade. Weeks of unemployment and being turned away with scorn from so many Factory offices had cured me of all that sort of nonsense.

But: 'I'm a Protestant. I don't know all these saints and martyrs, don't know their names, nor their histories . . . and in any case wouldn't I be expected to show a fervour that I do not feel in peddling their images?'

'Nonsense,' Mr Hutchinson had scoffed. 'You can learn about the saints. My daughter and I will teach you. As for fervour: did you feel much fervour when you peddled your – whatever it was – rice, beans, knitted socks, drawers? These pictures are no different. You will assume the fervour. It's not hard . . . Come, will you join us?'

Just now I was struggling to recall if São Damião was not so much the holy fellow who looked after the sick and the dying, but after those who were licensed to care for them. In other words the doctors. I lowered the image I was holding up a little and risked peeping over the top to see what it was that Maria Beatriz had drawn. Fortunately I saw that it was ambiguous. The saint – a sallow, rather ironical-looking gentleman, with a bald pate beneath his halo – was surrounded by the much smaller figures of ordinary human beings, some of whom were certainly unwell, being shown stooping, or bandaged, at the last extremities of life. In addition there was a set of rather portly, well-dressed fellows who may have been doctors. On the other hand it could be argued – I was certainly ready to argue – that they were victims of lesser diseases, of colds and catarrhs, just like my new friend was suffering from.

The main thing was that – as in all Maria Beatriz's works – the figure of the saint was large, dramatic and skilfully drawn. Even on a dark, damp Lisbon morning one could see that it would look very well, fixed to a wall in one's home, perhaps a candle or two throwing light upon the blessed countenance. Already I could see an acquisitive gleam in my new friend's eyes. I prepared myself to ease him towards what we both wanted – though he did not quite see it so clearly yet – the transfer of the sainted Damião from me to him, in return for a reasonable sum of money.

I forbear to trace exactly the stages by which I achieved this end. In most ways the selling of holy images follows the same pattern as the sale of anything else. When I had begun doing it, a few months ago, I mostly remembered the way the shopkeepers had once dealt with me: my tailor, my wig-maker and so on. And I employed what they had taught me: the deference that does not quite become so obsequious as to be sickening, the constant suggestion that it was just as much in my interest that the customer should be pleased by his purchase as it was in his, the insistence that our task together was to find something that suited him, and only him, in which my role was solely to advise and guide.

'I want you to be entirely satisfied,' I told my new customer. 'I shall be unhappy if in a while you find that it does not suit.'

'No,' said the businessman, having convinced himself far more than I had. 'São Damião. That's the fellow for me. What did you call him? A specific for what ails me. I like that . . . But what if he proves reluctant to help me? What should I do?'

'Oh, treat him like a dog. You cannot treat Damião too ill so as to bring him to the mark.'

'I have always wanted to put the Blessed Antônio face down in a chamber pot when I am angry with him,' my customer confessed, with a sort of guilty smirk upon his lips. 'But have never quite dared to.'

'You need not hesitate with Damião, your excellency. Stick him in the pot. It's the best thing for him. After treatment like that, he'll cure your cold in no time. And anything else that might be bothering your excellency . . .' I added with a lewd glance towards the front of the fellow's breeches.

I was rewarded for this rather shameful bit of pantomime by a dirty laugh from my customer and I was able to move him on smoothly then to the matter of payment. Because he had made such a fuss about being an important businessman early on, he was, as I'd hoped, too ashamed to object much to the steep price of one *moeda* I gave him for the drawing, which was worth then I think about thirty shillings. Still he looked a little appalled at how much his stop under the awning of the goldsmith's shop was going to cost him, and I quickly took a couple of *cruzados* off the price to show my goodwill. We shook hands on it. He gave me the sum demanded. I rolled the paper tightly and bound it with a bit of cut yarn. This he stuffed under his cloak and, after a somewhat troubled glance at me, which I could not exactly read, he made off into the rain.

In case he had any second thoughts about his purchase, I decided it was as well to shift myself from where it had taken place. I hurried away up the Rua do Oiro in the opposite direction from the one taken by my customer and soon dived into a side street called, I think, the Passagem da Santa Ana, and after that into the whole wild tangle of the Baixa in which once, long ago as it seemed to me now, I had wandered so often, hopelessly lost. Now I could find my way through with hardly a mistaken step along the way – and I assure you there weren't many natives of the Lisbon of nearly sixty years ago who could make the same boast.

Ten minutes after leaving the Rua do Oiro I was climbing to the second floor of Senhor Montesinhos' house. I admitted myself to my friends' apartment. It had been several weeks since I had last gone through the formality of knocking on the door to secure my admission. Maria Beatriz was at home, sketching in the parlour. For once, I saw, she was not at her everlasting labour of drawing holy images. She had set a bowl of fruit upon the table a few feet away from her and was sketching that. I tried to see how she was succeeding, but she was always shy about showing her own, unofficial work and covered up the paper she was working on with an embarrassed smile. This behaviour was quite at odds with her attitude towards her professional duties when she was forever asking my and her father's opinion of whether, say, she had put a sufficiently kind-hearted expression on the face of Our Lady of Compassion for the Wounded, or an adequately suffering one on that of Santa Teresa who in life had had a tendency to wear a particularly painful hair shirt, and flogged herself regularly too for the glory of God. But those, as Maria Beatriz would say, and the rest of her menagerie of saints, were 'only business', and she had no more concern for the task except to do it well enough so that the prints would sell.

At first she looked a little surprised at finding me back in the Rua do Parreiral so early, for even at this depth of winter there was still an hour or so of daylight left in which I could try to sell my wares. But then she saw by the state of my coat how inclement the weather still was, something that she had been too absorbed in her craft to notice. I told her that I would have stayed out even in the rain and wind, but that I'd had a piece of such good fortune that I thought I deserved to make a short day of it. With that, I laid out upon the table the many *cruzados* I had earned from the sale of São Damião. Of course she was delighted. Such a sum had not been seen in this apartment for many weeks. She praised me for my skill, my cleverness, my industry. I praised her for producing such work as made it easy and pleasant to sell. We smiled at one another. Truly, it was a shared delight, for aside from the few *réis* that I would keep back just to have something to jingle in my pockets, we both knew that the money belonged to our common treasury.

It was a time to celebrate. In spite of the weather, Maria Beatriz insisted on going out to buy a cooked chicken for our supper. She asked me to go in to see her father while she was out. And then with a wave and a smile that made her look suddenly very young, she was gone. I went into the sitting room where I found Mr Hutchinson swaddled in blankets, dozing in front of the usual inadequate fire. He heard me come in and seemed to shake himself awake. I asked him how he did, and he said he was rather poorly, which I could already see. His colour was certainly not good. I told him then that I had some medicine with me which might benefit his case, and with that removed from beneath my coat, where I had been hiding it from his daughter's gaze, a bottle that I had just bought at one of the local *tabernas*.

By now Mr Hutchinson was sitting up and looking much less morose than I had found him. I got our regular glasses and filled them both and we set to drinking. We agreed that the mixture was vile, and had some fun speculating as to what could have gone into it to give it its particular flavour. Mr Hutchinson claimed that he could taste dead cat, whereas I insisted on turnips. Nevertheless, we also agreed after a short while that, as far as intoxication went, the result was most efficacious. Certainly my brain was swimming when I was only halfway through the second glass, and it was probably fortunate that Maria Beatriz reappeared just then. She became very irate at the sight of us toping before the evening was well begun, and confiscated the bottle instantly. She left directions for me to set out the table while she went downstairs to Montesinhos' kitchen to prepare and cook some vegetables she had bought.

The chicken lay on a dish in the centre of the table and as I worked around it the fumes that were rising from its roasted flesh affected me so intensely that, with my moral sense distracted by the wine, I thought that at any moment I would forget about friendship, family and all the rest and just hurl myself at the meat and consume it all, ripping the legs and wings from the corpse as I gobbled it down.

To distract myself from this shameful urge, I turned back to Mr Hutchinson. I found he had grown melancholy again. At first I thought it was only because he had been deprived of his wine. But when, mainly to keep my thoughts from the sweet-smelling bird, I asked him what it was that seemed to be troubling him, he answered me in a mournful voice that he had been thinking upon death all afternoon. That was information calculated to sober me. I wondered what I could say that would comfort him. There didn't seem to be much. Young as I was, I worried about death myself pretty often, and were I as old as Mr Hutchinson and thus so near to eternity, I believed I would think of little else.

In the end I fumbled out a few words about the common lot of mankind, and that as I knew him to be devout in his Faith he surely could anticipate his end with less apprehension than most other men. He shook his head impatiently at that and said he wasn't thinking of death as it applied to himself, but of his daughter.

'Why, is she ill?' I cried, feeling an unexpectedly keen shock at what I'd just heard. He said that of course she wasn't, and I felt then equally surprised at how glad that news made me.

'She is not ill, Adam, but she is poor. And alone. My death will leave her without any support. She will have no father. She has no husband. She will have no one . . .' To my horror, Mr Hutchinson began to weep. 'And no money at all.'

'Sir!' I cried. I felt so agitated and unhappy for him that I leaned forward and took his hand. 'Mr Hutchinson, you must stop this. You are making me uneasy. It is the nature of life that we lose our dear ones as we go through it. I myself have lost a father who I loved . . .'

At which point I too was overcome with tears. Drunken tears, I daresay, but no less heartfelt for that. Mr Hutchinson gripped my hand tighter, and then suddenly, unexpectedly, uttered a great oath.

'Ah, Adam,' he mourned then, 'if I had a fraction of the sums I made when I was a young merchant in this town, I could leave my girl comfortable for the rest of her life. Instead of which she may starve, she may be reduced to become a beggar or worse, a servant. The daughter of Allen Hutchinson to be condemned to that! The beloved child of a gentleman who once earned seven thousand pounds from a single cargo of Madeira wine!' He took a deep, sighing, tragical breath – and then announced quite cheerfully, 'But I haven't despaired yet!'

'No, indeed,' I encouraged him, 'for while there is life –'

'I am always thinking of what can be done. While I have been confined in here, there is little else that I do. My hope is that I can leave her just enough money for her to buy a little shop here in the Baixa. That isn't a disgraceful occupation, is it?'

I assured him that it was not, that there were men in London who kept coaches and six and married their daughters to the younger sons of the nobility and yet were not ashamed to call themselves shopkeepers. This notion – coaches and six and everything – delighted the old man, and soon he was as full of glee at the thought of his daughter's future prosperity as he had been wretched a little while before in contemplating her poverty. It was not up to me to point out that he had about as much chance of raising such capital as would be needed to buy a shop from his third share in a street-peddling enterprise as I had of, say, ever gaining re-admission to the presence of my long-lost love Miss Gabriella Lowther. Instead I felt it was my proper work rather to feed the optimism that seemed to have brought him out of the realms of infirmity and spent with him many minutes discussing this shop – a stationer's we agreed would be just the thing for Maria Beatriz – and where exactly it should be situated.

When the lady for whom such a glowing, though – I feared – illusory, future was being planned returned to us, she was pleased to find we were in good spirits, though somewhat suspicious as to the source of them. However, when she had reassured herself that they were not the result of some fresh application to a previously hidden bottle of wine, she joined us in our good humour.

The little African girl had followed her upstairs with a tureen of cooked vegetables and she set it on the table next to the chicken. When the girl had gone, we three sat down to our meal, and I think that I have scarcely ever in all my life passed an evening so pleasant as this one was. The food wrought miracles within us, and indeed I believe that much of our generally rather lowered and depressed condition then was because we were simply ill-nourished, not to say, on the worst of days, practically starving. As our blood was replenished and thickened by the meat we ate, we perked up marvellously. There was a dessert too, for Maria Beatriz had brought in from the nearest *padaria* a tart made of sugar and preserved fruits. And when we had finished our food, she relented so much as to allow us both a glass from the bottle she had taken away, and at our urging poured one for herself too.

For half the night we ate, we talked, we even sang. At last, with much mutual congratulation on the good food and the good time we had enjoyed, I prepared myself to leave them and go up to my room. Maria Beatriz stood up and kissed me upon my cheek and it was very fine to feel her soft lips upon my skin. Mr Hutchinson sat watching us from his chair, smiling approvingly on our fond farewell. From him I got a clasp of the hand and I was so pleased to find how much more vigorous than usual his grip had grown. I slept a good deep sleep, and only remember waking once in the night to piss. As I did so, I heard the rain still drumming against the windows. Yet when I awoke in the morning I found that not rain but bright sunlight fell against the glass now, showing a promise for the day ahead that was confirmed when I went down to the street.

It was a beautiful day indeed, and the harbinger of a whole chain of other mild and pleasant March days. It seemed to me that I was experiencing the blessed bounty of the southern latitudes, which bring on spring so much earlier than in Britain. However, Mr Hutchinson and Maria Beatriz, when I met them for our midday meal, looked rather sceptical and advised me not to stow away my winter clothes too soon, in that they guessed the frigid season had not yet released its grip on Lisbon. But as day followed day of perfect weather I forgot their warning, or at least learned to dismiss it as only an example of the pessimism that I had observed seemed inevitably to be the accompaniment of age.

But I was young then and knew fine days would go on for ever, or at least till autumn came round again. Certainly the rising temperature was beneficial to my business. Men and women who had fled from my approach when the pitiless rain was falling or the damp cold eating at their bones now seemed much more disposed to stop in the street and hear what I had to say and look over my wares. That first beautiful day I sold five Santo Antônios, two São Cristóvãos, a Nossa Senhora dos Mártires, two São Franciscos, a São José, a Santa Joana Princesa, a Nossa Senhora da Boa Morte *and* a São Damião (to the same customer, a medical man), three São Cosmes – and sundry others I could not put a name to, but sold off anyway with the usual large promises as to their efficacy in curing whatever ailed my customers.

I brought back my haul of copper coins, with an occasional silver *cruzado* shining amongst them, to my friends in the Rua do Parreiral. They were loudly admiring of my proficiency. Maria Beatriz's sallow complexion became pink with pleasure, which I thought at first was solely a tribute to me. But then I realised she was also showing the artist's, the author's natural pride in the success of her creations. For though, as I have said, she was always businesslike and dispassionate as she turned out her saints and Nossa Senhoras and views of the church of São Roque, she could not help taking some pride in her contribution to the day's success, particularly after a long winter in which her drawings had hardly moved at all.

I did not begrudge her taking a share in my triumph. This was a season when I was not in a mood to begrudge almost anybody almost anything. The day was so beautiful, the next day the same, I felt so full of life, I could feel my whole body tingling as I went out into the street to begin my day's labour. I was happy, and must have looked it for people smiled at me as I went by. And they continued to buy off me. Maria Beatriz was able to purchase a chicken every night if she wanted, though of course she did not but interposed that dish with other good servings such as dried cod and onions, and sausages and cabbage, and pig's trotters, and veal stew, and a dish called *sarrabulho*, which she knew I liked much, made of liver and pork fat and blood. I hardly had time though to enjoy these feasts. I was so anxious to get back out in the street while there was still an hour of two of daylight left that I could use to sell a few more holy images.

While I was in this joyous frame of mind, something happened that at another time might have affected me sadly, for my friend and room-mate Bento took his leave of the house on the Rua do Parreiral just then. It was true that he was doing so for a happy reason in that he'd had the good fortune to win the hand of a lady, a comfortable widow who lived not far off in the Rua dos Odreiros, in a house that had been left her by her late husband. Yet I think had I not been in this marvellous happy state I might have taken the news that he was going rather hard, for I had grown very fond of Bento over the months we had lived together, and besides, there had been so many changes of circumstance in my life of late that I probably would have found it hard to endure another one so great. But as it was I shook his hand and wished him well with hardly a qualm. He was leaving the fourth floor that very day for, though the wedding was not to be for two weeks yet, he and his bride had decided there was no good reason to delay any more setting up home together when they both desired it so greatly.

He asked, before we parted, would I mind if he invited me to the wedding feast? I told him of course I wouldn't, how could he think I would mind? And added that I would be very glad to rejoice with him and his bride upon the happy day.

This was only a minor interruption to my joy in those days of blue skies and a warm though not burning sun. Mr Hutchinson, though not entirely abandoning his doubts about whether we had truly moved yet from winter into spring, was heard to say that it *looked like* the vernal season at least, and he was so encouraged by the lovely weather as to announce one morning that he intended to take up his trade again and share with me and his daughter the burden of keeping our little household afloat. This, I found, amounted to not much more than his finding a convenient spot in the sun a few yards away from Montesinhos' front door and sitting there dozing on and off, with some of Maria Beatriz's prints displayed on his lap, until the growing shadows of afternoon woke him up completely.

Not many sales could be expected from such a passive way of doing business, and not many is what he got. But I did not resent his behaviour. Maria Beatriz had said to me one evening after he had retired for the night that she thought he had lost considerable ground over the winter, and that she did not know how much longer he could last. And then, as I knew, Mr Hutchinson was himself contemplating his approaching demise. I did not want to make any difficulties for him in this very last part of his life. To doze away the hours in the sunshine, refreshed with the occasional cup of wine brought to him by myself or one of his neighbours, appeared to me the kind of dissolution that many much richer folk and in much higher places would envy. I was certainly not going to interfere with it.

2

One evening, as I was supping with the Hutchinsons as usual, we heard a great clap of thunder, which rattled the windows, and the next moment there came against the glass the first pattering of what proved to be a quite prodigious rainstorm. It kept going all through the night – in fact it hardly let up for days. There were intervals in its course, but they never lasted long before the rain returned, beating down on the unprotected streets and alleys with the same steady force. It grew cold again, the rain dropped from a bleak sky, the trees, which had started to show traces of green, seemed to become black and bare again almost as one watched – all of this justifying those old Lisbon hands, such as Mr Hutchinson, who had warned that the apparent spring we'd seemed to be enjoying would doubtless prove illusory, and that winter still had a few unpleasant jokes to play on us.

The old man's sensible response to the dismal weather was to retire to his bed. I was still out in the streets, dawn till dusk, with my urgent tongue and my bag full of images. But there came at last a day when the sky was so black and the rain so pitiless that even I could not think it worthwhile to go a-peddling. I lay on my bed for an hour or so after my usual time, listening to the rain spatter upon the roof. Then, hunger driving me to my feet, I went down to the kitchen and tried to beg a bit of bread and cheese for my breakfast, and some wine to wash them down. But Senhor Montesinhos' new cook, a hard-faced Angolan woman, would not let me have them and I actually had to agree to pay her for these pathetic scraps of food before she would. However, because I had no money on me – a fact I did not reveal until the articles were safely in my hand – she had to agree to give me credit until later.

Which 'later', I thought, as I made my escape, may very well never come. Godsokers! – as Mr Hutchinson used to like to say – it was only a bit of day-old bread and some bad cheese. Grumbling to myself, I went to the front door and stood a little way beyond it, under the arch, eating standing up, and looking out on a fluvial Rua do Parreiral. I wondered what I would do today. I could not face going back up to the fourth floor. I might choose to walk in one or other of the city's great squares, both of which were lined with covered walkways. But by the time I got to either of them I would be drenched through. I needed the company of others, I decided, and since the only other prospect was to go back down to the kitchen and teaze the cook, I climbed the stairs to the second floor and, as I had really known I would since the time I woke, knocked on the Hutchinsons' door.

The African girl let me in. She said that Mr Hutchinson was a-bed as usual but that Dona Maria Beatriz had told her if it was Senhor Hanaway at the door then she would be glad to receive me. I found my friend standing in the middle of the parlour floor. She had on a dress I had never seen before, a silk mantua, yellow in colour, and upon her head a high commode. She made quite a splendid figure and was enjoying the spectacle of herself for a tall mirror – which, like the dress, I had never seen before – had been propped up against a table and she was able to examine herself in it as she turned this way and that. Proudly, the little negress adjusted her lady's girdle and then, as I watched, tucked into it what the better class of women in those days insisted on Frenchifying as a *mouchoir*, which was only that common article the handkerchief by another name, though, as in this case, usually made of fine Flanders lace, and rarely employed at the useful task of wiping its wearer's nose.

Maria Beatriz, having given me every opportunity to admire her appearance, now gazed at me. She was a little apprehensive, I thought, as she waited for my verdict. I gave it very gladly and of course it was favourable. Happily, she turned herself all the way around so that I might enjoy her every aspect. I asked where she had been hiding this splendid dress. I could not help entertaining the rather mean thought that when, in the darkest days of winter, we three were resolving to sell off some of my fine clothes to get food I could not remember anyone mentioning that there was such a resource as this dress waiting in Maria Beatriz's wardrobe. But she cleared that question up by telling me she had rented it from a dressmaker in the Rossio, that it had arrived last night and must be returned there 'after the occasion'.

'What occasion?'

I really had no idea what she meant. She didn't answer me immediately. Now it was her turn to examine me closely. I shifted a bit under her gaze. I was not at my best, I knew it. I had on my plainest, most threadbare suit and my shirt had not been washed since . . . I could not put a date to it, some long time ago certainly and it was really quite unclean. On the other hand, I thought, why should I be primped and painted just because Maria Beatriz chose to be? What I was wearing exactly matched the dreariness of the day, whereas she was seriously out of step with it.

'Have you forgot Bento Ferreira's wedding feast?' she said.

Of course I had! Since my old garret-mate had invited me to it, I had spent one week of sunshine running about the Baixa selling everything I had in my bag, and another drenched in rain, lamenting the change in fortune, feeling myself lucky if I could unload a single image in ten hours of peddling. As for Bento – I had forgotten his very existence.

'Surely you won't disappoint our poor Bento?'

Of course I wouldn't! And I was suddenly so pleased to find that a day that had appeared utterly barren in prospect was now crammed full of possibilities. I did doubt, though – a glance at the rain-smeared window confirmed my fears – that we could get to the feast without nearly drowning on the way, and arriving among the other guests in a state of bedraggled confusion, which would hardly speak well for Bento's side of the wedding party. Maria Beatriz told me that I should not worry, that our landlord Montesinhos, who was also invited, was master for the day of one of those covered carriages called *caleches*, drawn by a pair of mules, and had promised to let her ride in it with him. She was sure that he would not object to my squeezing into the carriage too and, in fact, she added, she hoped I would keep as close to her as I could during the afternoon, at any rate whenever Montesinhos was near her. Of course I straight away wanted to know what she meant by saying that, but she would only promise, with a charming but somewhat anxious smile, to tell me at some point during the rest of the day.

I had about twenty minutes spare until the *caleche* would be ready at the front door and I used it as best as I could, washing my hands and face, changing into what remained of my better clothes, and so on. I think only my wig truly let me down after this transformation: a coarse affair made of horsehair, it was all I had left to me since that triumph of Monsieur Baye's art, my best periwig indeed, had been exchanged for three good beef steaks a month or so ago.

Senhor Montesinhos looked a little blank when I joined him and Maria Beatriz in the *caleche*, and I surmised that she had not told him that I would be coming with them. I had no idea why she had kept quiet so, but in any case there was clearly enough room for me and, as he had no reason to keep me out, Montesinhos made the best of it. We were a fairly comfortable, cheerful trio as we jolted over the terrible streets towards our goal. The feast was to take place in the house that had been left to Bento's bride by her previous husband. When we got near it, I couldn't help but give a cry of astonishment. I had no idea into what good fortune my old room-mate had strayed. The house was surrounded, as the better class of dwellings are in Lisbon, by a high wall, and this wall went on and on, bordering the street for perhaps thirty yards, or a little less.

Montesinhos nodded at my surprise. 'Old Machado was rolling in money,' he told me.

Vicente Machado was the name of the previous husband. I shook my head; I was still surprised by the scale of this house. I could barely see its roof above the wall.

'He was one of the few Old Christians in the jewellery trade,' Montesinhos further explained.

It says something for how far I had grown into Lisbon ways of thinking, both that I had no reason to ask him what he meant by that, and that, in knowing, I felt no surprise at all. Machado, as an 'Old', or as many would say a 'true', Christian, would naturally have a strong advantage among the pious wealthy of this city against his 'New' Christian competitors. These latter were descended from the Jews who had been driven into Portugal from Spain at the end of the fifteenth century and, in order to be allowed to stay, were required to attest that they had changed their religion to Christianity. However, even after two hundred years and more, there was still much prejudice against these *conversos* and lately the situation had been growing even worse. Even I, lost in my menial tasks in the streets, knew of this. The fathers of the Inquisition, encouraged by a king who, as my Uncle Felix had told me once, 'liked nothing better than to see a heretic burn before he supped', had been increasing their menaces against the *christãos novos*, both rich and poor. For the latter waited the dungeons and the stake. But the former did not get off scot-free either. Only the other day the news had spread through the Baixa that a very wealthy New Christian banker called Aquilino Branco had fallen foul of the Inquisitors. Half his wealth, including a great house that partly fronted on the Rossio and his *quinta* in Sintra, had been taken by the Dominican fathers. Most of the rest was confiscated by the state in return for allowing him and his family to leave the country unharmed.

Dismissing these sombre thoughts as best I could, I got down from the carriage and went to hand Maria Beatriz to the pavement. But I found that Montesinhos had got there before me, and was already doing the honours. I noticed that he gave me an odd kind of glance as he was helping our friend to get down, a mixture of triumph and prickliness, and altogether not the sort of look I was accustomed to getting from our genial landlord. We three hurried towards the gate. We spoke our names to a tall fellow who was standing there, holding above his head one of the then newfangled umbrellas – newfangled in Lisbon at any rate. He consulted a list he was holding in his hand, and then bowed us past him and into the passage, which at last discovered to us Bento's new home.

It was built, we could see, even in this tearing rain, in the pleasing old Moorish style of the country, with a great inner garden surrounded by buildings on all four sides. This way of constructing a house was perfectly adapted of course to the warm days of spring and the hot months of summer in which the fortunate inhabitants were likely to want to spend as much time in the open-air as possible. In the present conditions though this great inner space was somewhat redundant. We sped across the ground, with hardly a glance at all the magnificent plantings around us.

We reached the door on the other side, breathless and wet. We went inside the building. Maria Beatriz was immediately scooped up by a lady who she seemed to know and taken away to effect whatever repairs to her face and apparel the getting hither had necessitated. Montesinhos and I were left to ourselves and, though he attempted a continuation of the frosty address with which he had favoured me at the side of the *caleche*, really he could not keep it up. We knew each other too well (though not, it was to turn out a few weeks later, quite as well as I had thought). He was my easygoing landlord, I his decent and generally solvent tenant. How could we keep up a show of unfriendliness between us?

Besides, we had other things on our mind. We looked around us, marvelling at the scale and sumptuousness of what we saw – and remember we were only in the anteroom of one of these buildings. There were three others as big and, for all we knew, as handsomely furnished.

'*Merda*,' sighed Montesinhos, releasing his customary vent of garlick and decay as he did. 'That Bento has done shitting well for himself.'

I don't recall much about the wedding feast that followed, a lapse to which my old failing on these sociable occasions – the taking on board of too much wine, too quickly – no doubt contributed. I think I was introduced to Bento's bride – I must have been – but truly I do not remember it, nor anything about the fortunate lady, not even her Christian name. A little after the dishes had been cleared away, the tables were taken from the room, and a small orchestra began to play for the guests to dance. At this point several Portuguese gentlemen, evidently of the old way of thinking, removed themselves and their ladies from the proceedings. But more than enough were left to make the floor moderately crowded and certainly festive. Maria Beatriz – I am pretty sure in order to forestall a like invitation from Senhor Montesinhos – proposed that we take a turn about the room. As we danced, she confided to me why she was anxious not to find herself alone with Montesinhos. Astonishingly, it seemed the landlord had lately conceived a romantic interest in her and had actually asked her to think of him as a possible husband.

'That is absurd,' I said, very shocked at the news.

'I know. I have lived in his house for so many years and there has been nothing between us until now. But he feels he is getting on in life and you know his wife died years ago. Since my husband did the same – well, he says it is ordained.'

'I mean it's absurd that such a common fellow as he should dare to even think of making you his bride. How could he?'

I was very much on my mettle at this point. I took a truly familial interest in Maria Beatriz's fate and it seemed the height of impertinence for a scrubby sort of a landlord to propose himself in marriage to a lady such as Mr Hutchinson's daughter. At this distance I have no idea why I thought like this. Montesinhos was approaching his beloved with certainly much more in the way of fortune to offer her than Bento had to win his bride – and I had applauded Bento's daring for doing this and rejoiced in his success. And yet I could not seem to extend such generous thoughts to that same Montesinhos, who, if these things are important, certainly had the advantage in matters of face and form over my old roommate (always leaving aside his breath). Also, since I was by a good few years Maria Beatriz's junior, it was really the height of impertinence for me to carry on like this as if I was an elder brother or a father with the right to object to suitors on her behalf. I suppose that I thought unconsciously that, since she lacked a brother, and as her father was a poor, impotent, sickly gentleman who could not speak up for himself, it gave me an authority that was otherwise lacking.

We were passing near the orchestra now and because of the amount of noise they were making whatever Maria Beatriz was saying in my ear was somewhat lost to me. It seemed to be to the effect that Montesinhos had told her it would be 'safer' for her to join with him in marriage. Over her shoulder I saw the landlord watching us from a corner. Her he looked at with yearning, me more like with loathing. I did not think he had a right to show either emotion so plain and, forgetting that I had meant to get Maria Beatriz to tell me why the landlord thought she would be any more 'safe' under his protection than her father's – or my own – I asked her, as we drifted away from the band, whether she would want me to have a stern word with him, to order him to cease from bothering her. She told me she would never speak to me again if I did, which pretty much cancelled that line of action, and put me in my place besides. I concentrated thereafter on our dancing, and on how pleasant it was to face Mr Hutchinson's daughter so close, particularly to have the chance to study again her wonderful eyes.

I say 'study again' as if I had not seen Maria Beatriz for months instead of nearly every day through the whole of this winter. Yet it took us getting out of our normal round and usual surroundings for me to realise again what loveliness lay in her face and so I watched her eyes with such care and so gratefully as we hopped and glided about that room, interweaving with other couples, and occasionally touching each other's hands. Enjoying myself so much, I quite forgot the existence of Senhor Montesinhos and his ridiculous aspirations until he came to claim his right to dance with her. I thought of telling him to go to hell and let us alone, but there was such a beseeching look in his dark eyes that I could not do it. In any case I think Maria Beatriz out of pity would not have let me. I stepped back from my partner, surrendering her to our landlord with all the grace and friendliness I could muster.

As I've said, not much else remains to me of that afternoon when we feasted Bento and his wife. We three, Maria Beatriz, Montesinhos and I, stayed pretty late, long after the happy couple had left the room. In fact I think only the incapable drunkards were left by the time we went. Outside, we found the rain had stopped, though from the damp feel of the air it did not look as if it would hold off for long. Montesinhos had ordered our carriage for the homeward journey and so we went back to the Rua do Parreiral in the same way we had come from it, except that Maria Beatriz, after a cunning manoeuvre on the part of the landlord, was now sitting between us. As we jolted over the wretched streets I felt the warmth of her thigh pressing against mine. I was not, however, such an infatuated ass as to think she was meaning anything by this except that she was trying to remove herself from whatever unwelcome pressure Montesinhos was exerting on her other side.

When we arrived at the house there was some difficulty in getting the landlord to desist from his announced intention to conduct Dona Maria Beatriz to her door. It was pointed out to him that I would have to pass her apartment on the second floor to reach my own on the fourth, and so it was more logical that I should do the conducting rather than he. When this did not quite seem to defeat his resolution, Maria Beatriz added that she had asked me to stop off at her rooms because her father had requested she bring me in to see him when we got home. It was not true, either that she had asked me, nor I dare say that Mr Hutchinson had made any such request – I understood he was far too much under-the-weather just now for visitors – but she held steady to her story and in the end the landlord gave a defeated shrug and stamped off to his own quarters below the stairs.

Maria Beatriz and I hurried up to the second floor, giggling together at her narrow escape. Now I think of it, this seems such a mean thing to have done. While I hate even now to say anything critical of Maria Beatriz, I suppose Montesinhos was owed at least the respect due to a man who, though not fortunate enough to gain his lady's favour, had offered himself to her in an honourable and open fashion. We could have dealt with him better than by sniggering behind his back and running away from him. Or lying to him. I certainly include myself in the indictment. Montesinhos had been a good landlord to me; I lived really on his bounty. He could have got much more in rent even for the poor room I lived in than he obtained from me. He had not even tried to bring in a replacement for Bento as yet. I lived alone in the space that previously contained two tenants and yet I still paid the same as before.

However, at the time I was troubled by none of these thoughts. I suppose I can blame it on the universal excuse for bad behaviour. Maria Beatriz, I think, was a little drunk and I was much more than that, though the cool evening air on our journey home had calmed me somewhat. Still I had definite plans to go up to my bed and sleep off the rest of my inebriation, and was just bidding my companion a fond farewell on the second floor when she said that she wanted me to come in and sit with her for a while, that there were matters she wanted to talk to me about. Of course I could not refuse her, nor when I thought about it did I want to. I had liked her company so much this afternoon, and I was happy that I should continue to enjoy it. I was only fearful that the muzziness in my head would make me a feeble guest, and that I would not play a proper part in this talk she wished to have with me.

While Maria Beatriz went into the back of the apartment to see how her father did, I waited in the sitting room. I heard the low murmur of her voice and then, though I had to strain to hear them, her father's faint answers. It occurred to me suddenly that she must never know when she quitted their apartment for any length of time that he would still be alive when she returned. This was a sufficiently sharp and sombre thought to clear my brain of all the muddle and frivolity that the wedding feast had put into it. I sat myself down on my usual chair and looked across at the empty one where Mr Hutchinson used to sit when we were enjoying a bottle and a chat. I looked across at the other empty chair, by the window, where Maria Beatriz would sew and listen to us and smile to herself at our nonsense. I felt a horror rise in me, as if I was the only survivor of a terrible plague or a massacre that had taken away my best friends and left me desolate. Yet this was nonsense. I had just been listening to Mr Hutchinson's voice, and here was his daughter, alive and serenely beautiful, and standing now before me. I stood up, and asked her how her father did. She sighed and shook her head. Then said, 'It's of him I wish to talk.'

She asked first if I wanted wine, but it was my turn to shake my head, saying I'd had enough. Yet I was thirsty, and she went and poured me a glass of water from the pitcher that stood near her sewing-table. When I had drunk it, she motioned me to sit back in my chair and took her father's seat opposite me. She stared for a while into the empty grate, then in a voice so low at first that I had to strain to hear it, said, 'There is something weighing on his mind.'

I said that I had no doubt there was, nor what it was, considering that he was frail and old and that the inevitable consequence of having lived a long life would soon overtake him.

'It's not just that he thinks about dying. Of course he does. But it is something more than that. As if there was something left undone, or unsaid . . .' Her voice trailed away into uncertainty.

She sat thinking for a bit. Then, 'Yes, that's it. He has left something undone. What could it be?'

I suggested that the best course of action would be for her to ask him what it was.

'I have. He won't tell me.'

She sat for a moment or two more in silence, then lifted her entrancing eyes to study me across the room. 'You talk to him all the time. You are closer to him than anyone just now. Do you know what is troubling him?'

Of course I did. I recalled the conversation Mr Hutchinson and I had shared that day on which I had made my famous sale of São Damião for thirty shillings in the Rua do Oiro. Back in the house, he had told me, and I had believed him, that what he feared was not death itself but that he would be leaving Maria Beatriz penniless. I was sure it was this that was still afflicting him, and so it was in my grasp to clear up the mystery for her. But I hesitated to do it. I decided that it was really up to Mr Hutchinson to explain this to her. I supposed he had not done so till now out of feelings of pride, or of its close companion, shame. It is, I am sure, a wretched emotion to feel death approaching and know that one will leave one's dearest unprovided for – a terror I shall never know, thank God, for my sole descendant is well able to take care of himself. I resolved now that I would not leave Maria Beatriz in ignorance until her father was no more, but that for a little while longer I would keep Mr Hutchinson's secret.

'As I said, I can only think that he is finding death a fearful prospect and the thought of it lies very heavy on him.'

'But why?' said Maria Beatriz, looking truly perplexed. 'Padre Luís' – she meant the parish priest – 'will give him the sacraments when the time comes. He will die in the bosom of the church he loves. His life hereafter is assured. What is there to fear?'

I watched her for a moment, hoping to see some sign of irony in her eyes, but there was nothing like that. Her gaze was limpid and sincere, only – as I have said – discovering some bewilderment at her father's lack of serenity. So I shook my head and said I supposed that even the sturdiest Christian might find himself dismayed as the awful prospect of extinction approached – Jesus

Christ himself had had his moment of doubt on the Cross, after all.

This powerful example seemed to persuade her. Having resolved the puzzle of her father's behaviour, concern about it seemed to drop away from Maria Beatriz. Perhaps she had decided that she was unfairly afflicting me with her despondency. In any case, she became quite merry now. She wanted me to tell her about my own life.

'For you know, Adam, I see you almost every day and yet I think you keep many secrets from me.'

This said with a light and coquettish air which made her seem years younger in my eyes than she really was, almost my contemporary, and so someone I could easily confide in. She asked me how my family did and I mentioned my last letter from home. My mother and sisters' circumstances were reported as still being straitened. My father's old clerk, Mr Marks, had sent them a note for ten pounds at Christmas, which was most kind of him, but he could not be expected to do more than that for, my mother wrote, according to Marks trade in London was still slow as the effects of the great Bubble's breaking continued to be felt and demand for the kind of fine goods that he specialised in almost at a standstill.

The good news though was that my mother made no mention of my dismissal from my uncle's service; indeed she had added a postscript asking me to convey her very best to all her relations in Lisbon. So presumably those relations had either not written to her since I had been discharged from the firm, or else they were being discreet about the fact, for which I certainly gave thanks.

'But have you not told your mother you were let go? Oh, Adam, you must tell your mother. Think how she would feel if she was to hear it from anyone else.'

I wondered at how Maria Beatriz had unerringly launched her enquiry against one of my weakest points. Indeed my conscience had been pestering me for weeks at how deplorably I had been treating my family. I explained that I had hoped all this time to have had good news to tell them, and to be able to say that I had left my uncle's service because I'd been offered a better position elsewhere. It was the reason I had clung on in Lisbon after my uncle had dismissed me. I could not go back to England – to my mother – with my tail lodged so firmly between my legs. If I'd been taken on as only a low clerk in some ordinary merchant's house, I would have been able to gild the situation to make it seem like a desirable promotion, so that my mother should feel that her son, her beloved offspring – and incidentally her only hope of rising again in the world – was staying the course and that his future still looked hopeful. But I did not know how to make the existence of a seller of holy images in the streets seem anything like that, without lying outrageously to her, which I could not do. So I had taken refuge in silence, which I knew was a sort of lie but was the best I could manage.

Maria Beatriz listened to this sympathetically but still insisted that I should write the whole truth to my mother and I said, after some show of resistance, that I would. Probably. She studied me in silence for a few moments. I think she decided then it was unfair for her to be pressing me on a subject that obviously caused me some pain. It was not her fault, of course, that the next topic she raised also had the power to make me unhappy. For she asked me what had happened to that girl I had told her about once who I had seemed to be so enchanted with – 'Gabriella? Was that her name?' It surprised me for a moment that she did not know this story; certainly I had explained matters to her father when I had challenged him to tell me what those bad old words of his meant. But I saw that, no doubt from delicacy, he had kept this distasteful narrative from her. I was certain that I would not be any less correct. She should not learn about 'rump-sticker', etcetera from me.

But – I don't know how it was, but all at once my eyes filled with tears, and I wasn't sure then, nor am I now, whether it was for Gabriella I wept or for my mother or myself. All of them, I suppose, and for my poor old friend Hutchinson too. Maria Beatriz certainly assumed it was the first-named I was mourning. She leaned forward and took my hand. She asked me again how I had come to lose this special girl. And now, feeling so close and easy with her as I did, and perhaps also feeling a spurt of annoyance at Mr Hutchinson and all he had cost me, I decided it would be too fastidious to keep the reason from her. And so I told her almost everything of how quoting Mr Hutchinson's antique speech had lost me the friendship of the Lowthers and my chance at Gabriella, only refraining from mentioning the last and most deadly of the poisons her father had poured into my ear: the pipkin vent, in fact. However, by the time I'd finished she knew enough to see by how much the old man had injured me.

Looking up, expecting to see by her expression that she was sharing my indignation at her father's behaviour, I was surprised to find what looked very like the beginnings of a smile upon her lips, and that in her eyes as she watched me was an expression I could not quite define, and which I was sure only the fact that we had so recently been talking of my mother made me at first sight want to call 'maternal'. In any case, as soon as she saw I was looking at her, she composed herself. Her expression was concerned and serious now. It was as if she had never given way to that curious grin. She told me how sorry she was that her father had been the cause of my losing Miss Lowther, and that she did not wonder if I was angry with him. Hearing this, I felt quite a revolution in my previous dark, accusing thoughts. I said that, no matter what had befallen me from my connection with Mr Hutchinson, I did not regret it for one moment, that I loved him, that I thought I had learned from him too, not least how to face up to age and infirmity and – until this last sad illness – deal with them with a robust unconquered spirit.

I'm fairly sure I didn't exactly mean it for the purpose, but such words were the surest way to Maria Beatriz's heart. She told me she was so glad to hear this. That she had always believed that her father was worth much more than the world seemed to estimate him. That she thought he was a great man who had never received his just deserts. I must say I could not go along with her quite so far as this, but I didn't quibble, at least not out loud. In fact, I think I nodded and murmured that it was so, there was no doubting it. We talked on – I cannot remember what about. Many things. We laughed about some of them, some made us a little thoughtful and sad. And all the time, invisibly, without me at least really knowing it, little tendrils of sentiment and affection, and of desire too, were growing between us, reaching out, clasping us one to the other.

I said at last that I thought it must be growing late. Perhaps I should go up to my room? But Maria Beatriz pointed out that it was not so late as I thought, there was still a glimmer of light in the sky, I could stay for a little while longer, surely? She suggested again that I take some wine, just to speed me on my way if I thought I must go, and this time I agreed. She got up. Politely I did the same. We were standing a few feet apart, looking at each other. Who moved first? I like to think it was me; it was my place after all to move first. But perhaps it was she. In any case, in a moment we were in each other's arms. We kissed on the lips. We drew back, looking at one another, both I suppose alarmed at what we had done. But thrilled by it too.

We kissed again. Then she took me by the hand and drew me along the corridor beyond the living room. She opened a door, she led me into the little room where she slept. She placed the candle upon a small table, and left me there, I supposed to make a last visit to her father, who lay on the other side of the corridor.

I looked around me. It was the smallest of rooms. A bed and a table filled it. The enormity of what was happening began to dawn on me. And it also came to me that I had found myself in an archetypal Runaway circumstance. That is, my boldness had raised me to a height that I was sure my courage would not sustain. My next move – *his* next move – would certainly be to fly from the scene, and already I felt my legs tensing, ready for the word from his brain. But before that other Adam could really intrude himself upon this marvellous, unbelievable occasion, Maria Beatriz was back. She closed the door behind her. Told me that her father was sleeping. Came to me then. She let me – me, Adam Hanaway – undress her. At least start to undress her, for I soon got quite lost between her laced stomacher and her petticoats. After that she took over the operation, indicating with a tender smile that I should perform the same upon myself. When we were both naked, she blew upon the candle. The flame flickered and went out. In the darkness we fell upon the bed and, while defeated Runaway slunk off into the night, I at last divested myself of my so long unwanted virginity.

A prodigious surge of triumph, and a sense of having moved to a higher, better sphere of manhood – that is what I mostly remember of that first act of coition. As to how the experience was for Maria Beatriz, I really could not say. I'm not sure I even thought about it at the time. It must certainly have struck her that it was brief, under a minute, I fear. But happily, after a short interval, I was fit to engage with her again. And after that . . . but I am resolved not to turn this into a prolonged fit of old man's boasting. We lay with each other often enough so that I could lose at last my fatal self-consciousness, and be to her a proper, loving bed-fellow. Then came all the tender sighs and murmured endearments and long delightful caresses that had been signally absent from our first encounter. And at last, for the first time, I experienced that delectable state of being where one has so mingled oneself with a woman, and for so long, that one is no longer quite certain where the female half of this languorous equation ends and the masculine begins.

On and off, between fits of love, we both slept, and then I fell into a deeper, longer slumber than before. I awoke at last to find her looking down at me, and stroking my face. She told me in a whisper that I must be gone soon, that it was almost dawn and that her father always woke about this time and liked her to go in to see him. I started to scramble out of the bed, but she said I need not hurry by that much: her father would probably not emerge from his room for an hour or so to take his seat in the living room, and perhaps not even then for lately he had taken to spending whole days in his bed. So I dressed myself in a leisurely fashion, breaking off from time to time to kiss my love upon the lips. She was wearing a nightshift with a deep neckline that showed almost all of her breast to me. It seemed wonderful that I had lain my head there, and touched her there all this night.

When I was done, she led me to the door, looked out of it just in case the improbable had happened and her father was out of his room, then took me through the living room, and the parlour. At the front door, she clasped me in her arms and I put mine tightly about her. We stood like that for a long, loving moment. Then she unlatched the door, peered out into the corridor, and with a press of her hand upon my arm sent me out there. I looked back for a last glimpse at my beloved, but the door was already closed. I sped silently up the stairs, wig and shoes under my arm, praying that I would not meet anyone before I gained my room. The little African girl might for once have turned out early to begin on her duties. Or – horrors! – Senhor Montesinhos, perhaps after a sleepless night grinding over his ill success with Maria Beatriz, might have come upstairs to tell me his troubles.

But nothing like this occurred. I passed the rest of that day in a delirium of happiness. What I thought or did during it I cannot remember, nor at the time I think was I any clearer about my state of being. It was all incoherent, it was all wonderful. I surmise that I felt the usual misplaced beginner's pride in having done what the vast majority of my fellow-creatures had already achieved. I hope I spent a little time during my strutting and self-applauding to think of the lady who had consented to make me so happy – whether she was well, whether she regretted what we had done, whether she was easy in her mind at how our relationship had so marvellously changed. But I daresay I didn't. I was full of Maria Beatriz, but it was all sensual repletion: I thought of her body, her hair, her scent, the feel of her in my arms . . . I believe I am making this up now. Truly, if I concentrate, all I can remember is a joyful daze.

Evening came. I did not go to eat at the Hutchinsons'. I waited until I was pretty certain that the old man would be settled in his room. She opened the door a second after my first discreet knock. In her eyes I saw something that I almost thought might be a look of relief. I didn't know what it was doing there. I supposed it was because she was glad I had waited until now before coming to her. She drew me quickly into the parlour, closed the door. We kissed. She led me to the table, where she had set out a dish of cold meats and pettitoes for me. I said I wasn't hungry, which was the truth, but then had to confess I couldn't say when I had last ate. So she made me sit at the table and insisted I swallow a few mouthfuls. She poured me a glass of wine, then sat opposite me, watching me intently as I ate. She was wearing a dress I hadn't seen before, black and gold with a stomacher of dark-purple. It made her look very 'foreign', sultry. I could not keep my eyes from her breasts, which were pushed up high by the stomacher. I began to sweat. I was so hungry for her – and not at all for the food. I got up at the same time as she did. We positively ran through the living room, into the corridor beyond, and were in her room in seconds, our hands roaming all over each other, and pulling the clothes off our bodies.

That night was different from the first. Less of it was spent in love-making, though when we did come together our raptures were even more thrilling than before, for we were able to take our time, and explore each other's intimate places and desires much more inventively. There was no longer the sense, for me at least, of breaking in through a castle wall, with great exertion and lusty shouts, to get at the treasure within. Much more of mutual pleasuring and dalliance and laughter. It was very fine that second night, and even now it makes me glow to think of it. But what I remember most is that we spent long hours during it – touching each other certainly, holding on to each other – but really doing nothing much else than talk. And I think it was the first time in my life that I talked at length to an intelligent, sympathetic woman. The fact that at the same time my hand was upon her naked breast and hers was placed upon my unclothed thigh certainly added to the novelty and enjoyment of the situation. But it was the talk that mattered.

So in this way the night wore away. I left her bed without prompting as dawn began to show itself, and once more tiptoed up to my room, if anything feeling more satisfied and exhilarated than I had after the first night in her bed. Again I slept a long, deep sleep, longer than I'd wanted to for I had told Maria Beatriz last night that it was time I got out to the streets again and started selling for my living once more. I had not done that since the week before Bento's party, and that now seemed to me quite a distant epoch. I had said to my sweet mistress last night that I hoped I had not lost my skill as a peddler and she told me she thought it was most unlikely. So, when I rolled over and saw by the battered old clock that my old room-mate had bequeathed me that it was already quite late in the day, I gave a low groan of disgust.

The problem then was that I could not stop myself from groaning. Something was afflicting me. I felt it first, as I probed about in my being, as a physical ache, whose centre was located somewhere in my breast. Then it moved to my stomach and I thought I wanted to vomit. I scrambled out of bed and over to the pot, which I crouched before, holding my head so that I could discharge myself into the receptacle with the least risk of missing it.

But nothing happened. The disturbance had now moved on from my belly and was now – I didn't know where: my heart, my hands, shoulder blades, ankles? It wasn't anywhere as a physical symptom, I realised at last. It was in my brain, and what I wanted to excrete from myself was not bad food or too much wine – we had hardly drunk any last night – but the memory of what I had been doing, and with whom, all through that night and the one before. It was Maria Beatriz that I wanted to vomit forth; and her loving ministrations, which were the source of the pain and sickness I had felt since I opened my eyes this morning.

It is so hard for me to write these words. And from my present vantage point – thirty or more years older than she was then, and sixty years past what I was – my attitude seems utterly mysterious. Women who are of Maria Beatriz's age when I knew her seem to me the most delightful of creatures when they are handsome – and certainly she was that. They are, I see, in their prime indeed, and vastly to be preferred to the silly young jades who are so full of themselves and their pretended charms. But I am talking of how I was then. Now instead of sweet caresses and the joys of lying with her, I could only think this cursed morning of – breasts that sagged too much, arms that were too soft above her elbows, thighs that in my memory grew to become massive and disgusting like a hog's hams, breath that was not sweet sometimes when she yawned, a sleeping face glimpsed in the moonlight that was . . . was just *old*. As old as my mother's face! A dreadful notion. I seriously thought of returning to my place at the chamber pot when first it occurred to me. I had allowed myself to be trapped into bed with someone as old as that.

This is what I came to believe in explanation of my behaviour: that the guiding principle of my being then was a fear of looking ridiculous. There are, I suppose, few more puny motives for one's conduct than that, but I suspect it is common enough. When young, we have little enough to offer the world except our physical comeliness and our pride. And the pride is easily hurt for so little supports it. In my case, the disasters and upheavals of the last year had produced a particularly chronic example of the phenomenon. On this wretched morning, above everything, I was thinking that I could not bear the world to know that my mistress was old and wrinkled and flaccid. I could not stand to look so ridiculous as that.

That was the explanation that served me for a number of years. But I still went round and round on the matter, looking perhaps for more charitable reasons for what I felt, and mainly I think because I could hardly bear to remember how I behaved then to a person who I so admired and respected and whose memory had stayed green and luminous for me over all the many years since I knew her. Long after I left Maria Beatriz and all else in Lisbon far behind me, I came to wonder if the repulsion I felt that morning wasn't so much for her as for the situation I had got myself into. That I knew in my gut that I was too young and, frankly, too inadequate a man then to take on board a complicated, challenging, older woman. Not for any long-term prospect anyway; and that to get out of the situation a rapid Runaway escape was what I resorted to, disguising it from myself by making it appear as a concern about breasts and thighs and breath and so on. It was *me* who failed to come up to the mark indeed, and not she at all.

When I woke this morning I'd wanted to get out of my room as soon as possible so I could go back to work. But now I wished I could stay in it all day, so that I might avoid the risk of meeting Maria Beatriz. I did linger for hours, but at last hunger and boredom drew me forth. I went down the stairs with the same care not to make a noise as I had shown when I came up them at dawn. I couldn't help reflecting that I had crept along that last time from the impeccable motive of wanting to protect my mistress's reputation. Now it was to evade her.

I got down as far as the second floor. I went past the Hutchinsons' door not daring even to breathe. Had she been waiting at it, ears attuned to the least disturbance of the air beyond her door? Were her senses sharpened by a presentiment that things were not right with me? Oh, I sometimes wonder if everything would have turned out very different if only we hadn't seen each other that morning. An hour or two walking about the streets, clearing my head, might have put everything into a much better perspective. It was probably true that my time of rapture with Maria Beatriz was near over. I knew enough from talking to other boys at school and college who had taken mistresses that the first ardour can cool very fast. But I knew too that a steady period of fondness for the once-beloved can follow that more heady time. Passion can change into a friendship between two people – a friendship spiced with the memories of what they had been to each other as lovers. And, those aspiring gallants had explained to me, it might not only be in memory that these sports could still be enjoyed. A free afternoon, a rekindling of desire on either side, and the temple of Venus could once again be visited for a delightful hour or two. And, without the need to make every moment sublime and unsurpassed, very good entertainment could regularly be found between the sheets of the erstwhile love of one's life.

Into this easy, sociable, cynical phase, I say, my relations with Maria Beatriz might have moved – but, just as I was on the stairs leading down from the second floor, I heard her voice behind me, softly calling my name. Did she add 'darling' to it, or 'dear one'? I can't remember. It seems to me she did. I froze upon the stairs. She called to me again. She asked me if I had eaten yet. I had to turn to her, yet I knew I had no control over my face.

She read in one glance everything I was thinking, had thought, since I woke. Her countenance, that had been smiling down on me, now became rigid with shock. Her beautiful eyes clouded over, became opaque. They seemed sightless as if she was dead. I had done all this with a look.

I told her that I wasn't hungry. We looked at each other for a moment longer, then she nodded and turned back into her room. I went on numbly down the stairs. Outside the bright day mocked my unhappy mind. Indeed it was a beautiful day, the harbinger of many more to come. True spring had come at last to Lisbon. But not to me. I felt shrivelled, very cold; nothing could warm me. I plunged into the crowd in the Rua do Parreiral, let it sweep me along with it. We were all heading somewhere, I didn't know where. The road I lived on was usually more characterised by traffic, mules and carriages and so on, than by people. But now the latter had their dominion. It was a good-natured crowd, people calling out greetings as we went along. Even I was so saluted. Some hailing me as 'Senhor Hanaway', others 'Dom Adam' – to none of these friendly souls did I pay much attention. I only let them carry me with them. I think I nurtured briefly a hope that we were heading for the Tagus, for I wanted nothing more at this moment than to throw myself into it and let the waters close over me for ever.

However, it became clear that we were not now on course for the river. Unmistakably our path was directed towards the Rossio. I could hear music playing not far off, and the steady beating of drums. I wondered whether this heralded another of the devilish entertainments this town enjoyed so much and I would be witness yet again to some poor creature burning at the stake.

I did not think I would react as I had the first time. Indeed I remember all that – fainting, tears, confined to bed – with a kind of grim contempt. I remembered now that it was Maria Beatriz who had roused me at last from that state, she and Bento. She came to my room, almost to the top of the house, and sat with me, and talked to me until I was sane again.

Well then, I thought, I had better not get sick at the sight of charred flesh and screaming skulls this time, for I would have neither her nor Bento as kind attendants on me again.

But then it appeared I would have no need of them. From shouted conversations that I overheard, I discovered that the purpose of this surge towards the Rossio was not to roast heretics but to see the King review a regiment of his guards. Even though this would be my first, and as it turned out my only chance to view the celebrated Dom João V, the prospect did not attract me in the least. I had no time to spend on kings today. I tore myself away from the crowd and went down a little side street off the main road. In a moment I was back in the labyrinth of the Baixa. Behind me I could hear the tramp of feet and blare of trumpets as the soldiers were put through their drill, and the cheers of the crowd as they watched their sovereign going about his duties. Ahead of me though lay darkness and concealment in foul alleys and among multitudinous dungheaps, which were everything I wanted at that moment.

All afternoon I wandered through the city. I was in the Alfama at one time, at another I was climbing the hill of São Sebastião. Then I was walking among the neat streets and squares of the Bairro Alto. At one point I found myself at the beginning of the Rua Formosa where Gabriella Lowther lived. I had a wild notion to go to the house and ask after her, but luckily common sense kept me from doing that. Or perhaps it was shame. Having committed so great a folly with one of the women who had had the misfortune to pass through my life, I had not the spirit to invite another such disaster on the same day.

In the lower city again I stopped at a tavern – I don't remember in what street – and ate a slice of bread and drank some wine. I knew I had to go back to the Rua do Parreiral. I knew I would have to speak to Maria Beatriz at some point; after two such nights as we had spent together I could not ignore her. Yet I suddenly seemed to see it as a possibility. Maria Beatriz and I, living in the same house, never speaking, never acknowledging each other. I recalled that after some foolish muddle I had got myself into once with the Hutchinsons – I could barely remember the details now – I had done just that. Ignored them, hid from them. I could do the same now if I wanted.

Ah, but I argued with myself as I walked along, head down (I was out of the tavern by now, I was in the Rua dos Odreiros, not far from the Rossio; a crowd was streaming around me away from the square, so the great military review must be over), when I had behaved like that I had been a callow boy, a silly virgin, prone to the most ridiculous fits of misbehaviour. Surely I had progressed from there so that I need not insult any further a person I still admired so much and to whom, I had to acknowledge, I owed the kindness of releasing me from the virginity on which I blamed much of my earlier folly.

I suddenly remembered the cause of that original break with the Hutchinsons. The invitation I had slept through, the foolish, mendacious note I had sent to try to evade the blame of that fiasco. I actually stood still in the street, dumbfounded at this memory. The crowd flowed around me. I could not move. I seemed to see nothing but my own folly and disgrace. And I had come to this town a year ago with such hopes in my breast. I began to cry, the weak tears of self-pity. I had never felt so hopeless and alone.

So that when I first heard my name being called I thought it was a trick of the senses, that my brain, not being able to accept the state I had found myself in, was conjuring up imaginary companions to ease my sadness and loneliness. However, as my Christian name kept being repeated, and in the same shrill, girlish voice, I at last looked up to see if indeed this phantom attendant was something more corporeal than that. I saw that across the road, waving frantically at me, was a tall, dark young lady. For a moment my view of her was blocked by a passing cart, then she reappeared. She was trying to cross the road towards me, but kept getting pushed back to the side by the boisterous crowd. Out of pity I put myself out into the road and thrust across the current. As I got close to the girl, who had stopped waving and was now wearing a somewhat careworn smile, I recognised, under several streaks of dirt, the face of my cousin Nancy.

'Oh, Adam!' she cried out as I came up to her, and almost fell into my arms. I held her like that for a few moments and then put her a little away from me and looked her over. I saw that, even as she struggled to show her pleasure at finding me, she seemed prodigiously agitated. It occurred to me this might have been the first time in her cosseted life that she had ever been out alone and on foot in the streets of a city. I started straight away to ask her what she was doing here, but just then an impromptu band of small boys and girls, excited by the great military review, passed us banging on pots and pans and adding to the dismal racket with efforts to mimic the sound of trumpets.

I saw that we were standing just outside a tavern that I had been into myself a few weeks earlier in pursuit of a likely customer. I knew that it had private rooms for hire (by the half-hour) at a very moderate rate, and so I took Nancy by the elbow and steered her through the door of this establishment. The landlord, though he blinked somewhat at seeing my companion's obvious youth, proved amenable to renting a room on the second floor to me for a handful of *réis*.

'It's the military music,' he said understandingly over his shoulder as he led us up the stairs. 'It has that effect of warming a gentleman's blood.'

I wanted to throw him downstairs for his disgusting insinuations, but more than that I wanted to sit down somewhere quiet with my cousin and ask her what emergency had brought her into the streets. She could not out of propriety (a somewhat bitter joke in this place) sit in the public areas, so a private room it would have to be. When the fellow left us, after an almost intolerable degree of smirking and winking, I took her to a chair by the empty fireplace and sat her down. A bed invitingly occupied most of the rest of the paltry room – I ignored it and hoped very much it would not suggest to her what this space was ordinarily used for.

She took a moment to compose herself and then, with a wan smile, looked up at me, standing over her.

'Nan, do your parents know you are in the Baixa? Alone?'

'They wouldn't care,' she said bitterly.

'You know that isn't true.'

For a moment she looked as though she would start to cry. But then she seemed to hold herself more upright and put her head back like a soldier and I remembered that she had the reputation for being the braver and more resolute of my two cousins. There was a bowl and a towel on the table near the bed and I went and fetched them for her. She doused her face with the water and towelled herself dry and when she looked up she was the same doughty, bold-eyed girl that I had known from my visits to her father's *quinta*. I remembered then the last time I had set eyes on her, months ago, when I had walked over the hills to challenge my Uncle Felix's behaviour to me in the matter of the Gabriella fiasco, and had found myself turned away from the premises. Nancy had stood with me in the moonlight and talked to me at my time of trouble; now it seemed I had the chance to repay her, for her face once again seemed to have turned marvellously tragical.

'We are going home,' she said. 'We're going back to England. The packet sails tomorrow and we have taken rooms at an inn to wait for it. I could not bear to think of leaving without talking to you and so when they went to bed after luncheon I left the inn to find your lodging.'

'How did you know where I lived?'

She shrugged. 'I knew the Rua do Parreiral. I had heard you mention it – or it was my father or mother, I don't know. I thought it would be enough, but it is such a long road and it took me a while, asking people. Some of them were very impolite. But at last I spoke to a man who said he knew where the *mendigo inglês* lived and he brought me to the right house. What does "*mendigo*" mean?' she asked then curiously. 'I thought it was "beggar".'

'It doesn't matter. I am certainly not a beggar . . . So did you meet Montesinhos?'

'Who?'

'My landlord.'

'I suppose it was him. A pretty gentleman, with black hair and splendid eyes? But very foul breath? He said you had a room in his house. But he had seen you leave an hour or so earlier.'

'He could have let you sit in his parlour and wait for me,' I said, getting indignant.

'Mmm. Well, he didn't suggest it. He did not seem very pleased when I first mentioned your name, Adam.'

'Senhor Montesinhos and I are somewhat at odds just now over a certain matter. But it's of no consequence.'

'It cannot be very comfortable to be treated so by your landlord. Perhaps you should think of changing your lodgings?'

'Yes, perhaps I should. Nan!' I cried out, quite heatedly. 'What has happened? Why are you all going back to England?'

'Because my father has broken. Isn't that what they call it? He lost all his money – or rather, it was stolen by that beast Gomes. Do you remember him? We've got nothing now, Adam. We are as poor as you.'

I sank down on the edge of the bed, astonished at what I had just heard. Nancy looked at me as if she sympathised with my dismay, and seemed to wait for me to begin interrogating her. But I hardly knew where to start, or what questions to ask, and after a few moments she began considerately to supply me with the answers anyway. The trouble had broken over the family a few weeks ago. My uncle had used almost all his capital to purchase many bales of fine cloth from England that season in the belief that a string of forthcoming royal occasions – a betrothal, a baptism, a visit by one of the Queen's Austrian relatives – would create a vast demand for elegant suits of clothes among the *fidalgos*. I nodded when I heard this: I had never doubted that Felix was a shrewd businessman – except when he had cast away a fortune upon my father's promises – and the gentlemen of Portugal, be they never so impoverished, could always be relied on to sell a vineyard or a forest to make a figure at court.

The magnificent bales had come in through the front door of the customs house to actual applause from the other merchants gathered on the floor. Felix had enjoyed the tribute, but it had turned his mind too to other less happy matters. News of what was now filling his space on the Alfândega's floor was bound to spread. He feared the band of thieves who were known to operate in the customs house under official protection. He had suffered himself by their depredations, though never so much as had some of his unfortunate brother-factors. But now with such a valuable prize in his possession – could he really hold on to it? Truly he was a lamb, circled by wolves.

He talked over the problem with his trusted subordinate. To both his relief and his dismay, he found that Gomes very much agreed with his fears. Felix was satisfied that his concern was not just a result of a solitary lapse in nerve on his part, but unhappy to hear Gomes make very solid what had hitherto been only vague, unfocused dreads. The head clerk believed that the first period of maximum danger would lie in the weekend coming up, which on account of a religious festival stretched over three days. For this reason there would be far fewer guards and other personnel in the Alfândega in that period – though, Gomes acknowledged, given the usually larcenous nature of most of those officials, that might not be entirely a misfortune.

But not content with just raising the alarm, Gomes offered a remedy for the danger. In fact he volunteered to make up his bed at the Alfândega over the long weekend – and every night from now on, if his employer thought he should – so that he could keep an eye on the stock, until it was sold. Felix recounted this offer to the family at supper that night in the *quinta*. He got halfway through the story when he began weeping and could not go on till much later, for he was so overcome by gratitude for Gomes' loyalty.

When Felix came to the customs house on the Monday, to see how his head clerk was faring, Gomes was gone. So was the remainder of Felix's stock. Also, it was subsequently discovered, the sum of eight hundred pounds in Bank of England notes, which was held in the strongbox at Felix's office. The customs house investigators now sprang into action. According to an African worker who had been guarding a neighbouring location, Gomes and the cloth had left the Alfândega late on Sunday evening.

'They had to torture the black to make him say it,' Nancy reported. 'But not much. He was rather cowardly and they only put his feet in the fire twice.'

'Do you know the name of this negro?'

'The name? No, why should I? I remember the officer who came to tell us about it called him a "snowball" and said that he had worked sometimes for my father before now, but not this time, when he was robbed. So they had only flogged him and let him go.'

Suppressing fears that it was my poor friend Pedrito who had been used in this fashion, I begged her to go on. She said there wasn't much more to tell. The city authorities were alerted, enquiries began. Gomes was found to be missing from his usual haunts. A week or two later a message came in from a customs station near the border to the effect that a man answering his description had been seen on the road to Spain not long after the time he had been reported missing in Lisbon. He was riding a fine horse, with another behind him, and had attracted the attention of the customs officers because it was rare for a Portuguese, who was evidently not a *fidalgo*, to be so well mounted. However, not having at the time any reason to hold him, they had let him go on his way.

'And so we are ruined,' Nancy finished with a flourish that almost sounded cheerful. 'Father didn't only use his own capital to buy the cloth, he borrowed too. And he has no way of paying the people in England who supplied him with the cloth, nor his creditors here. It's all very grave. Men come to the house and sit with my father in his study and I can hear them asking him questions.'

'He is to be made bankrupt?'

'Not officially. The Factory sees that his difficulty is not entirely his own fault. It is because of thievery, and the blame is greatly on the part of the people here that they allow such crimes to go on in the Alfândega unpunished. Father has agreed to sell our house and everything and use it to pay what he can to his creditors. But that won't cover all his debts, and he has made promises to refund the rest whenever he can. We are to go back to England where he may have better opportunity to recover his position. But Mama says his shame will be known in London too, and no one will trust him. That horrible man has dealt us such a blow, Adam. What shall we ever do?'

She began to cry, and then bravely to fight against her tears. I really could not blame her for her distress. How melancholy this tale appeared. My blood boiled when I thought of the rogue Gomes. I thought I would kill him if ever I found him. I hoped he would one day be brought back to face trial for what he had done, and so that someone else at least would have the pleasure of taking his life at the end of a rope. But now, deep in the vast and populous land of Spain, with money – Hanaway money – to ensure him a pleasant and private retirement, it was not likely he would be seen in Lisbon again, or not for many years. I comforted my cousin as best I could, said that I hoped things were not so bad as they seemed, and that at least in London they would be better able to slip into a comforting anonymity, whereas here, with the Factory, and a community of a few hundred leading English families, it made it so hard to hide one's difficulties.

'That's true enough,' Nancy sighed. 'I know of at least two birthday parties I have not been invited to, and there is a ball next week at the assembly rooms that we weren't asked to. I saw you smile just then,' she said, tugging my sleeve in reproof. 'I'm not frivolous, you know, but there's not much else for a girl to do here except parties and so on, and I miss them. I shall be quite glad to go back to England.'

'And your mother? How is she?'

'Taking it better than I thought she would. She too says she is glad to have done with Portugal. We will be living mostly on an annuity she had from her own mother. It's not much. About three hundred a year. But it means that she is our breadwinner for the time being. And by the way, she has been ordering Father about lately. I can see she means to make the most of it.'

We both started to laugh at this, and I was struck by the good sense and temper that seemed to exist in my cousin very close to the surface, even at such a distressing time. She was about to tell me what condition her sister was in when there was a most violent beating on the door, followed almost instantly by its opening and the sight of the landlord's head looking around it. He was obviously disappointed that he had not caught his temporary tenants in any compromising or indecent positions but recovered sufficiently to instruct me that my time was up and did I want to take the room for another half-hour?

I wished very much I had strapped on my sword before coming out so that I could at least beat the knave with the flat of it for his impudence. Even unarmed as I was I thought very hard about going over and chastising him, and even took a step or two in his direction – but as Nancy pointed out, when we had regained the street, he was a 'big, nasty-looking fellow, Adam, and you could not be sure you would have beaten him'.

Arm in arm with my sensible cousin, I walked at ease down the Rua dos Odreiros. The crowds from the military review had melted away by now and, since all business in the neighbourhood of the Rossio had ceased in honour of the occasion, it was very quiet along this usually busy thoroughfare and we were able to talk without shouting at each other.

'You know,' she said at one point, 'we're all behaving quite well, considering. Except for Father. He is crushed.'

'Why did he not send for me?'

Though having said that, I could not for the moment think what particular consolation someone who was 'crushed' would find in my company. Indeed, at that moment I had a sudden dreadful thought that some kind of curse might be hanging over the entire Hanaway family when it came to business. Felix now had broken in all but name. My father had preceded him in disaster in an even more devastating fashion. Why on earth would Felix want to see his unlucky brother's unsatisfactory son at such a time?

'You *know* why Father cannot see you.'

'And that reason is . . .?' I ventured cautiously.

'Because he is so ashamed of how he treated you. He knows now that Gomes was cheating him all the time. Not just at the end. And that you were innocent of whatever it was he accused you of. And he knows he should apologise to you for that and for dismissing you – but he can't yet.'

'If I came to him now –?'

'No!' She said the word almost violently. 'He must be allowed to do this in his own time. Everything in his own time; that is what we have learned is best for him and so for us. He will try to make amends for what he did to you one day. Though not for a long while. But he has said he will explain to your mother what has happened, and apologise to her at least.'

We walked in silence until the road opened up into a square. There was a fountain in the middle of it, and it was so quiet here that we could hear the water falling back down on to the blue-tiled surround. I dropped Nancy's arm and turned her to me so I was looking down at her. Her dark, expressive eyes, gift of her Syrian mother, gazed back at me, curious as to what I had to say.

'Your father has no need to apologise to me. I failed him. I was a bad servant to him, Nan, and did not look out for his interests as I should have. Tell him from me that I hold no grudge against him. I think he was right to dismiss me, but not for the reason he did, for I never stole from him, though I know he suspected me of it.'

'Oh, Adam,' she said, putting out her hands to touch my

shoulders and then drawing me to her. 'That you should ever have had to say that.'

And she kissed me on the lips, an experience which – to my surprise – included my finding her tongue pressed quite deep inside my mouth.

When we were twenty yards from the inn's front entrance, she made me stop and we said our goodbyes. She told me that she was so glad she had found me, that she had been wretched before at the thought she would leave Lisbon and not see me. After all, she said, we are family, in spite of everything. I agreed with that, and we kissed each other tenderly but only as cousins should. I watched her tall, slim figure crossing the filthy road and heading for the inn. I too was very glad we had met again before it was too late, and I was particularly happy to know that my funny hoyden 'little coz' was growing into such an accomplished and comely young wo-man.

But when she was gone these tranquil, tender thoughts seemed to have gone with her. Certainly the images now in my brain seemed to have put on thirty years and more. No longer Nancy in all her young beauty, but the decidedly unjuvenile figure of Maria Beatriz reappeared before me. All that had happened, the muddle I had got into, the explanations that would have to be made, the arguments, the apologies: I felt overwhelmed both at what had gone before and what must lie in the future.

I walked very slowly back into the Baixa. Really, I wished my journey could have gone on for ever. But there was no helping it: at last I was in the Rua do Parreiral, then at the front door of Montesinhos' house. My plan was to sneak up to my room, just as I had sneaked down from it this morning, and stay up there until another day had dawned, when perhaps the prospect of explaining myself would appear less discouraging. However, I had as little success at trying to go up the stairs unnoticed as I had in coming down them. I had gone a few steps above the second floor when I heard the door open and a cool but not unfriendly voice say, 'Adam, can you come in here?'

I suppose I could have hurled an excuse over my shoulder and hurried on – but really I knew I had reached the limit today of making a fool of myself. So, with heavy heart, I turned round and went down the stairs again. She stood back to let me enter her parlour. When I had done so, she closed the door. We stood looking at each other. Then she smiled.

'I have been thinking, Adam,' she said.

I nodded. I thought I would do anything rather than say what I must say to her. I knew she would have to drag it out of me, word by word. It would be an ugly proceeding, for what woman can hear with equanimity that she has been cast off, dismissed from her lover's bed, abandoned?

'I have decided,' Maria Beatriz went on in the same calm, cordial tone, 'that we should not any longer behave with each other as we have for the past two nights. It is wrong,' she carried on, after I had made no greater contribution to the discussion than to gape at her. 'It is unfair to you. And not what I wish. And, above all, I fear it dishonours my father that . . . what has happened should have taken place under his roof.'

'We could go up to my room,' I said.

I felt like kicking myself. It was not at all what I had meant to say, and the last thing I believed I wanted.

On the other hand, I think it rather pleased Maria Beatriz to hear it. It certainly seemed to make her task less difficult.

'No, Adam,' she said. 'We can't.'

She rested a consoling hand upon my arm, then after a moment took it away. She sank down at the table and then murmured something that I could not hear. Indeed I was not sure it was a word she had uttered; it sounded more like a pitiful little moan, of distress perhaps, or pain. I sat down opposite her. She would not look at me. We sat in silence. I believe if either of us had begun to speak then we might have talked everything over candidly and without pretence, and however painful it might have been for one or both of us we would not have had between us that barrier made up of unsaid truths and evasions that we were to know for all the time that was left to us.

But neither of us, it seemed, was brave enough to speak the words that needed to be said. I felt very sad suddenly, and I knew I was mourning something. Not just the brief two nights we had spent in each other's arms, but the whole time of our knowing each other, our friendship – more, our partnership – seemed to be drawing to a close before my eyes. I reached out and touched her hand. She looked up. Her own eyes were filled with tears.

'Adam,' she said, 'I think you should leave here soon.'

I understood straight away she was not recommending that I should take myself up to my room. On the other hand I wasn't certain exactly what she was suggesting. At last I mumbled something about how, if she thought it would be improper for us to live under the same roof any more, then I knew of a room in the Travessa dos Fornos that was for rent at a price only a half again as high as what Montesinhos charged me for here.

'No. I mean that you should go home. Back to England. It's time you did.'

My first thought was that it was pretty hard to be expelled from a whole country because I had not fulfilled her expectations as a lover. But I soon saw in the way she looked at me, and how she stroked my hand as she spoke, that there was no desire to punish me.

'You've been here long enough. There's nothing more you can learn in Lisbon. You are only wasting your time. You should be with your own people and beginning your life as a serious man.'

I started on my old litany about how I did not wish to present myself before my family in a state of poverty that matched their own and certainly would not offer them any hopes of rising above it. I added that I could not see how, without even a little money behind me, I could do any better in London at securing a worthwhile employment than I had in Lisbon. To all this she offered no argument but only shook her head slowly. When I had finished, she thought for a moment, then said, as if she really was curious about my answer:

'And so you will be a seller of holy images in the streets here for your whole life?'

When she said this, the absurdity, even imbecility, of my present course came near to overwhelming me. What on earth *was* I doing here? How could I have lingered so long in this base condition? I muttered something about expecting that I would go home, of course, one day, some day, in the future . . .

'And why will that day be any different than tomorrow or the end of this month? Except that you will have wasted more time? Do you want,' she said, making now I think a great sacrifice of filial loyalty, 'to live a life as pointless as my father's has been? Do you want to look back one day on an existence as futile as that?'

'You are only saying this,' I burst out, coming close at last to what we should have been talking about, 'because you – you no longer –'

'Care for you? Do you believe that?'

And of course, looking at her, I knew I didn't. I sat in silence. I felt very tired suddenly.

'Truly I wish you could stay here,' she said then, not looking at me. 'If my wishes were what mattered, you would stay. But you can't, Adam, you know that. If you stayed much longer, you would despise yourself. And you would hate the people near you . . .'

'I could never hate you,' I said in a voice as low as hers. She looked up at me and there was a flash of pleasure in her eyes, and a disgusting little worm of lust invaded my brain as I speculated on how I could advance this moment into persuading her to take me once again to her little room along the corridor. But I fought the beast hard, and won the battle quite soon. I sat in silence, not moving, contemplating my situation, and the prospect Maria Beatriz's words had opened for me.

'Only, Adam,' I heard her say then, 'will you do one thing for me?'

I looked up. She was smiling at me again, but there was a fragility about the smile as if the slightest breeze of disapproval might blow it all away. I told her I would do anything she asked, and truly meant it. Did she wish me, for instance, to call out Montesinhos for his impudence in pestering her to marry him? She laughed at that as I had hoped she would.

'No, don't fight Montesinhos. It's just – I want you to stay.'

'You have just asked me to go,' I said, finding myself half mystified by her feminine indecision and half charmed by it.

'I mean – stay a little while longer. Until my father dies.' She shrugged, would not look at me. 'It's just – we have been like a family. The three of us. It would be unnatural that you should leave when he is on his deathbed. And then sometimes he seems a little stronger and he asks after you. Even though you hardly see him now, I believe it makes him happy to know that you are near.'

I gripped her hand again, and told her that I certainly would not leave for home before Mr Hutchinson's demise. Nor for as long after it as she thought she needed my presence. She said that she must learn to shift by herself in the world, and added that she knew we were not *really* a family, the three of us, that I had a proper family of my own waiting in England, and she had no right to demand from me any more than what I had first promised. And so we made the pact that evening, and I left her soon after, exchanging only a chaste kiss upon the cheek at the door, knowing that we were both now, as it were, upon a deathwatch. Our separate fates were bound up in the beat of an old man's heart, the breath passing into and out of ancient lungs, the opening of his eyes every morning on waking from death's imitator.

Mr Hutchinson

He had been born into a country at war with itself, and grown up in a time of revolution – old certainties thrown aside, new ideas thrusting to the fore. New people too. Many of those who had done well in the old days had been dismissed, replaced, were in exile. Everything seemed changed – and who was to know that a few short years would bring everything round again and the new people rendered in their turn as shattered and impotent as their adversaries were now?

But for the present they were doing very well. Among those enjoying the new dispensation that followed the King's defeat was Allen Hutchinson's family. Their leading representative was his Uncle John who had been a tremendous soldier for the Parliament, and had held the important town of Nottingham against the royalists for a number of years. He also had the distinction of being one of those gentlemen who had signed the King's death warrant – a fact that was not forgotten when Charles the Martyr's son came back to reclaim his throne. He was imprisoned, and died in captivity, a few years after the Restoration.

Still the memory of their great man lived on in the hearts of his family. If they had ever showed signs of slackening in their devotion, his redoubtable widow, Allen's Aunt Lucy, would have shifted heaven and earth to return them to their proper reverence. She was not content to keep this cult within the borders of her family either. For many years she was engaged in writing a biography of the dead regicide, which would explain to the world the quality of the man she'd had the great fortune to be married to. Given the temper of the times, it was hardly likely that this work would ever see the light of publication. Nevertheless, she stuck to her task, the number of pages grew, unwearyingly she built up her monument, not only to her husband but also to a time she remembered with such loyalty and devotion, when it was really thought that England could be changed, and men and women walk straight-backed in the light of Heaven, untroubled by the wicked machinations of kings and lords and bishops, and the distressing tendency of the English to grovel before all such creatures.

Allen Hutchinson frequently daydreamed in his youth of some-how penetrating to where his aunt kept this manuscript hidden and burning it up page by page. Lucy knew of his hatred for what she was doing; indeed she often remarked to Allen's face that she had two great enemies now in her life – one was Charles II and the other her sister's son. Allen returned this loathing, and with interest. Among his friends he was accustomed to referring to Lucy Hutchinson as 'that Puritan bitch *par excellence*'. It was the kind of thing that was bound to go down well among his particular set, composed mainly of the sons of the returning royalist gentle-men. He had gained admission to their company through the influence of another of his uncles, his mother's brother, Sir Allen Apsley, who had fought on the royal side in the wars, and now was a member of the obedient parliament of the new king's first years. In this heady period, Allen's set demonstrated their devotion to the monarch nightly by getting drunk, raising riot in the town, chasing whores and persecuting any poor soul they discovered on their rambles who they deemed to have an aspect too Puritan for them.

In the long years of his exile in Lisbon, Allen Hutchinson often wondered at this violent detestation of a sect and a people who after all were so fallen from their previous high position as to be hardly worth noticing, let alone persecuting. He came to the surprising conclusion that the main source of this rage was envy. After all, that generation of God-fearing English men and women had held tenaciously and fought hard for its convictions, however wrongheaded. His own believed in nothing, would fight for nothing, except for the right to drink and bluster and make a great noise in the world, mainly, the older Hutchinson decided, to conceal the fact that they had nothing else to offer, nothing they respected, least of all themselves. Even their vociferous protesta-tions of loyalty to the King meant little, Hutchinson concluded.

This particular king was hardly worth such devotion; his main value was that he threw a cloak of majesty over England's turning away from godliness and virtue by his own habitually lewd and cynical conduct.

Aunt Lucy was pleased to inform young Allen Hutchinson, almost every time she saw him, that he was a servant of the Devil, the Anti-Christ, the Beast of the Apocalypse. She warned him that he was in imminent danger of hellfire if he kept on as he was doing. Allen laughed particularly hard at that but still felt a bit of a qualm afterwards. Lucy in a Puritan fit was quite a sight. Prophetic. Terrifying really, for all that she was a small woman. Blazing eyes. He never saw their like again, until much later in life. Sometimes when his grown-up daughter Maria Beatriz was particularly angry with him, he thought he saw a little of her great-aunt there.

It became his fervent interest to find ways of teazing his aunt, and correcting her impertinence towards him. He lost no opportunity of mocking her great endeavour, the writing of her husband's story. He reminded her, though she hardly needed such reminding, of how she and her kind had fought so long and hard for England's future – and lo, here he was before her, her nephew, England's future become its present, and how did she like what she saw? He did everything, in fact, to undermine her – in her faith, in her religion, in her memories of her husband, and of the Cause they had both sacrificed so much for. But she kept her citadel quite as stoutly as ever her husband did that of the town of Nottingham. It used to infuriate Allen to the point of frenzy almost that, though he could make her wild with anger, she remained so secure in her wrong-headed defiance and her contempt for all he stood for. The struggle became an obsession with him. While others in his set were beginning at last to settle down and take up the careers that their births and backgrounds entitled them to, he was fully engaged in thinking how he could irredeemably and for ever infuriate his Aunt Lucy.

At last he hit upon the solution. He announced that he had become an adherent of the Roman Catholic faith. His father pleaded with him, his mother too. They were both heartbroken – indeed his father died from a seizure not long after this pretended conversion. Allen Hutchinson hardly noticed, though he had loved his gentle father in an offhand, pitying sort of way. But he was too busy having fun with Aunt Lucy. Who was, he was delighted to find, in despair. A lifetime of earnest Puritanism – and then the Whore of Rome appears right in the heart of the family. She actually stopped work on that interminable volume on her husband's life for she was so shocked.

Allen's effort to carry off this pretence had even included him ostentatiously taking instruction from a Romish priest he had found: Father Thomas, a rather simple young fellow from Yorkshire with dreadful table manners. When Allen brought him round for a family supper, it proved to be the last straw. As well as the wretched table manners, the priest had an awful insinuating way of looking at his betters. While Allen's mother, of course, could not help but receive her own son, he was told he would not be welcome any more at wider family gatherings. His Aunt Lucy positively banned him from her presence. He was a lost sheep who nobody was planning to search for. Or pray for. Everything had worked out very well, in fact, and it was time for Hutchinson to give up his pretence, and dismiss Father Thomas and his church from his mind and presence for ever.

Except that he found he could not! What was only meant in a sort of sport had become serious without his hardly noticing. Transubstantiation. Purgatory. The invocation of the Saints. The sacrifice of the Mass. The apostolic succession . . . all that Hutchinson believed he had been hearing from Father Thomas with no more attention than he might give to the babblings of a child he found to be lodged as firm in his brain as if it had been nailed to it. And all because he had wanted to teaze his Aunt Lucy.

What a shock this had been for Allen Hutchinson. A glorious shock, of course. Often in the years that followed he had trembled to think how he had almost missed his chance at Grace and his place in the life everlasting. From that moment on, he had never wavered in his Faith. He had married a good Catholic woman, and the two of them were able to secure eternal life for his daughter too, by bringing her up in the One True Church that the Lord had led him to when he was still young and thoughtless, instead of leaving him to rot within that ridiculous fraternity that calls itself the Church of England or, just as bad, inside the sect of baleful enthusiasts that his family had belonged to. Yes, how fortunate he had been!

On the other hand he could not deny that, on a personal level, this change of life also proved confoundedly awkward. As a professed Catholic, Hutchinson was no longer welcome among his old acquaintances. Indeed, he was hardly welcome anywhere in England now. The virulent Protestantism that had seemed to have been struck down at the Restoration was storming back across the realm, though its new garb was less holy and self-questioning and more mean-spirited and vindictive. It was time to be gone. Father Thomas, who had received his priestly training at the College of the Inglesinhos in Lisbon, had often spoken fondly to Allen of that city. Moreover, his uncle Apsley had connections in Portugal too, and though he liked his nephew's conversion to the wicked Old Faith of Rome not much better than the rest of the family, yet he agreed to lend his assistance one last time, and provided Allen with introductions to several important persons in the English Factory at Lisbon.

And so there Hutchinson went. He was twenty-four. Uncle Apsley's last gesture of assistance had included the provision of a fat purse to get him started in business. The introductions he had been given also helped establish him. The Lisbon factors, Protestant almost to a man, were no more enamoured of the fact of Allen's Catholicism than their counterparts had been in England. However, a well-born and handsome young man, with an influential relative at home, could not fail to win acceptance, as long as he kept quiet about his faith – which Allen Hutchinson was perfectly agreeable to. He settled down in the little world of the Factory, and to starting himself in business, for which, somewhat to his surprise, it turned out he had a certain aptitude.

All might have been well, and Allen Hutchinson might have lived out a decent, obscure and profitable existence in Lisbon for many years. But everything changed when he had the misfortune to kill a man – worse than that, it was an English merchant that he killed. The details of the case were not really important; in his old

287

age Hutchinson could hardly remember them anyway. Suffice to say that the man, name of Colston, was a friend of Allen's and that the dispute had been over an unpaid debt, though whether it was Colston who was in default or himself was long ago forgotten by Mr Hutchinson. But he did remember, always remembered, that the first act of violence had been done by his friend. He had seen – he *knew* he had seen – the glint of a blade against Colston's cloak. It was what had prompted him to get out his own dagger and plunge it deep into the other's breast. Witnesses to the calamity afterwards said there was no knife in Mr Colston's hand and called his own action a murder. But he knew what he had seen, he had never doubted the rightness of his action, though he did wish it had not been done to a man who was once his friend.

Mr Hutchinson had been detained briefly by the Portuguese authorities. But they did not bother him long. Under their law self-defence excused any killing and, though none could be found who were at the scene to testify for him, he got hold of a couple of Portuguese who, for a considerable sum, would lie for him, and say they saw Colston's dagger before Hutchinson had drawn. And though there were plenty who would swear that these two reprobates had never been near the scene when the killing was done, the judge was not much interested in a brawl between two foreign merchants, particularly when the slain party was a mere *herético inglês* and the accused, though also guilty of being English, had demonstrated that he belonged to the True Faith. It was obvious that the latter was innocent – and so Allen Hutchinson went free.

Yet he was finished in the Factory. A Catholic *and* a murderer? It was too much. No man would do business with him now. Few would even speak to him. He tried to hold his head up, to show he didn't care. He acted defiant. He paid bullies to accompany him to Factory gatherings in the hope that his presence and his attitude would provoke his countrymen to threaten him. But they did nothing but show the contempt they felt for him. He was raging against rows of backs.

He dismissed his bravos – on whom he'd almost exhausted his fortune, which had already been severely depleted in his legal defence. He went no more to Factory gatherings. He no longer pretended that he was in business. Or that he gave a damn any more about English respectability and propriety. He married a Portuguese girl (whose father was a stonemason), a year or so later found a couple of cheap rooms in a house in the Rua do Parreiral, moved there with his wife and infant daughter. And began what was no longer a life really, but bare survival. So far it had lasted for forty-five years.

Moments, episodes, sometimes came to him now out of that fog of time. He remembered when, through a courtier friend he had made in his time of prosperity, he had been granted a small pension by the generous Prince Pedro, given as to one who had suffered for the Faith. On this bounty the little family had limped along for many years, just managing to keep a roof over their heads and food on the table. Then there had been a brief period of prosperity when Maria Beatriz had married the furniture-maker Fonseca. The new son-in-law had pressed his bride's parents to join the happy couple in the big new house he had bought in the Rato. But Fonseca died after a year of marriage and it turned out that he had spent all the money he had and had gone into debt too in order first to win and then to keep his new wife: a course of action that Hutchinson had never understood, for Maria Beatriz had always been indifferent to money and once she had decided to accept Fonseca would doubt-less have been content even to live in a garret with him.

So it was back to the Rua do Parreiral and a bare existence on the pension. Maria Beatriz was contributing a little now too. A friend of hers, Tadeu Nunes, a printer, had been telling her that he got a lot of business running off woodcuts of a religious nature for sale in the city's streets. Knowing that Maria Beatriz had some gifts at drawing and colouring he invited her to see what she could do, and offered to try and place anything that she produced.

On a sad day for Portugal, and particularly for the Hutchinsons, the now King Pedro died at last. The new monarch, his son João, who quite lacked the quality of princely munificence that his glorious father had been so blessed with, caused hundreds of the pensions granted in the previous reign to be cancelled im-mediately, among them the measly 120 *milréis* a year, on which the

Hutchinson family had been subsisting like cockroaches for decades.

It was a devastating blow. (In later life it troubled Allen Hutchinson dreadfully that he remembered the day the pension was lost with even more sorrow and pain than he did that of his wife's death, which occurred after they'd been married fifteen years.) Something had to be done. After his expulsion from the world of the Factory, Mr Hutchinson had adopted increasingly the manners and outlook of a Portuguese *fidalgo* instead of those of an English merchant, and had lived virtually at leisure for the past thirty years. But now there were few resources left to preserve his shrunken family. Tadeu Nunes came up with another idea. His daughter brought it to him. By her expression, he could tell the pain it was causing her to reveal what the printer had suggested.

'Sell woodcuts in the street! Become a lousy peddler! Are you seriously asking me to do this?'

'No, Father. Of course not. It was wrong of me to . . . Of course you can't.'

But of course, in the end, he could. He had no other skills. He could not – really could not – work as a common labourer. If they'd had any money at all, or knew anyone who would lend them even a trifling amount, he might have tried to set himself up in some small business. But there was no one. Even Tadeu Nunes was only just scraping by. One day the same dilemma would be faced by Mr Hutchinson's unexpected and dear friend of his old age, Adam Hanaway. What else could one do? Telling himself that in a way he was indeed managing his own small business, Mr Hutchinson one day went out into the street with a bag full of his daughter's drawings, and began to sell them. Nearly fifteen years had passed like that.

And now it was over. He would never sell in the streets again, he knew that. His death was near. He had seen it in his daughter's eyes. Doctor Pessoa had finished with him. He should be grateful to be spared these last days, so that he could look back on his life and try to understand how it had all turned out. He dutifully researched his past. He thought of Aunt Lucy, dead now for so many years. He wished he could have told her once how much he had really admired her; though he would not conceal from her he had never wavered in his belief that fundamentally – he chuckled at the pun – she was a great pain in the arse. He thought of his own parents, and regretted that he had never properly mourned his dear father. He could hardly remember his mother at all: she had been such a gentle wraith, flickering through his boyhood and extinguished not long after her husband had gone to his grave.

He thought of the friend he had killed so long ago. William Colston. Had he really seen the blade that had caused him to draw his own? He thought he had, was sure he had. But . . . but . . . Well, he would find out soon enough. Yet Billy would not be there to accuse him. The poor fellow would be down in Hell with all the other Protestants, while his killer dwelt for ever in the light of Heaven.

The memories, the images, flickered in and out of his tired brain. But what made him happiest was that his thoughts were not only of the past. Ever since Montesinhos had come to see him, this had been so. The landlord had spoken to him almost without design, it appeared. He had just wanted to relieve himself of the burden of what was troubling him, and it seemed a sick old man would be just as good a receptacle as anyone else. But, as he listened to the man's dolorous complaints, Mr Hutchinson began to see a glimmer of hope that he might have found a way of reaching into the future. And though he would not be there to share it, there were others who would.

His mother had used to say to him that he should always try to leave a good taste in the mouths of whatever company he had just quitted. Well, he would do just that. His whole life might have been a failure and a disaster, but at the end Mr Hutchinson would leave a good taste in the mouths of those he loved. If only he could hang on for a little while longer, while his plans matured. If only Montesinhos could be persuaded that his troubles required the most drastic of solutions. If only Maria Beatriz . . .

But there's the rub. What to do about Maria Beatriz? She would never permit him . . . or Adam either . . . She was so tender towards him, would never allow the boy to face the least risk in however worthy a cause. His old heart pounded in excitement. He must be careful. In his bed, he closed his eyes. Concentrated with all his failing might. To live a few more days would be something, a few weeks would be almost too much to hope for.

Holy Mother of Mercy, he prayed, let me live for just a little longer, let me see my plan come at last to life. It is not right yet. It is still so shadowy and incoherent. It wants something more. I need luck. Need cunning. Something . . .

Adam

1

But this amazing old man refused to die. Instead he got better! A week after that conversation in which Maria Beatriz had told me I ought to go home, I had gone to the second floor as usual after my labours in the streets. I had taken up again the habit of dining at her table before heading upstairs to my solitary bed, as if there had never been in our relations a hiatus of wild love-making and intimate, unashamed talk. And for a wonder we both seemed to be perfectly reconciled to the abrupt ending of our pleasures. I could detect no sign of strain in her as we sat at the table, talking over the day's events just as we always had, eating the food she had prepared. I no longer entertained sly thoughts of getting myself back into her bed. I believed I was very content with how things had turned out and if I ever, for a moment, found myself wishing that matters could have been different, I only had to look at Maria Beatriz's calm and untroubled countenance to know how I should behave.

Was she as unaffected by the passing of our passion as she pretended to be? I don't know. At this distance I remember only two things that could shed light on what she truly felt. One was this show of serenity and peace of mind in the days that followed our separation as lovers. The other was that terrible moment on the stairs when she had seen in my face that I no longer desired her, and I in turn had seen by how much that knowledge had hurt her. She had looked pierced to her soul in that moment. And yet this was the same woman who now chatted easily with me of an evening and served my food, and told me new funny stories about Montesinhos, and the other characters of the neighbourhood, and what a woman who sold bread at the market had said that day to one who sold tobacco.

I remember though sometimes in these evenings, when our raptures were but a memory, looking up suddenly and catching her gazing at me so intently, with an expression in her eyes that I could not exactly read. As soon as she saw me studying her, she would look away very fast and her lips would fasten together tight as if she was annoyed at being thus caught out. Though what it was she thought she had discovered to me in these moments I could not tell.

In any case, as I say, I presented myself at her door on that particular evening. One small indication that perhaps things were not quite as they had once been was that I hesitated to let myself into the Hutchinsons' apartment as I used to. Instead I knocked. The door was opened. I saw at once that Maria Beatriz had been crying. This was a shocking thing. She had never even wept while we were in the process of disentangling ourselves from one another, and I had been grateful to her for it because I have always found it difficult to hold to a purpose in the face of women's tears. Now the unthinkable had taken place. Her eyes were red; fresh tears were starting in them. But luckily, before I could make a fool of myself by heaping her with my commiserations, I noticed that her lips were wreathed in smiles and that these were tears of joy.

She took my hand and led me through the parlour. Then through the living room into the corridor beyond, the very corridor . . . but, before I could become confused as to her purpose, she stopped at the door to her father's room and knocked on it gently. A gruff voice answered her. She smiled at me, then unlatched the door. Opened it and stood away so I could enter. I stopped in the doorway though, almost too startled by what I saw to stir.

'Well, get in and close the door, sirrah,' the old man scowled. 'Unless you are determined that a draught should carry me off.'

He was sitting up in his bed, nightcap on his head, shawl around his shoulders, a glass of *tinto* in his hand. I did get into his room as ordered, and closed the door behind me – Maria Beatriz had gone away somewhere. I turned back to Mr Hutchinson.

'Sir,' I said, when I could find my voice, 'I am truly –'

'Amazed to find me alive, isn't it so? Come, sit down, Adam.' He nodded at the chair by his bed. And as I was removing the candle that was resting on it, he raised his head and with a very good imitation of a bellow called out, 'Daughter!'

She must have been standing behind the door, for it opened the next instant and she looked in.

'Father,' she said sternly, 'you are not to tire yourself.'

'I'm in bed. How should I tire myself?'

'By shouting. You don't need to. You have a bell there.'

Mr Hutchinson picked up the little copper bell that was on his counterpane and wagged it facetiously at his daughter.

'What do you want, Father?'

'Not me. But Adam here. If we are to raise bumpers to my joyous recovery, damn it, the boy'll need a glass.'

She left the doorway. Mr Hutchinson grinned toothlessly at me. I told him most fervently that I was pleased beyond measure to see him like this.

'Would have been like this much sooner if *she* hadn't stopped my medical man from coming to see me.'

'You are only better,' said Maria Beatriz, reappearing in the room with a glass that she placed in my hand, 'because I stopped him from coming.' She sat on the edge of the bed, and smiled at me. 'He was so weak –' she nodded at the old man – 'and Doctor Pessoa still insisted on cupping him.'

'O Senhor Doutor Fernando Pessoa has been drawing blood from me for thirty years. And I have thrived on it.'

'And you would have died on it if I hadn't stopped him.'

Mr Hutchinson gave a shrug and a wink to me to show how little he valued female understanding of the mysteries of the faculty. He filled my glass and then, with a pretence of reluctance that was more comical than truly felt, also filled the glass Maria Beatriz had brought in for herself. He raised his own beaker, beamed at us both, and said, 'To the three of us. May we always be as fond to each other as we are now. Till death us do part, yes? And it appears to me, Adam, my dear –' He started wheezing and chuckling. 'As if you may be the one to separate us. You're looking somewhat broken down, my dear boy. Godsokers if you ain't!'

I drank the toast willingly and in the same chaffing spirit said, 'At least you are not looking broken down, Sir.'

'Indeed, I think I am not,' he said complacently. 'It appears this is not my time to die. Who knows when it will be? I feel well enough today to go on for years. But if it is only a few months – so be it. At least it is not *now*.'

After he'd said all that, I could not help giving a quick and somewhat apprehensive glance at Maria Beatriz. She understood exactly what I meant by it, probably sooner than I did myself. And very slightly she shook her head. She meant that she would not hold me to my promise of staying in Lisbon until Mr Hutchinson's death, if that event should be happily delayed by a matter of years, as he had just threatened. I was not sure even if I wanted to commit myself to the few months that were his more modest estimate. Her words the other day had fired me up. I was chafing at the bit almost. Home was the place for me now, I saw, and I would find any prolonged delay in getting there most onerous.

This was the peak of Mr Hutchinson's performance today, for soon after he seemed to become very tired and Maria Beatriz suggested that we should leave him to his rest, which of course I agreed to. But I was back the next evening and this time I found the old man up and dressed and sitting in his old chair in the living room. Now he was able to talk for a couple of hours before his fatigue overcame him. The next night it was as if it were the old days all over again. We three sat in our respective places and whiled away a whole evening in chat, and were merry together, quite as if one of us had not been lately under imminent sentence of death. He was most interested to know how our business was carrying on in the streets and I was able to assure him that the renewed fine weather had brought out pious customers in gratifying numbers.

And so a week went by like this, then two weeks. Mr Hutchinson seemed to improve on every day of them. The weather continued to stay fine and my sales in the streets and alleys were as bright as the weather. The coins my old and new customers had been keeping safe with them over the winter in case of any emergency were now released as confidence returned with the spring. Having talked the matter over with Maria Beatriz, I got her permission to reserve for myself a slightly larger share of the proceeds than before because I was now saving for my berth home. She also promised to let me have what few *cruzados* she would have to spare when the time came.

Even so, to achieve the sum I needed would take several weeks, but I found this time of waiting and working rather more pleasing to me than otherwise. My course was set firmly for home, yet I looked forward to going out each morning to my work in the place I would soon be leaving. Indeed I liked doing what I was doing so much that I even feared it would blunt my desire to go home. I took this trouble to Maria Beatriz one evening, after her father had gone to bed. After I had been talking for a few minutes I noticed that she was listening to me with, at best, only half an ear. She looked most preoccupied, and rather distant too. I stopped speaking fairly abruptly. She looked up after a while, saw me watching her.

'I'm sorry, Adam,' she said. 'I was listening. But not,' she smiled then, 'very attentively.'

'What is the matter? Is it bad news?'

'No, indeed. Good news.'

She got up and went into the parlour. When she returned she had a sheet of lilac-coloured paper in her hand. She hesitated before she gave it to me.

'Can you read Portuguese?'

I gave her a look to show her how redundant that question was – but in truth when I had the letter in my hand I found it more difficult by far than I had imagined it would be. I had learned to speak fluently a kind of Portuguese, a vernacular that – as the Hutchinsons never tired of pointing out – was full of Lisbon street words and slang and elisions. This formal flowery language that I was reading almost baffled me. After '*Minha muito cara Dona Maria Beatriz*' I was in trouble. Seeing my difficulty, Maria Beatriz took the letter from my hand.

'It's from an old friend Dona Antônia Joaquina dos Santos. We were at school together. She married a gentleman with a fine estate in the Alentejo, near Evora. Every other year I visit her there. We are still very fond of each other, and when we were younger and she lived more in Lisbon I was a sort of aunt to her boys. Of course they are grown up now, but the youngest son still lives with his mother, and the other not far off, and – oh, I so delight in seeing them all! Now Antônia writes to ask if I am coming to her this year and if I am tells me that I should start out soon before the hot weather grows unbearable.'

I told her immediately that I thought it was a very pleasant thing for her to have received an invitation from an old friend and I could not see why she seemed so troubled.

'How can I go,' she said then, 'with my father like he is?'

'But your father is well. He is quite recovered.'

'Is he?'

I said what I could to reassure her. That Doctor Pessoa himself had pronounced his patient out of danger. That even to the untrained eye Mr Hutchinson discovered many signs of a return to health: in his colour, in the brightness of his eyes, the easiness of his breathing, his whole air of restored vitality.

'He has had to go to bed again before it is nine o'clock. He never used to do that in the old days, did he?'

I answered that there was no doubt the prolonged bout of illness he had suffered over the winter had taken its toll. But that did not mean that Mr Hutchinson was not out of the shadow of his immediate decease, and indeed, looking at the case with a certain amount of optimism, as we who loved him were bound to do, there was nothing to say that a long period of convalescence, with frequent rest, decent diet and so on, would not bring him all the way back to his old rude health.

'What if he dies when I am away from him?' she asked, staring at my face, making me look into her eyes. 'How will I ever forgive myself?'

To that I really had no quick answer, and seeing it Maria Beatriz shook her head slowly. I concluded that she had decided that the risk was too great: she would not go to her friend's. A day passed, and I was back in the Hutchinsons' apartment. I had been thinking on and off about Maria Beatriz's dilemma since I left her. I saw the letter out on the table. I supposed she had been reading it again, probably many times since we'd last met. I said to her straight away that I could not think she was right to deny herself a holiday that she needed, that she had certainly earned, because of an eventuality that might or might not take place. Life, I announced confidently, could not be organised on such a basis, for any of us might, without warning, pass through the gates of death and how would it be if we were all unable to do anything that we wanted for fear that the universal and natural occurrence would take place?

This argument did not at all ring out so convincingly when I spoke it aloud as it had running around in my mind out in the streets. Maria Beatriz looked at me with even a certain amusement at my effort, which naturally irritated me.

'For God's sake,' I said, 'you heard him the other day, he was saying he might survive for years yet. Are you not going to leave the Baixa for years in case he should suddenly die?'

'He will not live for years,' she said, looking down at the letter.

'He might live for a year or two, or perhaps only a few months, but still . . .' I walked up and down the little living room. I was sure I should keep pressing. I felt her yielding. It was what she wanted to do if only I could find the right argument.

'How long would you be away?'

She thought about it. 'My friend will send me one of her coaches. It will take us three days to get there – the same back. I could hardly stay for less than three weeks.'

'So, a month altogether.'

'A month,' she said sadly. 'Too long.'

More pacing on my part, more sorrowful gazing at the letter on hers.

'Have you spoken to *him* about it?'

'Yes. He insists that I go. It seems very important to him that I do.'

She shrugged after she said that and when she glanced at me both of us silently acknowledged that her father had reached that unenviable state in life where a man could insist all he liked and nobody need listen to him.

Maria Beatriz sighed. 'I would so much like to go away. I have felt – so dreary over this winter, so troubled.'

There was a silence between us. I immediately thought she was referring to our abortive connection, conflating its brief length to that of a whole winter of discontent, and that I was being blamed for it. But she guessed suddenly what I was thinking, and smiled at me and added, 'Because of my father's illness . . . It would be so good to be with Antônia again. And the children are grown-up now but still I long to see them. Ah, what a pity I cannot.'

But in the end, she found she could. All of us – her father, me, Doctor Pessoa, her other Lisbon friends – were applying pressure on her to go. Even Montesinhos, she told me, came upstairs to say that she would be mad to throw away this chance to re-create herself and get away from surroundings that were always unworthy of a lady of her quality and position.

'I didn't like to point out,' she giggled to me, 'that he was talking about his own house!'

Together with her own strong desire to go, this pressure proved sufficient at last to carry the citadel. A letter was sent by stage to Evora, seventy miles away. Further communication took place, back and forth, and on a fine morning in late May, about three weeks after Maria Beatriz had got the first letter, she was being handed up into the coach her friend had sent by her father, who had been helped down to the street for the first time in months in order to perform this important office.

Several friends of Maria Beatriz had come to see her off, including dear Bento, who earlier this afternoon had rallied me that I had never yet been to visit him in his new shop in the Rua dos Douradores. I had promised to rectify that omission and soon – a promise, sad to say, I was never able to keep. Also come over from Douradores was our local lunatick, or as he preferred to be styled, Charles I, by the Grace of God, King of Great Britain and Ireland. Since his arrival he had mainly spent his time in blubbering near the coach door, apparently under the delusion that it was his Queen Henrietta Maria who was inside and that he was once again bidding her a desperate farewell as she went into exile from England.

I had thought myself, as I'd seen Maria Beatriz advance towards the coach and then as she had climbed the step and looked around at us with a lovely and affectionate smile, that there was indeed something truly regal in her person today, something very dignified and yet so gracious and kind. She was wearing a dress of apricot colour, glowing like a summer morning in Portugal, like this morning indeed, and holding a rolled parasol, apricot like her dress. She looked as if she should always be in fine coaches, surrounded by well-wishers, going somewhere grand.

It is a good memory I have had of her through the years: Maria Beatriz and her coach-and-four, in a beautiful dress, looking forward to a month away from the cares of home and family. I was thinking sadly that those cares certainly included me, when I saw her leaning forward in her seat and seeming to search over the heads of the crowd. I knew suddenly that she was looking for me and I straightened up and came forward through the people. She reached out her hand, and I took it. She gave me the kindest of smiles.

'Adam,' was all she said aloud. I bowed to her. We looked at each other for a time and it seemed all the calling and farewelling around us died away so we could not hear them, only each other's breathing. Then she said, but silently, 'You promised,' and I knew what she meant and I nodded, and then the next moment her door was shut, the driver flapped the reins, the coach moved off. It was so big that it almost brushed the sides even of the wide Rua do Parreiral. I watched it until it had turned the corner, then stood a little longer looking at nothing except the usual midday clutter of carts and dogs and mules and priests and people.

I was about to go back inside the house when I felt a touch at my elbow and a voice (that I still marvelled at hearing the revived strength and vivacity in) say, 'A word with you, dear Adam.'

I looked around. As if magicked away, the throng of friends and of the curious and the insane had disappeared. There was only Mr Hutchinson and I left standing outside Montesinhos' house. A fool on a skittish horse was bearing down on us. I put up my hand and pulled Mr Hutchinson to safety.

'Of course, Sir,' I said. 'Let me help you back to your rooms.'

'Don't want to go to my rooms. I want to go to a tavern.'

'Sir, is this wise? I can always send for a bottle –'

'I want to go to a tavern because I want to talk over a bit of business with you and that is where Englishmen meet when they are in earnest about a project. And that is where they seal their contract with a bumper. In a tavern, Sir, not in a damned parlour, nor a damned office either.'

I took all this babble about business and contracts and projects with a large pinch of salt, but in the end, after several other increasingly heated submissions by Mr Hutchinson, fell in with his wishes and escorted him to the Falcon tavern, which was the nearest one to Montesinhos' house. Seated at a table near the door, Mr Hutchinson looked about him with great relish. Everything, I saw, pleased him after so long an absence from such scenes – the counter with its dishes of olives and figs, the wine bottles arrayed in their racks along the walls, the dull polished wood of the tables and chairs. There were not many other customers. Over by the window was a party of four: small tradesmen, they looked like. They were sharing a bottle, and it was evident it was not the first to appear at their table. They were merry, and their laughter rolled across the room towards us. I could see that Mr Hutchinson delighted in it, and I guessed that, after weeks spent almost entirely in the company of a female, his daughter, however much he loved her, to hear men talk and chaff and laugh with one another again must be a welcome thing.

Mr Hutchinson took the fancy to order ale for once instead of wine: 'English ale, Sir! Fit for Englishmen to drink!' though what we got after a lengthy wait were two cobwebby bottles of Holland beer. While we were waiting for them, Mr Hutchinson, after several clearings of his throat and subsequent false starts, began what I supposed was his introduction to the 'business' he wished to do with me, or perhaps just to ask my opinion about. I did not listen to him very closely at first. It seemed to be more stuff along the lines of his worries about how he must leave his daughter penniless unless something drastic was done, and though I sympathised truly with his fears I had heard them more than once before.

So there we sat, two Englishmen in a tavern with our Dutch brew between us. Except for a brief swell of anxiety that he might be exhausting himself by so much talking, I was still ignoring Mr Hutchinson's words as much as I could so that I might explore my own concerns. I drank from the glass before me, gloomily comparing its musty, insipid taste with the delights of Sleeford's Lincolnshire Particular ale as served to me once by my lost love Gabriella Lowther's father. I found myself thinking that I would probably never know for certain what the real reason was for my being banished from the Lowthers' world – could it really have been only because of a few unlucky words? Or to put it even more accurately: because of two words only?

I was remembering now that, at one time during the second night I had spent with Maria Beatriz, very early in the morning I think it was, I had told her about the pipkin vent and the incalculable wrong that had been done to my prospects and career by it. I told her in a solemn voice, as befitted such a momentous matter, and was therefore most shocked when before I had finished she started to roll about in quite a paroxysm of laughter. She laughed so hard in fact that she nearly fell off the bed and I had to grasp her by her naked shoulders to keep her from crashing to the floor.

Thereafter, I might as well report, we tried to see if we could produce this famous phenomenon by our own efforts. But no sonorous blast of wind escaped from Maria Beatriz's private parts, however long we tried. I was made somewhat downcast at this, blaming myself, my lack of girth perhaps, for the failure. But Maria Beatriz assured me that it was just a silly trick and there was no reason at all to feel ashamed because we could not perform it. She added to this such a reassuring quantity of compliments upon my member and proceeded to demonstrate by how much she enjoyed having it within her so that I could not stay sorry for myself.

This I remembered now with much pleasure. But I had no delight at all in recollecting that, during those hours when I had become minded to reject Maria Beatriz, because she was old, flabby, wrinkled and whatever else I had conceived against her, I also decided to blame her for our failure to produce the pipkin vent. That she was too big down there, too loose, horribly loose, so that not even a well-endowed young fellow such as myself could fill her gaping abyss.

I shook my head, so deeply ashamed as I was of my mean, ungentlemanly imaginings. I had forgot for the moment that I was not alone. Mr Hutchinson's voice broke in upon my lamentable thoughts. He sounded quite anxious.

'What do you mean by that, Sir? Are you not with me so far?'

I looked up into the face of the father of the woman who I had bedded gloriously and then had despicably discarded. I knew that if he guessed what he was looking at he would take a sword – as he had not one of his own, I would have lent him my own – and put its point into my breast. And old and infirm as he was he would not have found it difficult for I would have helped him push the blade in as far as it would go.

Or perhaps not. I had for some time now rather taken leave of the extravagant flourishes and assertions of my younger days. But I was sorry to have been inattentive to the old man's speech, however repetitive. I resolved to do better from now on.

'Damn it, Adam! I believe you haven't listened to a thing I've been saying.'

'Not at all, Sir. You were speaking of your daughter, her poverty.'

'I left that,' the old man growled, 'long ago. Did you not hear me talk of Montesinhos?'

'I know,' said I cautiously, 'that you have been seeing him lately, you have told me so ... You are right,' I went on, choosing honesty at last, 'I didn't hear you talk of Montesinhos just now.'

Mr Hutchinson sighed in deep chagrin at this. He reached for his beaker and then discovered that it was empty. He knocked loudly on the tabletop to summon the landlord and when the man appeared seemed about to order another draught of ale. But then:

'Oh to hell with it. Dutch piss. Bring us some wine, landlord, and not your rotgut either.'

We waited. Mr Hutchinson had folded his arms across his chest. He was obviously very annoyed. I leaned forward and said as pacifically as I could, 'Sir, please tell me again about Montesinhos. I promise to listen carefully.'

I think he would have liked to continue his fit of spleen for a while longer, in order to wring as much regret as possible out of me. However, time was pressing – or, more to the point, he could not be sure how much longer his present vigour would continue. He waited just as long as it took for the landlord to bring us our wine and clear away the empty beer glasses, then when we were alone again he leaned across the table and spoke in the same low, urgent voice as before.

'I say I have seen Montesinhos. He is nearly ready to fly. The Holy Office is about to take him up, he's sure of it.'

'But why should Senhor Montesinhos want to fly?' I said, amazed. 'And what do the Inquisition have to do with him?'

'God's socks, Adam, do you really walk around in such a daze as this? Because he's a Jew, Sir. Call him a New Christian if you like, call him a *converso*, or a *marrano*, but the plain fact is that our respectable landlord is a Jew, from an everlasting line of Jews, and he properly fears the Dominican fathers. He dreads being put to the question, confiscation of his wealth, the rack, the *polé*, the stake, everything like that. And this is where our opportunity lies, my boy. Let me tell you how.'

When our interview was done, I returned Mr Hutchinson to his rooms. He still appeared invigorated by the excitement of having explained his 'bit of business' to me, and was able to make a greater contribution to his own ascent than I had anticipated. When I got him inside the apartment, though, his vivacity seemed to drop away. He looked around the empty parlour, then, when I had got him to his chair, around the empty living room. For the first time the full implications of his daughter's departure seemed to strike him and he looked suddenly very old and sad sitting there. I told him I would sit with him and be there to receive his supper at the door when it came up from the kitchen, and would stay with him as long as he liked thereafter. He said I was a kindly fellow and there was no need to burden myself with an old decrepit fellow. I said it would be no burden to me, but was a pleasure always to be in his company.

Indeed, I was saying truly what I thought, but it was also the case that I was bound to do this service. It was what I had promised Maria Beatriz: that I would look after her father while she was away. That I would for those four weeks 'keep an eye on him', as she kept saying. I think if I hadn't made this promise she would never have left town. It was also the case that in return she had agreed to make up whatever was lacking in what I needed to buy me a passage to England when she got home.

She was not so unreasonable though as to expect me to spend every waking hour with Mr Hutchinson and, after his meal had arrived and been eaten, leaving him dozing in his armchair, with a glass of *tinto* near his hand, and a chamber pot located not very far away, I stole out of the apartment. Just before I left him, the old man had opened his eyes for a moment and had asked me if I would think on what he had told to me. I said I was sure of doing that, that I scarcely imagined I would be able to entertain thoughts on any other subject for quite a while. Mr Hutchinson, with his eyes closed now, nodded at that and let me go.

Yes, I certainly needed to think. I had no relish for doing it in my room, however, particularly on a hot day like this. Instead I turned back downstairs and regained the Rua do Parreiral. Once away from Montesinhos' house, I started to wander, as I so often did, through the Baixa's warren of little streets and alleys. For once though I had not a bag of canvases under my arm, nor was I looking for likely customers. My mind too was free to ramble.

Montesinhos is a Jew, Mr Hutchinson had repeated. It is known by the authorities that he is, and so he must run.

But of course our landlord didn't want to leave his bit of capital here, where by law it would all go into swelling the coffers of the Inquisition. His only hope was to entrust it to a Christian, either a merchant of his own nationality, or a foreign one. He had been in negotiation with several such, and also some English sea captains, but the terms they offered were far too severe.

'Some of 'em want fifty per cent,' Mr Hutchinson reported. 'None of 'em will settle for less than forty.'

'Forty per cent of what?' I asked. 'Surely Montesinhos is not rich?'

'Rich enough. The house is sold, you know.'

'It is?'

'At a price much less than its value, according to him. But what was he to do? Everybody knows he is in trouble. The merchants know it and the sea captains and that is why they are attempting to gouge him. I estimate he is talking about £5,000.'

'Five thousand!'

'Perhaps a little less.'

I was sure Mr Hutchinson was plucking figures from the air. I could not think that even if Montesinhos had sold his house and everything else he owned he could be worth such a sum as this.

'Don't forget,' said the old man, as if reading my thoughts, 'that it is not only his money we are talking about. Some of it is his brother's. And I think he mentioned an uncle too . . . He sought me out as soon as he heard I was recovering. He offers a straight £1,000 down. Twenty per cent. Five hundred for each of us. Believe me, Adam, he's in great trouble. Things couldn't be better for us.'

Often thereafter I wished that I had understood more clearly what threat exactly was facing poor Montesinhos, and why it should be. I thought he risked persecution simply because, if Mr Hutchinson had it right, he was descended from Jews. I did not know then what I later learned that if Jewish ancestry was all it took to excite the attention of the Inquisition then a good part of the population would be under scrutiny, certainly of the noble part of it. For all the babble about their sacred *pureza de sangue*, the Portuguese nobility had been marrying among New Christians since their arrival in masses in the fifteenth century. It was the old familiar connection between title on the one side and money on the other, which has been one of the engines of material progress in my own country. Here it was concealed and denied: great oaths were sworn that no contaminated blood had ever entered a family's bloodstream. They had to be, for a number of important and prestigious offices, such as that of *familiar*, were closed to those who had any New Christian ancestors dangling from the branches of their family trees.

But Montesinhos was not a *familiar*, nor anything but a simple landlord, who also, I'd heard, had a small interest in a wine shop in the Travessa Ferraria. That he was of New Christian descent should have made no difference to him in these occupations. Something else was drawing the ominous notice of the so-called Holy Office to his modest house. As I say, I wish I had known what it was; it might have started the alarm bells ringing in my mind much earlier than they did.

But perhaps not. I was so taken by the scheme that Mr Hutchinson was laying out before me that I think I must have been deaf for the moment to almost any warnings. And why should I not be? It promised adventure, travel – and at the end of it I would be regaining my homeland, and would be doing it in a way that was not in the sneaking fashion of a pauper and a failure but with the proceeds of a smart bit of business in my pocket. Five hundred pounds! It would be in every way a creditable home-coming and I knew would make my mother very happy to hear of it.

However, there was one potential risk in this plan that I was not blind to, mostly because it might involve a threat to my own life.

'In what form am I to take this money out of the country? It cannot be in gold. I've heard there is a law here that makes it a capital crime to export gold.'

'Oh fie, Adam!' scoffed Mr Hutchinson. 'Kill an Englishman for such a little thing? Godsokers, they would never dare. Strip you of all your wealth and confine you for a long period in the Limoeiro perhaps. But kill you? Never.'

With that I decided our business might as well be concluded. I was not going to risk my life because Mr Hutchinson said I need not worry. I hoped I had many years left to me that I was looking forward to enjoying and while it might suit a very old man to risk the remainder of his life for five hundred pounds, it was not he who was going to be running said risk. And it was not, I decided, going to be me either. Not my life, nor the loss of the pathetic remnants of my property, nor a term of years in Limoeiro prison. I would hazard none of it.

I had started to rise from my seat, and would have next told him it was time to get back to our lodgement, when he placed a hand on my arm. I looked down at it. I felt a shiver along my spine as I did.

The hand was so bony and transparent; it looked, I was sure, just the way it would at the moment after the last breath had left Mr Hutchinson's body.

'He is not asking you to take it in gold.'

'In what then?' said I, sinking back into my chair.

'Will you speak to Montesinhos about this?'

'Of course. I would have to.'

'Then he will tell you. He'll tell you everything. And you will see there is no risk to you at all. Only opportunity!'

We concluded our business soon after and headed back to Montesinhos' house. Two hours later, when I returned to the same place after my long bout of walking and thinking in the Baixa, it was growing dark. On my way up the stairs I knocked on the Hutchinsons' door, and then remembering that there was now no Maria Beatriz to open it for me I turned the handle and went inside. I found the old man in something of a state. The ale and then the wine in the tavern and then whatever he had drunk since he'd been in this room had done their work upon his elderly physique. It seemed important for him to explain that the first time he'd had need to he had got himself over to the chamber pot – 'achieved the cursed jordan', in his phrase. It was just after he had settled himself down again following that expedition that disaster had struck. For he had discovered that he had not, as he'd thought, entirely voided the contents of his bladder and that a second visit to the utensil was imperatively called for.

'I thought I would just rest a little before I set out again. But when I did – damn me, it was too late.'

I told him it was my fault for leaving the chamber pot too far away from his chair, and that thought – which had not struck him before – seemed to cheer him mightily and make it easier for him to accept the necessary ministrations I had to offer in order to cleanse him, dress him in his nightshirt and finally put him into his bed.

'You are a thoughtless fellow, Adam,' Mr Hutchinson grumbled sleepily from his pillow. 'Not to put the damned jordan closer. But I forgive you.'

Just before I left him, he asked me if I had thought over 'our project'. I said that I had, and added that I would like to know more of it. He said that was good to hear, and that Montesinhos desired that I would call on him in his parlour in the basement tomorrow. Would noon suit me? I told him it would, and closed the door of his room. Up in my own, I brooded over this last part of our conversation. I presumed it showed that everything had been planned ahead between Mr Hutchinson and our landlord, that it had been in place when the old man had first broached the plan to me in the tavern. Unless Montesinhos had come up to the Hutchinson apartment while I was walking in the Baixa? But somehow I doubted it. No, everything had been calculated between them, perhaps days ago – including the fact that all would be revealed to me immediately after Maria Beatriz left town and not until then. With thoughts of cats and mice and what the latter got up to when the former were away, I fell into a deep and, as far as I could tell when I woke next morning, an entirely dreamless sleep.

At noon next day – or a little after that, for I thought it would not be good business for me to discover too much in the way of eagerness – I was knocking on the door of Montesinhos' parlour. He gave a quick glance into the corridor before he let me in. I could not imagine who he might have thought could be spying on us. There was only the little African girl likely to be down in the basement, and the cook, and perhaps Bento's replacement as casual labourer about the house, who was called Simão and lived with his parents in a hovel in a nearby alley. I did not think that any of those represented a threat to our meeting. But as I was shortly to find out, Montesinhos was in a great state of agitation, and anything was likely to set him off.

'You know they seized Diogo Wallenstein yesterday?'

I didn't exactly know who he was talking of, but thought I had heard the name in some sort of financial connection, of the loftier sort, as one heard in London of great bankers or merchants like Sir Matthew Decker or Sir Peter Vansittart without being precisely aware of what their greatness consisted of.

'*Wallenstein!*' cried my landlord in a sort of agony. 'He was banker to the Malafaia family. And to the Noronhas. He has lent to the court too – and yet they could not save him . . . So it is.' Montesinhos shrugged, sitting himself down abruptly without apparently thinking of asking me to do the same. 'He will pay a million *moedas* and they'll let him go off to Amsterdam. But what of poor fellows like me, Senhor Hanaway? They will have no mercy. I will be shorn like a lamb and then burned like a faggot. My brother too. Damn those priests – I truly believe they will be damned by God, and to all eternity, I hope.'

He was talking so wildly. As I settled, still uninvited, into a chair opposite his, I kept my gaze on him. The look in his eyes was distracted and he kept moving the muscle that directed his mouth so I was all the time expecting him to say something and then finding it was only this strange twitching he was exhibiting. Though we had had our difficulties of late, it made me unhappy to see him so.

'Senhor Montesinhos,' I said at last, when he appeared to have stopped going over the case of the wretched Wallenstein, 'it seems that I may possibly be able to help you.'

Twitch, twitch of his mouth, as he studied me. 'You have heard my proposition?' he said.

'To get your fortune out of the country. In return for £1,000.'

'Not so simple as that,' he said, sinking down into his chair. 'You will have to do a bit of business for me in London. Do you think you will be able to?'

'Since I don't know what it is,' I said, reasonably as I thought, 'I don't know if I can.'

The answer did not much please him. He frowned, shook his head. 'A businessman, a true businessman, should be able to turn his hand to any project that is to his advantage,' he pronounced. 'Senhor Hutchinson says you are that true businessman. That you come from a family well known in London. Also here. I know about Felix Hanaway –' Montesinhos frowned a little. 'He was a fool to allow himself to be imposed upon by that *filho da puta* Bartolomeu Gomes. That wretched –' And here he used a term that I did not at first quite understand. I recognised the word for 'children' but that which it was joined to – *estuprador* – I was not sure about. It seemed as if it might have something to do with *estupro*, which I knew meant 'rape'.

'. . . but for many years,' I heard the landlord saying now, 'your uncle carried on a good business here. He had the reputation of an honourable and charitable *fidalgo inglês*, and one should not condemn a man for one error of judgement.'

Child-raper? *Gomes*? And my uncle a *fidalgo*? I did not know how to respond to all this – but I did seize quite gratefully on the landlord's generous judgement upon Uncle Felix. It made me think that I could afford to reveal to him my own true situation, and hope for at least as kind a verdict on myself.

'Senhor Montesinhos,' I said, 'you must know I am only a street-seller, and have been so all winter. I failed when I worked for my uncle, and that really is all the business experience that I can lay claim to. My father was a great man in his time. But he never instructed me much in his trade because –' I found myself suddenly about to be overwhelmed by tears. I steadied myself, held them back. Remembered that they came only from self-pity, the least admirable of causes. 'Because neither of us thought I would ever need such knowledge.'

Montesinhos let me finish controlling myself, then took up the jug that was on the table and poured us both a glass of wine. He watched me sip at mine. It was, I noted, a pretty good swallow, not the usual rough stuff that came from his kitchen. He shrugged then.

'Still, it is in your blood, perhaps. And most important, you may have contacts in London that will allow you to do our business successfully.'

'Perhaps I do,' I said cautiously. I thought of the head clerk Solomon Marks, and of one or two other men, friends and associates of my father, who had stayed loyal to him until the end: the very few who had bothered to come to the funeral, in fact. But in all honesty I knew I could not promise they would support me as they had my father. I told this to Montesinhos. I added that it was my opinion that in so important a matter as his entire fortune he should find more experienced assistance than I could offer. In other words I gave the landlord every opportunity to take his business elsewhere, but before I had finished saying all this he was shaking his head.

'I have tried elsewhere. Only yesterday I was talking to another of those whores of sea captains. But now they know about Diogo Wallenstein their teeth have got even sharper. Now they demand sixty per cent of the proceeds. I am to entrust my wealth to a man I do not know who already proposes to rob me of much more than half my fortune? Which is already so diminished because of the price I was forced to accept for this house? I won't do it. I would rather trust you, Senhor Hanaway, for I know you and I think you are honest. I shall not like it if you fail me through incompetence. But I shall like it much less if I am beggared by a stranger who cheats me.'

With that he sat up straight in his chair and looked very fierce at me. The symptoms of distress I had noted when I'd entered this room – twitching mouth, distracted gaze, etcetera – were quite gone now, I was glad to see. Also I could not help but be flattered by his high opinion of me. At least of my honesty, at least compared with those 'whores of sea captains' who were his only alternative.

'Besides,' he began again, in a soothing voice, 'I am not asking you to do anything very difficult. Simply to shepherd my wealth out of the country. It will be in the form of a highly desirable commodity. When you arrive in London I should want you to try to place it. But if you are not offered fair terms then you will not do the business. The article is easily storable, with care it will not perish. I will be able to take charge of it when I reach London, or some other place where I can act freely on my own behalf. Do you have an address over there where I can write to you?'

I thought – I did not know what to think. In the end I gave him my mother's address in Kent, but told him that this did not mean that I had agreed yet to take part in this scheme. Montesinhos shrugged as if that was only an incidental detail.

'When I will be able to contact you . . .' He shook his head. 'I don't know. We may have to go into hiding here for a while. And then either we must strike overland across Portugal and into Spain and then through France, which I do not want to do, or I must try to take ship, which will not be easy for they are watching the wharves for our people. It may be that in a small port in the south I will be safer, but I can't tell. At least the bastards will not be able to seize my goods as well as myself, I will have been able to deny them that. Because of you, dear Senhor Hanaway. And for this favour I will pay a thousand pounds. And buy your passage to England.'

'What is it that you wish me to take to England?' I asked. Then, when he did not immediately answer: 'I have told Senhor Hutchinson that I won't carry gold.'

'Of course not. I would not put you to such a risk. Besides, if it was discovered by the customs swine, then it would all be lost, I might as well have let the Inquisition take it in the first place . . . No, I have transformed our family's wealth into the perfect article of trade. Exporting it brings no risk to you, it is easily transportable, and will certainly find a ready market in London. Or anywhere else in Europe.'

A project that involved no risk to me and for which I would be paid £1,000 (half going to Mr Hutchinson, of course): how could I possibly refuse it? Was it only a last flicker of my invisible brother Runaway's cowardly reluctance that made me mention Maria Beatriz's name now?

'But she is not here,' said Montesinhos.

'I'm aware of that. But I made a promise to her that I would watch over Mr Hutchinson while she was away. How can I do that when I am hundreds of miles away in London? Perhaps I could delay my departure until her return?'

'Impossible. I must leave Lisbon almost at once. And as soon as I am gone those devils of the Holy Office will be at my house and interrogating all my servants and acquaintances, looking for my wealth. And they will find it, they have their ways.'

Montesinhos seemed more than a little taken aback by what I had just told him of my promise to Maria Beatriz. He continued to watch me closely and in silence now. In his gaze was the same troubled uncertainty that I had seen when we began this interview, and to avoid it I looked again around his little room. The lamp was burning as I supposed it always must be in here when the room was occupied, for there were no windows. Over near one corner was an enormous closed sea chest, at least three times as large as my own, so big that it gave the odd impression of being larger than the room that contained it. It was made of a lustrous kind of hardwood and most intricately carved. On the wall against which it stood was a large mirror in which I could see a reflection of the woodcut that hung on the facing wall. It showed a female head, bowed in prayer, presumably that of a saint, though which one I was not sure, certainly not one of my steady sellers in the street. I recognised Maria Beatriz's handiwork anyway, which made me think again of how the landlord had once hoped to make her his wife. I regretted that I had been so scornful of his pretensions, and had even laughed over them in his beloved's presence.

It required several further meetings between Montesinhos and me before I found myself agreeing definitely to take on the job he had offered me. It counted for a great deal in securing my agreement when at the end of our first interview in his parlour he revealed to me what cargo it was that he expected me to carry to London. As he had promised it was nothing so dangerous to my liberty and perhaps my life as gold. But when I first heard him say what it really was I thought I had not heard him right.

'Cochineal?'

'Indeed, yes, cochineal. Why not?'

I really could not provide an answer to that, except to say the merchandise was completely outside my experience. Certainly Uncle Felix never handled anything so exotic. I was not altogether sure what it was I was being asked to carry. I knew the stuff was involved extensively in the process of dying cloth and other wares, of course, and too had seen stoppered bottles of it in liquid form in my mother's kitchen. It had always bothered me rather that, as I had been told, this substance that was sometimes introduced into our meals was made up of the ground-up bodies of a variety of insect life that was to be found only in Mexico. I remember it was a favourite among Grandfather Jack's repertoire of stories: 'What the nasty little beetle who lately decorated the cake Adam just ate is doing in his insides now.' But as to how this famous creature entered the great labyrinth of trade and how it was finally disposed of in a commercial fashion were matters I had simply never considered.

'My nephew who trades out of Amsterdam bought the consignment from the corsairs of Algiers last year and personally super-vised its weighing and packing. He was kind enough to allow a portion of it to be dropped off in Lisbon for I had told him I wished to exchange money and gold soon for saleable goods. Ever since, it has been lodged in a sealed compartment in a warehouse near the Mint. It lies there in the name of a friend of mine who is an Old Christian and so safe from the suspicions of the damned Inquisition. However, he has taken a risk in concealing my own-ership, and will be very glad that now I am able to arrange its release. It is a most excellent commodity,' added my landlord, 'and in demand in every port of Europe. It gets a high price in the market, and a very high one indeed in relation to its bulk. In fact it's said that, second only to gold, cochineal is the most valuable export from the King of Spain's dominions in America. It is easy to carry, easier to sell at the end of the voyage. Your only difficulty will be to protect the stuff from the designs of the villains on-board and onshore who will want to steal it from you, because they will well know its value. That is why we will not let it go on to any ship unless the captain has guaranteed its storage throughout the voyage in a compartment that has been sealed tight shut with tar. It should all –' here Senhor Montesinhos' desperate eyes became a little less so as he allowed himself a small joke – 'be plain sailing.'

As I have said, the great difficulty in these negotiations was my sincere conviction I had made a definite promise to Dona Maria Beatriz that I would look after her father in her absence, and so that without knowing it I had sworn away all such opportunities as Senhor Montesinhos was offering before they had even appeared. It was Montesinhos himself who showed me that this need not be so, and who pointed the easy way through the difficulty. I cannot remember all the skilful arguments that he advanced during the week or so that followed our first interview in his parlour, nor even perhaps a tenth of them. They were very many but almost all of them tended towards the one ingenious proposition that in taking up this excellent opportunity I would be most truly watch-ing over Mr Hutchinson's *interests* – the essential Mr Hutchinson, in fact – in that his hopes and mine were now so securely entwined.

And that indeed the converse of this was that if I let such a chance pass away from me then I would have failed my promise to Maria Beatriz absolutely. For the essential Mr Hutchinson would not then have been protected by me.

I cannot think that I was really deceived by such stuff at the time; certainly ever since I have regarded it as the most unconvincing compound of sophistry and balderdash that was ever presented to an eager, hungry, impecunious young man. But there it was; that was the great engine that was always pulling me into compliance with Montesinhos' scheme. His desperation drove him into being a most forceful advocate, and my need seduced me into providing a thoroughly credulous jury.

As to the knotty problem of what would happen in my absence to Mr Hutchinson, who I had – as I was now thinking of it – 'in a manner' promised to look after, Senhor Montesinhos had the complete answer for that too. While I was away 'looking after the old gentleman's interests', he promised to fill my place in every particular as his companion, nurse, drinking companion, friend. And for those few hours when he would be unavoidably absent from Mr Hutchinson's side, owing to some unanticipated bit of family or other business that needed attending to, then he guaranteed that his man Simão would fill the temporary vacancy.

'And what, Sir,' I argued, 'if you should suddenly have to leave Lisbon for good? If the Inquisition should –?'

'Simão,' the landlord said again and with even more emphasis than before. 'He is the key to our difficulty. I intend to allow him an extra gratuity so as to ensure his constant availability, and I will double it if I should have to leave this house permanently. And the best of it is that the Senhor Hutchinson actually likes the company of Simão. He will not miss you in the least, Senhor Hanaway,' Montesinhos cried, with what I thought was a rather hurtful note of conviction ringing in his voice.

However, I concluded that he had a point. The landlord's servant was a big, blubbery, patient boy who for some reason could always induce good humour in Mr Hutchinson whenever he saw him. He used to poke the fellow with his stick so as to see the flesh wobble. Simão seemed not to mind these attentions, and in fact appeared to hold Mr Hutchinson in an almost reverential regard, the reason for which, I finally understood when I came into the old man's apartment one afternoon and overheard him telling the boy the most ridiculous inventions about his own heroic life and fabulous deeds, a cavalcade which, according to its author, stretched as far back as the battles of the English civil wars when he had 'stood at the right hand of Oliver Cromwell himself, Simão, giving him the benefit of my advice, you know'.

No, there was not much doubt that I would be adequately replaced in Mr Hutchinson's service by the combination of Simão and Senhor Montesinhos. Really, I thought, if Maria Beatriz knew of the change of guard – and nobody, as I recall, ever suggested that a letter be sent to Evora explaining the new situation to her – she might well have approved of it.

Finally I had the assurances of the person most concerned, besides myself and my landlord, in my forthcoming exodus – Mr Hutchinson himself. He added nothing much to what Montesinhos had already said to me, except to remind me many times over that I had the future security and happiness of his daughter in my grasp. Five hundred pounds. A small, a very small fortune. But it would be enough to make real his old dream of leaving Maria Beatriz in some degree of prosperity at his death – proprietor of a stationer's shop, it might be, or whatever she desired, within reason.

What could I say? Every argument was for my leaving him and going to England, and only the small voice of conscience and the memory of what I had really promised to my dear friend Maria Beatriz, now safely far away, urged me in the other direction.

2

Montesinhos instructed me to prepare for my departure, which he said could happen at any time. I was not sure how exactly I was supposed to do that beyond making sure that I had stored in my trunk my clothes and few other effects, except for those that I would be needing day-to-day. There was certainly no one I had to say my farewells to. Those to whom I might have wanted once to perform this ritual were either gone home – like my family, supposing there were any who would have talked to me, other than Nancy – or gone away like Maria Beatriz.

I did finally, a few days after my last conversation with Montesinhos, seek out the address on the Rua dos Douradores where Bento had told me that the shop his loving and wealthy new wife had bought for him was located. I was greatly looking forward to this visit, for my feelings towards my old room-mate had always been warm, and also I liked the prospect of seeing him in the midst of his new prosperity. But when I got to the place I found that the door of the shop – Bento had said it specialised in jewellery, trinkets, fine watches, knives and forks – was fastened shut with a great padlock, and peering in through the windows I could see no sign of movement inside, nor indeed of any stock or tables or chairs or candles or any other accoutrements of the average shop. It was all bare and dark.

I asked the fellows who kept the shops on either side if they knew where Bento Ferreira had gone, but both said they had no idea; in fact they appeared to be suggesting that they were hardly acquainted with their late neighbour at all. Certainly could not say when it was he had quitted his place. It was all very provoking and mysterious, and I was rather hurt that Bento had gone away, without coming over to the Rua do Parreiral to mention his plans to Mr Hutchinson and myself. Indeed, he had not told us that he was even contemplating such a move when he had appeared outside our building to wave Maria Beatriz goodbye a scant three weeks ago.

As I came home along the Rua do Parreiral that afternoon – in rather a melancholy mood after my disappointing excursion – I saw the boy Simão was standing outside the house, looking this way and that. He seemed to be in quite an agitated condition, and was glad enough when at last he saw me. He told me, as we turned into the house together, that Mr Hutchinson had sent him to find me and to say that I would sail on the morrow, that I must be at the wharf at dawn, and so I should make myself ready in everything, and that he, Simão, was appointed to help me in that. It took him some while to tell me all this, for he was so excited. But at last he had settled himself, and I understood most of what he had meant to say.

'There's not much left to do. A bit of folding and packing. You go on ahead and start with it, Simão,' I decided. 'I will speak first to Mr Hutchinson.'

I found the old gentleman in his sitting room as usual. He got to his feet when he saw me and came and clasped my hands.

'Simão has told you?'

'Tomorrow. At dawn.'

'Yes. Everything is ready. The cargo goes on-board tonight, the passage for both you and it has been paid, and the captain has all the necessary papers. You have only to present yourself at the entryway and give your name and you will be admitted.'

'I can think of only one thing that is lacking then.'

'What is it?' cried Mr Hutchinson, looking and sounding quite distraught, for evidently he could imagine nothing that was left undone.

'You haven't told me the name of the boat.'

The old man shook his head at his forgetfulness. 'Why it is the *Holly*. Captain Speight commands. A very decent sort of man – I've heard.'

'A packet boat?' I asked. I had used to know the names of all the Falmouth packets. My uncle preferred to ship his goods by them for they were fast and well armed, which latter advantage was always appreciated by passengers and factors both, for even in those days of so-called peace pirates and privateers still lurked along the coasts of Spain and France. Yet I did not remember the *Holly* among their number.

'Not a packet boat. It's a two-masted snow, but very capable. Out of London . . . We could not get you a berth on a packet for so many English are going home for the summer. But the *Holly* is a *fine* ship, Adam. Fast, you know, and carries all the cannon you could wish. And Captain Speight –'

'Is a very decent sort of man, yes, you said.'

Mr Hutchinson frowned to see me brooding now.

'Adam,' he said, 'my dear boy, do you think I would send you home in an unsafe vessel?'

I did not think he would do that knowingly. On the other hand what could he know of the state of a ship that was tied up at a wharf almost a half-mile away from us when he was practically confined to his own apartment? He watched me for a moment, saw that I was still not convinced.

'Do you think then,' he asked quite calmly, stifling whatever resentment he might be feeling at my reluctance, 'that Montesinhos would see his whole fortune committed to a captain and a ship that he did not trust?'

That made some sense to me. While I was not quite convinced, it made it certain that I would go indeed to the wharf at dawn and see for myself how matters stood. I nodded, turned away.

'Where are you going?'

'To see Montesinhos.'

'Why?'

'Because – because I wish to say farewell, to thank him for this opportunity, to –'

'He doesn't require thanking.'

I turned back to the old man. He was frowning at me, looking very obstinate.

'But of course I must see Montesinhos before I go.'

At which point the voice of Simão, who had come into the living room without either of us noticing, broke in on us. He did not speak English, except for a few phrases Mr Hutchinson had taught him, but had evidently heard the name of his master and, trying to be helpful, announced, 'Senhor Montesinhos has gone.'

Mr Hutchinson scowled at the fat servant. I turned and gaped at him.

'Gone?'

'The *familiares* came for him yesterday,' explained Simão, who appeared not to have noticed – as I had – the warning stares Mr Hutchinson was giving him. 'He was out, and they said they would come again today and so –' The fat boy nodded in approval at his master's good sense. 'He went away last night.'

I turned back to Mr Hutchinson. He was looking awkward, as well he might. 'Is it true?' I demanded. 'Montesinhos has fled?'

The old man nodded unhappily. 'He had to. They had given him fair warning. He owes his life to the kindness of Dom Jeronymo da Silva. Another *familiar* would have waited until his return yesterday and snatched him up.'

'He has gone for good?'

'Yes. He won't be back. He did not tell me where he was going, so that I wouldn't have to lie about it when they asked me. But one day, I suppose, we shall hear of him from Amsterdam or Algiers or Constantinople.'

I sat down heavily upon the nearest chair.

'Then I cannot leave,' I said. 'I can't go on that ship. Because –' I almost shouted as Mr Hutchinson tried to intervene. 'Because my agreement with Montesinhos was that he would take care of you in my absence.'

'Sir,' said Mr Hutchinson, drawing himself to his full height – an effort which very soon required him to sit down on a chair, 'I do not need to be "taken care of" by you or any other person. Besides –' he added in a gentler voice. 'I will have Simão –'

To which Simão hearing his name stepped forward and bowed to each of us. Mr Hutchinson fixed him with a scornful glare.

'And though,' he resumed, 'he is the closest object to an idiot that you will ever find not actually one, yet he is attentive and industrious and he loves me. I will be in good hands, Adam. And you know my daughter will return in only a week's time. You need not concern yourself at all about me.'

I brooded over the matter as he watched me with anxious eyes. I ought not to go, I knew that all the time – yet always my ambition, and my desire to pursue it and catch up with it and so win back the place in the world that I had lost, drove me in the opposite direction. It would be such a grievous disappointment to have to give up now . . . And it was true that Simão, though a simple fellow enough, would do all in his capacity to look after the old man. In that endeavour he would provide the brawn and Mr Hutchinson the brains and the direction. Unless there was a very bad turn for the worse in the latter's state of health, then they should be – they ought to be – it ought to be all right.

'Adam,' the old man said then, leaning forward so he could touch my knee, speaking in a voice that quavered with age and emotion, and gazing at me intently from his rheumy, desperate old eyes. 'If you love me like you would a father – which I think you do, as I love you like a son – then you will go . . .'

'Why shouldn't I wait for a packet that can take me? Only a week or two – and then Maria Beatriz will be home. We can tell her everything that is happening.'

'You *can't* wait.' Now the old man was gripping my knee with a ferocity that might have amazed me coming from someone half his age. 'Because,' he almost begged, 'the goods must be got away before the Inquisition finds them. When they know that Montesinhos has fled they will do everything in their power to make sure his wealth does not vanish too for by law that now belongs to them. They've already taken everything of value they could find in this house.'

'They have?'

'Go and look in his parlour if you don't believe me. Simão tells me it has been stripped to the very walls.'

'I should like to write to Maria Beatriz,' I said, and Mr Hutchinson, seeing he had won the argument, beamed cheerfully, and released my leg and got to his feet.

'Yes, you write to her. I will give her your letter. And I will explain anything else to her that you do not write. What is it you want here, you silly gawk?' He rounded then on poor Simão who was still hovering behind us. The fat boy gaped at the annoyance he heard in the old man's voice and for a moment could not speak. When at last the words returned, he explained that he had not been able to open my chest and so I must come up and turn the key for him for he could not do it.

I left Mr Hutchinson, after assuring myself that he would be eating decently this evening. Simão said the cook had a shoulder of lamb in the kitchen, which had been reserved for Senhor Montesinhos' consumption, but now that he was gone she thought the rest of the household might as well enjoy it for else it would spoil.

About an hour later Simão left the house, sitting on the back of a cart with my chest beside him. It was to be stowed on-board to await my arrival on the morrow. Before he went Simão had kindly provided me with some good wax candles (also from our departed landlord's personal store), which threw a much stronger light in my room than the tallow ones I was used to. By their aid I hoped to write the letter to Maria Beatriz which would, among other things, justify my conduct in leaving her father to Simão's care, explain why I had to go so precipitately and that I hoped by going it would be to establish both myself and my dear benefactors on the high road towards prosperity. Finally I hoped that I might show, in a few elegant and well-chosen sentences, by how much I knew I had profited from my association with her.

I couldn't do it. The justifications and explanations tumbled in no time at all into ugly things that looked very much like lies and dodging. And the few well-chosen words in which I would assure her of my respect and, in an elegant fashion, my devotion simply refused to appear. Instead, when I tried to write them I was always assailed by memories that had nothing to do with such shallow utterances. I saw Maria Beatriz leaning over me in the dawn light, dropping one brown nipple into my yearning mouth. I saw her under me, her eyes tight shut, her breathing harsh and sibilant as I rode her to ecstasy. I smelled the smell of her at those moments, and felt again how we would cling to each other. She told me she always wanted to shout out loud or scream, but durst not because she feared her father, who lay so close to us, would hear her. I saw her too with her head back laughing in the same silent frantic fashion as I told her about the pipkin vent. I remembered waking when it was light and finding her raised on one elbow and looking down at me, her beautiful eyes suffused with tenderness.

And how she had tried to draw me once, posing me sitting up in bed, naked, herself sitting close to me, frowning over the board on her lap and her charcoal. But she could not do it. She said she was ruined for that sort of drawing, for every time she tried to set me down on paper my face turned into that of a saint – 'And you know you are not that.'

And none of this could I put into writing. Frustrated by my incapacity, and thinking that if I put some food in my empty belly it might kindle my energies, I took a candle down through the house. When I went to the door of the kitchen, however, to ask the cook if she could give me something to eat, I was stopped by the sounds of merriment from within. I heard laughter, loud talk, the clink of glasses. I supposed that Montesinhos was the inadvertent host of a party being held by his erstwhile servants and their friends. I wondered if Simão was among the revellers. I ought to confirm that he had delivered the chest to the right ship. But I was shy, I hesitated to break in on their entertainment. Besides, I was not certain of what reception they would give me if I knocked on the door. There seemed to be a spirit of levity, even insubordination, at large in Montesinhos' house, and I did not want to invite it upon myself.

I turned away from the kitchen door. Along the little corridor near by was the door to Montesinhos' parlour. Curious to see if Mr Hutchinson had given me good information, I went to it, and turned the latch. Inside was pitch-black. I stepped in, held up my candle, turned round. 'Stripped to the walls' was the right description. Table, chairs, the wall hangings, the woodcut of the saint, the mirror and, most startling of all in its absence, the great chest that had once overshadowed this room. All was gone. Those rascals of the Holy Office had taken everything.

Unless, I thought, as again I found myself near the kitchen door, and again listened to the small riot that was going on behind it, unless it was that these unruly servants and their knavish friends had seen their opportunity, between their master's flight and the reappearance of the *familiares*, to purloin everything they could get their hands on. Which seemed a dangerous game, I reflected, as I climbed the stairs up from the basement, for the fathers were not known to be gentle with anyone who threatened their own God-given entitlement to be the sole plunderer of the fortunes of hapless New Christians. But then the sudden chance to obtain wealth, even a little of it, will make poor people do reckless and uncharacteristic things. I only needed to look at what I would be doing tomorrow morning to show me the truth of that.

In a way it did not matter which set of scoundrels had made off with Montesinhos' property – except that I did not like the thought of leaving Mr Hutchinson in the hands of unruly, disorderly servants. However, since I had swallowed so much already in the pursuit of my own small piece of fairy gold, I doubted I would have strained much at this extra morsel of difficulty. Still I was very pleased when I opened the door to the Hutchinsons' apartment to find that Simão, who I had imagined revelling with the others below, was instead sitting in a deep chair in the parlour, half asleep. He came awake as I stood over him and endeavoured to get to his feet. I made him stop and sat down opposite him. He said he had been in the apartment since he'd got back from the ship. He had waited because Mr Hutchinson had told him I would soon be here, for that he wanted to assure me that my chest was on-board and my cargo expected there at any moment.

I thanked him for his consideration and his labours. I asked him then about the carousing I had heard in progress in the kitchen, and he said he knew who was party to it, it was some friends of the cook's: 'black fellows from her own country'. They had, he explained, broken into Senhor Montesinhos' cellar, and were engaged in drinking it dry or as near as they could get to that before they made themselves unconscious.

I wondered briefly whether I shouldn't go to find an officer of the law to take these rogues into custody. The problem was that I could probably spend from now until tomorrow's dawn and my time of departure before I found anything resembling that article. It was worse than in London where the officers of the watch, though too often old and broken-down, are at least known to be in certain places at certain times in the night and one may find them usually within an hour of starting to look for them. Here everything was in confusion, and I hardly knew even who it was I should be looking for.

So I abandoned thoughts of having those sots turned out from the bottom of the house. Instead I asked Simão, making my voice as solemn as I could, whether he really thought he would be able to look after Mr Hutchinson properly, 'in such times as these', until his daughter returned at the end of the week. He was silent for a moment – and I truly think if he had in any way wavered or fallen short in his response I would have given up this business, advanced though it was by now. But he swore to me then that he knew he could do the work, that he wanted to do it because he loved the old man, and that until Dona Maria Beatriz came home he would not let Mr Hutchinson draw waking breath without himself being close at hand. I was so pleased at his reply, and by the fact that for once sincerity had dispelled the cloud of confusion that usually covered the poor boy's eyes so that his gaze shone frankly and honestly as he looked at me. It made up my mind on the spot. I would go on the morrow, and I would go with a light heart for Mr Hutchinson would be secure in the care of this loyal lad.

I took out two *cruzados* from my pocket and tried to give them to him, saying that I wanted to show my appreciation for his conduct. He would not take them at first. He said he had already been paid by Senhor Montesinhos for the work. Then he said that what I was offering him was too much and I took this as a hint, whether he intended it or not, that he would accept a lesser donation. And so I pressed the two *cruzados* upon him once more and said that only one of them was for his own use, but that I would be grateful if he would take the other and go to a nearby cook-shop and bring me back a good supper for I hadn't eaten in so long. This he agreed to do. I remembered to ask him to fetch a bottle of wine back with it, for I no longer liked the idea of applying to the kitchen for a share of what was left of Montesinhos' store.

When he was gone I went through into the living room. I had thought from something Simão had said that Mr Hutchinson had already retired for the night. But in fact I found him sitting in his usual chair, beside the grate, though it was empty now, unlike those many times over the winter when I had sat with him in here and watched the fire crinkle and glow as we lazily discussed the events of the day, and – when Mr Hutchinson was in the mood – those of the last three-quarters of a century too. But on most nights now there was no need for fires.

I noted another variation from our usual practice as I sat down, which was that there was no bottle near the old man's hand. I told him that I had asked Simão to bring one with my supper, and that he would be very welcome to share it with me. I remembered then that I had not asked if he had eaten yet and was already half out of my chair to go and follow Simão and extend my order to him – when Mr Hutchinson said there was no need.

'You ate a proper meal? Or just picked at something?'

'Damn it, Adam. A proper meal. The lamb and some pettitoes and some sort of tart which Simão said was made from pears though I couldn't taste 'em. That cook I believe is getting very slipshod. I may have to have words with her.'

I did not think it worth telling him in what condition I imagined the cook to be just now, and that it was a small miracle that anything edible had come out of her kitchen in the last few hours.

In a little while we heard a knock on the front door. Mr Hutchinson made a fearful face and whispered to me that I should not answer it for it might be the officers of the Inquisition come to wreak still more havoc in Montesinhos' old home. I did not think, if it was the *familiares*, that they were going to be stopped from entering by a mere shut door. Of course when I opened the door it was to find Simão on the landing holding a tray with my supper on it. I thanked him and said I would sit up with Mr Hutchinson for the rest of the evening and see him to bed too, and that he should feel free to go to bed himself or – I nodded down the stairs from where could still be heard the faint sounds of savage merriment – to go wherever else he wanted. He told me he would certainly go to his parents' to sleep now for he must be up early tomorrow to wake me.

And so it was that the good ship the *Holly* received my person just after dawn of the following day. As Mr Hutchinson had promised me, there really had been nothing more for me to do than present myself at the entrance and give my name to the fellow who stood guarding it. Now, with morning well advanced, I still loitered near the entrance, watching all the bustle as the seamen prepared for the ship's imminent departure and my fellow-passengers accomplished their separate arrivals.

Wearying at last of this entertainment, I left the area and went in search of other diversions. Which was why I did not see the moment when the ship at last separated itself from the quay and we began to drop downriver. I, in the company of a couple of other passengers, was in mid-ships then, transfixed by a small local drama in which a cat, that we supposed was a member of the

Holly's crew, was clinging to a spar, which at this moment needed to be raised or lowered and was resisting all attempts to dislodge it.

When at last this interesting spectacle ended – the cat came down of its own accord and stalked away from us along the deck with its nose in the air as if to say it wondered what all the fuss was about – it dawned on me that the boat indeed was moving and that I should hurry towards the stern if I wanted a last glimpse of Lisbon. But the opportunity was already gone, for a mist now lay upon the river, and the city, though it was less than a mile behind us, was already almost invisible. Only the castle standing on its hill could be clearly seen. I felt very sorry to have left the place where I had spent nearly a full year without a backward glance, as it were.

However I was not allowed to indulge myself long in such regrets for I felt then a tap upon my shoulder. I turned to find the Captain's mate standing behind me. He said he came to me with a message from Mr Speight that the gunshot from the fort at Belém was anticipated momentarily, and that, once the ship had dropped anchor, the officers of the customs would shortly come on-board, and I should therefore take myself off to my cabin to make my trunk available to be inspected.

This gentleman added, as we walked together towards my berth, that he wondered to have found me at large on the deck instead of already beside my cargo, guarding it, for that he understood said cargo was a valuable one and I ought to beware the larcenous intentions of the other people on board the *Holly*. Most especially, he added, I should watch out for the crew, several members of which had been notorious jailbirds in their land days, some of whom indeed had only escaped the hangman by running away to sea. The mate went on to say that he would be very glad to arrange for an entirely trustworthy watch to be placed upon my cargo throughout the voyage by some particular acquaintances of his on-board, 'tough as nails and honest as the day', at very reasonable rates to myself.

I told him, in rather a lofty spirit, that I had no need of his assistance. That, once these ceremonies with the customs people were over, I had the Captain's promise that my cargo would be taken below and sealed up against all possibility of theft. To which the mate only made a curious face, difficult for me to interpret, tipped his hat over his eyes and strode away from me as he went, whistling a certain tune that was also, I remembered, a favourite of my poor father and was called, I think, 'The Maid Deceiv'd'.

I resumed my march towards my cabin in quite a pensive mood. However, I soon recaptured my spirits. As I had expected, the great bulk of Montesinhos' trunk still sat in the middle of the room, unviolated, with its padlock in place. Walking round it to make sure everything was secure, I heard the cannon fire from onshore, soon followed by the rattle of chains as the anchor was sent overboard. I sat down on the only place available to me – since the chest filled so much of the space – which was my bed. I waited the arrival of the customs fellows without apprehension. I had been assured by Senhor Montesinhos that all formalities had been completed before the cochineal had left its warehouse, and the duties agreed and paid over to the chief of the customs in that place down to the last *cruzado*. A receipt to this effect, together with a bill of lading that bore my name and showed exactly what I was carrying with me, had been lodged with Captain Speight. I supposed that the same process had been gone through in connection with all the other goods he was carrying.

This being so, I started to grow curious as to what exactly was the purpose or point of this new set of officers who, as I waited, were being rowed out to the *Holly*. There was a polite knock on the door just then. A young fellow of the crew, who I thought might be in the position of steward to the passengers, for I had seen him taking drinks and fruit to another of the cabins, put his head in and asked me if there was anything that I wanted. I told him not at the moment, and then before he could get away enquired if he knew what the officers from the shore might be seeking on the *Holly*.

'Gold and Jews,' was his succinct answer. He left me quite easy in my mind, for of course I was not guilty of concealing either article. Half an hour went by. At last I heard a knock upon the door. I got to my feet as Captain Speight appeared, ushering in two fellows, who looked me over in what I deemed to be a most impudent fashion. It was curious too: we had only just left the shore, we were still within the bounds of King João's empire, and yet already I was finding his subjects strange to look at, different, foreign indeed. At least I found these two so: in their ill-looking cloaks and wigs and with giant rapiers dangling from their belts, they appeared like characters in some play in a London theatre-house set in Illyria or Timbuctoo or some other illusory realm.

They looked to the Captain who then asked me to unlock my trunk and open it for inspection. I could not at first understand why these fellows had not asked me to do this directly, and bridled a little to think they were taking on such airs as to decline to communicate with me except through the Captain. Then I realised that, accustomed to the ignorance of almost every other English-man they had ever dealt with, they imagined I would have little or no command of their language. Also that the Captain himself had no reason to suspect that I understood Portuguese. I thought of embarrassing them all by demonstrating by how much they were wrong in that assumption and actually was preparing the words and phrases to show not only that I could talk their language but that I could throw in a few colourful epithets from the streets of Lisbon whenever I felt like it. But then it came to me that this would be a very minor victory and that it might irritate the officers needlessly. Though I had no particular reason to care whether they were irritated or not, it was better, I reasoned, to have contented, tranquil scoundrels looking through my goods rather than enraged and lively ones.

So, without speaking, I unlocked the padlock and opened the trunk. This is easier to say than it was to do. The lid was so heavy I struggled for a few moments to raise it. The officers did not move an inch to help me, but only watched my efforts with a faint sneer on their swarthy foreign faces. The Captain at last stepped forward and took a part of the lid and together we pushed it back until it rested on its hinges and the trunk lay open for inspection.

It was the first time I had set eyes upon the cargo that was to make – or at least be the beginnings of – my fortune. And yet of course I did not exactly see it now. The cochineal was bagged up in gunnysacks, I reckoned at about two or three pounds weight to each sack. All one saw was the topmost layer of them, and I supposed of course that this layer was repeated a number of times over until one arrived at the bottom of the trunk. As far as I could see there was no necessity to disturb their neat symmetry and I was correspondingly annoyed when the two officers began to haul away the bags on the top layer.

Just as I would have predicted to them, had they bothered to ask me, an exactly similar layer of gunnysacks appeared under the first. The officers, as if exhausted by their labours, paused at this point. One of them, who I had decided was the superior, glanced significantly at the other. Who pulled one of the bags of the second layer out of the trunk and, so fast that I had not time to stop him, whipped out a long-bladed knife from his belt and slit open the top of the sack. Inside was lined with paper, this too he made a cut in, then reached in and drew out a handful of rusty-looking powder, of which the individual grains were quite large, larger say than pepper when it has been ground. He rubbed these grains between his fingers and then applied his hand to his mouth and tasted them. He grinned up at his superior then and nodded and said, '*Cochinilha.*'

I was about to say that of course it was cochineal, he only had to look at the lading bill, but before I could the other fellow started speaking rapidly to the Captain. Who listened with an effortful frown on his forehead. I could have told him what the fellow was at as soon as the words were out of his mouth. But I was made so indignant by what I'd heard that I struggled to speak and by then the Captain had worked out the meaning of what had just been said.

'They want to take one of those bags with them. No,' he corrected himself, for the junior officer was holding up two fingers at this moment, 'they want two.'

'Certainly not,' I exploded. 'All the duties have been paid. They have no right to –'

'Otherwise they will search through the whole chest.'

'Let them. I have nothing to hide.'

My anger, if not my meaning, was conveying itself to the officers. They looked towards the Captain for enlightenment. They were starting to look a little annoyed.

'My apologies, senhors,' I heard the Captain say in halting Portuguese. 'He's just a silly young fool, who does not understand how things are done in this port.' Here he turned to me. I was about to upbraid him for his impertinence towards a passenger – to me! – when, in English now, he told me quickly that, if I did not give them what they wanted, it was likely that they would order the chest to be transferred to the shore. This would cause him, Speight, a short delay that he did not wish to endure. And for Mr Hanaway it would mean that his cargo and his person would remain on land until another ship had been found to take them off – and did I wish to go through all the inconvenience and expense that that would bring upon me? He added that he suspected that many more bags of cochineal than just two would be abstracted from my chest by one expedient or another while I waited to get away.

Of course I didn't want to go through all this, and so in the end I let them take the two gunnysacks. They made off with them at a fast rate, as if they knew very well they were thieves and villains and wanted to get back to their hiding-place as soon as they might. I went out to watch their boat heading for the shore. Captain Speight came and stood next to me. I suppose he was sorry for me. Perhaps he even regretted that he had felt it necessary to call me a silly young fool in front of those two garlick-stinkers. At any rate I had the pleasure that evening, when I was dining at his table, of turning to a Portuguese steward who was serving us and addressing him in his own language in the most confident and fluent style. The sight of bold Captain Speight spitting out a mouthful of hot soup in his dismay went some way to assuaging my hurt feelings.

However, that was a pleasure still some way off. Just now, watching those rogues scuttling back to shore, I could think only of my loss. Captain Speight moved away from me as I continued to stand there fuming. Gradually, just as the boat carrying the officers disappeared into the haze that lined the shore, so my anger too began to fade away. Still I was left with a feeling of discontent. I blamed myself for the debacle, though really I suppose there was no reason to do that. But it was certainly an unfortunate beginning to my independent career as a trader. I had handed over to those fellows what was not mine to give. I resolved therefore that Senhor Montesinhos and his family should not be the losers by my action. I would pay for those two bags out of my own share.

I saw now that the anchor was already back on deck. Obedient to the new shapes the sails were cutting against the hazy sky, the ship shook itself and started to move. I went towards the prow. We were heading for the river's mouth; beyond it lay the rock of Lisbon and beyond that, under skies as clear as those upon the land were now thick and murky, was the great ocean itself. I gazed towards these immensities of sea and sky in a most tangled frame of mind. I knew that a great opportunity was opening before me. I wanted to throw myself at it, and yet I wanted to turn back. New times, scenes, prospects were beckoning me onwards, but the pull of what I had left behind was growing stronger with every moment. I had a sudden foreboding that the less than twelve-month period I had passed in Lisbon, with all its difficulties and its great stretches of tedium and frustration, would be for me the most memorable of my life – and I was flying away from it and nothing that I did or said would turn this ship around so that I could claim my paradise once again. And this I was thinking even as I was making a concurrent desperate attempt not to remember the two people who I would most and for ever regret having parted from.

In the end, of course, I had to yield and admit them too to my memories. They were my family after all. Mr Hutchinson had been fretful last night, I remembered. After I had helped him into his bed he had lain there looking up at me and plucking at the coverlet. I had recalled that a friend of mine, who had seen his father die after a long illness, said it had been like that just before the end, the fingers plucking repeatedly at the bed sheets, as if the soul was already in agitation and trying to depart. I feared very much that the same was happening to Mr Hutchinson, indeed I feared it so much that my first thought this morning, when Simão had roused me, was that he had come to tell me the old man was dead. It wasn't so, of course, indeed Mr Hutchinson had seemed unusually vigorous when I went downstairs. He was standing at his door. He had clasped me strongly in his arms and smiled at me dry-eyed and simply said he wished me well, and then had turned back into his apartment without another word.

But the night before it had been quite different. He had not been vigorous but frail and, as I have said, seemed very agitated. I finally asked him if there was anything the matter. He did a certain amount of shaking his head upon the pillow, showing me he did not want to speak. But I had grown certain that there was something weighing on his spirit and that it would do him good to rid himself of it by telling me what it was. So I pressed him a little and at last it came out. He said that he had been wicked, that he had wronged someone. I asked him who it was he thought he had wronged and he said at last it was Senhor Montesinhos, and that he would never be able to make up for his iniquity, nor even apologise for it, for now the poor man had fled.

I did not know at all what he meant. I asked him what he thought he had done to harm Montesinhos, but he would by no means tell me that. At last, his distress still persisting, I told him what I believed absolutely to be the truth, which was that, whatever misdemeanour he thought he had committed against our landlord, by taking a part in this scheme to remove that persecuted man's fortune into safety, and so save him from the sink of poverty that he must otherwise have fallen into, we both were doing a very good thing, which would surely in Mr Hutchinson's case make up for any unkindness he might have shown before.

Oh, I had truly loved that old man, I thought now. And loved his daughter even more. All at once this thought came crashing in on me – much greater, stronger it felt to me than the waves that were now pounding against the hull below me. How much I loved her. How greatly I had injured her. How much I had lost . . . I knew that I could not even comprehend how much that was, but I felt it in my gut now as a raw pain, an agony tearing at me, making me sweat prodigiously even in the frigid breezes that roared in off the ocean.

The next moment, with that infernal intrusion of farce that in my youth always seemed to occur whenever I felt most deeply and sincerely about something, my stomach lurched, my mouth sprang open, a veritable eruption of vomit exploded out of me, to be almost instantly whipped back into my face by the roaring winds that the *Holly* was now battling against. A passenger who was standing to the left of me, and who had not seen my little accident, shouted above the gale that he would lay odds that our ship would be driven back into the river, and we should be tying up again in Lisbon before nightfall.

'And how should you like that, Sir?' he asked, turning to me just as I was trying to detach a notably undigested lump of vomit from my hair.

BOOK THREE

Dona Antônia

S he knew she should not despair. Knew that it was the common lot of women to be set aside in their husband's affections, particularly after they had passed a certain age, and were no longer comely. And in her case, her Nicolau, her lord and master, had behaved with absolute propriety and kindness. She had heard horrific stories of wives who were no longer considered worthy to decorate the marriage bed being sent into exile, or into convents, or even locked up permanently in an obscure room in the same house where their husbands were enjoying the new mistress – perhaps several mistresses, God save us – the noise of their revels penetrating even to the lonely recess where the abandoned old woman passes her gloomy, empty days and nights.

Nothing like this had happened to Dona Antônia, of course. If her husband had wanted to be cruel, thank God she had a pair of big sons who would not have permitted it. But there was no need. Nicolau had not banished her. He had simply withdrawn a little. And he had done it so apologetically. Regretfully. Only because she knew him so well did she understand what was happening. There was just – a little more space between them one day. And then more and more space. And he was distracted often. The faraway look in his eyes. He was thinking of *her*. She knew it even before the fact of his infidelity had been established for her without possibility of doubt. Her loyal maid, who through her family knew everything that was going on in Evora, told her; a candid friend who was 'so very sorry to have to tell you this, dear Dona Antônia, but . . .' had weighed in too. Oh, she knew all about it, perhaps even before he had pressed his ardour upon his new love to the ultimate moment. The deed itself. *A culminação*.

The woman's name was Teresa and she lived at the convent of

Santa Clara in the city. Was it her jealousy that made Dona Antônia feel that her husband's betrayal was made even worse by his becoming a lover of nuns? She had always found this style of seduction somewhat sickening to contemplate, and somehow ignoble, for all that His Majesty Dom João himself was the chief *freirático* in his kingdom, with his great whore Mother Paula of the convent of Odivelas. True, the girl that her Nicolau had taken up with was not a full-fledged *freira*, as she had not yet taken her final vows, but was what they called 'a little nun', a *freirinha*. Still she was at least nominally *religiosa*, and Dona Antônia knew there were zealots in the Church who whispered that hellfire waited for those who besmirched the brides of Christ by lying with them. She was troubled by the fact that when she thought of her dear husband being punished by satanic fires for this reason she couldn't help feeling a little pang of satisfaction.

Oh, but she didn't really want him to suffer. She wondered sometimes if her hatred for this Teresa had something to do with the fact that if Nicolau had not come to her father thirty years ago and asked for her hand then she herself might have ended up like this girl. It was the common lot of an unmarried female of the noble class to be mewed up behind the convent walls with a gaggle of other young women, dependent for their amusement on the gallants who came to the grille every night to flirt and play their guitars and accept the presents the nuns had prepared for them. Perhaps a love poem, or some piece of sweet pastry, the delectable *doces* – or, at last, for the gentleman-callers to be admitted beyond the grille and allowed the sweetest present of all in what lay between the legs of the sinful *freira* . . .

No, it was too much. Dona Antônia could not bear to think of it. What was that jingle she had heard once that was supposed to have been made up by Mother Paula of Odivelas, who bore the nickname of Trigueirinha, the little pepper-pot?

> You call me Trigueirinha
> I'm not scandalised;
> Trigueirinha is the pepper
> That is laid on the King's table!

Oh disgraceful. Oh shameful. How could Dona Antônia bear it? Why could she not stop thinking of it? Oh Nicolau. Nicolau . . .

It was the reason why she was particularly glad that this was one of the years for Maria Beatriz to visit her. Enough with the pitying, excited glances of her maids. Enough with the sympathetic eyes and secret delight of the Evora ladies who questioned her so intrusively. She desired to talk the thing over with her oldest friend, with whom she had never been anything but candid and who she had admired and loved since they'd been girls at school together, not only for her compassion and kindness but for her intelligence. Maria Beatriz would see through all the muddle and shame and come to the heart of the matter. And whatever she advised – however hard that advice might be to follow – would, Dona Antônia knew, be the right thing for her to do.

As she prepared to take her friend's morning chocolate up to her room, Dona Antônia remembered the days of their earliest friendship. It had not been a good school. Almost a school for paupers, in fact. Her own father had never had much money, had largely spent his life waiting for his two older brothers to die so that he could come at last into the inheritance of the family's meagre property near Abrantes. And Maria Beatriz's father's poverty, she understood from the first, was even more cruel than that of her own. Mr Hutchinson had only been able to keep his daughter in that school for one half a year – but it was time enough for the two little girls to become fast friends. And, amazingly, through all the years and the vicissitudes they had kept up their friendship, though now they rarely saw each other, and their love was expressed almost entirely in letters, which of course made their rare moments when they were together so precious. Besides, everybody in the family liked to have Maria Beatriz to stay. Her sons adored her. And Nicolau too had always had a soft spot for the 'tall *inglêsa*' with the enchanting eyes. Indeed in the early days of their marriage, when they lived in Lisbon and Maria Beatriz had been a frequent visitor to their home, she had sometimes felt a little jealous at the way her husband and her friend evidently got on so well, for she knew humbly that Maria Beatriz was much prettier than her.

But of course Dona Antônia had never had cause for anxiety. And the fears – product of her own amazement at her unbelievable luck at attracting the love of a young man as handsome as Nicolau, and with such prospects in life too – soon went away. She was left with her undiminished devotion to her friend. Unlike her own father, Nicolau came early into his inheritance. They moved back to his family's estate near Evora, and entered upon a life of ease and prosperity, surrounded by the respect due from every side for the young heads of a noble family, long renowned in the central Alentejo.

Maria Beatriz had passed through a very different course of life. Dona Antônia watched with anxiety as she saw from a distance how the Hutchinson family had to struggle even to stay afloat. She rejoiced when she heard of the marriage to Ruffino Fonseca, for all that he was only a furniture-maker and her friend a true gentle-woman. Nevertheless, she had been glad of the match, and to know that at last the shadow of poverty would be lifted perma-nently from the Hutchinsons. So glad had she been, she had even persuaded Nicolau to leave his beloved Evora and go back to Lisbon so that they could attend the wedding. That had been a good day, a wonderful day, one to treasure: Maria Beatriz's tranquil happiness, the man Fonseca's understandable pride, her own relief that matters had turned out so well and she need not worry about her friend any more.

Then had come another day, not much more than a year later, that brought a letter from Maria Beatriz in which, in the course of five brief sentences, she explained that Fonseca was no more. She told Antônia that she was all right, she knew that her friend would want to come to her but really she had no need of that. She would get through this sad time on her own. And with the help of her father, of course, who was the soul of kindness to her. She would write again soon.

Dona Antônia felt a little hurt that her friend would refuse her own comfort – before it had even been offered, she thought sadly. But those unworthy emotions were at once swept away by sympathy for her darling's loss. She wrote immediately to Maria Beatriz, a letter which her friend did not reply to. And in fact they did not correspond for many months after this. On the whole, Dona Antônia was glad for it. Happy in her own marriage, she had a superstitious feeling that she should avoid contact with someone who had been so cursed. It was the only failure in their long friendship, Dona Antônia sometimes reflected afterwards. At the time she had the excuse of believing that, now the worst had happened, at least Maria Beatriz's future was secure, for Fonseca had been so wealthy and all that he owned would now go to his widow.

When at last they re-established their relations Dona Antônia was horrified to find that her belief in her friend's prosperity was all an illusion. So far from being rich, Fonseca at his death was even deep in debt. It was not that Maria Beatriz complained about this. It all came out in jokey little asides in her letters. Dona Antônia was further horrified when she became aware by this means that Maria Beatriz – a gentlewoman! Her friend! – was forced to produce drawings that were sold in the streets to help keep herself and her father alive. And then, later, a further shock when Maria Beatriz disclosed – another humorous paragraph – that her father's pension had been annulled, and that he proposed now to replace it by himself going out into the streets and selling sacred images to whichever low people he could persuade to part from a couple of greasy coins.

'Imagine it!' Maria Beatriz wrote, having described this outrage. 'You are acquainted with a pair of peddlers, my dear and noble friend.'

Oh, she could imagine it only too well. Mr Hutchinson brought so low! And Dona Antônia had always admired him so, since she was a little girl and used to see at her friend's apartment the handsome man who was her father. And little Antônia had heard from his own lips of the great family in England that he came from, and a mighty soldier who was his uncle and a splendidly devout woman who was his aunt. And now he was a peddler in the Baixa?

She could not let this go on. She was prepared to make a regular allowance to her friend out of her own resources. In fact, as a first instalment, she did send a note for a substantial sum for Maria Beatriz to take to Nicolau's man of business in Lisbon. Maria

Beatriz sent it back, accompanying it with a frosty letter, as brief as that which had announced Fonseca's death, to say that she understood her friend had meant her action kindly, but she must never try to send money again. Dona Antônia was hurt by this for she really had meant well. But she refused to let it divide them. It was one of those years when Maria Beatriz visited her in Evora. They quickly cleared up any lingering misunderstanding over the money. Maria Beatriz promised her that it was not misplaced pride that had made her reject it. She said they – her father and she – truly had no need of it. They were happy as they were, just making ends meet. And though Dona Antônia looked carefully to see by how much this was mere bravado and concealment, she couldn't find any of that. Maria Beatriz did look happy, she *was* happy. Lord knows why, Dona Antônia thought.

And now, here they were, two old ladies. Both had celebrated their forty-sixth birthday last month – though celebrate was not the word that, on reflection, Dona Antônia thought was appropriate, for her at any rate. Life had passed them by. The end was in sight. Or perhaps they would live another forty years. In God's hands. Dona Antônia thought she could bear even a long life, as long as Maria Beatriz was there. Her husband had left her now, essentially. Her two sons – she could hear them now, in another part of the house, shouting good-naturedly at each other – they would leave her soon. Perhaps to be married. Or just to leave. José had already moved into his own apartment in Evora, and was always talking about going to Paris, and Timóteo would always go where his brother went. But as long as she had Maria Beatriz in her life, even as far away as Lisbon, she could manage.

She quickened her step as she approached the staircase. Such melancholy thoughts. Maria Beatriz's extinction, what Dona Antônia would do if she was not there. As she climbed the stairs it came to her why she was entertaining such notions. She had felt a faint but undeniable anxiety almost since the moment Maria Beatriz had arrived in Evora this year. Of course the journey here had been particularly arduous. The coach had twice had to stop for a wheel to be repaired. And there were rumours of bandits along the road, which luckily proved unreliable but had kept the convoy unsettled at night. It was no wonder Maria Beatriz had looked exhausted – ill almost. Hardly allowing time for their usual effusive greeting, Dona Antônia had done her duty and hurried her friend off to bed, with a maid to watch over her and, when it was needed, bring her drinks and apply cold compresses to her forehead and arms.

When Dona Antônia saw her again the next morning, Maria Beatriz had seemed quite recovered, and they spent a happy day catching up with their news. Dona Antônia did not think it appropriate, however, when they were both still so freshly delighted to be in each other's company, to speak of what was most on her mind, in a word her husband's cruel betrayal of her. Instead they talked only of cheerful things: how tall José and Timóteo had grown since Maria Beatriz had last been here; a great deal of Evora gossip that Maria Beatriz always enjoyed hearing; how Mr Hutchinson's health had vastly improved since the winter. Bad things, sad things could wait until the morrow, Dona Antônia had decided. But in fact the morrow came, and then a whole week of morrows and she still had not yet broached to her friend the matter of Nicolau's behaviour.

She was waiting for the right time. And that never appeared. Whenever she gathered herself to disclose the unhappy story, something in Maria Beatriz's eyes, or the way she touched her cheek and her temple, as if testing how hot or cold her skin was, or how she sighed often and so tiredly, would make her friend hesitate and then turn aside from what she wanted to say.

She *is* ill. Dona Antônia was suddenly sure of it. She flew up the second flight of stairs. The other morning she had gone into Maria Beatriz's room early, and had smelled something she had hardly wanted to identify, for her friend was always so very cleanly and fastidious. But it was certainly vomit she had smelled. The chamber pot was in its corner, looked spotless, was carefully covered. But still there was this reek, and Dona Antônia wondered if the unbelievable had happened and her poor friend had been incontinent, unable to get to the receptacle until she had voided the contents of her stomach – where? Dona Antônia's quick gaze had shifted over the carpet, the bed linen, where could it be? Of course, she didn't like to make enquiries – it was surely up to Maria Beatriz to be candid and tell all. After all they were the dearest of friends who should have no secrets from each other.

Guiltily aware that she was presently concealing at least one big secret from her friend, Dona Antônia approached the door. She had raised her hand to knock on it, when she heard through the wood the unmistakable sounds of retching from inside. *Yes*, she is ill, thought Dona Antônia, she's very ill. She felt as if she was about to unravel from the grief that overwhelmed her when she thought this. My poor darling Maria Beatriz. She threw open the door. Maria Beatriz was standing over the chamber pot. The same stink was in the air as before.

Her friend looked up, their eyes met.

'Well, now you know,' Maria Beatriz said, wiping her mouth with a handkerchief, closing the lid of the chamber pot. She went to sit upon the bed. From there she stared at her friend. There was a clear touch of defiance in her gaze.

Oh, what a fool I have been, thought Dona Antônia immediately.

But how is it possible, how –? Her brain was reeling. She brought the tray to the bed. Maria Beatriz took hold of the cup of chocolate, sipped at it, nodded gratefully at her friend. Dona Antônia sat beside her on the bed.

'Are you going to marry?' she asked at last.

Maria Beatriz shook her head.

'He is already married?' Dona Antônia asked, feeling a little twinge of anger in spite of herself when she said it.

'He's too young,' her friend said. Then, smiling, she took Dona Antônia in her arms. 'Don't look tragical,' she said. 'I am very happy. As long as you will not send me away as a fallen woman.'

'How can you possibly –?' Dona Antônia began to protest, when she saw that her friend was only joking. She felt Maria Beatriz's arms about her. She rested her head against Maria Beatriz's shoulder, just above her breast. As she had done, she remembered, a thousand times before.

'But really,' she said, 'how *can* you? How can it happen?'

She really wanted to know. Her own monthly periods had

ceased permanently two years ago. And even before that she had decided that she was long past the possibility of bearing children again. Five had been born to her, of which only her two sons had survived infancy. The girls had all died. She had been glad to know that she would never again have to deal with that sorrow. Yet she had also thought since then that her husband's defection might have had something to do with her becoming barren, even though they had never spoken of it.

'Well, evidently it can,' said Maria Beatriz, her lips against her friend's hair.

'When?'

'In December, I think.'

'And who?'

'I will tell you. But not just now.'

'Do you love this man?'

After a moment Maria Beatriz nodded.

'Of course you will stay with us until–'

'Of course I won't. My father needs me.'

'But–'

But Maria Beatriz pressed a hand firmly upon her friend's lips, silencing her.

'That's enough for now,' she said. 'I'm glad you know. I will tell you everything. But first I want us to talk about you.'

'Me! But I've done nothing. Nothing's happened to me . . . compared with . . . with what . . .'

Maria Beatriz pushed her friend gently away from her. Gazed into her eyes, searched her face. Dona Antônia could not look away.

'Yes, my darling,' Maria Beatriz nodded at last. 'Now I want you to tell me about you and Nicolau.'

Adam

1

I wish I had taken my fellow-passenger's bet, for I would have won it. The wind blew strong against us for almost an hour and then, as suddenly as it had roared into life, it fell away and we were able to proceed across the bar. We headed almost due west for the rest of that day and into the night, then turned towards the north and soon were skirting the coast of Spain and aiming for the Bay of Biscay and home.

After our struggle before the bar, we had only one further incidence of foul weather when a sharp blow rose up while we were off that portion of the English coast the sailors call the Downs, which lasted all of one day. Otherwise conditions were clement, the winds kind, and the Captain was able to bring our little ship to the mouth of the Thames in just under two weeks. Another day brought us into the river, and at about five o'clock in the afternoon we tied up at the dockyard at Rotherhythe. Waiting on land was found to be a number of merchant's runners, whose masters had been alerted by the signals along the coast which had begun wagging the information of the *Holly*'s safe arrival almost from the moment we appeared in home waters. I sent by one of these fellows, as he prepared to go back to the City to advise his master of the state of our cargoes, a message to Mr Solomon Marks at Royal Exchange, Cornhill. In it I announced my arrival, and added that I had brought with me a cargo that I believed to be valuable and concerning which I would very much welcome his expert advice, which I was confident he would not withhold from me for the love he knew my father had borne to him when he lived.

I guessed that by the time Mr Marks received this advice it

would be too late and dark for him to set out for where we lay, particularly as his journey would pass in part through some of the most infamous and dangerous streets and districts of London. No prudent man – and I knew my father's old clerk to be nothing if not that – would take such a risk. Captain Speight was so obliging as to allow me to remain on board the *Holly* for the night. He warned me very solemnly though that he could not guarantee my safety, nor certainly that of my cargo through the hours of darkness, for the waterfront teemed with rogues and cut-throats and it was possible that word of what I was carrying would have been conveyed to all the low taverns of the neighbourhood. He told me that he would have a guard, armed with blunderbusses, standing at the entrances all night to protect his own cargoes, but that I might think it appropriate to hire other sentries whose endeavours would be exclusively for my own interest. He added that he thought his first mate, who he recommended as 'an honest, upright sort of chap', had some friends among the crew or onshore who would be pleased for an appropriate fee to stand guard upon the cochineal.

I had no doubt that the mate would have brought half a hundred reckless bravos in to 'protect' me if I had shown him a sufficient quantity of *moedas* or sovereigns to buy his aid. However, I had no wish to have any dealings with that gentleman. I'd had great difficulty this morning in getting the men to raise Montesinhos' chest from its confinement below deck and to bring it up to its present location back in the cabin. I had known that I would have to give out some sort of presents to obtain this favour; the same had happened when at the start of the voyage they had taken the chest down to the hold. They had been satisfied then with a trifling sum, a matter of three or four *cruzados*, and I was prepared to let myself be imposed upon again to about the same amount. However, this time, the sum of money that was requested for doing work which, as far as I could see, was only the normal labour of their occupation, and for which they had already got or would soon receive recompense from Captain Speight or the ship's owners, was outrageous.

In the end, after Captain Speight had been applied to by me, and after that gentleman had declined to become involved in the affair, I was forced to pay what was demanded. Later, when the chest at last was in my cabin, I walked out on deck to compose myself with breathing in the cool river-air and with the sight of the fine estates and gardens I could see along the Kentish bank. I saw two of the men who had just brought up Montesinhos' chest standing not far away talking with the mate. He saw me looking, and motioned to the others and they walked away and out of my sight. When I went back to the cabin I found that a deep gash had appeared on one side of the chest, which was not there when I had seen it stowed away and which must have been made on its way back up. I hoped this was a result of carelessness rather than malice, but was not very confident of it. Indeed I assumed it had been made by the men to show what they thought of my resorting to their captain in our dispute.

In these rather troubling circumstances I settled down for the night. I had taken out my sword from my sea chest before I lay down and now it was beside me on the bed. I gripped its hilt as I closed my eyes and tried to compose myself. I thought I could never sleep but, as the wonder of that precious state so often discovers to us, in a moment I was enfolded by it without the least awareness of its approach.

It must have been quite a light sleep though, for I was waked from it by the merest rattling at my door. I had taken the precaution to lock it from the inside and to leave the key in the lock. Whoever was on the other side had found this obstacle and from the noises I heard was trying to dislodge it through the keyhole. I got up out of my bed, gripping my sword as I did. I thought to call out for help but did not, mostly because my throat was so constricted by fear that I could not get the words out. I saw in the faint starlight that was coming in my windows that the key was beginning to move and went to the door and seized it in my free hand. There were more fruitless attempts from the other side to budge it, but I held on for what, as far as I knew, really was dear life.

In the end the efforts of my unwelcome guests were in vain. I heard a series of hoarse whispers through the blessedly thick oak of the door. Somebody was urging somebody else to break that door down, for there was only 'a pussy young booby' behind it. I held on tight to my sword, I thought I would faint. It was an ideal situation in which Adam Runaway could do what he was best at – except that there was nowhere to run to. What I would do, I decided very fast, was to surrender the moment the door burst open. But then I thought – it was my future that was under threat and my chance to stop being the penniless plaything of fate that I had become, and was I to let go of that without a fight?

Thankfully, though the question had been plainly put, I was not required to answer it. From the other side I heard somebody swearing that they'd been told there'd be no problem about getting into the cabin, that it could be done without any fuss, not even waking the occupant, but look at how it was now. And besides he'd heard 'the fucking little arse-wipe in there' was possessed of a hanger and though he personally was not afraid of fighting any man, still 'the little cunt' might be lucky and cut somebody and it wasn't going to be him, 'not for a fucking fifth share' anyway.

Some loud wrangling went on after that, mainly about the division of the spoils, at which somebody finally said what was the point of arguing over something that they didn't have any-way and weren't likely to either, the way things stood? This dose of common sense seemed to have an admirable effect upon the gathering. There were some further remarks, but sounding much more subdued and peaceable than before, which I could not quite distinguish. And then there was silence. I presumed they had gone away, but of course did not dream of opening the door to find out.

I lay back on my bed, my brain a storm of conjecture and dread. I wondered if they had only gone to fetch some instrument or weapon that would make their task of opening the door that much easier. I tried to remember whether I had recognised the voices of any of the speakers I'd heard, so that should I be left alive after their next assault I would be able to identify them to the autho-rities. Only one of them was I certain of. I knew that he who had been most vociferous about the need to break down the door – though never once volunteering to do the work himself – and who had called me 'a pussy young booby' had been the *Holly*'s infamous mate.

Naturally I did not expect to get another wink of sleep for the rest of that night but again, such is the remarkable power of that gift of nature, sleep stole over me even as I lay quaking in my bed. The next thing I knew somebody was banging on the door and calling out 'Adam! Adam Hanaway!' It had been a year since I had heard that voice and so, with my mind still befuddled from sleep, did not recognise it straight away. Still I was reassured by the presence of the light that flooded in through my windows and, concluding that I was much less likely to be assassinated in broad daylight than in the depths of night, I went to unlock the door. I took up my hanger as I did so, just in case those villains of darkness had had the effrontery to come to my door and call my name as if they were friends of mine and so obtain by trickery what they had been unable to manage by their feeble show of force.

It was Solomon Marks, of course. Dear, good, loyal Mr Marks. His eyes shone as he first looked upon me. And then he put out his hand. He was not a demonstrative man, I remembered, and of course as the son I too had enjoyed a share of the deference he always paid my father. So I knew this outstretched hand was the equivalent of another man's warm embrace, and I clasped it tight. When he had got over a little his joy at seeing me again, he took a half-step back and looked me over. I must have looked a fright to him, just risen from my bed. I had not dared to undress in the night and the clothes I had been wearing from the day before were bedraggled and unclean. My hair too would have been sticking out in all directions. But I saw he was mostly concentrating on the blade I still held in my hand.

'Lord, Mr Hanaway.' He gaped at me comically. 'Do you plan to run me through?'

When I had, without going into much detail, begun to explain why I was choosing to answer my door this morning armed to the teeth, he told me I should put off my account until later, for that he had left in the great cabin a friend of his that he was desirous I should meet. I told him I would take just five minutes to clean myself and put on fresh clothes. He left me then and I went to my sea chest and in not much more than five minutes, arrayed in a more respectable suit, periwig in place and my face and hands sufficiently washed by dabbing over them a handkerchief I had wetted with my spittle, I was going through the door into the great cabin. There, sitting at the table with Mr Marks, was a thick-set, red-faced gentleman who I did not know. He got to his feet as I came up and said, 'Your servant, Sir. Michael Dutton. Glad to know you.'

'Adam Hanaway. At your service,' and I gripped the hand he held out to me, at the same time wondering why Mr Marks had brought this prosperous-looking stranger to share our reunion on the *Holly*. But I had not the time to consider it long for my father's old clerk had now jealously recaptured my hand and was shaking it hard. His eyes were a little moist I thought as he looked me over again, though he was smiling very broad. All in all he was not much like the Mr Marks I remembered, who always had seemed to me a very discreet, undemonstrative sort of man. I certainly hoped he had not turned frivolous since I had known him for I wanted his sober and expert advice upon the cargo I had brought from Lisbon. And which, last night, I suddenly remembered, I had been called upon to defend, perhaps at peril of my life.

Thinking on those vile men whispering outside my door and plotting my ruin, I could hardly hear the questions about myself and my family that Mr Marks was asking me, and cannot think how I replied to them. At last he saw that my attention was not really with him and taking my hand again he said gently that he had been happy to learn by my note that there was some business afoot that might give him the chance of being of assistance to me. He said too, and very gracefully, that there was nothing that would please him more, for as much as I had writ in my note that my father loved him so he had returned that love, and with it the greatest respect and admiration as to one who had been the means of first raising him in life and thus putting him at last on a sound and permanent footing.

After giving me some time in which to recover from the emotions that these kind words naturally produced in me, he mentioned that I had not specified exactly in my note what cargo I had brought, which was why he had asked Mr Dutton – nod to the gentleman at his side – who was his occasional partner in various ventures to accompany him hither, for he had more knowledge of certain branches of business and Mr Marks was better acquainted with others, 'So that between us, Adam, we should be able to answer all your questions.'

'And so,' Mr Dutton broke in at this point, 'what game are we after today, young gentleman?'

He had got up off his seat again, and Mr Marks too was watching me now with quite an eager, speculative look in his eyes. With these two experienced men of business waiting on my word, I felt myself suddenly very grown-up, responsible. It was with some pride and every hope that I would kindle their interest even further that I brought out the single word 'cochineal'. I was therefore quite dismayed when Mr Dutton sat down abruptly after I had spoken and laughed a little crossly and said, 'Well, you do not need me for *that*, Solomon.'

I could not understand what he meant by this. For a moment I feared that my seemingly bottomless ignorance had once more been imposed upon and that for some peculiar reason of his own Senhor Montesinhos had induced me to carry a worthless cargo from Lisbon to London. And yet what, I argued with myself then, could have possibly persuaded him to do that? Surely it was not worth paying for my own berth and for storage in a sealed hold simply to make a fool of me?

Solomon Marks, seeing my hurt, bewildered expression, reached out and touched my arm. I looked into his sympathetic eyes.

'Is cochineal not a good cargo, Mr Marks?' I asked sadly.

He laughed at that and Mr Dutton too threw in a couple of what sounded to me like exceedingly condescending guffaws.

'It's a very good cargo,' Marks said. 'You need have no worry about that.'

'Too damned good,' Mr Dutton put in.

Mr Marks, I saw, gave him a chiding look, then turned back to me.

'Dutton is only disappointed because it requires no skill at all to deal in cochineal. Everybody wants it.'

'The biggest fool in the world can make a good bargain with cochineal,' Mr Dutton put in. 'My Aunt Jane, who has been on her deathbed since King George's glorious accession, could make a decent bargain with cochineal.'

'And especially now,' Mr Marks added. 'For the Spanish ships that were bringing over last year's crop from Mexico were taken by the corsairs of Algiers and there is every reason to believe there will be a dearth of the product soon, so prices are very high.'

I did not know whether it was appropriate for me to mention that I believed some part of this stolen treasure was now sitting in Montesinhos' trunk. I feared Mr Marks' censure for that I was handling stolen goods. Even more I dreaded that he would turn moral on me and urge me to turn over the cochineal to the authorities. Of course were I as knowledgeable of the world of business then as I was soon to become, I would have known that had I told him where my cochineal actually came from he would undoubtedly have wished me joy of my good fortune and not put the least impediment in the way of my selling it on. But I did not know how these things were managed then, so I kept quiet.

'So the only matter to clear up, young gentleman,' Mr Dutton declared, still sounding a little regretful, 'is to find out how much of the blessed stuff you have to offer.'

'I'm not quite sure,' I confessed. 'Senhor Montesinhos – the gentleman who entrusted the cargo to my care – said that he thought about £5,000 might be cleared by it.'

Mr Dutton gave out a slow whistle. 'Deuce!' he said, getting again to his feet. 'That's a hell of a consignment. You must be careful not to release it all at once or the price may waver a bit. Was the article well stowed on this ship?' he asked then. 'Kept dry, was it?'

'As far as I know.'

'I suppose you didn't see it being packed?' I shook my head. 'So you can't say whether the scoundrels in Mexico or Algiers mixed anything in with the cochineal? Grit? Sand? Ashes? Anything like that?'

I agreed that I couldn't say. But I described the behaviour of the Portuguese customs officers when they had opened one of the bags and that they had seemed delighted with what they had found. Certainly it hadn't dissuaded them from making off with two of the bags. Mr Dutton grinned to hear that.

'Those villains! Still, Solomon,' he said, turning to my old friend, 'I suppose it's the best kind of testimony. Shall we offer it so? "As approved by some of the most discriminating rogues in Lisbon"?'

Mr Marks chuckled at that. Got to his feet and I followed him up. 'Let us go and see exactly what we are dealing with,' he said.

'Damn it,' said Mr Dutton, 'it's been a while since I've had to clamber up and down the ladders in a ship's hold. Not since my old father, God rest him, used to make me do it when he was in the coaling trade. Was I black at the end of a day of that!'

'You won't have to climb in the hold at all, Sir,' I said. 'For it is all in my cabin.'

I had thought this announcement would please the two merchants as it meant that they would not be put to the trouble of going below. Consequently I was surprised to find the both of them staring at me in apparent amazement.

'It's in Montesinhos' trunk,' I added diffidently, after a long moment of silence.

'In a *trunk*?' rumbled Mr Dutton – and in short to spare the need for any more explanation I led the way back through into my own cabin. The gentlemen came in after me and grouped themselves around the object that sat in the middle of the room.

'That is a prodigious great chest,' said Mr Dutton after a long moment's silence.

'And the cochineal is in there, Adam?' Mr Marks asked. 'All of it?'

'In gunnysack bags,' I nodded. 'Here – let me show you.'

And with that I took out the padlock key from its hiding-place and, with the two trading gentlemen's assistance, opened the lid of Montesinhos' chest – the first time, as I sincerely hoped, since it had been raised to admit the larcenous intentions of those customs officers. Messrs Marks and Dutton stood peering at what they found in there. As far as I could see everything was as it had been when the lid had been closed. Mr Dutton reached in, and gave a tug on one of the sacks.

'Three-pound bags?' Mr Marks asked.

'Feels like it. Cochineal at £2 a pound. Worth £6 a bag.'

'How many bags would you say?'

'At a glance – a hundred. Maybe ten more than that.'

'£600 sterling.' Marks turned to me. 'Are you quite sure, Adam? There's no more that was stowed elsewhere in the ship?'

I looked back at Mr Marks. My brain was whirling. I shook my head. 'No. Nowhere else.'

'What did this man who gave you the cochineal –'

'Senhor Montesinhos.'

'Yes. Him. What did he say exactly about the value of it?'

'He said –'

I tried desperately to remember. I remembered the little parlour, and the table in it and the chairs, and the wool hanging on the wall. And I remembered this chest that was now open before us taking up one side of the parlour. And remembered Montesinhos himself, his dark imploring eyes staring at me as I havered over my decision, his lips parted, the rotten teeth behind them . . . It was not Montesinhos, I realised suddenly, not he who had told me the value of this cargo. It had been Mr Hutchinson.

The two merchants were staring at me; I licked my lips. 'I was told it was worth £5,000. Perhaps less according to the price in London. Perhaps only 4,500 –'

Mr Dutton gave out with a shout of scornful laughter. He gestured at the trunk in a manner that indicated both irritation and amusement. '£600 is what you have there, Sir. £650 at best.' He turned to Mr Marks, evidently quite finished with me now. 'Well, there you are, Solomon,' he said. 'That's what comes from listening to the tales of a pretty young noodle who doesn't know which end to wipe himself. I'll be off now. Do you bring your fellows down from the City to fetch this chest this afternoon, it can be disposed of before midnight, and our friend here will have his 600 by tomorrow, which ain't a bad bit of business but not worth bringing a man this far downriver to give his opinion on.'

He looked back at me, I suppose to see that I had understood his advice. He appeared surprised to find me drawn up to my full height and staring at him very coldly.

'Sir,' I said, 'you will oblige me by giving me the names of your friends.'

'Adam!' cried out Mr Marks, seeing where this was leading. 'You did not say that.'

'I did say it. I have been called "a young noodle". And there was another expression used about me, most offensive. Mr Dutton shall withdraw both expressions and apologise to me or I will have satisfaction of him.'

After this there was what might be described as a pregnant pause. Mr Dutton appeared not to know quite what was happening around him. Or if he did his first move was not calculated to soothe my indignation, for he began to grin at me.

I will say that Dutton dealt with the situation in the end like a man. Seeing at last that I was in earnest, he ceased his irritating smiling. He seemed then to be brooding over his response, all the while resting four-square upon his stout, silver-tipped cane. When I attempted to prompt him to answer me, he said, 'A moment, young gentleman. I am considering your offer.' A few more seconds of thoughtful silence went by and then he firmly shook his head. 'I shall decline it, I think. In the first place,' he went on, ignoring my attempts to object to this, 'I know a little of you, Mr Hanaway. You used to be a pupil at Jonathan Cryer's establishment in Fenchurch Street, I think. It so happens my house has the honour of managing Mr Cryer's affairs. A shrewd enough gentleman,' he mused, 'but inclined to plunge a little deep in the China trade. But he told me once that he had the honour to have the son of the eminent Matthew Hanaway at his academy and that, as I remember him saying, if the young gentleman would only apply himself a little more thoroughly to the discipline he would be a very fine swordsman indeed.

'Now,' Mr Dutton carried on weightily, 'for my part I know nothing of that art and so I think you will agree it would be a case of simple murder for you to raise your blade against me. You will hardly object therefore if, as is my right as the challenged party, I make a choice of weapons that does not include the sword. Pistols then? I daresay you would prove a better shot too than I: you are younger, your hand steadier, your eye keener. On the other hand I may have a stroke of luck, I may put my ball between your eyes before you can do the same to me. And that is something I positively decline to risk doing. One blessing I enjoy at my late stage in life is that I know I have never killed a fellow-creature, nor even much harmed one of them. I should like to enjoy that knowledge until I die, which I hope will be quietly in my bed, some years from now, and surrounded by those who love me. And so if an apology is all that is wanted to avoid my being disappointed in this ambition then I give it very freely.'

He bowed then to me. And I, for some reason, bowed back. The thing was, I was so impressed by his calm and poised performance. It so exactly showed the sort of manly self-control that I had always desired for myself.

'Sir,' said Mr Dutton, in the same unhurried, almost cheerful voice, 'it was not my place on such short acquaintance to be calling you "a young noodle". Nor to be suggesting that you did not know which end to wipe yourself. It happened because I was greatly disappointed in this –' He nodded at the open chest. 'For I love a big, ingenious piece of business and here we have nothing like that. But still I should not have abused you so. I apologise for it.'

'Well,' said Mr Marks, his expression quite bathed with relief, 'that is over, and everybody friends, and we can now consider –'

'No, Solomon,' said Mr Dutton, 'it is not quite over. I have something more to say to Mr Hanaway.' He considered me then very coolly, and I might have resented it if I did not feel unaccountably diffident under his stare as if it was not I but he who had just triumphed and been apologised to. 'I have some advice for you, young Sir,' he said next, 'which is that if you propose to make any sort of figure in the world of business then you would be well advised to change your conduct soon. For we in the City are not pert young cocks always looking for a reason to stab at each other. We are a fraternity, and we like to speak our mind freely, yes, and sometimes we like to rail against one another and say things that people outside our number would wonder at and wonder even more when they find us sharing a bottle half an hour later and no harm done. And we would have no place in our ranks for a man who would threaten to fight another because he did not like what was said to him in a trading matter. We would not do business any more with him, and that is certain.'

Mr Marks at this point nodded solemnly. All at once I saw he was not just my friend and my father's old servant – he was a businessman, a colleague of Mr Dutton, and behind these two were all the serried ranks of those men who beneath all the flotsam and show really owned England, and its wealth and its parliament and empire too. Not just Dutton, I saw in a flash, but all this power and majesty I'd had the temerity to challenge, to wave my little sword at.

'It is true, Adam,' Mr Marks said then. 'We City men are very free in our language to each other and no lasting injury ever given because of it.'

'Nevertheless, Solomon,' Mr Dutton said, seeing, I think, that I was taking my correction very hard, 'Mr Hanaway was not to know that. And I spoke too harsh, there's no doubting it. Here, my good Sir . . .' He held out his hand. 'You have forgiven me, I hope. And I congratulate you on your cargo. It may not be worth £5,000, but it's a decent bit of business all the same.'

I took his hand. I must say I was feeling quite ashamed of myself and not just because I had offended against some law or mystery of the trade that I could not after all have been expected to know about. Clearly Dutton had no right to call me 'a noodle' – and yet, I reflected as I was still in his strong grip, who else but a noodle would arrive in London with a cargo that would scarcely fetch a tenth of what he had boasted it was worth? There was also the sobering fact to consider that my worldly prospects were now seriously reduced. Though I was not certain if I had ever heard Senhor Montesinhos put an exact price on his cargo, I certainly remembered him to have promised a thousand pounds to be shared between myself and Mr Hutchinson. Not even the most skilful mathematician could extract £1,000 from 600, and even if we confiscated the whole value of the cochineal for our own use – and I could see good arguments on both sides for that course of action – our gain would still fall far short of our expectation.

* * *

It was a mystery, we decided in my cabin on the *Holly*. Why had I been sent to London at considerable expense, why deceived? It had been clear to me that my going, and my taking this cargo with me, had been a matter of vital concern to Montesinhos. And yet here we were facing this lame and impotent conclusion to my odyssey – and it made no sense.

All three of us appeared to be taken up with contemplating this conundrum. Mr Dutton seemed to have forgotten his intention of leaving us and was staring at the great open chest in the same still posture and with the same fixed attention as Mr Marks and myself.

'Is the chest to be a part of the cargo too?' he asked suddenly, startling me, for after all I may not have been so focused on the problem as my 'colleagues' were.

'Interesting,' murmured Mr Marks. 'What do you say, Adam? Are you expected to dispose of the chest too?'

'I don't know,' I said honestly. 'Perhaps. I know Montesinhos was trying to sell as many of his possessions as he could before the Inquisition got hold of them.'

Mr Dutton got up and went for a walk around the chest.

'This is outside my knowledge. Do you know anything, Solomon?'

Mr Marks shook his head.

'Still, any man can see it's a fine, impressive piece. What a pity you did not bring it home in the Bubble year, Mr Hanaway. Everything sold well then, and a chest this handsome would have been snapped up at a very good price . . . What would you say, Solomon, at a guess? 500 for it?'

'Perhaps more.' Mr Marks was up now too and looking over the chest. 'This is very fine wood and the carving most intricate.'

'I think not more,' said Dutton. 'There's this damned deep gash over here.' He showed Mr Marks the present the crew had given me for being backward in giving *them* a present they considered adequate to their deserts. 'This'll take off a hundred or two from the price, I should think.'

'Couldn't a restorer do something with it?'

'A good one perhaps.'

'Then, if this is restored well enough – would you say £600?'

361

'At a guess – just about.' Mr Dutton turned to me smiling. 'Well, there you are, young Sir. How do you like this? You may have doubled your fortune.'

'It is still,' Mr Marks pointed out, 'a long way short of 5 or even £4,000.'

This was a cold splash of water to check my hopes, which had been rising a little as the two were speaking so intelligently about making money out of a resource I had not even known I'd possessed. But it was true, even if the chest sold I would still be far away from what I had expected and the mystery of why Montesinhos had sent me hither with such a disappointing cargo remained.

Solomon Marks' smooth and unemotional tones broke in on my speculations.

'Adam, did you say you had not seen the cochineal being packed?'

'I did say that. But it's all right, isn't it?'

Mr Marks ignored my question. 'You believe the chest is entirely filled with bags of cochineal?'

'Of course.'

'And yet you did not see it being packed.'

'Ah, very good, Solomon,' breathed Mr Dutton, his eyes brightening as he began to follow his colleague's drift. I must say I was still floundering about, lost.

'Do you think, Mr Marks,' I asked unhappily, 'that there may be – what did Mr Dutton say before? – only sand and grit in some of those bags?'

'It would make little sense for your senhor to ship out sand and grit that is worth next to nothing at all,' Mr Marks smiled at me. 'But there may be another article in some of them. Shall we see?'

In a moment we were standing at three sides of the chest hauling out the bags from inside and depositing them around us on the floor. There were no surprises in the first two layers. When we arrived at the third layer, things appeared much the same. Mr Marks got out a penknife and made a cut in one of the bags of this third layer. He felt inside and brought out a pinch of cochineal to show us, then laid this particular bag carefully to one side so that, I supposed, when we repacked it we would take especial care not to spill any.

I think Mr Marks was a little disappointed that we had gone in so far and found nothing extraordinary, though Mr Dutton was looking quite cheerful, so much so that I could not help glancing at him in some surprise as together we lifted out the third layer of bags. He saw me looking and chuckled and said, 'I can't help it. I love to handle cochineal. It's such a damned fine commodity. What a pity that you don't have more of it.'

'He may have even less of it than you think, Michael,' came Mr Marks' dry, unemphatic tones, making us look across at him. He had taken hold of the first bag from the fourth layer, perhaps a third or a half way into the chest. We could see at a glance that this was not like all the other bags we had encountered, which had a lumpy quality, soft to the touch. This gunnysack outlined something hard and straight that was within it, and as Mr Marks prodded it, it yielded not a whit.

'That ain't cochineal,' Mr Dutton remarked unnecessarily.

Again the penknife appeared in Mr Marks' hand. He lowered the sack to the floor. It landed with an audible bump. He opened it at one end. There was no crackle of paper as he felt inside. Then before my wondering eyes he drew out a long bar of metal that gleamed dully under the light from the windows. He reached into the sack again and drew out another bar, brother to the first, squared off at each end and slightly sloping at the sides. We three stared at these lustrous objects, and then looked at one another.

'Jesus wept,' breathed Mr Dutton.

It was certainly the case that I felt like weeping too. I sat down upon my bed, for the moment unable to take any further part in the uncovering of my cargo. The two merchants seemed to understand that it was not laziness that was afflicting me. I watched as they brought out layer after layer of gunnysacks. All the bags were the same, they looked hard and angular and I saw that to the touch they were unyielding. In the end, ashamed to not take my part in the work, I got up and added my strength to it. From the fifth, the seventh and the last layer, Mr Marks chose a bag at random and opened it. There were two solid bars of metal in each one. When we had got them all out, we rested. I thought the gentlemen deserved my bed, and went and stood against the wall.

'Adam,' said Mr Marks, 'can you lock that door?'

I said I could and showed him the padlock.

'It might be as well to lock it now.'

I did it, and we were silent for a little while, our eyes roaming over the neat stacks of gunnysacks, cochineal on one side – and on the other?

'Well, young man,' said Mr Dutton at last, 'you appear to have brought with you to London an entire year's production of the Minas Gerais! And very welcome you and it will be for it.'

I was shocked to hear this. I remembered how my Uncle Felix had once explained to me that the great gold mines of the Minas Gerais province in Brazil were the mainstay of Dom João's empire. That I could have been the unwitting means of abstracting so much wealth from the hapless Portuguese was shocking to me. I stared at the sacks on the floor, aghast.

Mr Dutton, guessing by my expression what I was thinking, started to laugh. 'I'm exaggerating, Mr Hanaway,' he said. 'This is a very little portion of what they take out of the ground in Brazil each year. Still it will do us well enough, eh, Solomon?'

'Is this a bit more like your "big, ingenious business" then, Michael?'

'By God it is,' beamed Mr Dutton. 'Outside my competence, of course, but still I shall enjoy watching how a master handles it. What say you to Martin Ruddy?'

'I say we couldn't do better. Mr Ruddy is a goldsmith,' Marks explained to me. 'Premises in Lombard Street, of course. He is a very shrewd gentleman and you could not do better than allow him to handle these goods.'

These goods! These sacks, and a few of them opened to show the muted lustre of what gleamed within. 'Would this have been captured on the way home by the corsairs, like the cochineal?' I asked.

'No reason to think it. The Brazil fleets are protected by warships, some of them British. Only in time of war would an enemy powerful enough to take a treasure ship appear on the ocean. No,' said Mr Dutton, 'I daresay your man Montesinhos legitimately purchased it in Lisbon. The difficulty, as I understand, is not the buying of the stuff there, but the getting it out of port. For if they catch you –' And, chuckling, Mr Dutton drew one stubby finger across his throat.

When we had replaced the sacks in the chest, the 'gold ones' in the lower part as before, it was decided that Dutton should return across the river to the City and speak to this Mr Ruddy in Lombard Street. After that, Dutton promised us, either the gold-smith would return with him in person or he would send someone he trusted who would know what next to do with my cargo. In the meantime it should stay here. I mentioned that Captain Speight had told me last night I must have it out of the ship by the end of this morning, but neither of my friends thought that was likely to be an obstacle.

Mr Marks proposed that, while we were waiting for Mr Dutton to return, he would take me ashore for breakfast, for he under-stood I had not eaten yet, and also so that I could stretch my legs. I said that though I would be glad to pursue both those activities I was not at all happy with the scheme for I felt I needed to be always on the spot to protect Montesinhos' chest, particularly now that I knew how valuable its contents were. I mentioned one or two of the incidents of the day before and especially of the night. I also told my friends how the crew had imposed on me by charging me so high for bringing up my chest, and added that Captain Speight had not been able to abate their greed, not least because he hadn't tried to.

There was a short silence after I finished speaking. Mr Marks said, quite mildly, that it was not intended we should leave the chest unprotected. Mr Dutton meanwhile was turning several shades of purple. 'God damn this Speight,' he spluttered. 'How dare he use a London merchant so!'

'Now then, Michael,' Mr Marks said soothingly. 'Mr Hanaway is not quite a London merchant yet.'

'No, it's not good enough, Solomon. I shall have to speak to this fellow.'

I said that I did not think Captain Speight was a man to be

'spoken to' in the manner Mr Dutton obviously intended, for though generally a quiet sort of gentleman I had noticed during the voyage he had shown a certain steel in him whenever he thought himself challenged or slighted. Even the passengers had not been excused his resentment on such occasions.

Mr Dutton chuckled to hear me say this.

'Him?' he said. 'He will shit in his breeches when I tell him what I think of him and his ship.'

'It is true,' Solomon Marks spoke to me, 'that he will not be happy to hear of our displeasure with him when he knows who we are. For, if we put the word about among our colleagues as to how he is treating merchants, we will ensure that they no longer send their cargoes to his ship. The owners will have to get rid of him if they want to continue to do business from London.

'And he will be on the beach for life with a black mark against his name. You'll see.'

I felt this was much too severe a punishment for a gentleman who had always been polite and reasonably friendly with me and would have asked Mr Dutton to restrain his anger, except that Mr Marks stepped in before I could speak and urged the same upon him.

'For you know, Michael, the less attention we draw to ourselves and this cargo the better, I think.' Mr Dutton, after considering the matter for a moment or two, shrugged his reluctant acceptance. Marks went on: 'You go now to Mr Ruddy's. On your way will you call in at the Queen's Head and get Old Doll to send us half a dozen fellows to watch this cabin? Have them bring pistols. I will send for the Captain and make sure we have his agreement that the cargo will stay here, and Old Doll's men will guard it from the crew.'

Mr Dutton left and Mr Marks and I sat on either side of the great chest and, as it were, conversed over it. About indifferent things mostly, for I think he saw I was still a little diffident about talking of my own affairs and what had been happening to me since I went away. He asked me about the voyage and I told him a few stories about my fellow-passengers and their various idiosyncrasies, which made him laugh. He said at one point that he had forgotten what a merry fellow I could be, which of course urged me on to new heights of anecdote. We were so engaged in this discussion that, though I think both of us heard the noises of what sounded like a scuffle out in the corridor and some angry shouts that seemed to come from the wharf, neither of us paid these commotions much attention and we – or rather I – kept talking. We were therefore quite astounded when, about ten minutes after hearing, without noticing, what I have called 'a scuffle', there came at my padlocked door a great pounding and a hoarse, angry voice calling out my name.

I got to my feet, went to the door and asked through it who was outside. When I heard the voice bawl, 'The Captain, damn you, open up!' I unlocked the padlock, removed it from the bolt, and opened the door. Captain Speight stormed in and shouted that he would have the law on me for bringing bullies on to his ship to fight against his crew. But before he did that he would certainly find one or two of his men who were still conscious enough to make a fist and leave them with me so they could teach me what was permitted to passengers on the *Holly* and what was not. At this point Mr Marks stepped into view from behind the chest. Captain Speight stared at him, then took a step back from his previous posture, which had placed his face about half an inch from mine.

'Do you know who I am, Captain?' Mr Marks said, very quiet and easy.

'Yes, Sir,' said the Captain heavily at last. He took another step back. 'I did not know this young fellow was entertaining a gentleman of your –'

'This "young fellow" is my colleague. He is under the protection of the brotherhood of London merchants. He has described to me the disgraceful treatment he has received at the hands of your crew and also your ineffectual attempts to control them, both of which have led me to order private guards to be placed on this cargo –' He nodded at the chest. 'They will remain on the ship until it is removed, which will be, I suppose, some time this afternoon.'

The Captain said the chest could stay on board as long as Mr

Hanaway desired. Mr Marks shook his head and told him aloofly that this afternoon would be enough.

After this, and after treating us to some quite embarrassingly fulsome apologies, the Captain left the cabin. We followed after a brief interval. I locked the door while Mr Marks spoke to a giant of a man with a brace of pistols stuck in his belt, who was to remain outside the cabin while we were gone from it. We saw several more of his kindred on our way out of the ship and there were two more waiting on either side of the gangplank. Of the members of the crew there was no sign. Mr Marks explained to me as we strolled away from the wharf that these valuable ruffians were in the general employ of a lady who kept an ale house near by who had used to be, as he delicately put it, a famous 'nymph of pleasure' in Covent Garden. Growing old and losing her beauty to the smallpox, she had retired to her native Rotherhythe, where she did a good business in many lines besides her ale house and was always employable because, as she once had been famous for her skills in bed, now she was celebrated for her shrewd business sense and her integrity.

'A bargain is a bargain with Old Doll,' Mr Marks sighed, so sentimentally that I even wondered if he had been one of Doll's satisfied customers during her reign of pleasure. 'And your chest will be as safe in her men's care as if you were sitting there watching it yourself.'

I had hoped that I would be taken to meet Old Doll and have my long-delayed breakfast at her ale house. But Mr Marks chose the less exciting venue of a coffee house situated in an alley behind the riverfront. It was much like those I remembered from the City and about the Strand, and appeared to be frequented mostly by well-dressed, canny-looking men, no doubt merchants like ourselves, who congregated around the tables and talked with one another in low voices. Mr Marks set me down at a free table and watched complacently as I devoured a beefsteak and coffee. He, as I remember, took only coffee. When we were done we went back to the river and hired a fellow to row us downriver to Greenwich.

We spent a happy hour or two strolling in the park behind the great new hospital there, telling each other how the year since our last meeting had separately dealt with us. I was a little shy, you may be sure, when I got to speaking of my months of labour in the streets of the Baixa, selling holy images, but Mr Marks professed himself pleased to hear that I passed through what he called 'such an apprenticeship', because, he said, it was the hardest thing to get a young fellow starting out in business to understand that at bottom all trade depended on just these sorts of man-to-man transactions.

'But, Mr Marks, I am only talking of woodcuts worth a half-*cruzado* at best. And my "clients" were the most ignorant, bigoted people imaginable and often very poor to boot.'

'So much the better that you were able to make a living selling to them. No, I think this was excellent preparation, Adam. Better almost than if you had made a success of your time in Mr Felix Hanaway's firm and had stayed there the whole year. Tell me, did you have any associates with you in this peddling project?'

Mr Marks waited with an expectant look on his face for me to answer him. But I could not for the moment. His words had suddenly evoked what, unbelievably, I had not thought of almost since the *Holly* had turned into the Thames' mouth. My associates indeed. The old gentleman who I had considered sometimes almost in the light of a father and she who I'd thought of as – sister, mother, friend, my lover. I had left them behind. And probably never would see them again.

Mr Hutchinson used to lament in the time we were waiting for my departure that I would go and would never return to Lisbon and so the day I left would be the last he would ever set eyes on me. I used to argue with him on this point, saying that I was sure I would come back. Once I told him that of course I would have to return for how else was he to receive his share of the money I would make on this voyage home? 'Bill of exchange,' was his succinct answer, and it was true a bill drawn on a good house in London, through their factor in Lisbon, would do the job very conveniently. Indeed Montesinhos' whole transaction, both the overt cochineal and the hidden gold, might have been done through bills of exchange and my voyage home rendered unnecessary, except that to have sold the goods in Lisbon would have brought a very much lower price than they would fetch in London. But there was no problem about sending a money amount in this form, and I knew, perhaps had always really known, that it was what I planned to do to get Mr Hutchinson's share of this venture to him. I had no intention of going back to Lisbon, and that too I had known all along.

'Adam?' asked Mr Marks, wondering clearly at my long silence.

I shook my head, and said that I was remembering the people I had left behind in Portugal. As I was speaking, I was thinking that *she* must have been back with her father now for a week and more. I wondered if enough time had elapsed for her to think of forgiving me. I hoped that at least what promised to be a fine success here, and the Hutchinsons' share in it, would do something to win me a pardon. Sadly, however, I did not think the money would count much with her when it came to weighing my behaviour.

Mr Marks did not press me on this matter and, I think, to give me time to recover from my apparent discomfiture, he spoke now of his own concerns. Of his haberdashery shop in the Royal Exchange, which he still kept, and of the various trading ventures that were taking up more and more of his time. One of them, which he had entered into with his friend Michael Dutton, to trade to the Levant, had been a very risky adventure because the pirates swarmed there in great numbers and, correspondingly, when the ship had returned last month with its cargo entire and unharmed, the rewards had been very great.

'You are looking at a rich man, Adam!' he smiled. 'And now I know the road to wealth I should like you to join me on it. It would give me so much satisfaction to be the means to set my old master's son securely upon his career. That is, if you still desire to be a merchant. And now, my dear Sir,' he added, looking at his watch. 'I believe it must be almost time for you to meet the excellent Mr Ruddy.'

2

And so I and the gold and the cochineal and the chest came home at last. Everything worked out with the bullion as Mr Ruddy told me it would at our first meeting on the *Holly*. The whole of it rested in his vaults that night, and the next day three-quarters of it was transferred to those of the Bank of England. I opened an account with Ruddy's house that very day and directly had the pleasure of seeing the sum of £1,787 recorded against my name. Within two months, on my goldsmith banker's advice, I realised on the gold that was in the bank and a bill for £5,315 reached my account. Mr Marks, who refused to take a commission on the transaction, took charge of the cochineal and raised £240 on it, and a man called Gore came over from Southwark at Mr Dutton's invitation and looked over the chest and took it off my hands for £800.

Even before this I had taken my £500 share from the general account and given it to Mr Marks, who had made an offer that I could hardly decline in that he proposed to put it in a venture to Holland, which if successful would quadruple my investment, and if not he promised to repay me the £500 in full. However, he was confident that we would do well by this adventure and for this reason he began to give me an allowance, which enabled me to live decently. He also afforded me a room in his house in Russia Street in the City, and what was much more valuable introduced me among his acquaintance, who included several very substantial merchants in various departments of trade. Most of them remembered my father and whereas I had feared that the memory of his failure would have rendered him – and by association me too – odious in the eyes of respectable City men, I found nothing like that. They made me feel very welcome in their company, and if they spoke of my father it was with a note of regret rather than scorn, and with something almost of admiration as if they were remembering one who had fallen heroically in battle, rather than because he had allowed himself to be swindled by cleverer men.

I should add that it was not only as the son of an unfortunate colleague that they knew me. My fame as the young man who had made off with a fortune in gold from under King Joaõ's eyes was spreading all the while and indeed the story was growing bigger in each retelling. Now I was reputed to have got £50,000 out of

Lisbon, and there were a few well-informed souls that had it up to £100,000, a veritable 'plum'. In fact I was enjoying a 'bubble' all of my own, and confided in Mr Dutton that I felt sometimes a little embarrassed about it. My new friend was kind enough to tell me not to be an ass, that every bit of favourable reputation is useful to a man in business and one should not disdain other people's high opinion of oneself even if it is not entirely merited.

'And after all,' he remarked, 'though you did not know you were transporting the gold, you would have paid the penalty for being caught at it all the same.'

As soon as I was able I coached down into Kent, where I had a joyful reunion with my family. Of course they wanted to know everything that had happened to me since I went away and I was made to feel rather ashamed – though not by them – when I realised how little I had ever said about my life in my letters, and how rarely indeed in the last few months I had even sent a letter home. I made them still more happy when I told them about the cargo I had brought back with me and that it had provided an entrée into the City world, which I hoped might bring prosperity within my grasp. Privately I told my mother that the first thing I wanted to do if I began to make a little money was to bring her and the girls back to London so that we could live together again in some decent dwelling. She said it was all she hoped for, that the past year had driven out many old and silly notions of what she and the girls were entitled to and a little house somewhere safe would be enough now. They could even do without servants if they had to.

When the girls were asleep I sat up with my mother and talked about the rest of the family. She said she'd had one visit from my Aunt Sarah who had told her that there had been an estrangement between my uncle and myself which now, according to Sarah, Felix much regretted. We agreed that we would do what we could to bring the family together again, an ambition that was indeed finally achieved when, by invitation, I visited the little house Felix had taken in Rood Lane one afternoon. Before dinner we apologised to one another for our old behaviour, vowed to do better in the future and sealed our promise with a warm embrace – and then all the others, my aunt, my cousins Betty and little Nancy, who had been waiting outside the room, came bursting in laughing and crying and enfolding me one after the other in their arms. At which point I became agreeably aware that 'little Nancy', though still slim and supple and girlish overall, was now marvellously well endowed in the area of the bust. It was my impression too that a similar welcome inflation had taken place in her posterior region, which before, from what I'd been able to make out, had seemed quite boyish in its leanness and angularity. Of course I was not so indelicate, nor so presumptuous as to seek to confirm this happy change by touching her there.

In all these excitements and in the stir of new opportunities that were opening for me it seemed almost every day, I had not much time to think of what lay behind me. So far behind me as it felt to me now. Mostly the past came to me in sudden unexpected glimmers. I might turn a corner in Fleet Street and expect to find myself in the Rua Nova dos Ferros and for several seconds be amazed to discover that only the shabby prospect of Fetter Lane lay before me. Or else I would be in what I would have sworn was a familiar alley in the Baixa – it was certainly crooked and filthy enough to be that – and be startled for the moment to find that everybody around me was talking in English. Or I would myself be in a chop house giving my order and only when I noticed the look of surprise on my waiter's face and saw that the other diners near by were staring at me oddly did I realise I must have been speaking in Portuguese.

These small lapses were perhaps only to be expected for I had not just been a visitor to Lisbon, I had lived there for many months and taken in the city and its people almost through the pores of my skin, and as they never caused me any real inconvenience I agreed with myself to find them amusing and benign. There were other memories that were not so inconsequential, or so droll, and from these I know I deliberately shut myself off for weeks and would not think on them. I mean of course those that concerned the Hutchinsons.

When I came at last to facing them, in some ways it was easiest to deal with the memory of Maria Beatriz. All that was behind me now, the story was finished. I might have played no very glorious part in it, I might have a lifetime of regrets before me – or more hopefully I would just have fond memories, but no matter there was nothing more, as I saw it, that needed to be added to the tale. My difficulty came rather with her father, and when I was brave enough to consider the business plain – lying usually after midnight awake in my room in Solomon Marks' house – it came down to what part I thought he might have played in the scheme that had sent me out of Lisbon port with a cargo in my possession that contained what, if discovered, might have led to my execution at the hands of Dom João's officers.

Montesinhos I did not much blame for it. It was a dangerous trick he had played – but then what after all did he owe to me? I suppose he saw himself as being in danger of his own life, and so why should he care much if another was placed in the same peril. He did not really know me, I don't even think he particularly liked me, if only because he saw that Maria Beatriz was fond of me.

So I could lay the thought of Montesinhos' deceit quite easily to one side. What I could not so cheerfully accept was the notion that Mr Hutchinson might have shared in this plot. That he who in our last days together was very freely calling me his 'son', and at the last had sent me away from him with a father's hug, the same man I had sat with on I don't know how many evenings talking and laughing in terms of deepest friendship, that this man might have been willing, in order to gain a little money, to have seen me seized, brought back to land, locked up in Limoeiro prison, and one fine morning, it might be, brought out to be hanged or garrotted before a cheering mob.

That was an unappealing picture to have to contemplate alone in my bed, night after night. With daybreak my thoughts gradually became less tragical. Clearly Mr Hutchinson couldn't have known what Montesinhos intended to conceal in his chest. I was sure as the sun shone through my window that the love between myself and the old man would not have allowed him to so behave. Besides, I thought I had a very good idea of his character and it was that of a gentleman – and no gentleman would ever put a friend into such a hazard. However, with the following night and darkness, I was back to my old suspicions. Mr Hutchinson could not even have pretended that I would not have minded taking the risk for the sake of the prize at the end of it, for I had always made it very clear to him that gold was the one thing I declined to take out of Dom João's kingdom.

And on the worst night of all it came to me, like truth writ in flaming letters, that he had dealt so with me because he had discovered the secret that his daughter and I thought we had kept from him – heard us at our joyous labours perhaps? Crept out of his room and put his head around Maria Beatriz's door? – that he knew she had taken me into her bed, and that this, though not exactly firing him up to take certain revenge upon me for dishonouring her, had at least left him not greatly concerned that, all unknowing, I would be risking my very life in agreeing to escort Senhor Montesinhos' cargo.

Again, with dawn, my apprehensions melted away. I was sure that this was all conjecture and fiction on my part, and yet the memory of the hours I had spent thinking them true never altogether faded from my mind. Mr Hutchinson might still appear in my thoughts sometimes as a 'father', but I was no longer always sure that he was a good father, or a trustworthy one to me.

Whatever my suspicions about Mr Hutchinson's part in the affair – and really for most of the time I was certain that he had been duped by Montesinhos quite as much as I had – my behaviour towards him now was scrupulously correct. I consulted Mr Marks as to how I could remit the £500 that was to be the Hutchinsons' share, and he confirmed that a bill drawn on a London factor would answer best. He mentioned several names, and we settled in the end on the house of Jarvis, Bird in Throgmorton Street whose counterpart in Lisbon was the same Jacob Tolliver who I had met at the assembly-house rout in the Bairro Alto and who was the father of the execrable Ralph. The idea of sending the Tollivers a commission via their eminent London correspondents rather amused me.

However, the pleasure was to be somewhat delayed because, in talking the whole matter over with Mr Marks, I discovered to him the somewhat haphazard condition of the house in the Rua do

Parreiral as I had left it: the late owner absconded, the servants in a state of near mutiny and liable to steal what they could get their hands on, and the Inquisition poised to make off with all that was left. Mr Marks recommended seriously that I first establish that the Hutchinsons were still residing at this questionable address, and if so whether they wanted the bill sent to them there, or placed directly in the hands of the Tollivers.

'Or they may have a friend whose address they would want to use,' Mr Marks suggested.

In accordance with his advice I sent a letter by a packet boat, addressed to Mr Hutchinson in the Rua do Parreiral. Without commenting in the least upon the immense fact of the gold I had unwittingly brought to London, I informed him that the cargo had been landed and a very satisfactory sum was now waiting in my account for whenever Senhor Montesinhos or his representative should arrive to collect it. Minus of course the £1,000 that was our reward, and of which I was now ready to send his share wherever he should direct me. A month went by, six weeks; I heard nothing. I wrote again, the weeks passed, summer was turning into a damp and smoky autumn, and still I heard nothing. A third time I wrote – and on this occasion we asked the courier to take the letter directly to the Rua do Parreiral. We got a report back from him at last that he had found there no people called the Hutchinsons, or anything like it, living at the house he had been directed to. The new owner claimed to have no knowledge of any such persons. Certainly he could attest that they had never lived in his house while he had occupied it.

Now I was quite alarmed. I proposed to Mr Marks that I should go to Lisbon to find out myself what, if anything, had gone wrong. It was not, I acknowledged when he pointed it out, a good time for me to go. Our Holland venture had paid off very well and I was on the point of investing much of my share of the profits in certain new projects that Mr Marks had brought to my attention. However, he did not want this time that I should simply trust to his advice but that I should involve myself in the fine details of the business, for as he said it was the only way for me to learn my trade. Otherwise I would always be only a mere speculator, subject entirely to fate's hazards and the skill and luck of other men.

He asked me if there was not someone who I could write to in Lisbon who was close to the Hutchinsons and would know their current whereabouts. I walked around with the problem for days. It did not seem possible that I couldn't put a name to any of the Hutchinsons' acquaintance that were also known to me. The pair had lived very quietly. Mr Hutchinson's connections, if they could be called that, were mostly among the waiters and drawers in the *tabernas* of the Rua do Parreiral and a couple of other streets near by. As for Maria Beatriz: I knew that she had a number of female friends, and I had been introduced to one or two of them, but for the life of me I couldn't remember their names now. If Bento had not left his shop on the Rua dos Douradores there would have been no difficulty at all in getting a letter to him. I wondered if he had quit his house too, but even if he had not it was of little use to me, for though I had spent a memorable afternoon and evening there on the occasion of his wedding I really had no idea where it was situated. There remained Tadeu Nunes, Maria Beatriz's printer. I knew he lived in the Alfama, I knew I had visited his place of work once, but again I could not remember where exactly it was located. Cursing myself for the lazy inattention that seemed to be all too characteristic of my Lisbon stay, I spent days on end searching through all the '*ruas*' and '*travessas*' and '*largos*' in my memory to see if I could match one of them with the printer Nunes. But I could not.

What I have said above is not really accurate. I did not spend whole days at this effort, but only a part of a few of them. My days indeed were very full at that time, and not only with my efforts to understand the business Mr Marks and I were set upon. My domestic life too was preoccupying me greatly. Since I had called at my mother's cottage in Kent, I'd been looking in an intermittent fashion for a home for her and for sisters Sukie and Amelia. It happened most fortuitously that the lease on the house next to my uncle's place in Rood Lane unexpectedly became available. As soon as I got the information from Felix, I was on the spot to make my offer and within the week, helped by a loan from Mr Marks, I had the lease in my possession with twenty-two years still to run. Within another week my mother and sisters were installed in the new house, and I too – after tendering my sincerest thanks to Solomon Marks for his kind hospitality over the past months – followed them to Rood Lane.

I need not say how happy the family – the whole family – were now become. Felix, though no longer a serious man of business, clearly enjoyed his new position as patriarch, not only over his own dependants but his late brother's too. My mother and my aunt, though in earlier days I remembered relations between them to have been often somewhat scratchy, evidently decided that there was no more time to be lost in petty squabbles, and became the closest and dearest of companions. And of course we, 'the children', were delighted with the change, and were always together, being in and out of each other's houses all day long. On Sunday was instituted a new tradition that we all dined together in one or other of the houses, taking it turn and turn about, and it was quite a sight to see all these Hanaways around the table, talking and laughing fit for several times even our actual number.

I have said that the younger generation of our united family was always together. It was so at first, but naturally as time went by small, harmless divisions appeared in our ranks. My sisters and cousin Betty made up one party and spent more and more time exclusively in each other's company, and on the other side were myself and my other cousin. I believe this partiality that Nancy and I began to discover for each other started with our finding that, unlike the rest of her family, she had many fond memories of her life in Lisbon and liked to talk about them with me, who also valued my recollections of that city.

So all these matters were distracting me from thinking about the Hutchinsons, and what to do about locating them, as much as I should have. Yet it was in my mind and perhaps it was because I was not entirely focused on the problem that one morning the answer to it flashed from nowhere into my brain. Dom Jeronymo! Of course! Dom Jeronymo da Silva. Maria Beatriz's friend. Her admirer indeed, at least at some point in her life. *He* would know where they had gone. And in the unlikely event that he did not, he had the position and importance to insist that they be found. I was not altogether certain whether he still commanded the cohort of bullies, all ready to do his will, that I had encountered early in my stay in Lisbon. But I was sure he could muster enough strength to cover the city in this enquiry. The Hutchinsons could not remain vanished for long.

And I even knew how to get a letter to him. For I remembered now that Maria Beatriz had told me once that the *fidalgo* occupied a house in the Rua Nova do Almada, near the Rossio. She said it was a grand house, but much in need of repair – two pieces of information, neither of which had surprised me by much. I was sure that a letter addressed to Dom Jeronymo in the Rua Nova do Almada would find him.

And so I wrote to this *fidalgo* telling him I was seeking to discover an address for the Hutchinsons for that I wished to know how they did, and further that I wanted to send them a certain document in settlement of a piece of business that Mr Hutchinson would know all about. I wrote in this oblique fashion on the advice of Mr Marks, who said that it would be as well to disguise a little exactly what I was meaning to remit to the Hutchinsons as it might encourage the avarice of other persons if they knew what it really was. I said that I had no doubt that Dom Jeronymo was a most honourable gentleman, who would probably die rather than purloin something that was not his own, and Mr Marks said that it was not unknown for letters in transit to be opened by un-authorised persons, persons who would not even be known to me, and who would make a point thereafter of looking out for any further letters from me that might contain the promised bill of exchange if I wrote it as clear as that.

I did what he said, the letter went off, I turned again to all the interesting and sometimes joyful occupations of my new life. Through the intervention of my friend Michael Dutton, I got into a very promising line of business in correspondence with a firm in Hamburg. It was my first venture in which I was not advised by Solomon Marks and you may be sure I worked very hard at it so that I could show the world, or such of it as was noticing me, that I was ready now to stand on my own two feet. At the same time my connexion with Mr Marks persisted and together we entered on several ventures in this period, most of which flourished though one did not, and in fact it failed so badly that it wiped away almost all the profits made by the others. However, Mr Marks was philosophical about these losses, and following his lead I tried to be too, though it hurt me to think that what had vanished in the unfortunate bit of business would have kept me and the Hutchinsons in luxury for at least two years in Lisbon.

This press of trading affairs did not mean that I was a stranger entirely to pleasures. Nor certainly were the seven other souls who lived in our two houses. Though winter in London is not conducive to those outings to the parks or pleasure-grounds or into the nearby countryside that my family had always enjoyed, yet we made sure that our merriment was not confined only to our dwellings. In January that year the Thames froze over and there was a frost fair upon it and the lot of us decanted from Rood Lane and went to see it. It is certainly strange to be standing in the midst of something that spends the rest of its time flowing strongly between its banks and I'm afraid I made a few mildly blasphemous comments about 'walking on water' and so on, which brought some protests from my mother and aunt and a wink of the eye, that may or not have been intended, for the wind was quite sharp, from Nancy.

It was surprising, for I had always thought of her as a nimble sort of girl, but she found it very difficult to walk upon the ice, much harder than her sister and cousins did certainly, and I was obliged to give her my arm for most of the time we were on it. Together we walked among the booths and saw all the little marvels of frost fair: the musicians and the hawkers and the oyster-sellers and the man with the bear cubs and the woman with two heads, though we both agreed she looked much more like a female with one head and a prodigious-sized goitre growing from her neck, which had been artfully painted and wigged. It was very pleasant to be walking so with my cousin and to feel her warm against me, pressing upon my side. I thought I could have walked with Nancy till the ice melted almost and the river ran free again – but when it grew dark the rest of the family wanted to go home and we had to go with them, though there were fireworks starting further out on the ice, and all kinds of other jollities. But there was nothing to be done: my uncle and I hired linkboys to light us back to Rood Lane and thus we came home.

It was in the same month of January in 1723, towards the end of it, that I received at last the long looked-for letter from Dom Jeronymo. The first two paragraphs were occupied with the most ridiculously elaborate salutations, which I translated with great labour, and at the end of them I had learned nothing whatsoever of any importance. The third paragraph however was quite another thing. It gave me the melancholy news that that '*o seu velho amigo Senhor Allen Hutchinson*' had passed away. At least I was pretty sure that was what was meant by his being '*recebido na presença de Deus e da Mãe de Nosso Senhor e de todos os santos triunfantes*'.

Further investigation confirmed that my first reading had been correct. The sad event had taken place in the summer, 'about a week after you left him alone', as Dom Jeronymo carefully noted, and two days after the 'inconsolable' Dona Maria Beatriz returned to the house in the Rua do Parreiral to discover her '*pai infeliz*' abandoned and on the point of expiring. Luckily Senhor Hutchinson had lingered long enough to explain what had happened, otherwise, as Dom Jeronymo took pains to insist at length, the lady would have been rendered even more '*desolada*' at my disappearance, 'after she had been given the most solemn assurances that you would not desert her father in her absence'.

Of course I spent an unhappy hour or two after that trying to justify my behaviour to the invisible presences of the *fidalgo* and even more of Maria Beatriz. 'What about Simão?' I remember I kept grinding out, aloud sometimes, to my imaginary audience. But at last I was forced into a sour acceptance that I had done wrong and not what I ought to have done. My whole attitude now could be summed up in a shrug. What had happened had happened. I was certainly very sorry to hear that Mr Hutchinson had died, and I knew I would be sadder still in the future when I was not spending so much emotion on defending myself for how I had left him. But his death had long been anticipated, could have come as a surprise to no one, not to Maria Beatriz, nor to me, certainly not to Mr Hutchinson himself. The thing now was to consider where we went from here. And about this Dom Jeronymo was uncharacteristically concise. Dona Maria Beatriz knew about my 'document', he said, and it would be as well if it was forwarded, as I had suggested, to the offices here of the Englishman Senhor Tolliver. Of course since it would be inappropriate for a lady to enter a place of business, another person, 'worthy of trust', would be sent to arrange the exchange of the bill into coin of the realm.

I wrote a brief letter back to Dom Jeronymo saying that I was sorry that his letter to me had not enclosed even a note from Dona Maria Beatriz. I added that I had never wanted to injure her and that I hoped the 'document' I was sending would at least make her life easier and more prosperous in the future. And I asked Dom Jeronymo to convey to her my deepest sympathies on her father's sad death, which I too regretted most extremely. I wondered whether to add anything about how I had loved him, had even considered him for a time as like a father to me. But I could somehow see the caustic expression appear in Maria Beatriz's lovely eyes if she was ever to read such words.

I concluded by saying that the Tollivers' corresponding firm here would be given their instructions this very day and that the document therefore might be expected in Lisbon by the next packet. And that, I decided, would have to be that. I sincerely hoped that Maria Beatriz in time would forgive me, at least enough to get in touch with me without the medium of Dom Jeronymo. But it was in her hands, I concluded, and I regret to say there was a part of me that was not sorry that she had chosen for the time being to proscribe me. With all the new and absorbing elements of my new life, there seemed not much space left over for a maker of holy images in a place like Lisbon, which increasingly, now that I had re-entered the modern world, appeared to me the city of a dream: strange, antique and indistinct. And when I looked around me here and saw the freshness and modernity of a girl like Nancy – well, of Nancy herself, in fact – then I could only wonder at my old attraction to a woman deep in middle-age, who dressed by English standards in the clothes of another age, and who knew nothing of the latest jokes and catches and ideas and gossip and fashion that make London the only place in the world to be for a man or woman who wishes to live at the very summit and vanguard of our Age. What could a lady who lived most of her life in the back room of a tenement in a noisy street in the Baixa offer compared with this?

And so I decided to put aside all thoughts of Maria Beatriz, at least till a better day should dawn between us. However, a few days after I had writ last to Dom Jeronymo, Nancy surprised me sitting alone in the living room of my house, and discovered that my face was bathed in tears. I had not even known I was crying. She asked insistently what these tears meant and at last, though I could not talk to her of Maria Beatriz, I told her about Mr Hutchinson, how I had lost a dear friend, and I feared I had not done right by him at the end. Nancy comforted me and told me many kind but unmerited things, complimenting my kind heart and so on. She even wept with me a little over Mr Hutchinson, though she had never met him. As I say I could not explain to her that I was crying certainly for him, but even more for a woman I had loved, still loved, and knew that I would probably never see again.

After this I wrote a letter addressed directly to Maria Beatriz at Dom Jeronymo's in which I said – all the things I was desperate to say. My regrets, my shame, my love for her. I sent it off the next day. It may have gone in the same packet boat that carried the bill of exchange for £500. I never got a reply.

3

In time I almost forgot that old story of Maria Beatriz and her father. For a while I hoped sincerely that she would write to me, and I would often catch myself wondering how her life was now, whether she had used the money I'd sent her to buy herself an establishment, or gone into partnership with Tadeu Nunes, or what she had done with it. Once or twice when I was offered a particularly promising bit of business I actually found myself thinking that this would do very well for Maria Beatriz, that I would write to her and explain what the venture involved and I was sure I could at least double whatever she invested and would be very happy to put in five hundred or a thousand on her behalf, she had only to send me the word, of course I would trust her for the money . . .

But it was only a daydream. By her silence the lady had showed what she thought of me, and that she had no intention of renewing our friendship, whatever – and I could see the scornful curl of her lips as she thought this – whatever bribes I might hold out to her. The verdict upon me was clear and final and – I acknowledged it – she had the right to make it.

However, one cannot at twenty-three live always in a state of troubled guilt, not even when the guilt concerns one's folly and misbehaviour towards one who, if only for a day or two, I had thought might be the love of my life. And my load was appreciably lightened when I came to believe that after all my life's love might be not behind me but now, in the present, and I hoped in the future too. My friendship with Nancy, forged that afternoon in the streets of the Baixa, renewed when I came home, grew ever warmer. We used to like to hug each other almost any time we met in one or other of our houses or in the lanes and alleys around them. But there came a time when we grew self-conscious, we scarcely touched one another. And this new reticence was accompanied on my part by the beginning of an overwhelming desire to kiss her, a temptation to which at last I succumbed one spring morning, about a year after I had come home, when I found her in the living room of her house, making such a pretty picture as she played with some new kittens on the couch. I was in fact rather surprised to find her there for Mother had told me that my aunt had told her that Uncle Felix desired to see me in his house. I understood he would be waiting for me in the living room but when I got to it there was only Nancy and the kittens, definitely no uncle.

And it was there, in her father's living room, on that spring morning, just after we had finished our first delightful spell of kissing, that I blurted out some sort of proposal that we should be married. And she agreed straight away, without any maidenly sighs or tears or hesitations, and so we fell to kissing again. Later, when we had convinced ourselves that no one was going to come into the room while we were in it, we went in search of the rest of the family. The adults were waiting in my house, in the other living room, and they looked as if they'd been holding their breaths all morning. When we told them what we wanted to do, the joy was immense. The thought of a union that would bring the two sides of the family even closer was a joyful one for the older generation to contemplate. At sixteen Nancy was certainly eligible to be wedded. There were of course no legal or moral grounds against such a union in that though 'cousins' we were not so by blood. And whereas once in my aunt and uncle's eyes I had been little better than a rascal, and a lazy one at that, I had in the months since I'd come home shown myself in a very different light, a proper substitute (though never a replacement) for my father and with evident aptitude and liking for the world of the City.

The only condition Uncle Felix and Aunt Sarah placed on us was that we should wait a year before we wed, so we might be entirely sure at the end of the period that this is what we truly wanted to do. This stipulation my dear girl and I agreed to on the spot, without any misgivings or hesitations as far as I can remember. Perhaps we didn't even know what we were promising, we were in such raptures with one another.

And so everything in my life, domestically and in my business affairs too, was moving ahead at great speed, and on the whole successfully, though that did not prevent me sometimes from feeling dizzy almost at how fast it was all going forward. In this rush of affairs, if I ever thought at all of Maria Beatriz, it was in a kind of wonder that I had ever known her, or – with a stir of apology towards Nancy when I thought this – ever loved her, and lain with her.

She came back into my full attention though one morning in March of 1724, when I had an unexpected visitor. Which bare statement hardly suggests the dimensions of the thunderclap that was about to break over me and mine. I was in my bedroom, which also served as a storage place for those papers that I could not fit into the little room I was renting above Mr Marks' shop in

Cornhill. I had come back from the office this morning to locate some bills of lading I needed to examine and which I had thought were at Cornhill but could not find there. I was in the midst of this search when the little serving-girl who we had just taken on to assist my mother about the house knocked on my door to tell me that I had a visitor below, a lady. Perplexed, for I really was not accustomed to female 'visitors', except my own family, I went down to the parlour.

In there I found indeed a lady, who was sitting very upright on one of our cane-backed chairs. The day was cold, and the fire in the parlour not yet lit, and she was still wearing her coat, a most handsome-looking garment, tipped with fur. It had a hood that was up and around her face, which I could not therefore see. What I could see was that even shielded by this coat her figure appeared to be that of a young woman and I guessed a comely one – there was something in the way she held herself that made me think that. Conceiving her so, naturally I felt a stir of interest. Though I sincerely loved my Nancy, it did not make me completely insensible to the charms of other women. A couple of times my dear intended had had to reprove me when we were in the street and she had decided that I was taking altogether too much interest in the passing displays of female pulchritude.

'Madam?' I said at last when she had made no move to rise on my entrance or look at me or show by any means that she was aware I had come into the parlour. I very much hoped I could soon make her look at me at least, and then drop down the hood of her coat so that I could see whether I was correct or not in ascribing an unusual degree of prettiness to her presently invisible features.

'Mr Hanaway,' she said, and in a voice that I did not exactly recognise but that somehow reminded me of something long ago.

The next moment she turned to me and did what I was so much hoping she would. The hood slid down from her head to her shoulders. She looked up at me.

'Don't you know me, Adam?' she said at last in a voice that would have been pitiful except that it had such a harsh note of defiance in it.

I kept staring at her, unable to take my gaze away, though I wanted to very much. I did know her at last, though at first had not recognised her at all for she was so terribly changed.

'Miss Lowther?' I said, wishing indeed it was not.

'Miss Lowther it is,' she said with the same mixture of sorrow and boldness in her voice. Now she got up, she extended a gloved hand to me, and I took it. I could see now all the lineaments of that beautiful face that had once so enraptured me. I had then such a clear vision of us both in her 'dolls' house', her lovely face turned towards me and she smiling as I listed for her all the old-fashioned nonsense that Mr Hutchinson had told to me. Not willing to dwell on that now almost heartbreaking memory, I asked her abruptly as I still held on to her hand:

'When did this happen?'

'This?' She took away her hand, touched the abomination of scars that had become her face. 'Do you remember when you came to our house – we spent some time together that afternoon? I woke up the next day with my face – not like this yet feeling as if it was on fire. We were worried that I might have spread it among the guests. But after all only one fell ill like me. Do you remember Mary Mills?'

I nodded. Memory of an ordinary pretty girl, fair-haired.

'She caught it. But not near as bad as me. Except for that there were no other casualties. My father got me away from Lisbon straight away. I told him, ill as I was, that it was an underhand thing to conceal my sickness from those who ought to know of it, but he was accustomed to doing whatever suited him and so though I was very poorly he took me twenty miles out into the country and nursed me there himself. Afterwards, when I was better' – here she paused as if to relish the irony of that word – 'he was ashamed of what he had done and searched to find any others that had been injured by being in our house so that he might make some amends for it. But as I say, there was only Miss Mills. Oh,' she remembered, 'and there was a Portuguese maid died from it, but since she was thought to have brought the smallpox into the house in the first place, my father declined to involve himself in the case.'

'Then it wasn't you who was playing the harpsichord,' I cried out, suddenly distracted from her sad tale.

She looked at me curiously and I told her how I had gone up to her house on the Sunday afternoon after her father's 'tea', had heard the harpsichord being played behind the doorkeeper and had assumed it was Miss Lowther who was playing it.

'Not me,' she said. 'I was gone by then.' She shrugged. 'Perhaps one of the servants, I don't know . . . You came to the house? No one told me of that.'

I was hardly hearing her. I was lost in memory, old defeats, old shame. 'And so it wasn't the pipkin vent then?'

'I beg your pardon?'

'I thought your father had taken you away because – because it was believed I had been telling you things that were improper, and he desired to remove you from all possibility of our meeting again.'

'Ah yes,' she nodded, and for a moment I could see a glint of amusement in her eyes, which had before only shown strain and unhappiness. 'I remember now. The pipkin vent. Father told me about it when I was – not so bad as I had been. We used to talk about almost anything,' she explained then, seeing my astonishment. 'I had no mother and so he was father and mother both to me and we placed no confines upon our conversation. Yes, it was the smallpox and not the pipkin vent that took me away. Though we did wonder why you should be saying such indelicate things to a young lady. Are you a satyr, Mr Hanaway? The ravisher of maidenly innocence?'

'I am nothing of the sort. I had no idea what I was talking about,' I confessed, sitting myself upon the chair opposite hers. 'I was just trying to impress you, God help me!'

It was remarkable. I could see her poor ruined face plain before me and yet the old thrilling connection still seemed to be there, but like a shadow now. I felt myself drawn to her, I even amazingly, for one instant, wished I were a free man so that I could flirt and smile with her again with a clear conscience. Yet this was a face that I was certain no man could ever love now. The tragedy of it welled up inside me. She was a living ruin of what she had once been. And what had she done to deserve such wretched luck? She had been rich and careless and had thought well of herself, which she was certainly entitled to do. But she had been humorous too and clever and original. And she had been wonderfully, memorably lovely. And now she was this.

'Father always knew how to turn a situation to advantage, so he gave out that it was your behaviour that had made it necessary to take me away from Lisbon. The hope was that the pox would leave me without many marks and I could come back almost as if nothing had happened. But it was not so kind to me as that, as you see.' She was silent for a little while and I – I could think of nothing to say. She looked up then, smiled at me. The effect was almost hideous. Without thinking I looked away from her, repelled. When she spoke next her voice was remote, bitter. 'I hope my father's lie didn't cause you too much trouble.'

I thought of the rupture in my family, my being cast away from my uncle's protection to fend for myself, the many months lived as a virtual beggar, everything that my imprudence and Mr Lowther's falsehoods had led me to.

'Oh not too much,' I said.

'He would have been glad to hear that. For you know he liked you.'

I shook my head mutely. She regarded me from shrewd eyes, seeing I am sure beyond my apparent bland acceptance of her father's iniquity.

'Truly,' she said, 'I did not know what he was doing until it was impossible to stop him. He so much wanted to protect me that he didn't care who else he wounded.'

'Really, I do forgive him,' I said, almost believing what I was saying. 'Please tell him from me.'

'Oh, it's too late for that,' she said almost lightly. 'He is dead.'

It was almost as much of a shock as the sight of her poor face. I don't know why it should have been, except that on the two occasions when I had met him Mr Lowther had seemed to me a particularly vital sort of man.

'I'm sorry,' I said. 'Was it –?'

'Smallpox? Not really. Perhaps if you look at it in one way. For I was the apple of his eye and now the apple was – rotted.'

'No!'

'Oh indeed, Mr Hanaway. Unless your sight has completely failed, you must agree with me. Anyway, Father couldn't bear it. He seized upon the first bad attack of distemper that winter and let it carry him away from me. He cared too much about my beauty, you see. And the fine match it was going to make for me . . . But all that was gone now and my father did not care to stay to see the final act. In which I am indeed to be married, you know. A Portuguese gentleman. He is very poor and rather old – but still he cost me a great deal of money. But luckily my father left me a great deal. My beloved insists that we do not live in either his country or mine, so we are to live in France, somewhere quite remote, where nobody will know us.'

'I give you joy,' I said soberly. I thought to mention that I too was soon to be wed, but I did not want to put a merry gloss on something that appeared to me desperately serious and sad. I was wondering too if my uncle knew of Mr Lowther's death. It would be strange if he didn't, they were old friends after all, and yet I could not see why he should keep the information from me, unless indeed he had thought the memory of the Lowthers, of Gabriella really, would distract me from my duty to wed his daughter. This thought rather irritated me and, though she was quite blameless in the matter, I actually found myself thinking harsh things of my poor Nancy as well as of her over-scrupulous relative.

'Now, Mr Hanaway, you will be wondering why I have paid you this visit.'

I started to say that of course Miss Lowther was always welcome in my – and so on. But she waved me away with a show of impatience that rather reminded me of the old proud Gabriella.

'Yes, it must seem odd to you. And it will seem even odder when I tell you that my entire visit to England has been undertaken only because of you.'

Had she desired to teaze me, and astonish me by this mysterious approach to her goal then she had certainly succeeded. But I think it was more awkwardness than a wish to make fun of me that governed her tortuous advance, and certainly she had a devious tale to tell and one in which she did not figure in an entirely blameless light. She took a few more moments to collect herself, then she said, quite brightly, 'Sir, I am here to deliver your son to you.'

It would be a weary matter to go through all the degrees of shock, confusion, incredulity and so on with which I heard this announcement. They must be imagined so, and as always increasing rather than lessening as Miss Lowther – uninterrupted by me, who was really too astonished to speak for many minutes – told her tale. By her account she first knew of the existence of the child in June of last year when she was in the house in the Rua Formosa. Her father had died six months before and she had decided at last to remove herself from a place which, though it had many happy memories of childhood for her, was where the sickness that had changed her life had struck, and where her father died. She planned to move in with her grandmother at her *quinta* in the Buenos Ayres district.

'Because I thought marriage was quite out of the question then,' she remarked. 'And I would be as well living at Grandmama's for the rest of my life as anywhere else.'

Meanwhile she was spending much of her time in the old house, trying to decide which of its contents might be sold or lent and which she would want to take with her. One morning one of the serving-girls came to tell her that there was a Portuguese gentleman at the door who apologised for the unconventional manner of his approach but that he wished to speak with the lady of the house on a matter of great importance.

'No,' she said then, as if interrupting a question that I really would have been quite unable to ask even if I'd thought of it, 'it was not the *fidalgo* who has done me the honour to ask for my hand. He was still unknown to me then. In fact, Mr Hanaway, it was a friend of yours. Or at least you know him. When I received him – for I was so weary of my own company that I would have admitted the Devil himself to my drawing room if I thought he might distract me for a while – I discovered he was a short gentleman with quite remarkable moustaches. He told me his name was Dom Jeronymo da Silva.'

Giving me a few moments to move past the strangled gasp of surprise with which I had greeted that name, she went on with her story. Dom Jeronymo had started by paying her many extravagant and uninvited compliments. ('And what was even more polite, he pretended not to notice my repulsive condition.') At least she had thought they were compliments, but given the extremely flowery nature of his language she was not absolutely sure they were so. In the end she was forced to tell him 'rather abruptly' that if he wanted her to know what he was trying to tell her it were best if he spoke to her in a much simpler sort of Portuguese. He did this and, after many circuitous side excursions, came at last to the reason he had appeared at her house this day.

He said he was the emissary of an unfortunate lady who had given him the name of Dona Gabriella Lowther, as one who might perhaps be so kind as to assist her in her present difficulty. Thinking that the *fidalgo* was here only to get her to contribute to some charitable institution, perhaps in aid of fallen gentlewomen, Gabriella had remarked then that her father had always given to the charities that were administered by the English Factory, and that she thought she would do the same from now on and so she would not be persuaded to give alms to any other foundation, no matter how laudable its aims. She was preparing to get up and bring this interview to an end, with a certain amount of regret, for Dom Jeronymo seemed to be an amusing sort of fellow and she did not receive many visitors now, certainly not gentleman visitors, when he mentioned a certain name.

'My name?'

'Yes, Sir. Your name. He said he believed I was a friend of yours. I told him I had met you once or twice. I'm sorry to have had to put it that way –'

'No, You were right. We met each other once or twice, that's all.'

'Yes, still you looked a little discomfited when I said it. So did Dom Jeronymo. He said he understood from this lady that you and I had been closer than that. He used the word "*namorado*". Do you know it?'

I nodded dumbly. *Namorados, namoradas*, sweethearts. I knew too now who this 'unfortunate lady' was. She'd had to listen to my hymns to the divine Gabriella more than once, and how the pipkin vent had deprived me of my fondest hopes.

'Did Dom Jeronymo say what trouble this lady was in?'

'Indeed. Very bad trouble. He said the Inquisition had taken her.'

'Ah, Jesus. *Why?*'

'A charge of heresy is what he said.'

'But – it can't be. She was the most devout of –'

'I'm only saying what I was told. The Inquisition took her up . . . And there is worse. Dom Jeronymo said that she had died in their keeping.'

The groan that came from me then must have dispelled all lingering doubts she may have had that I truly knew or had cared for the poor lady who apparently was no more. For she reached out urgently and touched my hand even as I began to rock to and fro in my misery. 'But the thing is, Adam,' she said, 'I am not sure if she is really dead. He kept talking of her in the present tense as if she was still alive. And said many things as if she was waiting still to hear from him the outcome of this visit to me.'

'She is still alive?'

'Alive perhaps. But the Inquisition has her, it seems certain.'

I was on my feet. I was walking around the room. The assaults first of despair when I thought she was dead, and then of hope when I was told she might be alive, had quite distracted me. When I turned back to Gabriella, she apologised for taking so long to get the story out, but that she had not been quite sure whether or not I did truly know this woman. She went on to say that Dom Jeronymo had told her that the woman –

'Her name is Maria Beatriz,' I snapped.

'Yes,' said Miss Lowther gently. 'I was told that.'

The *fidalgo* had said that Dona Maria Beatriz had been taken up by the Dominican fathers in June of last year. She had given birth while in their custody. The child, a boy, was now two months old and it was near the time – 'because she is dead', as Dom Jeronymo ingenuously put it – when he must be taken from the Palace of the

Inquisition to be brought up by strangers. Dom Jeronymo gave his personal opinion that it would be for the best, as only the most devout and respectable Catholic persons would be chosen to raise the boy. However, his friend, 'who I love – loved', had been insistent that the child not be raised in the Church nor in Portugal if it were possible. But as an Englishman and a Protestant like his father. It was something that was detestable to Dom Jeronymo to contemplate and he had serious doubts whether he should be assisting her in this wish, for as far as he could see it was only delivering the child to a life of error and thereafter to the ever-lasting torments that a merciful God reserves only for heretics. However, he had agreed, reluctantly, to make this one attempt to relieve her anguish.

'I asked him,' said Miss Lowther now, 'why he did not get in touch with the supposed father himself – that is, you – and he said that Dona Maria Beatriz had lost all contact with Mr Hanaway. That he had gone away to London and abandoned her and her father and she had never heard of you again.' Miss Lowther shot me a reproving glance, then seemed to soften it a little. 'Of course, as Dom Jeronymo admitted, it was unlikely that any message from England would be received by a prisoner of the Inquisition even if you had known where to send it.'

Miss Lowther had asked the *fidalgo* what it was he expected her to do, for she did not know where Mr Hanaway was either, not even that he had left Portugal. Dom Jeronymo, as if it was quite an obvious thing and that he could not understand her mystification, had said, 'Why, madam, take the baby, of course. Dona Maria Beatriz says – said – she had been told that you were wealthy, that you lived in a big house with many servants, and so that a child would present no very great difficulty. And if you should some day wish to inform his father of his existence then that she leaves to your judgement. Only she wants your assurance that the child would grow up as an English boy and in your faith, not hers.'

This offer, and the almost serene way it was made, quite dumbfounded Miss Lowther. Which must be why she did not rise up before the *fidalgo* had even finished speaking and tell him: no, no, it was preposterous, impossible. Another reason, she said frankly now, was that the long, tedious stretch of time she had passed since her father died and the almost inconceivable extent of tedium that she guessed lay ahead had rendered her so dissatisfied and weary of her life that any diversion however absurd and even distasteful was welcome. Also, as she thought the matter over, the proposition came to seem a little less outrageous. She knew that among her Portuguese acquaintance, of the genteel sort, there was a degree of relaxation in the way they regarded these matters. Children were, so to speak, passed around informally; often you found one or two growing up in a household that was not their parents', and sometimes these arrangements went so far as to lead to the adoption of a child whose natural parents were still living and who quite approved of the new situation.

On the other hand – no, it was ridiculous. She was a girl, barely eighteen years old, and what did she know of babies except that she had always rather disliked those who had happened to be present in her father's friends' houses when they went visiting, or else went with other families on excursions into the countryside? Nevertheless, she did not want to show herself as completely heartless, or unmoved by the sufferings of this poor lady, whether dead or alive. She told Dom Jeronymo that she would make what enquiries she could as to where Mr Hanaway had gone. She thought there was an uncle who he had worked for once – but the *fidalgo* told her that the uncle had gone to London too. She said then that there must be somebody in the Factory who would at least know of this uncle's address in London and perhaps through that means the absconding father could be tracked down. As she had promised, she would find out what she could.

Dom Jeronymo, by his expression, showed that he was unimpressed by her offer – which was hard for she had thought she was making quite a sacrifice to agree to go among the people she had once known in her prime with her now ruined face and disappointed hopes. But he told her it would by no means do, that the child had only been removed from the palace of the Holy Office with great difficulty. He had been keeping it for the past few days in the care of a wet nurse he had employed but he knew that suspicion must fall on him soon for he was known to be an acquaintance of the heretic Maria Beatriz Fonseca. If the child was taken back into the care of the Dominicans it would disappear for ever, perhaps to live a life as a peasant's son on the plains of the Alentejo, or a fisherman's in Setúbal, or even taken across the sea to be raised for a priest's vocation in a mission in Brazil or Goa. If she was truly interested in sparing him from a fate that was abhorrent to his mother, then Miss Lowther must take him and take him now. There was no possibility of delay.

'Why, what do you mean?' asked Gabriella getting to her feet in her alarm.

'He meant,' she said now, 'that he had the poor little thing out in the driveway of my house. He led me outside, keeping a hand on my elbow, which I was thankful for because I thought I would fall into a faint if he didn't support me – and you know, Adam, I was never someone who did silly girlish things like that. There in the driveway sat a coach that looked to me incredibly old-fashioned, a hundred years old at least. And the driver looked almost as old, sitting up there on his box.'

There was a coat of arms on the door, faded into nothing more than an heraldic glimmer. Dom Jeronymo flung this door open. A young woman of the common sort was sitting in there, staring at Gabriella with bulging eyes. In her arms was a baby, or at least the shape of one for it was hidden almost by the cloths it was bound in. The woman gave Gabriella a scared grin, and then turned back the topmost cloth so that the child's head could be seen. The little mortal opened his eyes, peered feebly at this new person that had entered his life, belched loudly, and began to cry.

'And after that I could not send him away. I engaged his wet nurse – Francisca – and found a room in my house that could serve as a nursery and where she could sleep beside her charge. The other servants were very curious, of course. I told them the baby belonged to a dear English friend of mine who was leaving him in my care while she went home for a few months. By the way, his name is John. Dom Jeronymo told me that the mother had insisted on that for it was the same first name as that of a relative of her father's, who had once been a famous man in England. "A great general of the Republic", according to her. I have no idea what she meant by that.'

'She meant her father's uncle. Colonel John Hutchinson.' I was hardly looking at her now. 'He held Nottingham for the Commonwealth in the civil war, and signed the King's death warrant. Mr Hutchinson told me about him once.'

I do not know how long we sat in silence after that. I do recall that at one point Miss Lowther left her chair and went to the door and called for our serving-girl to come. She did so, and I remember seeing her standing in the doorway looking at me with a scared expression on her face. At Miss Lowther's command she went away again, to return a minute or two later with a small jug of wine and a glass. Gabriella, I remember, administered the wine to me like medicine, insisting that I swallow every drop that was in the glass.

The first words I really recall myself to have uttered thereafter were, 'I am a father?'

It was, I suppose, the nub of the matter, and the most important question I could have asked, though sometimes afterwards I wondered why it had not been more directly about the fate of Maria Beatriz. Yet the news of my fatherhood, coming out of the clear blue sky instead of with the many months of mental preparation that are normal in these matters, was so immense to me. I had always been the son, never the father. My father was – dead. My second father – also dead. I had known how to be a son to them when they were alive. But I'd had no practice at this other trade.

I noticed that Miss Lowther was stirring somewhat in her chair, and that on her face was an expression I could not exactly make out. It was strange – I no longer thought of this face as 'ruined' or 'pitiable' or anything like that, her news had taken all that sort of dross away. I was only interested in trying to interpret what it was, willingly or not, trying to convey to me.

'Do you think,' I asked, 'that I might not be this child's father?'

'How am I to know that?' she said with some difficulty. I had actually found a way of making bold Gabriella a little timid. And yet I think now it was concern for my feelings rather than prudery that rendered her so shy of saying what she meant. But she did it in the end.

'Only you can know if your relations with the woman – with Dona Maria Beatriz – were such that a child might result from them.'

To that I only nodded and was silent.

'Then, Sir, perhaps you should consider whether you are certain to be the only possible father of her baby.'

I was silent still, mainly now in amazement that such a question could have been asked about Maria Beatriz. Gabriella saw something of this in my face for she said then, 'I'm sorry, Adam. But somebody must ask this of you and it might as well be me who you are not likely to see ever again. I don't know this lady, or her character. All I know is that she bore a child out of wedlock. Surely you know that in such cases women who have been indulgent to more than one man often cast around for the likeliest "father" to lay the charge of her baby against. Even though we shared only the briefest of acquaintances in the old days, I should not like you to be a dupe, that is all.'

I did believe that Miss Lowther meant well to me and so I only shook my head and told her that Dona Maria Beatriz could not have done what she was suggesting. I would give my life that she was honourable and chaste – or at least that she had known no men while I knew her but me. And that Gabriella need not concern herself over it any more. She nodded and seemed to accept what I said. Later I was to understand that her urging the possibility that the child was not really mine had something to do with the fact that she would have been happy enough if it had made me repudiate him so that he could continue in her possession. But she was sufficiently honourable not to press the matter when she saw I was convinced the paternity was mine.

She said then she had her own confession to make. That she had really intended from the start to try to discover where I was so that she could inform me about the child. But she had kept finding reasons for putting off the task. Not least that she really did not know whether it was fair to the child to put him in the possession of the particular father that fate had caused him to have.

'For you must remember, Adam, that all I knew of you then was that you had done something very bad at your uncle's firm, which had caused him to dismiss you, and I remembered too that somebody had told me that you had become a beggar in the streets –'

'I was a peddler,' I said, with as much dignity as I could find. 'It was not a dishonourable occupation. And though I did not match up to my uncle's expectations, yet I never behaved dishonestly to him either.'

'I guessed it was so. But still, the whole business seemed rather murky . . . Anyway I let the time drag by with all these excuses for not doing anything about finding you. And –' Here she hesitated for a moment, before it all came forth in a rush. 'And I had come to love the boy, there it is. For the first time I found something that was more engrossing to me than my disaster. *He* did not know how I was meant to look, and when I was with him, or thinking about him, I forgot about it too.' She bowed her head for a little while. Then looked up and smiled at me. There was just the trace of a tear in her eye. 'I'm sorry, it was selfish. In the end I decided I must do something, I was no better than the woman who steals a child from the streets because she is unable to bear her own. And now, unexpectedly, it seemed that I might after all have my own chance at motherhood. For I had met, been wooed by, and had accepted Dom Oliveira Francisco Miguel de Sousa de Azevedo. My intended, Adam.'

She was still smiling at me and so I risked teazing her a little. 'Who is poor and old.'

'I'm afraid so. But he assures me he is still in possession of his manly vigour and as he fathered three sons on his previous wife he reckons he can manage a couple for me before he is through.'

'You will have a husband and three sons to support from the day you marry?' I marvelled.

'And a pair of unmarried daughters too. It will be expensive, there's no doubt of that. Not much left of the wealth of the Lowthers when Dom Oliveira is finished with it, I should think. Oh, it's not so awful as I pretend,' she said then – I think because pity had again crept back into my gaze, though not for her ruined face this time. 'He is a very decent sort of man, and I think will be kind to me and maybe keep me from becoming too perverse or cruel. For you know I used to have a bit of a disposition towards those vices in the old days and I can't think I was likely to improve much as I grew older, whatever happened, unless someone appeared who I could accept as my spiritual guide, and certainly a priest wouldn't have answered. It was my *fidalgo* in fact who insisted I did try to find you, that I had waited too long to do it. He said that we could not raise another man's child without his permission, it was unfair both to you and to dear little John. Which is why for the first time since that night you came to our house I went to an entertainment where the Factory would be present in numbers.'

She fell silent after saying that. I didn't know whether I ought to prompt her or not. I decided it were best to let her tell the story as she wanted, including as slowly as she wanted. Besides, I was again losing myself in contemplating this extraordinary new circumstance that I found myself in. Adam Hanaway – a father!

'I'm sorry,' she said then. 'I was remembering that night – of course I knew that the change to my face must mean that I would be treated differently by those I had used to know. But I really had not understood – though it is a truism, I know – quite how much a woman's, a young woman's existence is governed by how she looks. Oh, they made a show of welcoming me at first. But that died away pretty soon and I could see in many of their faces that they felt I had done ill to bring my ruin to their Merry Christmas party. These silly people who I used to treat so lightly, to laugh at indeed, and too often to scorn. Soon they could not bear my presence any more and I was left alone. *I was left alone*! Who used to have men so thick around me at these routs that I had to go and sit with my father just to give myself breathing space. And the other girls all wanted to be my friends in those days – even though I made it clear that I could hardly bear most of them – as if they thought they could share in my popularity if only they could stand near to me.'

She paused. She bit her lip, shrugged.

'Oh well . . . after about ten minutes of my own company I was just deciding that I would go home, I couldn't stand this any longer, when Ralph Tolliver appeared before me. Do you remember him?'

I nodded.

'I think his father had sent him over. Sent *them* I should say because he dragged his witless wife up to me too. She soon could bear me no more and squawked out some feeble apology and made off. Which left poor Ralph. He did appear monstrously ill at ease. Could hardly look at me. He used to look at me once, oh yes he did!' Gabriella nodded, and from the look in her eyes I knew at last that I had been right in thinking when I had first seen them together in the assembly house that they had been lovers. I was sure of it now.

'So there he was,' she went on, 'humming and hawing and wondering how soon he could get away from me. I thought I might as well make this unpleasant encounter as useful to me as it might be, so I asked him if he knew anything of what had become of Mr Adam Hanaway who used to attend such parties as these. And though Ralph was the most possessive sort of fellow in the old days and scarcely liked to hear another man's name mentioned in his presence, he quite brightened up now to hear yours. Perhaps he thought it meant I would be devoting my unwanted attentions to someone else rather than him. Poor fool!'

Which was said with very great scorn. I was about to tell her that I was indeed known now to the Tollivers, father and son, by reason of the bit of business I had done through their firm in sending the bill of exchange to Dom Jeronymo – when she told me of it herself.

'He said he gathered you were doing very well in London. That you were the customer of a substantial firm there, for which he and his father were happy to serve as correspondents in Lisbon. And that by a letter that had accompanied a bill of exchange they had learned that Mr Hanaway was well thought of in the City as a rising young man of business, with several important connections who had brought him into certain promising ventures of late. Did I want the gentleman's address?'

After that, Gabriella knew what she had to do. With her

intended's reluctant permission – 'He thinks I and my fortune are bound to be snapped up by some fop in Piccadilly before I have been home two hours, dear man' – she booked passage on the first packet of the new year. She did not write to me because she saw no reason to; she would be home as fast as any letter. Nor had she sent any warning when she arrived in London because, she said, she could not bear to deprive herself of seeing me when I first heard the news. ('Did I not say I had a perverse streak in me, Adam?') And more soberly, she did not do it because she wanted me to see the child before I decided what I wanted done with him and she thought that a letter, even from within London, would give me time enough to harden my heart against him.

'Harden my heart?'

'Why yes. You might reject him. I will tell you frankly that I would not be very sorry if you did. I would love to have the raising of him. He is a promising boy and will be treated as well as any of my stepchildren or as well as those children that I may have one day. I will even engage to raise him in the Protestant faith as his mother wanted. For my *fidalgo* is not much bothered about that sort of thing, and says I may do what I want.'

'You've discussed this with him?'

'Yes. I have.'

'Reject my son . . .' I said to myself then, so low I thought she could not have heard me. But she was listening with painful attention and taking everything in.

'Yes,' she said. 'You may. But see him first, or you will always regret it.'

'See him? Why is he here?'

She laughed when she understood what I was meaning, which did something to break the tension that had grown between us in the last minute or two.

'No,' she said, 'I have not copied Dom Jeronymo's example. John is not outside in a coach, I promise you.'

'On a day like this,' I said, trying also to smile, 'I'm glad to hear it.'

'I'm staying at my aunt's house in Leicester Fields and he is there, with Francisca in attendance. My aunt, of course, has not stopped cooing over him from the moment I carried him in through the front door. You may see him whenever you wish.'

My mind was everywhere now, and I did not know which thought to grasp first . . . Maria Beatriz. I had to know what had happened to her. Whether she was alive or no. (O Lord, how I prayed she was.) It meant I must go back to Lisbon as soon as I could. Dom Jeronymo was my only likely source of information, yet I knew now I could not trust him to tell me the truth in a letter. He had lied to me. He had lied to Gabriella, probably. And he had not, I realised, done anything to tell her where I could be found in London, which he must have known long before he had delivered the child to the Lowthers' house, for we had established a correspondence by then.

Maria Beatriz. Even if alive, in the hands of the bloody Inquisition . . . And yet almost in the same moment I seized on this theme it was blown from my hand, and I was thinking of this child who had, as it were, erupted into my life. Bringing implications and consequences with him that I could hardly begin to weigh. Gabriella Lowther was watching me as I sat struggling to find my way through this maze. There was pity in her eyes and I was so distracted that I did not even think there was something peculiar in that *she* should be pitying *me*.

At last I calmed down sufficiently so that I could face the one element in this story that now seemed to me the most important of all. I thought that Miss Lowther might be able to advise me here, for she was a young woman too, and also soon to be married, and might have the best perspective in which to view my quandary.

The maid came back in to light the fire. When she was gone, as the short day's light faded beyond the window, and the rain dribbled down the glass, I started to tell Miss Lowther about Nancy.

There is nothing in all the years we spent together that made me more proud of my wife Nancy than the way she received the news that her husband-to-be not only had once enjoyed the favours of a mistress, but that the offspring of this connection lived, was now in London, and that I was even contemplating raising him as my own son. And, unless she chose this occasion to repudiate the promises she had made to me, he would be her son too of course. Before we had even lain together we would have a family of our own. It was not a prospect, I think, that many young ladies would have contemplated with much or any pleasure, and indeed when I first told her of it she swore one very surprising oath and marched right out of the room we were in, which was the little parlour of my uncle's house. I sat on in there in a considerable degree of misery, thinking that all my hopes of a life with Nancy had suddenly been dashed, wondering too if I could resuscitate these expiring hopes by repudiating my little son. For that reward I might do it, I thought. And I knew that the child would continue to have a good home in the care of Gabriella Lowther. Yet I could not stop myself thinking that there was something craven and unfeeling about this course, and that I owed more to this little stranger.

At this point Nancy reappeared in the parlour. She came and sat with me and held my hand and began to talk very fast. She said she was sorry she had behaved as she had, that it was the surprise, the shock of hearing the news. She knew perfectly well that young gentlemen customarily had experiences of women before they married. She was glad at least that I had not been to a prostitute –

'She was certainly not that,' I promised, gripping her hand as tightly now as she had held mine. 'She was a pious, cleanly, decent, lovely –'

'There is no need,' cut in my bride-to-be, 'to go on like that. I am sure she was a very good sort of a woman.'

'I was only going to say, dearest, that she was lovely for a woman of her age.' And I told her what I guessed that to be.

Nancy's eyes widened at this and almost a sympathetic look came into her eyes. Evidently she saw me now as a young innocent who had been caught in the toils of a much older, more experienced female. And such was my need to justify myself in Nancy's eyes that I started to feel a little this way myself, and that Maria Beatriz had quite taken advantage of me. At the same time, great waves of fear for her were sweeping through me so that I could hardly listen to Nancy. And there was so much to do. I had gone out to a maritime coffee shop this morning and arranged a passage to Lisbon by the next packet, which sailed in two days' time. I had to put my affairs in some sort of order before then so that I could make this unexpected voyage without throwing all my ventures into disarray.

'The child –' Here Nancy's voice began to quaver and she looked very tragic. 'The child is hard for me to think of, Adam. No,' she said as I tried to say something apologetic, soothing. 'Let it be. It is a surprise, and not what I would have wanted. But if you are certain that the baby is yours then of course we must keep him and raise him as our son. We could not do anything else.'

I started to say that we had the opportunity to see the child first before we made a decision, but she would have none of this, saying that it would be monstrous to treat the matter as if we were buying a horse or taking on a servant.

'We must make up our mind before we see him. It is the only proper thing to do.'

'But what if he doesn't want to leave Miss Lowther and come to us?' I asked.

'He is a child,' she said, demonstrating the kind of sturdy, unsentimental common sense that I was to witness often enough from her in our marriage. 'It isn't up to him what happens.'

After this it seemed easy enough to tell her that I must go away. She said she understood and perhaps she did. 'I must know if she is really dead or alive,' I said. She asked me then if I found Maria Beatriz was alive: 'Will you come back to me?' I started to say that of course I would, how could she imagine – when I saw she was even smiling, so little did she think that the attractions of a woman of fifty could threaten the hold of a now seventeen-year-old on me.

'Ah, don't smile,' I said. 'I believe she is in a poor way even if she lives. Perhaps I can do something to help. And I would like at least to assure her that her son –'

'*My* son,' said Nancy sternly. 'Yours and mine. If we decide to take him, he is to have no other mother than me.'

She said then she had only one reservation about letting me go, which was that I might not return in time for our wedding. It was late in March now, and we were to marry in June. I said that I thought I could manage it, though of course I would not pretend to predict what the weather at sea had in store. But I would do everything in my power to be back in time, and would linger in Lisbon no longer than it took to satisfy my apprehensions over Maria Beatriz.

We went to Leicester Fields the next morning, a day before my departure for Portugal. I had sent a note by runner to tell Miss Lowther that we proposed to visit and had decided we would take the boy to raise him as our own. I supposed that she would be receiving us at her aunt's house but when we got there we were met only by a housekeeper who informed us that the two Misses Lowther had left the house early and were not expected to return before nightfall. She added that the child was in an upstairs room and ready to depart with us. We climbed the stairs, both of us I think feeling somewhat taken aback by this method of transferring custody. Indeed Nancy wondered audibly, 'What on earth does Gabby think she's doing?' Some time afterwards, when we were less jangled by the tensions of this moment, we realised that poor Gabriella had gone away, not because she was impolite or uncaring, but as she could not bear to watch us take away the little boy she had cared for. Nancy, I must say, had one other side explanation which I rather deprecated when she told me of it.

'For she always looked down on me as a funny little stick and couldn't have endured to see me triumph over her. Her with a horrible face and everything.'

The little boy was sitting on his bed. He looked up as we came in, held us in his gaze for a moment, and then – wondrously – smiled at us. Nancy came at him with cries of joy and swept him up in her arms. I was mostly engaged in dealing with the fact of this sturdy little stranger. For some reason I had thought of him as the baby that Gabriella had described when Dom Jeronymo brought him to her. But of course several months had passed since then, in fact a year and more. And there he was, no baby but an undoubted little person. He eyed me curiously over Nancy's shoulder; I gave him a little wave and came up to him and patted his head.

At this moment, the nurse, Francisca, who had been standing in the background unnoticed, came forward. She showed us the packing she had done of both the young gentleman's clothing and of her own. It was the first time almost that I had considered the fact that she would be coming with him. I thought immediately that it would not do to stay any longer in the same house as my mother and sisters, as Nancy and I had expected to do in the first months of our marriage. A new house or apartment must be found for us and that would be another worry on my mind as I sought to make everything right. I wondered if Mr Marks could be induced to look for a place for my suddenly enormous little family while I was away. Meanwhile my departure would at least free up my room in the present house. John – John! – and his nurse could stay there for the while.

And all this was going through my head as I was smiling and waving at the now serious-looking little boy in Nancy's arms. He looked as if he was just starting to contemplate the implications of the great change that was coming upon him, and I certainly felt at one with him there.

4

Next day, after a loving farewell from Nancy when it was yet dark, I crossed to the Deptford dock and went on board the packet at one of those unearthly hours in the morning favoured by sea captains who like to start early on the business of teazing and dismaying their passengers. Some sort of reputation had evidently preceded me for I noticed that I was treated with a degree of deference rather above those of the other passengers, who were generally accorded little or none. I was sat next to the Captain at table, for instance, which was not wholly to my liking as this officer had a habit of spraying food when he laughed, which he did quite often. He also too often made such comments to me, accompanied always by a little laugh and several winks, as that he hoped, 'I wasn't planning on smuggling any more gold away from the bastard Portingales, eh, Mr Hanaway?' but that if I was, he believed he could accommodate me on his vessel where there were hiding-places that the 'sons-of-bitches' would never detect in a hundred years. This facility was offered of course for the most modest of fees.

Because I did not want to lose all credit with him and so be relegated for the rest of the voyage to the condition of the other passengers, I said that, while I had no definite plans to convey anything dangerous out of Lisbon this time, my designs might change and I was glad therefore to know I had available the consideration of a discreet and gallant captain such as himself. He said he understood: 'Nuff said between gentlemen, Sir!'

The weather on this voyage was not kind to us, and it was a full four weeks before we found ourselves standing off the Rock. Still I believed that if the journey back was only as slow as the one here had been, I was almost certain now I would be able to return to London before June the 14th and my wedding day. It must be said though that the nearer I got to Lisbon, the less did I care about that. All my thoughts now were with Maria Beatriz, and if Nancy could have seen into my mind she would have got a very doubtful impression of man's constancy. But then, I told myself, when I felt guilt for this, my dear girl was in no sort of trouble, whereas my – my whatever-I-would-call-her – was either dead or in great peril.

I grew very angry when I thought of Dom Jeronymo's conduct in this affair. After his letter to me I had heard nothing from him, not even an acknowledgement that the bill of exchange had arrived and been cashed. However, Mr Marks, wiser than me, had asked to be informed about this and one morning we had got a note through Jarvis, Bird in Throgmorton Street that the bill indeed had been cashed at the Tollivers' counting house in Lisbon, though by a *fidalgo* rather than the lady it was made out to. This Portuguese gentleman had said he was a friend and adviser to the lady and had brought with him proofs of what he said. His explanation for her non-appearance was that of course a lady of distinction and virtue in Lisbon could not be expected to appear in the masculine surroundings of a counting house. However, her signature had been procured in receipt of the money and this receipt the Tollivers had the honour to also forward to us. Mr Marks called me in to verify the signature. I knew it certainly. I had seen it on letters she had written and sometimes on her drawings, when she thought she had made a specially good one. It was Maria Beatriz's hand, no doubt of it.

But I wished now I had brought the letter Dom Jeronymo had sent me. Was there a hint in it, even one, that the poor lady had been in any danger? I was sure there wasn't, still I would like to have had it before me. If there wasn't such a hint then I could not have responded to her need any sooner than I was doing now. Which might well be too late for her, but still the knowledge would do much to quiet my own conscience in the matter.

With so many contrary notions and emotions chasing each other around my brain – and I have not even mentioned yet the one that still overshadowed all the others, which was my continuing astonishment at the fact of my unexpected fatherhood, of my son back in England, my little John – it was scarcely to be wondered at that my first sight of the city of Lisbon, after an absence of nearly two whole years, should have had far less effect on me than might have been expected. While my fellow-passengers were gathered on deck near the prow of our ship, exclaiming at the wondrous spectacle emerging in the sunlight before them, I was somewhere towards the stern, pacing up and down, going over what I wanted to do as soon as I set foot upon the quay.

We came into the river at about two o'clock in the afternoon and I thought I might have time enough even today to call on Dom Jeronymo. But I had forgot all about the wretched health officers and their inspections and their infinite ways of wasting other people's time. When the passengers were allowed ashore at last evening was upon us and I had to give up hopes of interviewing Dom Jeronymo today.

Once on dry land I took one of the little two-wheeled mule-drawn coaches, and had myself and my baggage driven to a good inn I knew of in the Largo da Picheleria. They had a room free, which I took for one night, and with the opportunity to stay longer if I wished. I sent a message by one of the hotel's servants to Dom Jeronymo's house to alert the *fidalgo* that I was here in town and that, *com licença*, I would wait on him tomorrow morning between eleven and twelve. I went over then to a coffee house in the Rua Nova dos Ferros where I knew merchants and sea captains were accustomed to meet and do business. There I fed myself well and at the same time ascertained the days of sailing of at least half a dozen London-bound vessels. The one that left soonest was in two days' time, but I had the names of others now for two weeks ahead. The gentlemen I spoke to said there would be little trouble for a single passenger to find a berth on any of them, even up to the hour of sailing, for it was too early for the great summer exodus of the English and the ships were leaving half empty of passengers.

It did indeed seem a long way from summer when I regained the street. A keen wind was coming off the river and I was glad to go back to my inn and my warm room. I had thought in the coffee house that I might walk through the Baixa first to pay a visit on what had once been my home, Montesinhos' house in the Rua do Parreiral. But the cold convinced me that this was not a good idea. Besides, what would I be visiting but the ghost of the building that I had known, with new owners and probably servants and tenants too, who would not have the faintest idea who I might be?

Just before I set off for my inn though there was a little necessary business I wanted to conclude. There was a mercer's shop I knew of not far from the coffee house that dealt in the finest varieties of merchandise, and I went to it and found it was still open and there bought myself the sort of great swirling cloak that I had often coveted during the winter I had spent here but had never been able to afford. Now warmed and protected by these many yards of fine-woven Spanish wool, I came out of the shop and hired a boy to carry a torch before me and light my way back to the Largo da Picheleria.

As I came in off the streets, the innkeeper handed me a bulky package sealed with some sort of crest and addressed, 'À Sua Excelência the Earl Lord Hanaway, MP.' And though of course both I and the fellow who gave me the letter knew this was only an example of the Portuguese fashion of flattering whoever they were addressing, still it gave me a glow of satisfaction when I read this preposterous salutation and noted also its effect on mine host.

I took the package up to my room, broke the seals and discovered inside at least three large sheets of paper. Even so, it was a short note I read for the gentleman who wrote it had an extremely generous hand and managed no more than a dozen lines of writing per page, though he covered both sides of them. Cut down to the marrow, and translated as best I could from his highly formal Portuguese, Dom Jeronymo da Silva's note to me expressed surprise that I had arrived at Lisbon without letting him know in advance of this 'joyous event'. He said he would be glad to see me on the morrow although it could not be until the afternoon as it would be Sunday and he preferred to spend the mornings of '*o dia sagrado*' entirely at prayer, whether privately or in attendance at Mass. He regretted that he could not invite the Senhor Hanaway to accompany him to the latter but understood that the errors of my religion – 'though doubtless sincerely held' – prevented me from enjoying the blessings offered by the 'True and Only Church' to its faithful followers.

I was already in bed when I was reading this note, with its odd mixture of cordiality and provocation. I set it down upon the bedside table, snuffed out the candle and fell almost immediately into a sleep that lasted until I was awoken next morning by the appearance of the maid with my hot water.

I took breakfast not at my landlord's table but at a coffee house in the Rua dos Escudeiros. Afterwards I wandered about the town, revisiting some of the places and streets that had been my familiar surroundings in the days when I worked here in one trade or other – with the exception of the Rua do Parreiral. I was still loath to see again Montesinhos' house, though I scarcely knew why. I promised myself I would go to see it after my interview with Dom Jeronymo.

I was down by the Alfândega for a while. I made no attempt to go into it, but I thought of the people who I had known there and laboured beside. I thought of Senhor Gomes and wondered where he might be now. In Hell, I hoped – but I supposed he was more likely to be still in Spain where he was thought to have fled after purloining my uncle's money. Had he spent it all by now in riotous living and was dragging out the life of a penniless fugitive? Remembering that cold and calculating man – the '*escorpião*' – I thought it was much more likely that he had used it to make a good investment and was presently enjoying the existence of a gentleman of substance and prospects. Wherever and whatever he was, I damned him anyway.

After this I could think of nothing better to do than go back to the inn. There I told the landlord that I desired my room for another night and he said it was good that I had told him in time for there would be plenty of people looking for lodgings all over the city before long on account of the festival tomorrow. I did not ask him what festival it might be, for the Portuguese are always having them, or processions or street pageants. It was bound to be religious in any case, and in my present mood not of much interest to me. I only requested that a bit of food now be sent up to my room.

When I'd eaten, I washed myself in the water left over from this morning and dressed in a fresh suit of clothes. It was a dove-grey suit, sober yet most elegant, that I had ordered before Christmas from a tailor in Clement's Lane, recommended to me by a City friend, Mr Vellicott of Turner, Vellicott and Short. There were still thirty minutes before I was due at Dom Jeronymo's. I had considered the advantages of arriving before his doors in a good coach, but the display seemed hardly to warrant the expense. Besides, the journey by foot to the Rua Nova do Almada where he lived was not far and the roads there in tolerably good repair and cleanly. A walk would do me no harm, I decided.

I put on my fine new cloak and examined myself in the looking-glass. I thought it gave to my appearance a definite flourish, even wearing it, as now, over my sober City suit. I did not attach beneath it the sword that in the old days I had always thought an essential part of any gentleman's attire when he was on formal business. Since Mr Dutton's advice to me on board the *Holly*, I had rather given up wearing this article. I was no longer, as they say, always 'spoiling for a fight' (or, as Adam Runaway usually contrived it, spoiling for one that at the last moment I found myself unable to participate in). I was in fact much less the bold fop of old, and when I thought of the sort of clothes I used to wear on important occasions they seemed like the plumage of a peacock compared to what I wore now.

And so, bundled up in my cloak, I left my inn and headed towards the Rossio. It was the first time for two years I had walked in the great square. I saw now that it had always been my favourite place in Lisbon, so open and busy, and yet without that rather forlorn sense of infinity that sometimes fell on one in the wind-swept emptiness of its rival beside the river. Today the Rossio seemed busier and noisier even than I remembered it, and I guessed that tomorrow's festivities were bringing in the crowds early. There were men and women carrying flowers and tree branches that were radiant with the bright-green leaves of spring. They looked quite incongruous on such a bitter day as this, but certainly cheered up the scene with their promise of warm days to come. The fountain and the lamp standards were already garlanded with flowers, and in the houses around the square bright-coloured banners were being hung out in celebration. Only the forbidding bulk of the Inquisition Palace sat in dour indifference, black and undecorated, as if to remind the poor wretches that were under its jurisdiction that their frolics and flowers were only the baubles of a moment and that what it offered was for eternity, and it was death.

Made somewhat subdued by these reflections, I left my dear Rossio and walked along the Rua Nova do Almada. I asked a street-vendor the way to Dom Jeronymo's house and she pointed it out. I went up to the door she had indicated and knocked on it. After that I took a step or two back and looked over the property. As Maria Beatriz had told me once, it was a substantial house, but old and much in need of restoration. It was faced with marble but, as they do it here, wherever the noble stone was cracked or had greatly decayed a pinkish sort of mortar or mastic had been applied to cover the wounds. Here the repairing substance so predomi-nated that the whole building seemed to be made of this dusty, dingy pink. There were other sorts of repairs visible as I looked up at the house. In several of the elaborately carved arches that formed the windows fronting the street the glass was broken, and some-thing like brown paper or discoloured pasteboard stuck up in its place to keep out the winds. It made me think how cold it was likely to be inside, and that I would probably have to keep on my cloak even if the *fidalgo* thought me impolite.

Nobody coming to the door to answer my knock, I smote upon it three more times before at last hearing a creaking and a turning of key in lock. The door opened; a very old man looked out at me. I

413

was reminded suddenly of the man Gabriella Lowther had seen on Dom Jeronymo's coach on the day baby John had been brought to her door and who she had said looked to be at least a hundred. Whether or not he had actually reached that miraculous age, he certainly looked extremely old, and I really wondered that he should be exerting himself on such a day as this even so far as to open the door for me. But he had, and so I gave my name promptly and did what I could to help him open the door wide enough to admit me and then to close it from the other side.

A very sombre feeling crept over me as I followed in the darkness behind the old servant. He was creeping towards a chink of light at the end of the corridor, which discovered the presence of another door, slightly ajar. It was as cold in here as I'd guessed it would be, perhaps colder even, and the smell of mould and damp was almost overpowering. My thoughts now – I almost said at last – were entirely with Maria Beatriz, and yet I did not like at all to associate her with these forlorn surroundings. I wanted to think of her as I had seen her last: on a late-spring day that was not icy like this one, but warm and bright. And she in an apricot dress, warm like the day, taking her seat in a fine coach, and then looking out to smile at the crowd of folk who loved her and had come to see her off.

Dom Jeronymo, I remembered, had not been present on that morning among her other friends. It seemed a melancholy circumstance that of all those who had known her it was only this man I could locate. For he did not make me think of the Maria Beatriz I had known. He was not part of the humdrum friendly life of the Baixa. Probably he had looked down on us who were. He kept himself apart in this great old falling-down house. Served by this antediluvian creature – who now with visible effort pushed upon the door we had reached. Slowly it opened for him. He stepped aside and nodded me through into the room beyond. I found there, standing beside a huge fireplace in which smoked the smallest of conflagrations, the *fidalgo* himself. He appeared to have posed himself for my entrance, with one arm resting negligently on the mantelpiece and the other holding up to the light a small volume that he seemed to be reading.

He gave an affected start when, as if by chance, he looked up from his book and saw me standing there. Followed by a deep bow which I returned as well as I might, having rather got out of the habit of bowing deep in the past two years. He said he was delighted to see me, then laid his book aside on the mantelpiece with an audible sigh as if he could hardly bear to be torn from his studies.

We regarded each other without much more warmth than was thrown off by the wretched little fire that smouldered between us. The last few years seemed to have dealt harshly with Dom Jeronymo. His wig was quite worn away and what was left of it appeared greasy and uncombed. He had not been shaved for several days at least and his beard was coming in not grey even, but pure white. And there was some infection that was troubling him in his eye – his left as I remember it – for it was red and weeping, which discovered an additional note of distress in his appearance, and indeed to our whole interview that day, for the phenomenon continued throughout it.

However, I had no leisure to contemplate Dom Jeronymo's condition, and so when he had at last concluded various enquiries concerning my health, the speed and comfort of my voyage hither, whether or not they were treating me properly in my hotel, etcetera, I put to him directly the question I had come a thousand miles to ask.

'Is Dona Maria Beatriz really dead?'

He gazed at me in apparent astonishment as if he could hardly believe what I had said. His left eye worked furiously, the tears ran down his whiskered cheek.

'But certainly she is,' he said. He was stuttering when he said it as if I had caught him quite off-guard.

'Truly dead?'

'Truly. Did not Miss Lowther explain that to you? I am sure I told her that when I brought her the child.'

'Miss Lowther explained it indeed. But she also said that when you told her of it you spoke sometimes in a manner that suggested to her that Dona Maria Beatriz was still alive. You spoke of her as existing in the present.'

Dom Jeronymo shook his head. 'I could not have done that.'

'She was most clear that you had.'

'I do never like to contradict a lady,' he said, 'but she is wrong . . . What may have happened – as is the case with most of the English, Miss Lowther's command of my language is not great.' Another polite bow. 'Not as yours is, for instance. She may have misunderstood some things I said.'

We stared at one another.

At last he said gently, 'Senhor Hanaway – she is dead.'

She was dead. Truly, finally dead. And I realised in that moment that all along I had kept inside myself a hope that she might not be, which was so strong that it amounted almost to a certainty. So that it came as an unanticipated blow to my heart to know that she was really gone. Why, I remember thinking, I will never see her face again. And though in truth after I had left Portugal I never really thought I would see it, yet the knowledge that I *could not* seemed suddenly insupportable. I felt so weak under its influence that I groped my way towards the nearest chair. I was about to settle on it when, even in the midst of my sudden new misery, I noticed the face of the *fidalgo* as he looked down at me. It was suffused with consternation and I suddenly knew that this chair, and probably every other of its brethren in the room, was not able to face any more the necessary duty of bearing the weight of a human being.

As I have mentioned before, most of the serious events of my life in those days seemed tinged with a discolouration of farce, a circumstance that I generally tried at least to treat with a degree of rueful humour. But this time it would not be amusing at all. It would be insupportable if after the news I had just been given I were to go sprawling on to the naked floor.

I turned away from the chair. I heard the *fidalgo* sigh with relief that his poverty was not to be exposed even further. I came to stand again with him at the fireplace. When I looked up, I saw he was regarding me with a much more natural and sympathetic look than the quizzical hostility that he had shown before. I guessed this change had come upon him because he recognised by how much I had been pained by what he had told me. I don't know in what light before he had considered my relations with the Hutchinsons, with Maria Beatriz in particular. Of course, because of the child John, he knew I had been her lover. But she had probably explained to him the truth, which was that I had been so for only a couple of nights. As for how he saw the rest of my acquaintance with that family: perhaps he had imagined me as one of those useless and unimportant hangers-on that Portuguese families of the better sort tend to collect around them.

Perhaps too he had guessed that my coming to see him so unexpectedly was for quite different motives than I knew them to be. I did not think so immediately, but I am sure the matter of the bill of exchange for £500 – which was the only cause of our communicating with each other previously – was much on his mind. I do not wonder at that. It is never a convenient matter to have to make an accounting of a long-ago transaction at a day or two's notice.

'Tell me,' I said, looking away again from the *fidalgo*, for I really could not bear to see the sympathy in his weeping gaze, 'how did she die?'

Dom Jeronymo shrugged.

'She had a child.'

'She died in childbirth?'

He hesitated.

'Not exactly. A month or so after she gave birth, there were complications. There was nothing surprising about it.'

'Where was this?'

'Where she died? In the Palace of the Inquisition.'

'In a cell?'

'Of course.'

I groaned to hear this. Dom Jeronymo bent over and poked at the fire with a stick to make it glow a little brighter. I suppose he did this because he did not like to be staring at me when I was in such evident distress.

'Was the child too born in this cell?' I asked when I had recovered myself a little.

'No,' he said, clearly glad to be able to reassure me on this point. 'In the hospital of Todos os Santos. She was very well cared for there. You know it is just across the Rossio from the Palace of the

Inquisition, most convenient –' He stopped there as if he was not entirely pleased with his choice of words. Then: 'A week or so before she was brought to bed of the child, she was carried in a litter – very gently – across to the hospital. Be assured, Senhor Hanaway, your son was not born in a prison cell.'

'But they were taken back to it afterwards?'

'Yes, of course. She was facing serious charges. It was a wondrous act of mercy on the part of Holy Mother Church that she was allowed to leave her place of confinement and bear the child in Todos os Santos.'

I really thought I could not stay in this terrible cold room a moment longer. It made every sorrowful detail that Dom Jeronymo was telling me seem ten, twenty times more pathetic. And yet I knew I had to listen to many more of them, for I would never forgive myself if I came this far and did not find out everything there was to know about the melancholy end of my poor Maria Beatriz. I owed it to her and – unexpected and strangely cheering thought – I owed it to our child. If I could just have a glass or cup of something, hot coffee or tea preferably, I knew I would find the ordeal appreciably less trying. I really wondered that I had not been offered something already. The Portuguese of every class are punctilious in their hospitality, and a glass of wine and probably a few choice morsels to eat were invariably provided for a guest before he had been in the house five minutes.

Looking up again at the *fidalgo*, I saw that his features were pulled into what I interpreted as quite an agony of embarrassment – and all at once I thought I knew why he was being so remiss in his hostly duties. He had not a bottle of wine in the house, I guessed, and even if he had there was probably not a decent glass in the place to serve it in. Of course I could politely ignore the situation but my need for refreshment, even more my need to get out of this terrible house, was very pressing and made my brain fertile in discovering the way to fulfil both my desires.

I told him that it was the custom in my country for a guest to bring presents of food and ale or wine the first time he set foot in a gentleman's house. But that my mind had been so occupied by thoughts of what I was coming to find out here that I had clean forgot these important civilities. I implored him to forgive me and added that I could not think of proceeding with our interview unless he allowed me to repair the damage by taking him to a hostelry I knew of not far from here. I assured him that it was a very select establishment I was proposing, which only accepted the best sort of client, and that I was sure that Dom Jeronymo would not feel in the least dishonoured by adding his illustrious presence to the assembly.

After a prolonged show of reluctance, the *fidalgo* graciously accepted my invitation. I thought we would have to wait a little longer while he summoned his creaking servant so that his coat or cloak might be brought to him. But apparently he had no need of either. We went straight from his freezing house into the slightly less freezing street. I took him to a place I liked to use in the Rua Nova dos Ferros, in fact the same coffee house as I had gone to last evening. We settled down at a free table. Dom Jeronymo looked around him with great interest. The usual clientele of English merchants and sea captains was all about us. I had instinctively wanted to be in their comforting, familiar presence. For Dom Jeronymo though I suppose everything appeared quite exotick. The waiter coming over to take our order, I told my companion that my perturbation of mind had also made me quite forget to eat today and that I was prodigiously hungry. I asked if he would allow me to order him a chop too as it would trouble me to have to eat alone, and again he graciously acceded to my request. Poor devil, I suspect he really had not eaten a thing all day and I had my doubts about his yesterday too.

The warmth, the smell of coffee in the air, and then the soothing influence of the food when we began to eat, all contributed to the growth of a strangely agreeable atmosphere between myself and the *fidalgo*. He asked me at one point if this was at all like the coffee houses in London that he had often heard of, and I said it was very like. He said then that he had always longed to visit London and I asked him why he did not. He hesitated for a long moment, and then shrugged and with a charming, regretful smile said that it was too late for him to go travelling.

'Surely not,' I said, wondering at the same time how old he was. Forty-five, I thought, trying to look behind the signs of disrepair, perhaps fifty. Old indeed, but not too much so. On my voyage from Lisbon to London in '22 we had a couple of gentlemen in their seventies among the passengers, who put the rest of us to shame with their vigorous morning and evening tramps about the deck.

The *fidalgo* was shaking his head. 'Too old,' he insisted gently, 'and too poor.'

This information, freely offered, rather bewildered me. I had come from a community where the last thing one wished to be known was that one was poor. I had forgot that here a gentleman might see his poverty almost as a proof of his gentility.

'Yes, it is all gone now, Senhor Hanaway,' Dom Jeronymo went on complacently. 'I have lived off the family estate ever since it became mine, as my father and grandfather did before me. There was always a field of pasture or olives or a farm-house to sell so that I could maintain myself for another year. But there's nothing left now. It was a fine estate in the beginning, granted to my great-grandfather by Dom João IV, but there is nothing left of it. The last to go was the house you have just done me the honour to visit. I must move from it before the month is out.'

'What will you do?' I asked, feeling very sober suddenly. Since I had myself not long risen out of abject poverty, the thought of someone else descending into it could not be comfortable to me.

'I shall go to a monastery.'

'You will become a – a monk?'

'I don't know. Perhaps they will just allow me to live there and work for the house, maybe in the fields, or the bakery or the laundry, wherever I can be of use. You see, Senhor Hanaway, I have discovered at last that of all the things I have loved in this world – hunting, fighting, eating, drinking – nothing has meant half as much to me as my love of Holy Mother Church. Yea, passing even the love of women, I love my Faith.'

At this Dom Jeronymo smiled again his charming, shy and always gallant smile. For a moment I could see him as he would have been twenty-five years in the past when he was a young and wealthy *cavalheiro*. He must have been devastating to the fair sex back then. I wondered again if he and Maria Beatriz had ever been lovers. Whenever I had accused her of it – tenderly, when we ourselves were lovers – she had always dismissed my suggestion, saying that Dom Jeronymo had only paid court to her like any other young spark with a long cloak and a guitar, and there had never been anything serious in his love-making. And yet I always wondered how such a trivial connection could have lasted over so many years. Dona Maria Beatriz had been fascinating to me from the moment I had first known her; I hardly dared to think what effect she must have had on men in her youth.

I was thinking of her, and the warm, familiar surroundings of the coffee house seemed to waver and shrivel around me. Dom Jeronymo saw the change that had come upon me but, such was the perfection of his manners, that he waited for me to declare what had suddenly afflicted me. I hesitated, not wanting to go forward, knowing all the same that I had to.

'Dom Jeronymo,' I plunged in at last, 'I must know more about what happened to Dona Maria Beatriz.'

'Of course,' he said, setting his plate aside, leaning towards me. 'You were her friend. You are entitled to know.'

'When did the Inquisition take her up?'

Dom Jeronymo considered. 'It was in the week after she came back from Evora. Not long after that, a few days.'

'Her father was still alive then?'

'He died the day after she came home. Did I not write to you about this?'

I nodded.

'They were able to take a proper leave of each other,' he promised me. 'Her father never knew what danger she was in.'

'And she was in the dungeon of the Inquisition from – when? – June of that year until she . . . she died?'

'Yes.'

'Eighteen months then?' I shook my head. 'I don't understand,' I said. I knew there was little point in going on, I knew the *fidalgo*'s opinions were unshakable in these matters and that he could hardly even understand my own. Yet I owed it to something, someone – Maria Beatriz, humanity – to make my point.

'How could a woman who was blameless be made to suffer eighteen months of imprisonment – in surroundings that most probably contributed to her –'

'She was not blameless,' Dom Jeronymo said quietly. And, when I tried to dismiss his intervention, said again with the same quiet force, 'She was not blameless.'

We stared across at one another. The waiter chose this inappropriate moment to appear to refill our cups. Neither of us glanced at him.

'Did you not know that her mother was a New Christian?'

I had known. Maria Beatriz had said once to me that on her mother's side, in the distant past, had lived ancestors who were known to have been Jews. I think it was on one of those nights we lay together that she told me, probably the second, when we were talking, casually, intimately, between our passages of love-making. She'd mentioned it in passing, as something incidental, just another detail in her account of her mother, who as a child she had adored.

'You are saying,' I said heavily, 'that because she committed the great crime of being born to a woman who had some Jewish blood –?'

'That wasn't the reason she was taken up.' Dom Jeronymo reached out for his cup. Sipped at it. There was a gleam almost of amusement now in his eyes as he gazed at me. It seemed so disgracefully out of place; I wanted to pluck it out of him. 'Do you think the Holy Office can be troubled with such trivialities as that? Half the population would be languishing in the dungeons of the Inquisition if they did.'

'That was what I understood,' I said slowly. 'And so why was Maria Beatriz –'

'Dona Maria Beatriz – Montesinhos, her landlord – a man called Bento Ferreira and his wife – another called Tadeu Nunes, a printer – a pair called the Lourenços – several others, male and female.'

'What of them?'

'Did you really not know, Senhor Hanaway?' And when I

almost shouted, so that the good merchants at the next table looked up at us and frowned at our noise, '*Know what*?' he shook his head and said mildly, 'Strange. I would have thought she would have told you. Her lover.'

I did not respond to that. I said at last, with lowered head, 'Mr Hutchinson told me that Montesinhos was of New Christian stock. I didn't know about Bento and –'

'I've told you. That didn't matter. What mattered was that they were in the habit of gathering together in Montesinhos' house and practising the Jewish rites. They were not "New Christians",' said the *fidalgo* with a sudden ugly leer upon his face. 'They were Jews. *Circuncisos. Relapsos. Heréticos.* They were people who had been offered the peace and glory of the True Faith and the hope of Heaven hereafter – and instead had crept into a vile corner to revive the abominable practices of their forefathers.'

Some dishes arrived at the table next to ours. A muttony-flavoured aroma wafted over to us. It was thick in my nostrils as I stared across at Dom Jeronymo. He shook his head; there was an expression of pity almost as he considered my bewilderment.

'It's true. They met regularly in Montesinhos' house. In the house you lived at for – how long was it? A year? About that? And yet you saw nothing?'

If there was a hint of menace in Dom Jeronymo's words I chose to disregard it. I was an Englishman. I now had important connections in the City of London, which was as good as saying that I had a serious voice at the Court of my Sovereign and in Whitehall and Westminster too. There would be a hell of a fuss if the Inquisition attempted to lay its bloody paws on me. Yet in fact it was none of these thoughts that rendered me speechless for a little while. But was rather that, when he had stated that I had seen nothing, there came to me in the same moment a sudden distinct memory. I am on the ground floor of Montesinhos' house, where the kitchen is. I am in the corridor that leads from the kitchen to his little parlour. I see at the end of it the parlour door open wide. Beyond I see a table laid with a white cloth and on it are tall tapers burning in golden candlesticks. I think I hear a murmur of voices, perhaps somebody laughs. I am getting close to the parlour – then

Maria Beatriz appears in the doorway and I stop. We look at one another, and then slowly she closes the door upon me. The light dies, I am left in darkness.

All this I had seen. Yet only now did I know what I had seen. If I had known any earlier – what she was doing, what danger she was in – could I have done anything to save her from the fate that waited for her?

Dom Jeronymo had not ceased from watching me. And when I looked up now, he nodded and said, 'You did know then?'

'I can't tell,' I said slowly, 'what I did know. What I saw . . .'

How envious I had felt of the warmth and joy that I sensed lay behind that closed door. This happened in that period when I was quarrelling with the Hutchinsons after I had forgotten to go to dinner with them as I'd been invited, and had then made matters worse by sending them a ridiculous note that attempted to cover up my error. When Montesinhos' parlour door had closed on me I had interpreted it as another attempt to slight me, and punish me for my folly. I had gone away cursing Maria Beatriz's unforgiving nature. Of course she had only been trying to protect her little group of co-religionists. And perhaps protect me from knowledge that could have done me no good, might have brought me into some danger myself.

'How did the Inquisition learn about Montesinhos' house?' I asked.

The *fidalgo* looked a little uneasy at this point. He shrugged and said, 'In the usual way.'

'Which is?'

'A denunciation.'

'Somebody denounced these people?'

Dom Jeronymo shrugged again. Then inclined his head.

'Who was it?'

Dom Jeronymo touched his fine moustachios which, in contrast to the white whiskers on his unshaved cheeks, were of the deepest black. Since I'd first set eyes on him today I had suspected him of employing lead or coaldust to keep them looking dark and young. When he took away his hand I tried to see if any stain now adhered to it . . .

I had no idea why I was entertaining such inconsequential thoughts at so serious a moment as this. He was maintaining a grave silence. I probed a little deeper.

'One of the servants?'

'Not in the first instance . . . Senhor Hanaway,' he said, 'you might not be pleased to hear the answer to your question.'

'I am sure I would be obliged to you,' I said, 'if you would tell me who was the low bastard who sent Maria Beatriz to her grave.'

'Now I am sure the answer will not please you.'

Dom Jeronymo spoke so seriously that I could not but consider what he said. But of all the candidates for treachery that presented themselves to me – had it been Tadeu Nunes who had turned on his fellows? Or one of the Laurenços? – I thought there was none who I would be so shocked to discover as the traitor that I would rather have never known his name. Though I did hope it wasn't Bento.

'Dom Jeronymo,' I said, as earnestly as I could make myself sound. Indeed as earnestly as I really felt. 'For my peace of mind, I should like to know. Otherwise I shall always wonder.' And then, when the *fidalgo* still did not speak: 'And I should want to know for my son's sake too.'

It felt very strange to say that 'my son'. Dom Jeronymo stared into my eyes.

'You will tell him?'

'I don't know yet. Perhaps. I think he will want to know what became of his mother one day.'

'I think it would be very wrong to tell him.'

'Well, so you may, Dom Jeronymo,' I said. 'But you will give me leave to decide that for myself. After all –' Again the hesitation, the sense of disbelief that what I was about to say was really true. 'After all, I am his father.'

I saw that I had won my point. Dom Jeronymo nodded. He looked about him for a moment, and I followed his example. All around us were the beefy, self-satisfied faces of wealthy Britons talking over ships and cargoes and ventures to Massachusetts and Muscovy, and other excellent matters fit for men of the modern world to discuss. And here we were, Dom Jeronymo and I, raking up the disgusting embers of ancient hatreds and prejudices. All at once I wished that he would not tell me what I had demanded to know. I wanted to finish this meeting, to go away, flee this city, go straight back to where I knew now I belonged absolutely.

But it was too late for that. Slowly, making sure that I understood everything he was saying, he told me of the day he had received a message from Senhor Hutchinson asking him to call in at the Rua do Parreiral. He had been glad to accept this invitation for he had hoped it would mean he would be seeing his dear friend Dona Maria Beatriz. It was only when he got there, and had been received by her father into their apartment, that he discovered that she had gone to Evora several days before. He was at first rather hurt that it had not been thought necessary to tell him of her plans.

'Of course in the old days I would have been made aware of it in any case by my attendants throughout the city. But nowadays –'

He gave a shrug. I guessed he meant to say that his leadership of a gang of cut-throats and bullies was among those luxuries his poverty had forced him to do without. He did not linger long in regretting the passing of his glory. He told me now that he had set aside his disappointment over Maria Beatriz's absence, and settled down to speak with Senhor Hutchinson, though not very cheerfully because, he admitted, though he yielded to no man – no man, Senhor Hanaway – in his admiration for the daughter, he had never particularly cared for her father. However, he was resolved to make the best of circumstances and merely hoped that he could get through the visit without descending into one of those foolish wrangles about nothing that he so often got into with this particular old man. But before he had half concluded the normal civilities that must occur between two gentlemen when they meet, Senhor Hutchinson had blurted out what he wanted to say. That there were Jews who were meeting regularly in the basement of this house. He gave names: Montesinhos – Bento Ferreira – the Laurenços upstairs . . .

'Dear God,' I breathed now.

'Yes, indeed. Through these unworthy lips, God had shown us the way to trap a nest of vipers.'

The *fidalgo* had not known at first whether the old man was being serious. And then whether this was simply another sign of deteriorating mental health, that he was imagining these secret meetings, these Jewish rites. Often as a *familiar* of the Inquisition, Dom Jeronymo had used to receive information of mysterious and suspicious goings-on. When these phenomena were investigated, they were most usually found to have an innocent explanation. Or else it was clear that the denunciation had been done out of malice and also had no substance in fact. Yet Senhor Hutchinson continued to maintain the truth of his story, and he was very clear about what he knew. That there were Jews in the house, they were holding ceremonies here, the taint of heresy was within these walls.

Dom Jeronymo had done what he could to shake the old man's story. He reminded him how seriously such charges would be considered by the Inquisitors. He reminded him too that he was making them against friends, neighbours who he had known for many years, most of them. And he asked him what he thought his daughter would think of his conduct. At this point the old man had started to seem uneasy. He said he was doing it precisely to help his daughter. To make her a fortune, he said. And then, when the *fidalgo* continued to probe his motives, he had come out with a story about Montesinhos and how he wanted to frighten him, to make him more alarmed than he already was. And then Hutchinson was shouting and weeping and all sorts of nonsense was pouring forth.

'He talked about you a great deal, Senhor Hanaway. About how this was all to do with business. Which we Portuguese could never understand. That he was an Englishman, thank God, and was in business with you, another Englishman, and that I could not know that sometimes in business one had to do things in the dark that one might be ashamed of in the light of day. Of course he was right,' the *fidalgo* shrugged. 'Not I nor, I hope, any other Portuguese would understand an occupation that encourages one to betray one's friends. If this is business, we are most fortunate that we are such incompetents at it.'

'It is not business,' I said, through teeth that were almost clenched together. 'Not as I have known it. And in any case,

Mr Hutchinson had had nothing to do with business for many years. He was only a sick old man. You should not have listened to him.'

'I am not free to choose what I hear and what I don't. If I've received information of behaviour that may insult and endanger Holy Mother Church then I must not keep it to myself. My oath and my honour require me to take it seriously.'

And seeing that Dom Jeronymo was indeed taking him seriously, Mr Hutchinson had crumbled absolutely. He revealed the plot, as it existed in his own mind – and in no one else's, he insisted, certainly not in Adam Hanaway's. Dom Jeronymo would please to make it clear to Montesinhos that he had definitely come under the suspicion of the Inquisition. The landlord would be terrified of course and forced to flee his home directly, but not before he had finally acceded to whatever business proposition Mr Hutchinson had been urging on him.

'I did not ask what it was. I had no desire to know. But this was the strategy, Senhor Hanaway. To use the Holy Office to frighten this wretched man into trusting Hutchinson and you! He kept saying Diogo Wallenstein wasn't enough. I suppose you know what he meant by that?'

I did know. Montesinhos must have tried the old man's patience too much, vacillating to and fro as to what to do with his person and his fortune. At sometime in the middle of a sleepless night the brilliant idea must have seeped into the old distracted brain. And in a way I had to acknowledge its lucid shrewdness. For what else could force an intelligent fellow to entrust his whole fortune to a foolish old man and an ignorant boy? Only the immediate prospect of the rack, the hot pincers and the stake would do for that.

'By now he was in a very distressed state of mind,' the *fidalgo* reported. 'He wanted me to forget the things he had said. But I couldn't do that. Whatever is said to the Holy Office or its representatives cannot be made unsaid. I would have to act therefore in my official capacity. He implored me, for the love he knew I bore his daughter –' Here Dom Jeronymo fell silent for a little while. Then took in a deep breath. 'He asked me to allow the people time to get away at least. And so he wept and begged and called on the name of his daughter and – and in the end, to my eternal shame, I gave way. I will have to ask forgiveness for this every day of my life and before the throne of Lord Jesus Christ thereafter.'

Dom Jeronymo agreed to send two men, known to be lay-servants of the Inquisition, to watch the house on the Rua do Parreiral, and not to be too careful about concealing themselves. He would give Montesinhos a few days, no more. When after those few days Montesinhos still showed no signs of departing, he had arranged for a brother *familiar* to visit the house in his absence and demand to speak to the landlord. That had done the work. On the next visit it was found that Montesinhos had gone.

'In fact, all the birds were flown by now,' Dom Jeronymo reported, sounding I thought quite gloomy at the memory. 'The word had got around from Jew to Jew. Ferreira, the Laurenço couple, the printer fellow, another man called Pardinho who had a toyshop in the Rua do Oiro, all those who were used to meeting in Montesinhos' basement – all gone. Except for one. Dona Maria Beatriz who was many miles away from Lisbon when this was happening.'

Of course, said the *fidalgo*, Senhor Hutchinson had not de-nounced his own daughter. He was not mad or cruel or greedy enough to do that. Indeed he was entirely ignorant of her in-volvement. His knowledge of what was happening in Montesin-hos' parlour had been picked up in dribs and drabs from the servants over the years, what they had seen, what guessed. His daughter's name had never been mentioned, perhaps out of compassion for him, to protect his ignorance. It only came to light after some of these low people had been seized by the agents of the Holy Office and encouraged to reveal what they knew. Most of them gave the information freely, but one of them, a brazen young lout called Simão, had had to be 'tortured a little' before he would speak.

When Dom Jeronymo heard that Maria Beatriz's name had been mentioned in this unhappy context, he did everything he could to warn her. He had learned from her father that she would be returning from Evora any day now. Dom Jeronymo had sent men

– 'at my own expense, Senhor Hanaway' – to watch the ferries, with orders to bring her straight to him, not to let her go on unawares to the Rua do Parreiral. But the party she was travelling with had chosen not to take the ferry that crossed directly to Lisbon, but another to Cascais in order to visit friends out there. Afterwards they came back into the city through the Alcântara gate where none of Dom Jeronymo's people were watching for Maria Beatriz. And then she had come on from there to her home, and it was too late.

The Inquisition in the house, her father on his deathbed – I could not bear to imagine what this homecoming must have been for her. And that she knew who was the cause of the disaster – no, it was too much. I shook my head, I wanted to cram my fists into my ears, not to have to listen to any more of this. But the *fidalgo* was remorseless. I had asked to be told. He had not finished telling me.

'Some of my colleagues were for taking her up right away. But I persuaded them to wait. It was clear that the old man had very little time left. We stationed guards outside the apartment door, and some in the street below in case she tried to escape by the windows. Yes,' he nodded, hearing the disgusted snort I made at that suggestion, 'I told them that it was not very likely but they insisted and as it made no difference to her I did not argue much. I don't know what happened between her and her father then. She has told me since that he never knew or guessed that he had brought her into such danger. I believe from what she said that it was a peaceful death. God showed mercy, and whatever one might say about Senhor Hutchinson I knew him always to be devout in the Faith, a humble servant of Holy Mother Church. I think indeed that a part of the reason for his first mentioning the Jews in Montesinhos' basement to me was because he could not bear any more to know what sins were being committed in the very house he lived in. I think that was as important to him as this "business" he was so proud of.'

I had – nothing at all to say to this. I was thinking now that at last I knew what the old man had been meaning when on our last evening together he had accused himself of having harmed Montesinhos, and said that he would never be able to make amends for what he had done. But this did not seem to be a memory worth sharing with anyone else just now, and so I kept silent. The *fidalgo* waited courteously for a little while to give me a chance to speak, and when I did not he nodded, stirred the cold dregs of his coffee, then said:

'She came out of her rooms after a few hours and told us that he was dead. She was dry-eyed. Standing very tall and straight. She looked like –'

'A queen,' I said, and the *fidalgo* nodded.

'If all queens were really as proud and beautiful and noble as she looked then.'

Thereafter Maria Beatriz had settled into the actually rather humdrum existence of a prisoner of the Inquisition. She was placed in a cell – 'not the least comfortable, by any means' – and every week or so was brought before the judges for an examination. She was not allowed to have any books, but some painting and drawing materials were permitted to her, as long as what she produced pertained only to holy matters. So she spent a great deal of time drawing the faces of the Saints and of the Virgin, just as she had used to do when she was free. The results were so pleasing, seemed so filled with sweetness and piety, that several of the officers and priests of the Holy Office were pleased to accept them as gifts, even from the hands of a Jewess.

About this time I interrupted Dom Jeronymo's benign portrayal of Maria Beatriz in the hands of the bloody Inquisition to ask if she had been tortured. He shook his head and begged me earnestly to believe that she was not.

'There was no need. She very cheerfully confessed to taking part in Jewish rites. She said her mother had taught her them when she was a girl. Had taught her in secret, not even her father had known of it. And that she had never wanted to lose or set aside that which she had been taught. She told us she had got her sincere belief in the Jewish religion from her mother – and her equally sincere belief in the true Catholic Faith in Jesus from her father, and as she loved both parents equally she did not wish to part herself from either set of teachings, for that she believed in each of them with equal fervour.'

'That is not logical,' I said.

'Which is exactly what was pointed out to her by the merciful judges who examined her. In any other religion, no doubt her first utterance of such heresy would have sent her directly to her death. But these goodly men argued with her and tried to break down her stubborn resolve over many months, using only the methods of argument, reason and prayer.'

I refrained from making any smart remarks concerning the *fidalgo*'s misapprehensions about the bloodthirstiness of other faiths – of mine, for instance. I tried to imagine Maria Beatriz before her judges. I suppose she heard them with the same appearance of tranquil self-possession as she had often shown when listening in the evenings to my and her father's nonsense. I wondered if she had sewed while she listened, as she would often do with us. I suppose the judges wouldn't have allowed her to.

'No, there never was a need to torture her to extract information, for she gave it so readily. Except . . .' Dom Jeronymo hesitated. Then: 'She would not agree to tell us the names of those *heréticos* who had worshipped in Montesinhos' basement with her. Not even the name of Montesinhos himself. None of them, though she was told we knew them all anyway, and that they were all now fled to safety – except for the shopkeeper Pardinho who was taken up in Setúbal and was now in a cell on a lower floor where he was quite happy to give the names of every one of his fellow-*relapsos*, including hers. But even when she was told of this, she would not budge. She would name no one.'

There were some who thought that an application of the *polé* or the rack might be in order to combat this particular feature of her obstinacy. For, though the Holy Office already had all the names that she might have given, it was always deemed important that a penitent should prove the value of his conversion by surrendering up to justice any others who had sinned with them. However, a young priest who had been among the foremost admirers of Maria Beatriz's artistic skills had argued that, since she was not *penitente*, but was still maintaining the heresy that she could love both faiths equally, then the naming of others by her would prove nothing about her own spiritual health. Most of the fathers agreed with this argument – and then when it was discovered that the prisoner was at least three months pregnant the desire to put her to the question grew even less fervent.

'For Holy Mother Church,' reported Dom Jeronymo solemnly, 'would never wish to hurt the innocent unborn in chastising the errors of the living. It was ordered that Dona Maria Beatriz should be left unharmed until after she had given birth.'

'And then she would have been tortured?'

The *fidalgo* shrugged. 'The question never arose.'

'Because she died.'

'Yes. Because of that.'

'Did she die unrepentant?'

For a moment my companion's eyes seemed suffused with sadness. He nodded. 'Entirely. To her death she would insist that she needed the comfort of both beliefs and would not be parted from either of them.'

'But that was madness,' I said, feeling inside me a sudden spurt of anger at the authoress of her own unnecessary doom. 'Not to do the little thing that would have saved her. Especially when she knew she was pregnant – and then a mother. How could she do this?'

'Have you never wanted to sacrifice everything for what you believe in, Senhor Hanaway?'

'No! I haven't.'

'Strange,' mused Dom Jeronymo, 'it is what I have wanted for myself since I was a boy . . . You must understand that even if she had escaped death she would not have been set free. She had been found guilty of the crime of Judaising. The child would have been taken from her, she would never have seen him grow up. And she herself would probably have been sent to the Angola colony for many years.'

'Are you saying that she preferred to die?'

'Only that, perhaps, she found few temptations to live.' There was a silence between us. Dom Jeronymo studied me. Then he shrugged. 'She was resigned, Senhor Hanaway.'

But what had she been so 'resigned' *about*? Because it was her own father who had betrayed her? Because I had abandoned her?

'She was obstinate.'

I had used the word *obstinada*. But my companion shook his head.

'No, she was *resoluta*,' he said. 'She is resolute in her error.'

Resolute. Yes, that fitted Maria Beatriz. 'It was a very great sorrow to all of us,' Dom Jeronymo sighed, 'and especially to the judges of the Inquisition who strove so manfully to rescue her soul. But she is unyielding. She will not be persuaded.'

I let a few moments drift away. It hardly seemed worth mentioning at such a time, yet I knew it would nag at me for ever if I did not.

'Sir,' I said, 'I think you have committed the same mistake with me as you did with Miss Lowther.'

He eyed me curiously across the table.

'You have,' I pointed out, 'spoken of Dona Maria Beatriz as if she is still alive.'

'I am sure I did not,' he said, quite indignantly.

'Sir, I am sure that you did. More than once . . . However, it doesn't matter.'

I let him ponder the question in silence. At last he shrugged. 'If I did make such a mistake – and I do not for a moment doubt that you believe I did – it was only because I find it so hard to think that she is really no more.'

His thoughts chimed in so well with my own that I felt in my breast an immediate surge of sympathy for him. I wondered myself if I ever would get used to talking of Maria Beatriz in the past tense. In this town at any rate she was still so vivid to me, so alive. As she was, I saw, for her poor *fidalgo* who had adored her for so long.

Yet sympathetic though I felt to the man, there was still one item of business that I had to get through with him. I feared it would disturb the atmosphere of quiet fraternity that had grown between us in the past few minutes, but I knew I had to do it. Again it was something I would have worried and wondered about for years if I failed to ask him now.

'And the bill of exchange?'

'The bill of exchange?' repeated Dom Jeronymo. He sounded

puzzled and looked rather hurt. I did not care. I realised I'd had enough of the tone of gentle regret with which he was dressing up this disgusting story. I wanted to jerk him quite out of this mood, and I could think of no better way of doing it than by subjecting his refined ears to talk of hard cash.

'Yes. A bill for £500. You cashed it at the Tollivers' counting house, and showed them a signature that was claimed to be hers. Was it a forgery?'

'A forgery? – *I*?'

'If not, then the signature was obtained from her when she was in prison. Was she tricked into signing it? Cajoled into handing over to you money that was hers by right?'

'Sir – Sir –!'

The *fidalgo*, so calm and composed only a moment or two ago, was actually stuttering in his distress. I did not care. I thought: By God, if you have stolen her money, even not so as to pocket it yourself but to give to your poxy church, then I will have the law at you.

'You cannot think . . . No, you cannot. The money was all devoted to her service. I swear – I should not have to swear to it. Even in the dungeons of the Holy Office much can be bought with a generous supply of *moedas*. Better food, a better cell – and do you think every woman in there who is brought to bed of a bastard child finds herself in the hospital of Todos os Santos at the moment of birth? No sir, most of them expel their burden in darkness on to the filthy straw of their bedding. Would you have wanted that for the mother of your son? It cost money to obtain that mercy, Senhor Hanaway, a great deal of it. I could not have afforded to make her life bearable out of my own resources. Your bill of exchange came as a miracle, a gift from God. I would no more have thought of purloining it for my own use than I would think of getting myself drunk on communion wine.'

I had wounded him, I knew, and was sorry for it. I was sure now that he had done all he could to make Maria Beatriz's last months as comfortable as they could have been. And I should not have suspected him of stealing from her. I had been away from Portugal too long and had not remembered that for a *fidalgo* who was like him, like so many of his fellows, at the extremity of poverty, his honour was the last thing left for him to care for, and he would never have given it up.

We finished our interview a little later still with a sense of strain between us, which made it impossible for me to do what I had been planning during the meal, which was to give him some money and ask him to use it for his own necessities. Still I believed I could find a substitute for a purely cash gift and as we were standing by the table and adjusting our dress I asked him if he would mind accepting my cloak and using it for his own. For I pointed out, quite truthfully, that such a garment was not really in the mode in London nowadays and I did not think I would be returning to Lisbon for many years, if ever. He would be doing me a great favour by taking the thing off my hands.

He hesitated long as I knew he would, but the sight of this fine cloak, which I had bought only yesterday, proved too much for him and he accepted my gift at last. It was a pleasure to watch him wrap it around his little form, and see how well he looked in it, and to know that he would be measurably warmer in his body now for as long as this unseasonable cold weather lasted – unless indeed his other exigencies forced him to sell the article, which was entirely his own business, of course.

Outside in the freezing street we faced each other for what I guessed was the last time. He asked me when I thought I would be leaving the city and I told him I believed there was a packet boat sailing on the morrow and, if I were able to get a berth, I would sail with it. There was nothing else for me to do here. I had thought to visit the graves of Maria Beatriz and her father, but really I could not face it. Besides, I dreaded to ask where Maria Beatriz's remains might be – I did not know exactly how they disposed of heretics when they were dead; probably she was dust now, perhaps blowing about the courtyard of the Dominicans' convent, or in the Rossio itself. As for Mr Hutchinson – well, what did it matter?

He seemed most relieved to hear what I had said, which I thought was strange. What could it matter to him how long I lingered in this place?

'I think it is good if you go tomorrow,' he said. 'You would not like to be in this city then.'

'Why not?'

'Didn't you see that a festival is being prepared? Don't you know what will be the climax of the day?'

Of course I did. I had simply not wanted to think of it. The '*culminação*', he had called it. The high point, the masterpiece of tomorrow's celebration. The piles of faggots and the stakes. They were all being prepared behind the gay flags and banners I had seen in the Rossio. I had walked past them an hour or two ago – on Maria Beatriz's dust? – and had willed myself not to recognise the signs, to pretend they only represented the outpouring of innocent piety and exuberance.

And the people around me there, so full of barely suppressed excitement. They could hardly wait for the morrow, and the stink of charred human flesh.

'As I recall, Senhor Hanaway, you do not favour this necessary sacrament of Our Faith by which poor deluded victims of the Devil are released from their earthly torments and sent to the judgement of a merciful God.'

I stared at him. In spite of his confident words, his face appeared very strained, unhappy – and I thought I saw that he was trembling or shaking in a sort of convulsion in spite of the protection of his fine new cloak.

'It is not my faith, Sir,' I said then. 'Thank God. And no, I shall never be reconciled to the idea that there is merit in burning living human beings under any pretext whatsoever.'

I must say I was ready to go hammer and tongs with him on this matter once again. But then the oddest thing happened. He looked away from me. He was shaking his head. And then I thought he was weeping copiously – until I remembered that his suffering eye must be in a state of great torment under the keen wind that blew around us. Still it did *look* like weeping . . . He said at last, 'Senhor, forgive me, I no longer have the heart – I don't know any more . . .' And with that he bowed pretty stiffly and left me.

And yet even that was not the last of our encounter. I watched until I had almost lost him among the jostle of the pavement and in the shadows of the arches that hung over the street, and then I ran after him. He turned round and glared fiercely when he felt my touch upon his cloak as if he expected to find a footpad behind him who intended to rob him of it.

'Dom Jeronymo,' I said, when I had recovered my breath, 'did she not leave any message for me?'

He looked at me out of his weeping eyes. 'For you?' he said at last. And then, heavily, 'Nothing. She left nothing at all for you . . . Except her son. Is that not enough, Senhor?'

He seemed to consider me then, my agitation, my distress. He shrugged, hesitated, then said in a voice low enough so that I had to strain to hear him, 'She told me once that it was the greatest joy she had ever known when she found out in Evora that she was with child. She said it was a miracle, and she was a second Sarah. She meant the wife of Abraham,' Dom Jeronymo explained considerately to the foreign heretic, who he must have supposed had little or no acquaintance with the Scriptures. 'But she was exaggerating. She was not ninety like Sarah was when she conceived, and I have known of women who have given birth when they were even older than Dona Maria Beatriz.'

'How old was she?'

The *fidalgo* eyed me sternly as if, even though he had said the lady was no more, he suspected that my question was both intrusive and indelicate. I suspected much the same – but if I were being charitable to myself I would say I had asked it because I so wanted to know every last detail about her before it all vanished into nothingness. And who else in the world now could I ask about Maria Beatriz?

'Did she never tell you?'

I shook my head. 'But I always thought she was about fifty.'

'Well, she was not as old as that,' was all he would grant me. 'And so,' he went on quickly, as if leaving a distasteful subject behind, 'she was happy in Evora. She said she knew her father would die soon, and that you would go home, yet if the child lived she would not be alone. And she felt so fortunate, so blessed . . . Was that a message to you? You may take it so, I suppose, Senhor Hanaway, if you want to.'

Once again I watched him walk away from me, his new cloak swirling and billowing behind him. I did not know if it was a message from Maria Beatriz to me or not. I would think about it for years and never satisfy myself. But more immediately I could not mistake the edge of scorn I had heard in the *fidalgo*'s voice. Again I slipped into the easiest mode by which I could abuse him. People-burner, I muttered to myself, as I saw him go. Bigoted savage . . .

Really I had no right to behave so superior towards the poor man, nor to condemn him so roundly for what I then believed to have been the peculiar barbarities of his faith. A little more than ten years from this date, summer of '36, I was to arrive with my wife and our son at the port of New York to begin our new life over there. It was a prodigiously hot and close day, such as I had never known even in Portugal, and I noticed that a strange, sweetish, fatty smell seemed to hang in the still air over the little city. When I remarked on it at the boarding-house where we spent our first night I was told quite casually that it was because they had been 'burning up some negroes' the day before, and that 'they stink worse even than Indians once they're on fire'. A further question obtained the information that, yes, these were living negroes who had been put into the flames, and they had perished most suitably for their crime was arson, and they had been found guilty of starting fires at the homes of three white families.

This awful account made me feel very low. I supposed that the executors of this savage punishment must almost all have been brave Protestant folk of my own blood. And perhaps there were Protestant divines lurking about at the scene to give their church's blessing upon these sacrifices, just as the Dominicans had always delighted in offering their ministrations at the *autos-da-fé* in the Rossio. It seemed to me there was nowhere in the world, no matter which faith predominated, where I might be safe from witnessing or hearing about such an abomination. I had come three thousand miles to find it flourishing in this fresh new place. I would have done as well to stay in Europe. I remembered Dom Jeronymo then, and thought I owed him an apology for blaming his religion alone for something I now knew to be a universal sin.

But of course I knew nothing of that on this freezing cold day in Lisbon. Still full of my Protestant pride and self-righteousness, I walked back into the coffee house and approached the man I knew to be the agent for the packet line, who would get me out of this godforsaken town. I secured a passage on the next boat which, as I had already established, would leave from its wharf not long after dawn tomorrow. After this I had an evening and a night to get through in a city that was for me suddenly made horrible by the thoughts of what would take place in it the next day.

I soon decided what I would do with my time, and it was not to the Rua do Parreiral that my steps then took me. Instead I walked over to the Rua Suja, where brothels and other houses of pleasure were to be found. It would be the first time I would visit such an establishment in this town – but not, I must admit, in London. I had not been able to remain entirely virtuous during the long wait before my wedding. Nancy and I had discussed whether we should anticipate the pleasures of marriage, but had decided not to in the end. She had a desire – which she could not understand but also could not quite shake off – to be a virgin when she wed, and I confessed that I would prefer her to be intact too, though also I could not exactly say why. Besides, even if we had wanted to let our natural desires overwhelm us, there never seemed to be the time or the place. Both our houses were so busy, so full of folk coming and going.

We did what we could in terms of touching and toying with each other and that was very pleasant. Yet I wanted more. Maria Beatriz had taught me to want much more from a woman. And so in the end I had gone to a house recommended to me by a City acquaintance and had my pleasure with a girl there. And then I went back, several times, several girls. I always enjoyed these ladies in armour, for I wanted no threat of illness to hang over us when at last I would be physically joined with my Nancy. Tonight, in the Rua Suja, I found myself without that necessary item in a free-roving gentleman's wardrobe. But luckily the lady I picked out as she was sitting in an upper window looking down on the street had a full range of sheaths in her room, every size, thickness and colour. It took her a moment to have me suited up, and a moment after that I was mounted and riding her pretty hard.

Afterwards we lay quite at ease and talked. She was a *mulata*, a light-brown girl, very pretty, fine small breasts and a full belly and posterior. She said she came from Recife in Brazil where there were very many of her colour. She said she had been brought to Lisbon with some other girls last summer. In all her life she had never known such cold as during this past week, she said. She hoped I would stay the night with her and keep her warm.

'Besides,' she said, 'you can't go back out into the street without even a cloak to cover you. You must stay.'

I lay and listened to her, quite content to pass a few lazy hours in her company. She talked on about herself, and Brasil, and how she missed someone called Banguela, who I understood to have been her protector or her husband, and someone else called Felipe who may or may not have been her child. I could not quite understand everything she said for she spoke in an accent unfamiliar to me, which I supposed must have come like her from America. What else I could make out was the usual whore's chatter of ribbons and dresses and customers and the foibles and treacheries of her fellow-inmates in this pleasure house.

In a little while we both drifted off into a sort of doze. When I woke from it I found myself inside her again and all unconsciously copulating with her. And after that I did not see much reason to cease from an activity that seemed to give us both much pleasure and for which we both agreed we were still full of prowess. So we went at it yet again. I felt no pangs of shame at this behaviour. This morning I'd had a lingering hope that Maria Beatriz was still alive and that I might be able yet to save her. With such a solemn purpose before me, it would have felt most disrespectful to even be thinking of sensuous matters. Now everything had changed. My dearest Dona Maria Beatriz Fonseca-Hutchinson was beyond my help, all possibility of help.

I do not seek to justify my presence in a whore's bed on this particular night. I know that in one light all I was doing was to satisfy my carnal desires, and for her there was probably not much else in it than the silver *cruzado* I had agreed to give her at the end of her performance. But still I do say that I felt then that the shades of death that I had watched gathering around me all day – not only the deaths of people I had loved, but of those unlucky strangers tomorrow in the fire in the Rossio, *todos os mortos*, all the dead – those shades, I say, retreated just a little away from our bed as we devotedly and repeatedly performed that joyous activity I once heard Mr Hutchinson refer to as 'brangling all the way to Hairyfordshire'.

Gomes

I n his cell one night, about a week before his execution, it happened that Bartolomeu Gomes was employing his time in looking back, with the greatest of pleasure, on the day he had slain his first employer, Captain Merriweather of Farquharson's Dragoons. Really everything that came to him in his time of prosperity stemmed from that deed. The money he was awarded for his meritorious conduct gave him the chance when he was back in his own country to bide his time until the right opportunity appeared before him. He was not forced into some such undignified struggle for existence as becoming a porter or a stable boy or a fellow who collects the pots and sweeps the floor at a *taberna*. He was sure he could do better than that, *was* better than that. In particular he believed that the good command of written and spoken English he had got while serving with Farquharson's Dragoons would be bound to secure him promising employment in a great trading town like Lisbon.

It proved harder than he had expected to get a start. He had not reckoned on the racial pride of the English, which made them much prefer to hire a lubberly boy from home, one week in the country and without a word of the language in his head, than a Portuguese. It was much the same with the other foreign firms. But in the end his persistence paid off. Three months after his arrival in the capital, Gomes got his start – a house called Morrell, Cuthbert and Simms – and began on the career that led at last to his being employed by Felix Hanaway. Which in turn, particularly after he became head clerk, allowed him to steal from his factor on a limited but regular basis. He was also in a position to collect commercial information around the Alfândega that he could sell on to the doorkeeper's men. And finally it gave him the greatest opportunity of all when one day Felix confided in him, with huge and what Gomes soon saw was justified excitement, that he was proposing to throw all his remaining fortune on the purchase of a number of bales of cloth, manufactured in England from fine Spanish merino wool.

'The *fidalgos* will shit themselves, Bartolomeu!' cried Senhor Hanaway with uncharacteristic vulgarity. 'They will sell almost everything they possess to get their hands on a length of my cloth.'

Senhor Hanaway was so happy. Gomes thought it was almost a shame that he was going to have to steal his precious cargo from him. But of course he did not let such unhelpful thoughts divert him in the least from his goal. He made his plans, he matured them over many weeks, he kept his secrets, and late one night, in the middle of a long weekend, when hardly anybody was in attendance at the Alfândega, he got the bales of merino out into the streets and into the possession of those traders he had selected weeks ago for the honour. He did not tell them that nobody else in the Alfândega knew about this theft. By the time it was discovered that he had cheated not only his employer but also the doorkeeper and his rapacious agents – who had been making their own plans to seize the cloth as soon as they saw it come into the customs house – Gomes was far away from Lisbon, astride a fast horse in the direction of Spain.

In the saddlebags of his mount, and of the accompanying horse, was what he had for so long desired and believed he deserved. What he had thought his Captain Merriweather was bound to deliver to him, and whose failure to do so had earned him his death at Almanza, much more than his making his servant play the part of a *maricão* with him. What he had now was enough to 'set him up for life'. Like a retired dragoon with a good piece of loot to take home, he could now buy that little *taberna*, or perhaps a shop of some sort, in a small town somewhere across the border. It was not a great ambition. Gomes had never thought of himself as a greedy man. He had just wanted to be set up so – and never again to have to take orders from anyone, English, French, Portuguese, Spanish, no one at all.

He lasted little more than a year in Spain. He never bought a *taberna*, nor a shop, a stable-yard, nor any other kind of business. In the little town he first chose to settle in, fifty miles beyond the frontier, he did his best to find such an opportunity. He was shown a number of establishments. Nothing attracted him. He went to look for the right place elsewhere. For months he trailed over the countryside, seeking what he wanted in the little towns of the Estremadura: Cáceres, Guareña, Hinojosa del Duque, Almandralejo, others. Nothing that pleased him. He found many reasons to explain to those who desired to sell these places why he would not take them off their hands. But what it really always came down to, as he looked over the ninth or tenth prospect that he had seen in a week, was the feeling of boredom that overcame him, the sense of tedium, the questions that sank like a stone through his mind: Why am I here? Why am I wasting my time? What has happened to me?

A number of the places he saw certainly earned such a response, for they were mean and shabby and hopeless. But there were several, at least three or four, that any reasonable man would have been proud to own. Their situation was good, the buildings sound, the business excellent – yet Gomes rejected these too in the end, and moved on to yet more prospects, more little towns: Brozas, Barcarrota, Los Santos, Zalamea de la Serena . . . Still nothing.

If only he could do what he had planned and hand over the money and settle down in his new possession. At least he might have slept again for a few hours put together if he did that. Since he had arrived in Spain, he had hardly passed a night when his sleep wasn't fractured and his dreams wretched, for he was so frightened that the money that had made him independent would be stolen from him, just as he had stolen it from Felix Hanaway. For fear of being discovered, he never visited a town large enough to contain a merchant or banker with whom he could deposit the cash. In any case he did not think he could bear to trust such a creature with his fortune, for almost all of them, he understood, were secret Jews and so by nature and the Devil committed to betrayal and theft.

So he had to keep the money-bags with him, at all times. Every night they surrounded him on the bed as he lay and twisted, trying to find an hour or two of untroubled sleep. During the day they were in the saddlebags of his horse, and he could not bear to let the beast out of his sight for five minutes. He longed to hand over the money. But then once again, in Garovillas or Plasencia or Cabeza del Buey, he found himself standing in front of a pretty little inn or a fine big drapery shop, and he only had to say the word and it was his – and he could not. Could not.

He began to drink heavily, at first only to induce a state of mind in which he could slip insensibly into sleep, pure sleep, without dreams. It didn't work. He concluded that he had not yet drunk enough and so he swallowed more of the filthy Spanish stuff. It made him quarrelsome. There were some fights. It was during this period that he committed the second and third of the four murders he had been guilty of in his life. Two Spanish louts who had made the mistake of insulting him at a bad moment. Both killings were done out of sight, as it were, out in the country, and the corpse buried and covered in branches and leaves almost before it was cold. Actually, in his memory, he had not been drunk when he had killed. He had just been overwhelmed in each case by the need to strike out, to kill – something or other.

Usually his behaviour did not approach this level of violence. It was more show than serious. Challenges were issued, which he never thought would be picked up, for as he shouted at the company, as he heaved himself through a tavern door – or else was jostled out by the other customers who'd had enough of his truculent nonsense – the Spanish were all cowards, fucking *poltrãos*, and one God-fearing Portuguese could deal with twenty fucking *galegos*, no problem, no problem at all – this last usually delivered at a door that had just been slammed in his face, waking all the echoes of whichever damned little town he was in. A crowd would collect. Boys would throw stones at the drunken foreigner as he heaved himself up on to his horse. 'Go home,' they would shout after him as he went down the street. 'Go back to your own stinking little country.'

Go back. But how could he? How much he wanted to, though. Gomes could hardly believe it when he considered the matter during his sober moments. He was actually feeling that wretched *saudade* he had often heard about and had never until now known what it was. He would prefer it was Lisbon he went back to – but

446

that was impossible, of course. Still he thought he would be happy if only he could go a little way across the frontier. Back into his old home province of the Alentejo, which he had so despised when he was growing up, and to get away from which he had gone after Farquharson's Dragoons long ago. Yet he longed for it now. At any rate he longed to shake the dust of this paltry country off his heels, and return to where the language he spoke was spoken and where the saints he worshipped were most happy to have their homes. São Bartolomeu he *knew* was much happier when he was in Portugal.

Fifty miles away . . . yet it would be so dangerous. He could not go to any of the towns along the frontier, those so-called 'dry ports' where there were customs posts. His name and the crime he had committed would certainly have been circulated among the frontier officers by the envious agents of the Lisbon Alfândega. If he was identified and caught, death awaited him, no question about it. Yet he longed to go. Yet he could not . . . and so he drank again, and again got into a fight and had to leave yet another little town in a hurry. His money was slipping away in this wasteful pointless fashion. He told himself he had only to throw aside his longings and settle down into the humdrum but comfortable life here that his wealth could still buy for him. He had always in the past been able to train himself to do what he thought was necessary to achieve the future he had planned. But then he thought of Portugal, and how he longed to be back there, and his resolution failed him.

And so at last he went back. Slipped over the border in the rough country between Elvas and Campo Maior. Rode all through the night to get himself far from the frontier posts, passed into the valleys of the Sierra d'Ossa. He came to rest at last in the little town of Estremoz. It was a beautiful day, sun shining but the air cool enough at this altitude. All around him were the faces of his countrymen, and he could understand every word they spoke to one another and to himself. He was home.

And yet, he had to acknowledge after his first joyful month in Portugal, he was back in Spain too. That is, his situation had hardly changed. He was still wandering from one little country town to another and once again considering business propositions that interested him not at all. The only thing that was really different was that by coming back to his own country he had put himself where the King's justice at any time could carry him away to trial and execution for his thefts from Felix Hanaway. A slip of the tongue, a too close enquiry into his antecedents, even his face recognised in the street by someone who had known him in Lisbon and knew what he had done – and Gomes in a short time would be kicking his life away on the scaffold, or else feeling the cord of the garrotte tightening around his throat.

He had to stop what he was doing. He must come to rest at last, find a town, settle down, cease being always the stranger – otherwise he would have no chance of melting into his surroundings. He agreed on the spur of the moment to buy a *taberna*. It was in Portalegre, a larger town than he had considered before, but he was growing very tired of the little hamlets – church, five hovels, tavern – which had been almost all he had seen for the past fourteen months. In spite of the possibly greater risk of discovery, he needed more bustle and variety than that. So he bought the place, almost without looking at what he was buying and – the previous owner being so anxious to get away – he had the keys and was in possession within a week.

The purchase was not a success. The tavern was ill-sited, and there was plenty of competition. It might be that another man, with a more easy-going, welcoming disposition, might have made a go of it. But Gomes was not that man. And when he finally got around to closely examining the accounts, and discovered how poorly his business had been doing for so long, he was even less able to put on hospitable airs. I've been cheated, Gomes thought, as he sat alone, night after night in his tavern. Which was true – and yet he knew he had exposed himself to the fraud. Until his third cup of wine of the night, he was honest enough to acknowledge that. After that, he was insensible to reality. He was furiously angry. People looking in at the door with ideas of coming in to spend a quiet half-hour and swallow a glass or two took one look at his irate, dangerous face and backed out again.

It was then that he had killed his final victim, the Portuguese. This murder might have had serious consequences. It had been done in his own tavern, when a fellow who had pretended he had come into it for a drink showed that he was more interested in being insolent and in mocking Gomes' ill fortune. Gomes had got the body out of his place without being detected, and hidden it in the forest, in a deep pit he dug a couple of miles out of town. Yet suspicion had come close to him. The missing man – his name was Antônio Parente – had invited his friends that night to go over with him to the tavern to 'have some fun with that ill-looking booby Gomes'. His friends had declined the invitation. One of them said afterwards that he thought Parente was going home to bed, the other had the distinct impression that he planned to go over to Gomes' tavern by himself. In the end, since nothing could be proved, and besides there was no body found, the affair was allowed to lapse. Yet Gomes could not help but know that his reputation had sunk to an even lower level than before.

Which hardly increased the popularity of his establishment. He was losing money now very fast. And yet he could not get out of what his imprudence had betrayed him into, for nobody who had an ounce of common sense would agree to buy a business that had never been sound, and whose present owner seemed committed to driving entirely into the ground. So he lost himself in drink, and ugly dreams.

There was one other vice that he indulged himself in at this time. It was his old frailty, which his one-time position in Felix Hana-way's household had once offered him so many opportunities to satisfy. For it had given him privileged access to the young girls who came to work as servants under his authority. He had been able to indulge himself occasionally on his travels in Spain, choosing for his victims the country girls who worked in the fields, chasing them down and having his will there and then among the furrows. By the time they were able to report what he had done to their families or their masters he was far away, kicking his horse into a steady canter, removing himself into another district entirely.

When he came at last to settle in Portalegre this method of

indulging himself was not so easily available. He could and did ride out into the country and find what he could in the fields near by. But he always had to come back to the town at night. It was no longer the case that he could remove himself to a distant safety far from where those injured country girls were sobbing out their stories of rape. On the other hand Portalegre was just sizeable enough to have its small quotient of street children, bound to no household, living by the scraps that were thrown at them by more prosperous folk. And on what they could steal, of course. Gomes found some more or less willing collaborators among the older of these children, who would let him do to them what he wanted for a handful of *reis*.

One of the things he wanted to do had to be explained, or else pretty forcefully demonstrated to his new bed partners. He had never lost that old partiality for making his entrance to a young girl's body through the less frequented portal. The street girls he used soon became accustomed to his unorthodox tastes, and since he always added a few coins more to their tip when he had enjoyed them this way they rarely made any objections. Their male counterparts were not so unconcerned. Gomes sometimes heard mutters of '*maricão*' and '*sodomita*' as he went past them in the street. They did not bother him. He knew he was not a filthy *maricão*. If he had been in the least concerned about these slurs he might have grabbed one of those insolent boys and explained to him that his bum was entirely safe from him. That what he chose to do with a bitch differed from true sodomy even more than ardently kissing a female on the lips differed from doing the same to a man. And the proof of this was that while the law, through the sacred Inquisition, punished those guilty of practising this form of intercourse upon boys with the utmost severity, the same activity when done with a female was never even spoken of as a crime at all.

How did it happen that in his case one night the two so separate worlds became intermingled? He was sure it was a cruel trick. Perhaps played on him by the father or brother of some girl who he had mistakenly thought was abandoned by all her kin and so had used her as he liked to. Or perhaps it came out of the resentment in the town that he knew his surly, churlish and often drunken behaviour had created since he'd settled here. Or – very likely this – it was done by those who suspected him still of doing away with Antônio Parente. Anyway, *someone* had had to tip off the Inquisition's local *familiares*, so that early one morning they had burst into the tavern, and climbed to the sleeping platform above to find there Gomes, waking out of a sodden sleep, blinking up at the cold faces that surrounded him. And then turning to look at what lay beside him in his rumpled bed. A street urchin of about fourteen. Unfortunately it was apparent – cock with an unusually long foreskin poking out of a bush of russet-red hair, small tight sack of balls descending – that the child in question was a boy. Gomes thought he had heard the other children call him Pedro. He would remember until the day of his death that as Pedro had looked back at him his face was wreathed in knowing smiles.

To the *familiares*, to the priests, to whoever would listen, Gomes insisted that he had been deceived. That he was certain it was a girl he had taken to his bed the evening before that unlucky morning discovery. Pedro had replaced her in the night while he was sleeping. Someone was playing a dirty trick on him. His listeners heard him out. He saw in their faces that they did not believe him. And what was really unfortunate was that he was not quite sure he believed himself. Had he really had any idea what had been between the legs of the body he had lain on top of that night? Girl, boy, boy, girl – it was all a haze, engendered by the many cups of wine that, as usual, he had swallowed before taking his pleasure upon his night's companion. He too clearly remembered that he had visited, as he liked to, his partner's *bunda*. But had it been a female *bunda* he had penetrated? Male *bunda*? Girl? Boy? Oh, he shouted aloud sometimes, in the dark cell they were holding him in, I am not a *maricão*. No, not I. No! It's a mistake! I am innocent.

He did a lot of shouting in these early days of his imprisonment. Shouting, screaming, begging. He shouted a lot when they transferred him to the Inquisitorial palace in Evora. Shouted when they brought him before his judges. Begged them to understand that he was the most sincere of Christians. And that what had happened – a trick. A mistake. He loathed the thought of the *sodomia* as much as their excellencies did. The walls rang with his shrieks of outrage and fear when they condemned him to be 'relaxed' to the secular arm, that is, to be held imprisoned until the day when he would be brought forth and his unworthy body delivered to the fire that would consume it.

For some time now Gomes had not bothered with all that. No more shouting. The change came when he was told that he would be moved to Lisbon, where his execution would now take place. The father who gave him the news was quite chatty about the reasons for it. There was a dearth of candidates for the next *auto-da-fé* in the capital. A number of *relapso* Jews, caught trying to flee the country, who were expected to be part of the sacred ceremony, had been thoughtlessly done to death by mobs of the faithful in the places where they were being held. The King was not at all happy to hear that the celebration he loved to watch should be so impoverished. The summons was sent out to Evora and Coimbra, the other towns where the Inquisition maintained courts and prisons, that they should send any *heréticos* they had in their keeping who deserved to be relaxed or otherwise severely dealt with to the capital. Evora was contributing its mite to the general budget in the shape of Gomes and three others.

'I am not a *herético*.'

'I know, my son. They are willing to take *sodomitas* too.'

'I'm not –'

What was the point? Everybody had heard his noisy protests and explanations in Evora and it hadn't swayed them. He might have a different reception in Lisbon but he knew that was the faintest of hopes, hardly a glimmer. He had been tried, condemned, and that before – as his judges had kept telling him – the mildest and wisest tribunal in the Christian world. Besides, the King required his presence in the capital so that he might be burned for the greater glory and sanctity of his kingdom, and Gomes, as a loyal subject, could hardly oppose the royal pleasure. Gomes had felt like telling the friar who had made this argument to him that he couldn't give a *burro's* arse for the King's pleasure – but considering that such a treasonous and impertinent expression would crush any lingering hopes he had that he would find mercy somewhere else than in cruel Evora, he kept his mouth firmly shut.

The convoy set off at last: soldiers riding at the head and in the rear, priests with their crosses and the *familiares* in their costumes, all excited to be making the trip, and in the middle of the procession the open cart containing the prisoners. The weather was beautiful on each of the three days that the journey took. Cool and sunny, autumn in the air. The crowds came out along the route. Gomes had expected to have curses and reproaches – and probably other items much more solid – flung at him and the other prisoners. But for the most part the country people watched the procession go by practically in silence. It had startled Gomes the first couple of times it happened, but then he saw that it was awe that was silencing these clowns, not disgust, and much of that wonderment was directed at himself and the other prisoners. The priests called out to the people to repent and take warning from the impending fate of the wretched men and women they saw passing before them. The people looked up at Gomes as they kneeled beside the road. Some of them held out their hands to him. They seemed to want him to bless them, and so he did, making the sign of the cross above them. He didn't feel strange to be doing this. He felt it was entirely appropriate. For the first time in many a month, he felt content to be himself.

It might have been thought that arrival in Lisbon and consignment to a small dark cell in the Paço da Inquisição would have snapped him out of this contentment. But it was not so. The jailers and the priests who patrolled the corridors and cells of the Palace commented to each other and to him about his tranquil demeanour, very rare in their experience among the prisoners they dealt with. Of course he was not subject like so many others to a regular submission to the two varieties of torture permitted to the Inquisition, that is, the rack and the *polé*. Gomes was particularly pleased to have missed the second of these exercises – during which, with hands bound behind their back and attached to a rope, prisoners were hoisted ceilingwards and then dropped abruptly. He had heard it was exquisitely painful, and usually resulted in permanent damage to the prisoner's arms and shoulders. However, he was not excused these ministrations because of any misjudged inclinations to mercy on the part of his jailers, but because as a sodomite (he had almost given up denying the charge) he was not required to go through the process of spiritual repentance and denunciation of himself and of others that was demanded from heretics, and for which of course torture was an excellent and God-given instrument in the hands of the Inquisitors.

'So you see, Bartolomeu, that the Holy Office is not a repository of casual cruelty and unrestrained violence as the Jews and Protestants pretend to maintain,' remarked Father Manuel on one of his regular visits to Gomes' cell. 'For you, so strong in the faith as you are, need not fear for a moment that you will be put to the question.'

Father Manuel, who had taken it upon himself to examine Gomes on his spiritual health over the week or two after his arrival in the Rossio, had pronounced his finding among his brother priests that the prisoner was blessed with 'the faith of a little child'. Thereafter Gomes had been the recipient of many smiles and kind words from those holy brothers who chose occasionally over the six months he was with them to come into his cell and relieve his loneliness by passing the time of day with him. Nobody was so assiduous in their attendance as Father Manuel. Gomes concluded after studying the priest for some time that this kindness stemmed from a certain – call it 'ambivalence' that his holy friend had towards the crime for which he had been condemned. And that this attitude grew in turn from the fact that Father Manuel was one of those priests who found their vows of celibacy lay very light on them, for that they were not particularly, or at all, troubled by the allure of womankind.

Gomes had not in the least relaxed his contempt towards the sexual practices of those degenerates who were called *maricões*. But as his friend never exhibited any desire to involve Gomes in these dirty games, he came to trust the father and looked forward to his visits. There was also the fact that Father Manuel sometimes brought him titbits from the priests' refectory, and even delicious sweet *doces* from a nearby convent. He was a plump, smiling fellow of about Gomes' age. One side of his face was covered with a dark-purple birthmark. He told Gomes once that it was because of this disfigurement that he was so alert to any signs of fanaticism or uncalled-for severity as he went about his work. For when he was born the ignorant peasants of his village had declared his mark to be a sign that the infant belonged to the Devil and had wanted to kill him forthwith. But the village priest had stepped in, told his would-be murderers to desist and depart, and then under cover of night had smuggled him away to a far-off village and the house of a pious *fidalgo* to be brought up where he would be safe.

As the day of the *auto-da-fé* at which Gomes was to die drew near, Father Manuel began to talk enthusiastically of how lucky he was that he would be involved in this great celebration. For such fortune was certainly not the lot of most sodomites who usually were handed over by the Inquisition to the civil authorities early on in the process and turned off without ceremony by some local executioner in whichever obscure locality had been the scene of their crime.

'I am not a –'

'Yes, yes. But think of it, Bartolomeu! In Lisbon – before the King himself – and the Inquisitor General – and all the priests and *familiares* and the people. Dressed in the black *sanbenito*, with your face painted on it and the flames arising.' (Gomes had already noted the painter of the *sanbenito* garment, worn by all those prisoners who were to appear at the *auto-da-fé*, watching him through a hole in the door of his cell, committing his face to memory and his sketchbook.) 'Why,' said Father Manuel, 'if all those guilty of your crime were to meet such a splendid end, I think we could never keep their numbers down. There would be as many sodomites in Portugal as there are Jews, I think. More!'

He gave an anxious little giggle after saying that, and soon afterwards got up to leave. Gomes guessed that his vision of an ever-swelling population of compliant *maricões* had rendered the priest in urgent need of relief. He considered idly for a moment seeking his own release. But, as always, he was proud to know that the thought of the *maricão* persuasion was disgusting to him, and not at all stimulating. In any case he decided he would wait until dark as usual, for it was easier to keep one's motions secret from the prying eye at the holes in the door. Last night he had thought of a little girl he had known called Doroteia who had come to work at Felix Hanaway's house in town long ago. He wondered what had happened to her. She'd had to be let go, of course, but he had kept her longer than he had most of her kind. He decided he would keep Doroteia a little longer still, at least in his imagination, at least for one more night.

But darkness came and he did not think of her or of any other girl. He lay awake, listening to the night sounds that penetrated to his narrow cell. The pad of sandalled feet as the priests went by in the corridor. Muffled weeping from a nearby cell where a woman – an apostate New Christian, according to Father Manuel, due to be condemned for life to the Angola colony – mourned the children she had been separated from. Hoarse shouts from a lunatic, another *cristão novo*, who had been loudly protesting his 'innocence' for the past several nights, and would do so for the next few until the priests' servants came in and bound his mouth. He had been denounced, Father Manuel had said, by his own sons.

Bells rang in the Palace and beyond its walls. Gomes lay on his trestle and stared at the ceiling he could not see. He wondered himself at his own tranquillity as he saw the prospect of his death become ever more real. He had not known he could be so brave. Violent, vengeful, cruel – he knew he was capable of all that. He had four dead souls to his credit to show that. But this strange – what was it? – this *fortitude* that was keeping him so steady now . . . that was unexpected. Yet he did not conceal from himself that the death he had faced for many months was an agonising one. He had seen the condemned burn at other *autos-da-fé* in the Rossio and over at the Campo da Lã, the other of the Holy Office's execution grounds in Lisbon. The wretches would cry out as the flames began to grill them, 'Mercy for the love of God!' And the crowd beneath the pyre would laugh with glee and echo their words mockingly back at them. 'Mercy for the love of God!'

He didn't think it was the fact that, as he had been told a couple of weeks ago, he would not after all have to face quite so dreadful a death that kept him tranquil. Father Manuel, beaming all over his plump, disfigured face, had brought the news to his cell. Mercy had been decided upon in the case of the sodomite – 'It was because they know you are such a faithful son of the Church, Bartolomeu, I am sure it was that' – and moments before the fire was lit beneath him as he waited on his pyre, the executioner would step forward and he would be garrotted. That was good to know, of course – but still he did not feel that the real explanation for the calm resolution with which he faced his own death lay there.

What it could it be? He puzzled over the problem this night, and for almost all the nights that were left to him. At last, on the very night before the day he was to die, he thought he had found some answers. The first of them came to him when he was not even thinking of the main question. Some time in that night, when he had woken for the third or fourth time, he found himself looking back to his time of exile in Spain, and to its equally unsatisfactory aftermath when he had returned to his own country. He was wondering again why it had been impossible for him to settle in any of the places he had visited, or to be satisfied to take on any of the likely businesses he had been offered. And it came to him that he could not do those things, those little ordinary things, because he had tasted once what was not ordinary at all. He had lived and worked amidst the buzz of great deeds, great coups, huge wealth and the chance to make even more of it – and none of these could ever be found in a neat little *taberna* in a pretty village like Zalamea, or a horse farm in the wide-open country beside the Rio Guadiana. Gomes had been like an actor who after an elaborate leave-taking from the metropolitan stage finds he cannot bear the life he has reduced himself to, dragging about the provinces, appearing in smaller and smaller theatres, and with fellow-actors whose talents invariably are far below his own.

Of course he had always known, if only unconsciously, that this was at least a part of the reason for his unwillingness to settle for a small fate in a small provincial town. Yet now it appeared to him as not only an explanation for his past behaviour, but a way of illuminating his present too. For he saw in a flash that it was the same reason why he could not be bothered to fear his own death.

He, the Gomes he cared about, had died many months ago, when he had stolen from his employer and set off on the road to Spain. From then on he could never again live and work in a place in which the fruits of the entire world were admitted, judged and sold onwards to the highest bidder – and Gomes had been a part of this gigantic process. From now on the best bit of business he could ever hope to do would be to make a good deal on some hay or find a cheaper supplier for his wine or his cheese or his eggs.

What a fool he had been. He had raised himself by his own efforts to his position at the Alfândega – and because of crass, greedy stupidity had tossed it away. Gomes began for the first time to remember his employer with something that actually approached affection. He had always been a gentleman, Senhor Hanaway. Kindly, trusting, too trusting, of course – but that need not have been a fatal flaw. If only he had chosen a head clerk he could have relied on. They might have made a formidable pair. Felix with his position in the Factory and his undeniable nose for business, Gomes who could supply everything else: the ruthlessness, the command of the account books (which he had exploited for all the wrong reasons), the instinct for combat.

Oh they would have done well together, Gomes reflected. If only, on an unlucky day, he had not conceived the plan of robbing his employer of all that he possessed. And what use had that been in the end? How often had he found himself standing in front of a pretty little inn or a fine big drapery shop, and he only had to say the word and it was his – and he had remembered the Alfândega, how the light fell blue and gold and dusty from the windows in the roof; how the factors and the clerks had cheered when those fateful bales of merino were brought in and he had felt so proud to think it was his own firm that was dealing in such fine merchandise – even though he was planning to steal it; how Senhor Hanaway would touch him on the arm sometimes and tell him that he could not do without him, you are the finest clerk a man ever had, Bartolomeu, my dear friend, as good as an Englishman any day.

He remembered this now. It was a glad thought to know that he had lived at this peak. And it did not matter, he saw, what happened to him now. He had drunk the good wine, and the lees might as well be thrown away, he had no use for it. A momentary pain as the cord tightened around his neck – and then oblivion, which he would take any time over a long life dragged out in Garovillas or Gavião or Cabeza del Buey.

The occasional random noises from beyond his cell door were growing more frequent now, and more purposeful. In a few minutes they would be coming in to prepare him for his ordeal. He would be dressed in the *sanbenito*. Then Father Manuel had promised to hear his confession. And then the rest would follow . . . But Gomes was not thinking of all that now. It had come to him that the priest had once given him the clue to whatever still remained a mystery concerning his calmness as his end approached. For what had he said to Gomes? Hadn't he told him how lucky he was that he had been brought to die in Lisbon? And it was so, Gomes thought, the joy at his good fortune stealing up through him as he sat at the edge of his bed. How terrible it would have been if his last breath had had to be drawn in a wretched hole in Spain, or even in Portugal. He had come from the Alentejo, from the dreariest district in all that dreary province, and he would die in great Lisbon. Only for that he was entitled to see his life's story as a success.

No further use for a life that had turned sour – and the gift of a quick death in Lisbon, a town worthy to receive his sacrifice. No wonder he had been calm all these weeks. His mind, without unravelling the situation exactly, had known that it was right for him to be at peace.

They came in to him at last. Fitted him with his penitential garment. Looking down, he was able to see that the artist had made a wretched job of rendering his features. He had done better with his drawing of the flames that were licking around Gomes' painted head. Presumably the hack was much better at drawing flames because he had to do them all the time, whereas each face he attempted was an individual challenge. Father Manuel saw him looking, discerned his disapproval of the artist's efforts. He told Bartolomeu that he must not mind, that all the other prisoners had been equally ill served.

'Except for one woman who is an artist herself, and has been allowed to draw her own face. It's a most creditable performance, you must look out for it today.'

Gomes thought he would probably do no such thing. He would have other things on his mind. The acquiescent glow with which he had woken to the day seemed to be fading fast. He felt his legs were turning uncertain, his knees had a tendency to buckle. He was glad to kneel on the floor of his cell to make his confession to Father Manuel. It was not a long one for, as he said, how many sins could he commit in a little room with a locked door? He did not think it worth troubling the priest with his carnal night-dreams, about Doroteia and the others. They stood up. Gomes felt better, steadier. Father Manuel enfolded him in a hug. He was weeping, Gomes noted. The priest smelled pleasantly of chocolate and cake. Of course the fathers always did themselves very well at the time of the *auto-da-fé*. Tonight Father Manuel would be feasting off pork and lamb, and Gomes would be – where?

'Oh, Bartolomeu,' Father Manuel sighed. He stood back then, he regarded the prisoner. Remarkably Gomes found a look almost of joy in the priest's eyes. 'Outside they are saying it is going to snow,' Manuel announced triumphantly. 'Imagine! Snow here in this month, on almost the last day of it. It is a miracle!'

It was certainly cold enough to snow. Gomes was shivering as he followed Father Manuel and the other priests down the corridor. He was brought into a large quadrangle, somewhere near the palace walls. He was handed a candle, unlit. Then instructed where he should stand in the procession that was now forming up. The Dominican brothers were in front, grouped around the banner of the Inquisition, which bore on one side of it the image of St Peter, and on the other a crucifix between an olive branch and a sword. Then came the ranks of *penitentes* who, having admitted their crimes and so been judged deserving of a lesser punishment than death, were placed ahead of his own group, which consisted of *negativos*, who had denied their sins, or *diminutos*, who had not confessed enough of them. Both types were rightly regarded as being worthy of death, as, obviously, was the lone sodomite.

Gomes' group was the smaller of the two, being composed of

only three persons. One was a fellow from Brazil, who had owned a sugar mill there. He had dwelled for a time in a cell along the corridor from Gomes, who used to sometimes hear him shouting to the effect that the Holy Office had only taken him up because the fathers wanted to get their greedy hands on his mill. At one point he had been taken away to the dungeons for, Gomes was given to understand, a regular course of the *polé*. It certainly seemed to have quietened him down. He stood there now, a quiet and pensive figure, his gaze fixed upon the cobblestones. Gomes knew that the torturers of the Inquisition were required not to leave marks on their victims that could be seen when they were brought forth before the public on the day of their execution. Certainly he could see no marks on the Brazilian. Yet he was not holding a candle like all the other prisoners, and Gomes surmised that this was so because, after his ordeal in the palace dungeons, he could not.

Gomes' notice was first attracted to the other sharer in his doom today because of the *sanbenito* the person was wearing. This must be, he realised, the woman Father Manuel had told him about who had been permitted to draw her own image. It was strange, Gomes remembered, but when Manuel had been speaking of her there had been a curious note of respect, even admiration in his voice. Later he had told Gomes that the woman had been condemned because she could not be shaken in her belief that it was correct for her to espouse both the Christian and the Judaic faiths.

'Then she must be mad,' Gomes had said.

'Of course.' The priest had hesitated. 'And yet she does not appear to be mad,' he said, a kind of wondering note in his voice as he spoke.

Gomes now looked up at the madwoman. He knew that she was due to burn without the merciful prior release of the garrotte, for she would not accept that she had committed a mortal sin by her beliefs, nor ask forgiveness for what she had done. As the priest had said, she certainly bore no evidence of her insanity. She smiled at him as she saw him looking.

'You draw very well,' Gomes said at last.

'Thank you. I've had much practice. Only I fear I may have flattered myself too much.'

Gomes shook his head. He wanted to say not at all. If anything she had underestimated her beauty in her drawing. In particular she had failed to – not wanted to? – convey the loveliness and strangeness of her eyes.

These eyes were settled on him now. He wanted – wanted to say . . . that he was afraid. Afraid of death, he could not bear it. All his boasted tranquillity – gone now, quite gone. He would shame himself when they left the Palace. Before the people of Lisbon – his people – he would be dragged, screaming, and begging and shitting himself . . . If only – if only he could walk beside her, and perhaps touch her hand.

'Dona,' he said to her. And again: 'Dona . . .'

Luckily a harsh voice broke into his trance, otherwise there was no knowing what foolishness he might have committed. He was on the point of falling to his knees before this strange woman, when:

'No talking there! It is forbidden for the prisoners to talk.'

Gomes pulled himself together. The woman was taken to stand behind him by the *familiares* who were assigned to each prisoner during the procession. His own two took up their stations on either side. At least, thought Gomes, he could be sure that those who were allotted to him would be of high status, true *fidalgos*. The fellows up ahead, the mere *penitentes*, could not be certain who on earth would be walking beside them; it might well be some jumped-up merchant or lawyer, allowed into the brotherhood of the *familiares* because he had paid someone well for the privilege. But the *relapsos* who were to burn, and whose *sanbenitos* showed the flames consuming them, were always given attendants of the very best quality. He saw with satisfaction that on one side the gentleman wore the habit of the Order of Christ, on his other that of the Order of Avis. This was the real thing. You did not win admission to these brotherhoods unless you could prove that no one in your family had worked for gain for at least five generations.

Gomes felt his weak fears – his *womanly* fears – subsiding gratifyingly fast. He no longer thought of the madwoman with the glorious eyes who, for a moment, he had believed was the only one who could see him through the ordeal that lay ahead. Between two such upstanding guardians of the faith and of the realm of Portugal as attended him now, he knew he would make a good show today. He heard the mutter of the multitude outside the palace wall. He was almost impatient to begin, to show them how Gomes could die.

The great gate was flung open. The Dominican friars began to chant. He could not see him now, but he knew Father Manuel was among them. He would be with him till the end, he had promised Gomes this. The procession moved forward. Gomes' candle was still unlit. But then everybody else's was too. The keen wind made certain of that. As he stepped out into the courtyard of the Paço da Inquisição, snow began to fall thickly around him. Snow at the end of April. Manuel's miracle. The next moment, the sound of first one, then of several guns boomed forth from the castle of São Jorge, so high up they sounded as if they were being fired in heaven. Their noise was taken up then by guns all across the city. Looking up, Gomes saw that a small flock of cranes, probably startled by the guns, was flying slowly south above him, leaving the city behind. He did not envy them.

As the echoes of the guns died away, the crowds began to hoot their contempt and rage. Gomes began to smile. All this noise for him! A boy from the Alentejo.

Adam

I left my little whore in the Rua Suja when it was still not quite light, and joined my ship. My mood on this voyage home was to be sombre, though not to any excessive degree. I was very sorry of course that my mission had been essentially futile, that I had found that Maria Beatriz had really died, many months ago, and was beyond my help. Often in the years that followed I would wonder whether, if I had come back to Lisbon in time, while she still lived, I would have been able to save her. I could never make up my mind. On the one hand the Portuguese and their Holy Office were forever concerned to keep the foreigner out of their particular business. On the other, they also had a healthy regard for the power of England and the propensity of its agents to involve themselves in their dependencies' affairs, and these might indeed have found that they had a proper interest in the case of Maria Beatriz, for she was the daughter of an undoubted Englishman, however notorious and even infamous a one he had been. It was just possible that, to save themselves the bother of a quarrel with King George, the Court and Church in Lisbon would have reluctantly let go of one unimportant woman, even though by letting her live and not burn they were condemning her poor soul to everlasting torment.

On board ship that morning I resolved that I would not despair, and would even discover some crumbs of comfort for myself in what I, who was still living, had done for my dear dead, however fruitless. I thought, in other words, that I had done the right thing in coming out here, I had not hidden at home, I was ready to accept my responsibility. That this was not needed after all, I would not lay to my conscience. At least I had not behaved as I am sure Runaway would have, and made a giant noise with his boasts of what he would do, and then straight away run and hidden from the consequences.

And I would say that I date from this time the moment when Adam Runaway ceased to trouble me seriously. It was Maria Beatriz's last gift to me, though given all unconsciously. I am not saying that I was free thereafter of the ordinary moments of faintheartedness, even cowardice, that are a part of every man's existence. But I no longer felt Runaway as an incubus inside me, ready to take me over whenever he willed it. We were no longer joined together. Indeed, I think I may have killed him.

There were other incidents and scenes from this period that contributed to this happy murder, I am sure. I remember when Mr Dutton had declined to fight with me but had showed me that in his refusal was more strength and courage than had been in my challenge to him. Then I think of my whole course of life in the two years before my last trip to Lisbon: the reputation I had won, however inadvertently, as a brave man who had smuggled gold from Portugal at the risk of his life; then the steady growth of my knowledge and understanding of my trade, and the success I had earned in it – all of which helped to make me less fearful in the world, more steady. And then there was Nancy – and my new son . . . so many good reasons to send my old and hateful and cowardly companion to hell for evermore.

I got home in good time to prepare for my wedding and on a pretty day in June I married my Nancy. I had managed to persuade her not to go on with her original plans for a church wedding, and so we were spared the attentions of a gawking congregation during the ceremony and the vulgarities of a so-called 'charivari' after it, with a horde of low people of both sexes following us home and banging on drums and sawing on fiddles until we would pay them to go away. To avoid these horrors, Mr Dutton offered the use of his fine house in Essex, and there in the drawing room, in surroundings of tranquillity and dignity, with all our family and dear friends present, we made our vows before the local parson and received his blessing on our match. Nancy looked lovely, as a young bride should, and I had no reason to believe that my own appearance detracted from the spectacle we made. We were a fine young couple on the verge of life, in truth. Meanwhile, our new son John sat on his nurse's lap in the front row of seats in perfect silence and watched the ceremony with apparent close attention.

And this really completes my account of my time in Portugal, for I never saw the place again. Thereafter the course of my life bent me always away from that period of it I had spent in Lisbon, and I came quite soon to think of it as not much more than a transient episode, almost as just an incident, though sometimes unawares I would be caught by an unexpected pang of – something or other, perhaps even the famous *saudade*, when I remembered a particular face or a building, or a perfect day when the breezes were coming off the river, the sunshine sparkling but not too fierce, and the customers were buying Maria Beatriz's drawings almost before I had started trying to sell them.

Only one important dilemma from those days remained unsettled, and it was to cause me considerable unease and even distress over the years as I sought to find an honourable way through it. It was also, as I shall explain, the thing that was to save my reputation, even my life perhaps. I had always believed that Senhor Montesinhos was taking no great risk when he had entrusted his fortune to my care, and that was very true – up to a point. The fortune stayed intact in the vault where it had first been placed, while I waited for my old landlord to appear in London to claim it, or to send me directions as to where I should send it to him. After the first couple of years, acting on Mr Marks' advice, I began to place notices in the newspapers, first only in London, then abroad, anywhere we could think of where Jews were known to congregate. We advertised particularly in Amsterdam for I had remembered Montesinhos had told me he had a nephew who traded from that city. We even sent by an East Indiaman notices to Madras and Bengal.

I always couched these advertisements in the most neutral and unexciting terms, such as 'Mr Adam Hanaway seeks news of Senhor Onofre Montesinhos' followed by my office address, for I did not want to be plagued by a host of fraudulent applications. After more years had gone by and I still had not heard from my old landlord, I changed the wording to something more like 'seeks Senhor Onofre Montesinhos for whom he has some welcome information'. As I had expected, this brought in more than a few replies, some of them signed very confidently 'Onofre Montesinhos'. They were all easily detected as frauds, however; none of them brought me any closer to discovering the real Montesinhos' whereabouts.

I was forced to conclude at last that the likeliest explanation for this silence and absence was that Montesinhos had been caught in trying to escape, whether before he had left Portugal or afterwards. And that, most likely, he had perished at the hands of the Inquisitors – or else was being held in some dungeon from which it was not likely he would ever emerge. And it was not only the landlord who had disappeared, for I remembered that Mr Hutchinson had said to me that other members of his family had contributed to the fortune I was to take away from Lisbon. Presumably they would have been told where their money was bound and with whom it had been placed, and yet not one of them ever appeared to claim it from me. It was as if a tempest had destroyed a whole family. And I – what was I? The sole survivor? The rightful heir? Was it proper indeed to for ever leave the money useless and unproductive in a vault? I wasn't sure it was. Was it proper then to take it and use it for my own purposes? I was almost certain it was not.

In the end it was a commercial disaster that fell upon me some ten years after I had arrived back in London – two ships that foundered on their homeward voyage, an unlucky decision to enter into the world of marine insurance for which I had neither the aptitude nor the understanding – that brought me to the necessity of invading Montesinhos' fortune. One Monday morning I found I was on the point of breaking and perhaps being sent to debtors' prison by the Wednesday if I did not come up with the sum of £2,000 in the interval. I could not bear for it to be so crudely a case of 'like father, like son'. I knew that extreme measures were required. Mr Ruddy, who had first given a home to Montesinhos' fortune, was now dead. His son and successor apparently knew nothing of how the money had first reached his vault. Nor seemed to understand that, though it was entered in his books against my name, I was not its rightful owner. At any rate he betrayed no signs of surprise or contempt when I obtained a bill from him for £2,000, thus reducing my – Montesinhos' – account to the sum of £5,000. And having done that, and used it to preserve my name and family, it was not hard, when my wife and I settled that we would remove to New York and start again in life, to decide to take another bill from Mr Ruddy junior for the remainder of the account, which bill I placed the day after we arrived in America with a good Dutch house in Water Street on Manhattan Island, the agents there for a firm in Rotterdam I had previously done much business with.

I told myself then, and often thereafter, that Montesinhos' money would never really be lost to him, that when I was back on my feet as a merchant I would always keep a sufficient balance in my accounting so that if he should, remarkably, appear in New York, I would be able to take him by the hand and show him that his money was still safe, even after so many years, and that he could take it away whenever he felt like it. I really did hope that he would so appear one day or write to me, though the passing years made that ever more unlikely. Still almost the first thing I did when I became prosperous again was to send out a new batch of advertisements to newspapers in all the principal American cities giving my present address in New York and saying that 'Mr Hanaway seeks news of . . .' etcetera, etcetera. Again all I got was another collection of fraudulent replies, and the only difference was that I found the American impostors by far exceeded their European counterparts when it came to issuing imaginative and impudent inventions.

This ambition to keep Montesinhos' fortune intact and distinct from the firm's lasted for as long as I had control over the business, but at last, a number of years after we had moved to Philadelphia – which followed my poor Nancy's death, when I could no longer bear to live in a New York that so much reminded me of her – my son John told me that we could no longer maintain what had become almost a fiction, 'a castle in the air', he called it, and was certainly proving an obstacle when it came to fairly and cleanly making up our accounts. The Montesinhos fortune would never be collected by its rightful owners, he said, and as we had been its guardians for so long and were owed something for our steward-ship, we might as well regard the business concluded by absorbing the money into our own account.

After some soul-searching I agreed to what he had proposed to the extent that while I thought we might reasonably keep half of the Montesinhos money for ourselves, we should send the rest to a synagogue, or to some leading Jewish family, so that it could be administered for the benefit of their community. John was a good enough son so that he acceded to this proposition finally, though he made it clear that he took a rather less sentimental view of what we owed to the memory of the Montesinhos family – which was reasonable for he had never known my old landlord, never experienced his kindness, nor watched his palpable anguish for love of Maria Beatriz, nor indeed ever smelled his endearingly horrible breath. We eventually sent in his and our name the sum of £2,500 to a charity for assisting poor Jews to settle in America, and were profusely thanked for this gift by the gentlemen who administered it. I must say that I could not help thinking their thanks would have been somewhat less effusive if they had known we had, as it seemed to me, bilked them of more than half of what should have been theirs.

But this sort of opinion I kept to myself, for John, though a good son, had really not much patience for what he used to teaze me was my habit of 'libelling myself' whenever I had the chance. I spent my days thereafter with my memories, and serving on the few charities that interested me – and, like many others, waiting in a kind of frozen dread while the menace of an unnatural war between two branches of the British race gathered around us.

Now that scourge has broken over us. John is a 'patriot', whatever that means in this particular colony where there appear to be at least four sides to every question. And I – I am nothing. Memory and the past is where I belong now. I am so old I can no longer be expected to take any serious part in the present-day. I feel the marks of my approaching end are with me. I think it is quite close. Perhaps I will die this very night. I think I wouldn't mind that.

But if I should not, I hope I have a pleasant night, without pain, and perhaps with sweet dreams. Most of all I wish I could dream of Lisbon. That is: of Old Lisbon. My beloved city. It is gone now. The great earthquake and fire of twenty years ago levelled to the ground almost everything that I once saw, and I've been told the restoration of the city has completed the work of transforming it utterly. (Oddly that restoration was done under the command of the famous Marquis de Pombal, the King's first minister, who when I first knew of him was called Sebastião de Carvalho and was the young leader of a particularly ferocious gang of street-fighters. So everything changes.)

I am glad I do not have to see this new city. I cling to the old one that I loved. I tried to say what it meant for me in a little book I paid to have published in Philadelphia, a while after we had moved here. (Many copies of this work are with me now, for sales were far below even the modest estimate my printer had made.) It was called *A Visit to Portugal in the Time of King João V*, which I signed proudly as being by 'a Pennsylvania Merchant', thus giving the lie to my son's repeated jest (I think it is a jest) that I have 'never really left England'. In this book, which differed markedly from the present account in having almost nothing of the personal in it and being mainly confined to descriptions of buildings and monuments and streets that I remembered, I opened my narrative by describing the view the approaching traveller would have of the city then: the lofty white houses, palaces, churches, rising from the water's edge, and the castle on its hill looking down on everything. And I wrote too of how, if the wind was blowing strong from the land, the scent of oranges and lemons would flood the whole town, even out as far as the ships on the river. (Surely that one ancient blessing still survives? For even if the orchards were uprooted or burned during the cataclysm, they must have grown back by now, and sometimes the air will be as sweet as it was sixty years ago. I long to believe that is so.)

This is the lost city I want to remember tonight. Not exactly the city the approaching traveller saw, but how I viewed it for the last time, when I was leaving it, in that strange season when the northern winter seemed to have taken up its abode amidst the southern spring. Oh how cold I was as I stood at the stern of the packet boat looking back at the marvellous sight. We had not left at dawn, of course. Even packets never leave when they are supposed to. It was mid-morning by now, an overcast sky but no haze and the city was clear behind us. I looked at it all, from side to side, from west to east, from Belém to the far edge of the Alfama. Other passengers were also standing near by, all drawn to the fabulous vision we were sailing away from.

Just then we were assaulted by the noise of cannonfire. At first I thought it was only the customs gun, but then I considered that it had come from high up, perhaps from the castle battlements. The sound of another cannon careered across the water towards us then, and this I thought came from a battery in the Terreiro do Paço. Then other pieces from other parts of the city joined in the celebration, and soon the whole world was echoing with the noise. Flocks of birds rose startled into the sky. I saw a half-dozen cranes flapping slowly one after another towards the south; they must have been visible all over the city.

I knew what this racket meant, and it was certainly nothing so ordinary and innocent as a summons by the King's customs. It meant that some notable point had been reached in the devilish sacrifices that were presently underway in the Rossio only half a mile from where we were. Perhaps the priests had started to harangue the luckless heretics who were paraded before them; perhaps the few who had resisted all calls to repent were being tied to the stake; perhaps the executioners were applying torches to the faggots . . .

But as I stood there, while the echoes of artillery died around me, I resolved that I would not think of unhappy things, and things I could not help nor change. I would look only at the beauty before me and forget the horror that was behind it. And to help me in this – would Maria Beatriz have thought this was a miracle if she had been there? Then would she have drawn for me whichever saint it was that had the kindness to arrange it? – something happened that was to drive all thoughts of suffering and wickedness from my mind that day. It began to snow. In Lisbon, in April, it snowed. An old fellow, a stalwart of the Factory, who was standing near me, said that he had lived in this place for forty years and had never known it to snow like this. Though he had seen it happen in this month once in a great while, dusting the castle's roof, on the summit of its hill, it had never been general like this, down to the waterline, even out to where we were in mid-river. It may never have happened before, this veteran said. It probably never would again so late in the year. We were very lucky to be witnesses to it.

I was lucky. I saw snow falling late in April upon the Tagus river. And that is what I would like to dream of tonight. The snow coming down so large and dense, and the miraculous city of Dom João V retreating behind a veil of white, hiding its face, as if it knew in its stones that it was doomed.